CLEARCUT

A Novel of Bio-Consequences

"A deep, satisfying thriller in the tradition of **Mount Analogue** and **Wizard of the Upper Amazon**, **Clearcut** argues compellingly for the interconnectedness of all life forms, and the latent powers of nature which humankind has ignored at its own peril. The book's herbal revelations and their poignant timelessness suggests that all human ills might yet be solved with ecological clarity and loving patience."

—Michael Tobias, author of
Voice of the Planet and *World War III*

Other books by Bill Hunger:

Hiking Wyoming
When Two Saints Meet

CLEARCUT

A Novel of Bio-Consequences

Thanks for caring

BILL HUNGER

Bill Hunger

HAMPTON ROADS
PUBLISHING COMPANY, INC.

This book is fiction. The events and persons portrayed in the story are fictional; any resemblance to any person living or deceased is coincidental.

No medical claims, implied or stated, should be derived from this book. Self-diagnosis using herbal remedies is often ineffectual and occasionally dangerous. If interested in pursuing herbal natural healing, the reader should consult a competent herbalist, naturopath, herbally trained chiropractor, or holistic M.D.

The author acknowledges the producers of the
documentary video discussed in Chapter 27:
Hoxsey, Quacks Who Cure Cancer,
© Project Cure, 1987 (Realidad Productions).

Cover art by Louis Jones
Cover design by Marjoram Productions

For information write:

Hampton Roads Publishing Company, Inc.
134 Burgess Lane
Charlottesville, VA 22902

Or call: (804) 296-2772
FAX: (804) 296-5096
E-mail: hrpc@mail.hamptonroadspub.com
Internet: http://www.hamptonroadspub.com

If you are unable to order this book from your local
bookseller, you may order directly from the publisher.
Quantity discounts for organizations are available.
Call 1-800-766-8009, toll-free.

ISBN 1-57174-049-X

10 9 8 7 6 5 4 3 2 1

Printed on acid-free, recycled paper
with linseed oil in Canada

Dedication

Jill, to you, my love.
Couldn't have happened without
your tolerance, love, and support.

Thanks for inspiration to a long line of
environmentalists, healers, farmers,
loggers, and spiritual friends.
Thanks to Hampton Roads Publishing
and Frank DeMarco for following the vision
to publish such an inspiring line of books.

bio-consequences (bi'ō-kon'si-kwən(t)s), *n.* 1: the direct or indirect impact of varying influences on living matter or organisms. 2: the effect, result or outcome of the interaction between living organisms and the biosphere. 3: the degradation of an ecosystem by living organisms due to bio-waste. 4: the effect of a degraded ecosystem on its living organisms. (Greek *bios*, life)

CONTENTS

BOOK I   ALLIS

1   Disease 12
2   Doctor 19
3   Healer 27
4   Newstime 34
5   Environmentalist 43
6   Cure 49
7   Denial 53
8   Newstime 60
9   Payback 69

BOOK II   DECISIONS

10   Loggers 84
11   Alone 90
12   Newstime 94
13   Planning 104
14   Reaction 110
15   Destiny 116
16   Loggers, II 128

BOOK III   SEARCHING

17   Gurner's Gang 136
18   Newstime 145
19   Intuition 156
20   Flower Talk 166
21   Committee 176
22   Education 182
23   Newstime 188
24   Conflict 195

BOOK IV **RESPONSIBILITY**

25 Earthview 202
26 Newstime 213
27 Experience 221
28 Communication 234
29 Loggers, III 237
30 Causes 243
31 Reflections 254

BOOK V **COOPERATION**

32 Newstime 260
33 Energy 266
34 Blackness 276
35 Standoff 278
36 Homeopathics 287
37 Newstime 291

BOOK VI **VICTORY?**

38 Newstime 300
39 Disbelief 303
40 Repeat 315

BOOK I

ALLIS

♣ 1 ♣
Disease

December 31, 2007, 2:20 P.M. The office of the Head of Fraudulent Practice Investigations, United States Food and Drug Administration, Washington, D.C.

Those walking past the doorway leading into Jim Bowerns' office automatically stepped to the far side of the hall. The chief of the FDA's Special Investigations Division was well-known for his clarion voice. It now rang loudly and authoritatively, carrying itself through the closed door and a fair distance down the surrounding hallways.

"Damn-it-all, Johnson! What's going on? This is the third time I'm having to talk to you about this character. He should have been skewered and barbecued long ago. This department has too large a load to be concentrating so much time and energy on one sorry phony."

A second, softer voice attempted to hold ground against overwhelming animation. "Mr. Bowerns, I'm in the same boat I was in a month ago. There's no solid evidence. There are no nails to drive this case home. Nails? We can't even find the hammer. And now there's—"

"You mean you still haven't found the man's advertising?"

"There *are* no ads, sir. There are no written claims. Gurner is totally QT about what he does. And now there's—"

"And no records of massive, ridiculous payments for his, quote: 'services and healings'? Come on, Johnson, those things must be sticking out like welts. They always do."

"Mr. Bowerns, we've done our homework. The man charges considerably less than similar practitioners. If his clients are financially strapped, he doesn't charge them at all. According to his tax statements, his bank account, and his lack of credit cards and financial references, Gurner isn't even at the poverty level. And now there's—"

"Well, *what about the records?* Look, Brian, you know as well as I that these health-hypocrites, especially the sincere, goody-goody kind, always keep detailed patient record books they're going to use to save mankind. We've bagged a lot of quacks through their records."

Brian Johnson could not equal the vocal capabilities of his boss. But his news was pressing. Willing into being all the power his small-framed body could convey, he returned the stare of the iron-faced man in front of him. "Sir, our men have 'burglarized' his house. Twice. It's just a small cabin in the mountains and easy to search. There was no stash of cash, no stockpile of illicit drugs. Also no records, no patient data, no diary explaining what he's doing. No *anything* along those lines. And now there's—"

Johnson slapped the director's metal desk with both hands as he saw Bowerns inhale. "*No!* Now listen! You've got to let me finish here. We went the course on this guy. We interviewed several of his clients and we could find no incriminating evidence that would stand up in court. In fact, it would be counterproductive to bring those folks to the witness stand. They had nothing but praise for the man. We can't document a single case where Gurner hurt anyone. No doctor in the area has had to repair any damage caused by him. I must note that several of the people I talked to stated that Gurner undid a few mistakes the doctors made. And now there's . . . now there's evidence that something Gurner has given, or done, to a few people has reversed or eliminated their symptoms of ALLIS."

Thirty seconds of intense staring and burdened silence passed before Bowerns again spoke. "Ha ha, Johnson."

Johnson looked apprehensively at his supervisor. "Mr. Bowerns?"

"I said 'ha ha.' I appreciate your adding a little humor. But let's focus on the business at hand and get this so-called healer off the street."

Johnson could no longer match Bowerns' stare. His eyes dropped to a notebook lying on the director's desk. "Sir, if you'll just look at this interim report I've put together. There are some facts here that—"

"The *facts,* you addlebrain, are that you are supposedly a top FDA agent assigned to gather evidence against the latest phony-baloney healer/magician acquiring notoriety for himself. And you are failing miserably at the task. *And* if that statement about him healing ALLIS carries any conviction behind it, I'm going to seriously consider transferring you to a less demanding position. Cripes, the best scientific brains in the world haven't figured out what *causes* ALLIS, much less been able to even *start* working on a cure. No snake charmer is suddenly going to poof the thing away."

"Sir, I have talked to three different people whose stories and medical records show—"

Bowerns didn't even try to hide his sarcasm. ". . . show that they were in varying stages of ALLIS and now have none of the symptoms. This, of course, because Gurner gave them something or did something to them. Cripes, Brian, you've been in this field for fifteen years. How many times have you seen an incurable disease suddenly be unexplainably cured, and later it turns out it was temporary hypnotism, or mass fanaticism, or outright lying about the original circumstances?"

"Too many times, sir. But there's something different, something genuine about both these cases and this person Gurner."

"Genuine. Hah! With this new disease running rampant, we're going to be plagued with all kinds of hotshot healers and wonder potions and magic pill dealers, and now my best man sounds like he's been sucked into the same current."

Bowerns had directed the U.S. Food and Drug Administration's special Fraudulent Practice Investigations Division for ten years. One could not successfully hold that prominent, taxing position without effort, a fair amount of callousness—and insight. Bowerns' insight suddenly came into play, and his voice softened, mimicking concern. "Johnson, you're looking tired. And you've lost weight. What's happening?"

Johnson's eyes left the desk and traveled floorward. He scuffed some black heal marks onto the polished linoleum, but remained silent.

"Come on. Something's up. What?"

Suddenly, Johnson seemed to collapse into the limits of his spare body and lost all pretense of fortitude. "Mary . . . Mary is displaying the first signs of ALLIS."

"Mary?"

"My wife."

"Brian, no!" *No wonder this guy is not with the program.* "Is she showing the loss of muscular strength?"

Johnson stood closed-eyed and motionless, offering only a nod.

"Body temperature drop?"

"Yes."

"How many days ago?"

"Three."

Enthusiasm surged into Bowerns' voice. "Well that's different! You know as well as I do that they're never positive about a diagnosis until there's been at least five days of symptoms. She could have any number of other bugs or diseases. A lot of people panic, thinking every little sniffle is ALLIS, but lots of times it isn't, you know."

Johnson again offered a closed-eyed and very distant nodding agreement.

"I mean it, Brian. It's very likely *not* ALLIS your wife has." *But if it is, she's got ten days to live. Twelve, maybe. Then the funeral. And he'll probably need a couple of weeks off after that. So Brian's out for a month, and us with more work than a chemical factory has lawsuits. So who do I put on this Gurner character in Brian's place? Unless . . . ?* "Brian!"

The elation and ardor in Bowerns' voice forced Johnson to look up from his internal grieving. He noticed the branching vein in his supervisor's forehead begin to bulge, which happened only when Bowerns was either very angry or very excited.

"Listen. Let me pour this idea out while it's fresh in my head. The AMA is getting antsy about him, and I'm the one catching the flak. We've *got* to snag Gurner, but you say you haven't been able to scrape together any evidence.

"Now, you know what we've done in the past sometimes. We've had to resort to—what would you call it—compiling our own facts. It's ethically questionable, but it's better than some impostor out there stirring up false hopes and robbing people's pocketbooks. Besides, it's our job."

Not only was Bowerns' forehead vein growing more livid, his face began to flush with excitement. "Look, Brian, you take Mary to Gurner. Let him claim that he'll heal her. Let him treat her. And then when she . . ." Bowerns waded through a short throat-clearing. ". . . Well, you know. If she *does* have ALLIS, and he can't do anything for her, both you and this agency will have the proof we need to fry the faker. And . . . uh . . . of course, if she doesn't have the disease . . . which she probably doesn't . . . Gurner will boast that his magic methods were the reason she lived, and he'll be sticking his neck all the further onto our chopping block."

Bowerns' forehead vein receded slightly, but his chest puffed out like a proud rooster about to crow. "What do you say? Personally, I think it's brilliant!"

Johnson remained stock-still as his mind tried to catch up to see if it could believe what it had just heard.

Bowerns left no pause for thought to happen. He became soothing and fatherly. "Brian, look, you've been kind of stuck in the same old job status for several years now. But there is word of a possible assistant administrator position opening in the near future. And though I'd plug for you anyway, it would really float well with the higher-ups to see a scalp like Gurner's on your belt. Think seriously about this idea, my boy. Take my advice, get Mary to Gurner ASAP. You've got the agency's resources at your disposal. You're a veteran. You know how to handle these situations and extract what we need to complete the case."

Johnson gave Bowerns the kind of look Ukrainian peasant women threw at Nazis after the soldiers shot their sons. But Bowerns paid no more attention than the troopers had. He was looking at his watch and calculating other matters in his head.

"Brian, in about half an hour some television and newspaper reporters are coming up for an interview and a Q-and-A session on where our department is with the ALLIS situation. I've got to brush out the place and tidy myself up. Get with me later on what is happening with Mary, and of course with Gurner. OK?"

With the charm of a talk-show host, Bowerns escorted Johnson to the office door. "I'm really glad we had this chance to talk. And you know, every scientist and researcher in every country of the world is chasing a cure to this disease. I heard that both the Chinese and the CDC down in Atlanta are on the verge of discovery, and within a few days they'll have a positive track to follow. It'll work out for Mary." *You can tell he loves her. And you can tell he knows she's a goner. But she's not the only one . . . she's not the only one by a long shot.*

The office door clicked shut, and immediately the man, the man's doomed wife, and the man's job assignment disappeared from the director's thoughts. Stepping before a full-length mirror tucked into a workroom corner, Bowerns began to straighten his tie and brush his suit, and began also to prepare himself for the journalistic dissection he knew lay ahead.

Ah, mirror, mirror on the wall, who would have ever thought this body would get so portly? Or that my mustache would start to turn gray . . . even before the hairline receded?

Anyway. So, I've got to talk here to ABC and NBC and Newstime and all the majors and minors. About these . . . rumors. That's the key word in this speech: "rumors."

President himself calls me this morning: "Jim," he says, "the press is starting to speculate that the ALLIS disease was caused by a safety breach at Army Biological Warfare. Let's quell that idea before it becomes really uncomfortable. Say whatever you need to." So. Rumor it is. Unfounded. No proof. I ought to be able to bark on that angle for quite a while.

Bowerns possessed a remarkably quick and sharp mind. He had an almost phenomenal ability to classify and grab facts out of the most distant memory, and he could readily organize these facts into an impressive speech on a moment's notice. When he really concentrated and put this ability to use, and when he incorporated his naturally strong charisma and powerful tone of voice, he became a brilliant orator, one who could easily convince people to doubt what they knew to be true. To a fragile and in-need-of-an-answer public, he was the perfect person to calm fears and lay to rest any screaming doubts.

Communists. Blame the "rumors" on the Communists.

Bowerns' mirror image frowned at that idea.

No. That won't work. Hardly any Reds left. Well, how about Greens? Environmental alarmists, pushing panic buttons but really not knowing what they're talking about. That ought to work.

Both the reflective icon and the director received a brief hair combing and a quick spray of breath freshener.

And end on a positive note. Johnson had to know I was full of it when I said Atlanta was about to hit on something, but I think the public will swallow it a couple more times. Something along these lines: big money, crash efforts, top priority given to this research; sunshine just below the horizon but ready to rise and all that.

The razor-sharp mind sometimes pitted itself against him, asking questions; prying, probing questions, questions a firmly opinionated government superior should not ask. But rather than examine the questions, Bowerns avoided them, managing his thoughts so that he never had the time to think too deeply. Ignoring the hidden queries had become second nature.

Thus when an unanswerable question flashed before the face

in the mirror (*Cripes, what if the Army did unleash an unnatural and uncontrollable germ upon us?*) it received a customary non-acknowledgement and silently passed into oblivion.

One more minor adjustment of the tie and a final look at the teeth to see if they were clean; the inspector felt ready for anything. The first of the reporters were arriving. Bowerns left an imageless mirror to deal with unanswered questions.

♣ 2 ♣
Doctor

December 15, 2007, 11:15 A.M. A lecture auditorium at Ashford Medical School, Baltimore, Maryland.

Oh, crumb. This is sad. Five hundred people could fit in this lecture hall, and there's maybe twenty here, and it's already past time to begin. Poor Dr. Meyers. Just like his nutrition classes. Extracurricular and voluntary, and so nobody comes. Crumb, if they were offering these budding sawbones a new method on how to jam a tube up someone's ass, these sessions would be piled with surplus interns.

Stephanie Peters was wallowing in exasperation again. As a flower blossom suddenly poking its head above several inches of snow does not fit a January day, she did not fit into the medical school scene that had claimed so many years of her life. Through four years of basic college and a Bioscience degree; through the following years of pre-med schooling, and then through the four grueling years of med school itself; through an intense first-year residency and an even more strenuous surgical residency at a major hospital; now she was back in the original medical institute's classrooms, placing some finishing touches on her acquired art of body carving. After a dozen years of rigorous schooling and inevitable mental conditioning, she had never lost the burning memory of why she had started this long road in the first place. She was an uncommonly idealistic humanitarian. People around her were sick or in pain, and she wanted to help. People near her hurt and needed professional medical aid, and she desired to be the aid-giver. Now, twelve years of intense work and self-sacrifice later, with just a few more hours of trauma-repair surgery training to complete, "Doctor" Peters would soon be free, legal, and able to wholeheartedly offer herself and her services to a world of human aches and pains and diseases. But the closer that important date drew, the more she found herself overpowered by helpless and scared feelings.

It was her main residency that opened the doors to these fears. It was the stint at that hospital, Mercy, a big one located in a big city, that grafted her onto a mental tree of self-doubt and inadequacy. Medical school's thousands of hours of textbook anatomy and chemistry test tubes and cadaver-carving courses couldn't begin to numb the potential doctor's tender emotions or caring thoughts. But the months on the Mercy Hospital cancer wards and intensive care units abruptly shattered all her preconceived notions.

Not that the hospital, by all accepted standards, wasn't one of the most modern and most efficient in the country. Not that they didn't do their job and do it well. But to a med student whose dreams also carried a goal of personal and individual patient consideration, Mercy Hospital acted as the dragon that awakened the princess from her idyllic sleep.

She couldn't wholly accept standard medical procedure; that was her problem.

She questioned when she and a staff doctor administered a powerful and new anti-cholesterol drug that did diminish a patient's atherosclerotic risks but also, as a side effect, damaged his liver and kidneys.

She hurt, terribly, when she watched cancer patients of all varieties waste to skeletons and grow bald and spend their days in nausea and listless existence—a meager mode of being stemming more from the disease-countering chemotherapy and radiation treatments than from the cancer.

She felt the injustice when five days of life in this hospital, forced upon a person because of an accident, left him financially strapped and hopelessly in debt for years to come.

She wept the night a patient's eyes both hemorrhaged, leaving her blind for life. Yes, the potent blood thinner she had prescribed weeks earlier—under the auspices of a senior doctor and twelve years of medical school pharmacology training—did indeed list vessel hemorrhage as one of its possible side effects.

Time and again she watched people cured of one ailment be readmitted to the hospital in need of treatment for a second or third malady, disorders often caused in part by the drugs or surgeries given to handle the original problem. She often felt she was observing an endless therapy session that cut off a person's limb in order to save his ambidexterity.

So few in the hierarchy of physicians and surgeons questioned the procedures. On your patient you try an appropriate chemical from a long listing of appropriate chemicals; if it doesn't work, move on and try another. Often, to her great satisfaction, the patient was healed, was given a new lease on a malfunctioning body. Then she felt proud to be part of the procedure that allowed such a miracle. Just as often, though, when the chancy game of long-term chemical therapy failed, the costs in human health and happiness were too much to comfortably ignore.

Prior to Mercy, the hospital she graced during her first-year residency was a small-town, rural medical center located near an Indian Reservation in southern Arizona. The central beehive of Mercy Hospital would later make this experience seem like that of a lone worker bee placed in the wide-open flower fields. But even here the pharmacy orientation, the surgery gods, the high costs, and the other doubts began to demand her consideration.

Because her sympathetic concern never remitted, she questioned when the standard medical methods employed didn't appear to embody the Hippocratic Oath. Because she questioned, and took that questioning seriously, she became an active observer rather than a go-with-the-flow participant inside the giant beehive of activity called the modern hospital. Because she was such an excellent observer, she saw, besides the drug gambling games and the over-cut overkill and the beyond-fathoming expenses, two other facets and facts of medicine-patient life that left her seriously doubting her choice of joining the medical profession. And because almost half of her life and all of its goals were suddenly being seriously cross-examined, she was an internal mess by the time she left Mercy Hospital.

One of these major misgivings presented itself when she realized that there was no way she could sustain, in modern medical practice, her ideal of individual caring and health giving. Mercy hospital later irrefutably proved this. She had ten to fourteen hours in a day when her wits were sharp and her mind able to intently concentrate on the medical problems and the persons placed before her. In those hours she had twenty, thirty, even forty or more people needing to be treated, evaluated, examined, rechecked, tested, etc. With five to ten minutes rationed to each person, with a never-ending line of people, hour after hour and day after day, there wasn't much chance for idealistic patient care. She found herself, like her colleagues, in those five or so minutes of patient contact, having to skip past the inner patient personality; having to focus solely on the specific disease or problem; having to skim the lab reports and x-ray pictures; having to grope for a medicine among the list of drugs that pharmaceutical companies say treat a specific symptom; having to simply hope the prescription would work; jotting the current information onto the patient's chart; washing her hands; saying goodbye and good luck to that one; saying hello, piece of meat number 61, you're next! The over-whelming requirements of a doctor's practice forced her to deal only with relieving disease symptoms. But then, her years of schooling hadn't exactly trained her to seek the roots beneath the plant of disease . . . even if she had the time to do so.

Her second major doubt arose in regard to the patients themselves—specifically, their resigned apathy toward whatever the doctor said. If the woman whose eyes hemorrhaged had but asked—demanded—to know the consequences and side effects of the prescribed drug, she and her doctor both could have looked it up in the *Physicians Desk Reference* and discussed the dangers and possibilities. Then the patient could have at least made an educated choice.

But most patient reaction to any decision handed them was an automatic "OK, Doc."

Here, take these pills . . . OK, Doc.

Here, we're going to x-ray you again and again and again . . . OK, Doc.

Here, we're going to open you up and rearrange a few things . . . OK, Doc.

Here, we're going inject a powerful poison into your veins . . . OK, Doc.

Here, we're going to cut off your nose and sew it to your navel . . . OK, Doc.

The sad part was that when people allowed that kind of treatment, one tended to give them that treatment.

The Arizona hospital experience also injected another qualm into her wavering mind. During her rotation there, the medical center found itself treating a larger-than-normal influx of reservation Indians, almost all of them severely sick with major bronchial disorders and various cancers. This disease trend among the tribal members had been in process for several years, and Public Health officials were in the concluding stages of a report citing a direct link between an abandoned uranium mine and the reservation members' 25 percent greater-than-normal incidence of radiation-related sicknesses. The report suggested that the mine's massive piles of unreclaimed, uncovered tailings, and the simple fact that most of the reservation lay downwind from these tailings, might have something to do with the statistics. Environmental Protection Agency workers traipsed over the contaminated countryside, agreeing with the Public Health reports but denying that it was their responsibility to see that the tailings were covered and somehow made safe. Bureau of Indian Affairs officials and representatives from the mining company that owned and formerly operated the pit made several appearances, each time loudly and vehemently denying that the tailings or they themselves were responsible for this unfortunate disease occurrence. A few Indian Legal Aid lawyers nosed through the hospital center records, verifying the statistics and consoling the dying with promises of lawsuits and strong compensating actions. (They failed to mention to the victims that this process would take years.)

But soon-to-be-Dr. Peters, who spent the hours peering down the throats of the men coughing up blood, or feeling the weakening pulses of the children slipping away from life due to leukemia, knew in her soul that these people were victims. They didn't ask for this, or do anything to bring it on, but they had received it in full.

A new and confusing thought process triggered itself in the young doctor's mind. Radiation and its bone sarcomas and many other cancers; asbestos and its mesothelioma and lung damage; pesticides and their deadly, lingering aftereffects; mercury and its brain and central nervous system paralysis; lead and its kidney, liver, and heart damage; the carcinogens of nitrates and nitrites; carbon monoxide, acid rain, ozone depletion, chemical spills . . . "Environmentally Caused Diseases" was an insignificant, two-hour med school class that nobody paid much attention to, what with heavies like Advanced Biochemistry, Anatomy IV, and Beginning Surgical Techniques weighing down the semester. But here in the real world, environmental degradation formed a blazing, fiery sun of a health hazard. She spent many hours wondering how many people needed to see her because they had been burned by that man-induced fire.

Full of questions, void of answers, she returned from the Mercy

Hospital residency to her alma mater, there to pass all the final tests, receive her M.D., and undergo a further semester of post-graduate courses. Outwardly, she stayed at the school as a means of polishing her education; inwardly, it served as a breather from having to go back into the real world and face more unanswerable questions.

It was during this final, extra term that she met and fell under the sway of the newly-resurrected Doctor James Meyers.

Most of the stories circulating the school about J.W. Meyers, M.D., were rumors, and most of the rumors were false. The facts before the rumors everyone knew. Dr. Meyers had been teaching at that school for over thirty years. He represented a foundation pillar of the class, credibility, and character of the institution. She had taken a few of his classes in her mid years. But even at that time the good doctor was looking wan and acting with less enthusiasm and sharpness than one would expect from such a renowned and multi-awarded professor.

Then he was hospitalized. Pancreatic cancer with cancerous lymphatic metastasis. Radiation therapy cooked him, and chemo-therapy ran him through the wringer. But the cancer won the rubber match, and the doctor was given his prognosis. He left the area, presumably to die. The school's Board of Trustees sadly prepared to rename halls and parks after their fallen colleague.

The halls, however, retained their long-standing and original names. One and a half years later, Dr. Meyers returned to the university in full vigor and complete health. And he returned a changed man.

He never really stated, at least to his fellow medical professors, what exactly had cured him. The arch-druids of the school were too deep in shock to feel honest excitement about his return. By all accepted medical proclamations, he should be dead. This strange renaissance did not portend well.

The Board read the omens rightly. Dr. Meyers immediately began teaching again, only now he was injecting a new philosophy into his standard classes. Students, much to their amazement, were shown more than orthodox procedures for surgically removing or chemically treating cysts, moles, tumors, diseased organs, and the like. They suddenly found themselves being tutored in alternative methods of healing. And some of the programs the doctor suggested were pretty bizarre: massage, herbal poultices and teas, vitamin and mineral nutritional balancing, and dietary changes, to name a few.

Dr. Meyers owned such credibility, tenure, and acclaim that his new course of thought might have been overlooked by the school directors as the erratic (and hopefully temporary) behavior of someone miraculously returning from the dead. He might have even gotten away with initiating extracurricular classes that focused on preventing diseases as a means of treating them.

"Don't you see," he'd almost yell at the few students participating in these classes, "that a doctor who simply treats a disease or the symptoms of a disease isn't tackling the cause of the disease. That kind of doctor is merely a repairman."

Maybe he'd have squeaked by with those aberrations, *if* they had been temporary. (One trustee did loudly snort out that Meyers must have been cured of cancerous pancreatitis by a cerebrotomy, because all he talks about is quack nonsense.) But James Meyers burned his bridges with the school medical establishment the day he told a packed lecture hall the story of his healing.

One doesn't even mention the name of an AMA-blacklisted doctor who has moved (or fled) to Mexico to continue his controversial, "unscientific and unproven" cancer treatments. Much less does one admit to the whole school that this condemned doctor treated oneself. Very much less should one ever conclude that these treatments were the healing grace that saved one's life (even if the living proof is standing behind the podium). One does not "blather" on about unorthodox therapies like fasting, diet changes, sweats, laetrile, wheat grass juice, enemas, and herbal combinations as if they're the new saviors of the modern, infirm world. And for triple damn sure one does not challenge an entire auditorium of students to question and investigate the methods of current research and medicine they are being taught. One doesn't ask them to be open to alternatives, to be pioneers, or to explore new ways. One does not.

Dr. James Meyers did.

It took only a few months after that. Sudden evidence proved beyond all argument that Dr. Meyers had misdiagnosed several illnesses in the school hospital, and it was feared he was no longer capable of a medical practice. Evidence established beyond a shadow of a doubt that Dr. Meyers had misappropriated and used for his own purposes school funds that were designated for research and learning. Rumor from highly reliable sources held that Dr. Meyers frequently partied with several of the female med students, pressing his status and professorship on them to his advantage (and although what a man does in his private life is his business, we still don't want that kind of image generated here). Evidence, as they say in medical school, had Dr. Meyers by the genitalia, and he was soon down the road, disgraced in his field and by his peers, banned from practicing medicine in that state . . . and with no gold watch to commemorate his many years.

But in the few extra-curricular lectures his tenure had permitted him to present, he touched a few of the latest generation of physicians and surgeons. A few listeners questioned, and a few of these questioners investigated some of the statements he made. One young and emphatic woman in particular was set ablaze by the claims and challenges presented by Dr. Meyers.

Prevention! thought Stephanie Peters to herself after the twenty people in the mostly empty hall had adjourned from Dr. Meyers' lecture. *He said that a good portion of the people sick with degenerative diseases wouldn't be in such a boat if they had only been taught and followed the essential facts—not the government facts, or beef- or dairy- or sugar-industry facts—but the essential facts of nutrition, diet, exercise, and clean living. And he said that our eight hours total training in nutrition on the four food groups, on getting enough protein, and on a couple of elementary basics on vitamins and minerals wasn't even a beginning for an uneducated person, much less for a doctor. He said that many of the folks currently beset with modern diseases could be treated more effectively, more successfully via alternative, less invasive, and less technical means.*

He said, heh, he said, "Get with it, guys"—and five women frowned—"Get out there and prove it and don't just take my word for it." Twelve years in this school, and something tells me my education is just beginning.

Dr. Stephanie Peters mentally programmed herself to make time the next day to visit an off-campus bookstore and see what alternative reading was available in the health section. Another thought lightly passed through her mind, a thought on which soon every chiropractor, naturopath, holistic M.D., nutritionist, and healer in the world would in some form also dwell.

Crumb, I wonder if this alternative stuff would prevent or cure ALLIS?

· 3 ·
Healer

December 27, 2007, 11:15 A.M. Along an isolated trail east
of McKenzie Pass, near the Three Sisters Wilderness Area,
in the Deschutes National Forest, Oregon.

Ever-present thoughts swirled through the lone man's mind,
whirling like the wind-driven snow flurrying through the winter
forest in all directions. So intent was this hiker's mental activity
that he hardly noticed the shin-deep snow he shuffled through.

*I don't know anything! Do You hear me? Nothing. Most of the
time I don't feel as though I've the knowledge to pop a blister
appropriately. I certainly don't know what I did . . . or even what
I didn't do that somehow did something.*

Occasional pitch-encrusted blaze rectangles located the buried
trail. Tall and ancient fir and spruce trees hushed the countryside
yet augmented the wind's moanings. The man's thoughts wildly
raced.

*C'mon, God. Remember me? Your old friend, Gurner? I've
talked to You so many times before like this. And You've never
really answered me very clearly. You've always maintained a
suitable silence and discreet distance. But this one is serious. You
got to talk back; You got to open up and let me know what's
happening here.*

A whirlwind of snow eddied around the hiker, momentarily
causing him to pause in both his steps and his thoughts. When
the mini-tempest subsided, the man's step, mind, and inner conversation again resumed their paces.

*Look. I know and You know that when We get back to my
cabin, life is going be a hectic mess. This trip has been nice,
watching serious winter settle into these mountains. But the snow's
getting deep, and I didn't bring my skis . . . and You and I simply*

can't be backpacking forever . . . and that answering machine is going to be chock full of call-me-back messages . . . and that damn phone I never should have gotten will probably be ringing off its hook. What if it's that magazine reporter wanting to do an article . . . an article on me, Gurner, the supposed healer? I'm not a healer. Every healer I've ever read about seems to have super mental concentration powers, a special dispensation from You, or at least an absolute and unwavering faith in You. All I ever get from You is silence.

The mostly unknown and reclusive herbalist named Gurner spent a large amount of his free time exploring forgotten trails and untrammeled side-drainages in and around his home state of Oregon. His ongoing quest was to scour the landscape for new medicinal herbs. During these isolated times, he generally carried a running conversation inside his head. The current debate created a stormy tirade of thoughts.

And yes, maybe if I could penetrate that silence, I could find the place where a sure faith in You dwells. But as You well know, every prayer and meditation I've tried has been firmly ignored. You REFUSE to come down to my level and talk. You repeatedly ignore my prayer to grace me with a hands-on healing power. I just cannot and do not trust the silence. And I AM NOT A HEALER!

Gurner's long and lithe body easily glided through the gathering snow. A lifetime of country living and wilderness conditioning meant that almost no mountain slope or outdoor circumstance could hinder his sure pace. His naturally ageless facial features did, however, portray a weathering when deep lines of worried reflection creased them. As he paused under the semi-shelter of a thick cluster of spruce trees, these lines edged into deeper existence.

What has happened here? How did I get to this point of confusion on what I am and what I really have?

It seems that a few years ago I found, or developed, or was latently gifted with an unusual capability, an ability to listen to the rhythms of another person's body. I know, I know, try to explain that one to the courts. I can't even fathom how it works. But somehow, intuitively, I could mentally run through the workings of a person's body. And from that tuning in, I could compose what seemed to be an accurate profile of the weaknesses and strengths, balances and imbalances in the person. As a result of this special ability, wonderful healings happened, like the man with shaking hands who feared he was getting the same Parkinson's Disease that killed his dad. The problem, according to my mental vision, proved to be a toxicity in mercury. And there was the woman with a violent body rash that no dermatologist-prescribed cream would alleviate. It was simply caused by a serious mineral deficiency and malfunctioning kidneys.

Gurner pulled a plastic bag from his parka pocket and, hunching under the thicker tree branches, unconsciously munched some dried fruit. He watched the flying snow.

Well, that would have been stars if I'd have just left the ability at tracing problems to their source. But no, I had to get engrossed in some old herb books, and some new nutrition books. Their simple philosophies made so much sense: "First, prevention as a cure; second, treat the whole body and person, not just the symptoms of an ailment; and finally, treat it naturally when possible, because God did know what He was doing when He made herbs and whole foods."

I then managed to expand this ability to listen. First I could determine the hidden or main cause of a health problem, and then, by listening even harder, I found I could sense what natural remedies would specifically work for that problem. I could individualize it. I could hear—and I guess I still do "hear"—what specific herbs work on the specific weaknesses of an individual person. So instead of suffering through innumerable frightening tests, the man with the mercury-induced shaking drank a cleansing tea especially tuned to him, and the tremors stopped in a few months. In place of what could have amounted to years of allergy tests and trials with possibly ineffective, expensive chemical creams, the woman ingested an herbal remedy that her own kidneys "told me" would rebuild and heal it. The rash was gone in three months, apparently for good.

Now, over the years, many, many people have been helped, been relieved of a wide variety of pains and problems. And because of such successes, I thought I had been given a special gift of healing from God, and all would be yippie-spippie as "We" set out to heal the endless grievances of the world.

Gurner peered upward through the tree branches at the presumable Recipient of his mental conversation and voiced a thought aloud.

"Hah."

Gurner then shook his head and lowered his gaze to the disturbed white fluff piled around his boots. *I'm beginning to believe I'd be more suited for a hermit's life in a secret mountain cave.*

The wind gained a more permanent power, and the snow decided to seriously pursue its task of covering the landscape. The healer Gurner hunkered deeper into his parka, eased out from under the tree's bower, and resumed his hiking pace.

Then when did it start? When did my gift catch up to me? . . . Or, when did the world start catching up to my gift?

I want to say the turning point occurred when that fellow with the ALLIS thing came to see me. Good God, I've worked on all kinds of weird conditions, but that one? With cancer, people at least have some time, and whatever healing route they choose to take, they've also got hope that it will work. Even with AIDS, people don't die the next day. And science is making leaps and bounds in finding a cure, so they have hope. But this poor guy had suddenly been told he contracted the wildest disease of the century, there is no known cure, and that he had six or seven more days to live. He needed a psychiatrist. He needed a real healer. He got me.

I agreed to look at him, to try "listening" to him in my own way. And I found nothing especially wrong except weakish-feeling endocrine glands. He did display an impairment of metabolism and a loss of muscular strength, but I've heard those are the standard ALLIS symptoms. All I could think to do was intuitively give the poor guy some strengthening herbs and say call me in seven days. He didn't think that was funny. Neither did I.

Then in seven days he called me. And three days later he called me again. And he's still calling me every once in a while, weeks later.

He lived! No further symptoms. No complications. The doctors of course said they misdiagnosed the case, but I don't think so. I think something I gave him reversed the disease. That meant I suddenly had a listing of four herbs, one or more of which may have healed the incurable. Inwardly, I guess, I really desired another ALLIS victim to experiment on, to see if I did have something viable.

Gurner abruptly halted his walking, stared up into the confused gray sky and yelled his thoughts, as he often did when internal thinking simply did not emphasize a point strongly enough. "Damn it all. I didn't mean for the victim to appear so fast or to be so far advanced into the disease . . . or to be a kid. Oh God-of-mine, You occasionally supply a man's wants too well."

Five years old and with maybe four days to live. Distraught parents, clinging to any hope. Heard about me from the first fellow. Flew half way across the country and came to my door with this near-dead child draped in their arms. I tried. I tuned in. I listened. And I got the most contrary information. That little girl didn't have any of the same indications the first man did. When I went to give her that herbal-four combination that worked on him, my entire self went into rebellion. Those herbs didn't feel right, somehow. Finally gave her folks some simple nervines and tonifying plants. I also gave them a lot of doubts and no promises.

"And she lived! I don't know how, but she lived!"

Unfortunately, it's a small community I live near. Everybody soon knew. The doctors said nothing, but it wasn't long till my house was broken into, and again a week later. Nothing stolen, just everything torn apart and scattered around.

Shoot, I never have advertised. I only receive clients via word of mouth. I've seen too much of the razor's edge we have to walk—real healers and aberrant M.D.s and guys like me who don't know what we are. The meds calls it protecting the public from quackery. But a lot of honest, effective, and sincere pioneers in healing have been eaten like bugs by the big medical hens. They won't tolerate chicks wandering away from their clutch. I'm scared. If I'm on their blacklist, if they're seriously sniffing me out, I've got to leave my place.

Gurner lived alone. He had never opted for any other lifestyle than being alone and outdoors. Perhaps for this reason the healer often tilted his head back and loudly voiced his most profound thoughts and questions to That which he assumed was beyond sky. He now howled into the wind.

"Do You hear that, God? We're leaving. Soon as We get back to the cabin, You and I are packing up and heading to some unmarked nook in this world where nobody knows Us . . . Well, doesn't know me. They very well may know You. But I am NOT going to jail for saving lives."

After such vocalizations, Gurner habitually paused to listen for any response. None came.

So a third ALLIS person came to me. Nothing in common with the other two. Something inside said give him herbs. But EVERY-THING inside also said that the herbs I'd given the other two wouldn't work on him. So I didn't give him anything! My insides told me to not give him the herbs that had worked on someone else, but I didn't really know what herbs to offer.

So he died. Five days later he died.

And I wept, because I didn't pursue the voice that may have been his gift of life. I swore to never ignore that intuitive voice again, no matter how insane it seemed.

Of course, right away it had to seem completely insane. Two more ALLIS near-fatalities were brought to my door, and that crazy sixth sense of mine was wanting to give them some herbs that again were unrelated to anything I'd found or done with the previous persons. I had to follow my inner precepts. I had to give them what my insides said they needed.

Gurner lifted his arms in a gesture of exultation. "And they lived! My God, they lived!"

Gurner dropped his arms in a wave of exasperation.

Then it really grew crazy. Telephone calls from newspaper reporters, wanting to be the first to interview me. When I wasn't refusing to meet the press, I was dismissing business baboons trying to tell me how much money "we" would make when "we" patent this cure and move it into mass production. Not to be left in the dust, the various psychos of the Lord occasionally called to let me know that my healing was certainly of the Devil.

Talking quietly, as if a companion were beside him on the trail, Gurner voiced his next thought. "I'm a loner, God. You know that. You're partially the cause of that. All that attention and hubbub sure left me yearning to play the magician's role and vanish. Besides, I didn't know what I was doing that prompted the curing of ALLIS."

Then my client-friends started getting anonymous calls asking questions about me. Said the callers were trying to get them to agree to inaccurate and slanderous information concerning me. Seemed to me that the flea-bitten FDA dog was about to bite. So, in typical Gurner reaction mode, I split. I've been in these beautiful mountains for a couple of weeks, cold but happy, trying to talk this whole thing over with my Friend of Friends. But He's been Mr. Mute the whole time, and trying to get advice out of Him is like trying to whittle down an iron rod with a blunt knife. The only thing I know for sure is that I'm heading home simply to pack up and leave. And if they . . .

Gurner stopped in his tracks and peered earnestly into the

stormy sky. His face suddenly acquired an inspired glow, as if the thousands of surrounding snowflakes had transformed into miniature light bulbs. Then the herbalist stomped his foot in the snow, raised one fist to the air, and loudly yelled into the monochrome sky.

"YOU ALWAYS DO THIS TO ME! You let me agonize for weeks about something and You never say a word, and then at the eleventh hour some very subtle flash pops into the background of my mind, and I've got an answer. There WAS a common denominator with those ALLIS victims! In fact there were *two* things common to every case. Oh thank You for finally showing me!"

Got to go back and see if it pieces together. Got to try! True healers would go back. They wouldn't run just when the answer might be presenting itself.

The potential healer doubled his already brisk pace along the trail, still yelling, still holding his fist in the air.

"But I'm taking You with me, God. I'm not going into the shit-hit fan alone. Do you read me? . . . Do you hear me?"

The wind wailed louder, actually accentuating the quiet of the forest.

"Hello. Do You hear? Are You there . . . ?"
Dead silence. Again.

♦ 4 ♦
Newstime

January 2, 2008. Excerpts from *Newstime* Magazine.

A LETTER TO THE GENERAL PUBLIC
FROM PUBLISHER MILES LOTTER.

The frightening AIDS epidemic and the successive affliction of Lyme Disease have placed newsmagazines in a quandary concerning reporting procedures on such subjects. AIDS reporting, we were told, was often blown out of proportion, was journalistic sensationalism, was a media-induced bogey. Statistics do prove that compared to other historic, worldwide disease plagues, AIDS was relatively minor in both the number of its victims and its technical difficulties in transmission.

Lyme Disease, on the other hand, appeared to warrant minimal media coverage. It was an antibiotically-controlled Richettsia, not a mysterious, untouchable virus; it was transmitted by ticks and not by controversial sexual and drug-related practices; it seemed a disease that deserved the standard and sometimes cursory coverage allotted such "ordinary" subjects. Compiled statistics then revealed a large percentage of the U.S. population to be afflicted with Lyme Disease. Again the public let us know that we blew it, that we missed a big one.

Damned if you do and damned if you don't notwithstanding, the affliction nicknamed ALLIS has earned this issue's feature article. The worldwide staff of *Newstime* has arduously compiled as many accurate facts, statistics, and opinions as now exist on this mushrooming threat.

Reporting on any disease is an incredibly complex process. Because ALLIS is so new a subject—less than six months since the first cases were detected—exact information becomes that much harder to obtain.

Will this issue be a repeat of the AIDS-type reporting band-wagon? The emerging statistics of ALLIS, and especially the enormous lack of knowledge about ALLIS, adequately answer no to that question. By presenting what is currently known, and by informing people early in the game, we hope to prevent later confusion.

Sincerely,
Miles Lotter, for *Newstime*

. . . . .

ALLIS, A HISTORY OF:

If one were to strike a up conversation about a new and frightening disease called RDMS, few persons would have an idea what these four letters represent. But say the word ALLIS, and every ear in hearing distance will turn and listen to what is being said.

RDMS is the medical abbreviation for the ailment officially titled RAPIDLY DECLINING METABOLIC SYNDROME. But "ALLIS" is the accepted and popular name for the disease.

In early August of 2007, Alice Cherskin, a housewife living in Sweet Home, Oregon, visited her family doctor after suffering five days of intense chills and sudden muscular weakness. Instead of the fever and other typical flu symptoms he expected to find, clinic physician Dr. Markham Bates discovered that Mrs. Cherskin's basal temperature was more than two degrees below the 98.6 F considered normal. He ran extensive blood and urine tests on Mrs. Cherskin. Before the results of these tests returned, Alice Cherskin's body temperature had dropped another two degrees, and her strength had ebbed further. She was rushed to a major medical hospital in nearby Corvallis, and extensive medical testing was again performed. Before the results were available, Alice Cherskin died, eleven days after her first reported symptoms. The complete results from both series of lab tests were thoroughly reviewed, but revealed nothing traceable as the cause of death. Neither did the autopsy.

Three days after Alice Cherskin had contacted Dr. Bates in Sweet Home, another Alice, Alice Whitaker of Bellingham, Washington, sat in the St. Luke Hospital emergency room, wondering why for the past three days she had been so deeply chilled and why she couldn't rouse the energy to continue her work as a fitness instructor at a local health spa. Doctors' preliminary examinations found nothing wrong with her other than a noticeable loss of strength and a basal body temperature two and one half degrees lower than normal. They admitted her to the hospital for further testing, and for the next ten days the medical teams at St. Luke's ran every manner of test available to that modern facility. The final two of those ten days they also attempted every life-support technique known to medicine. To no avail. Ms. Whitaker slipped into what resembled a hypothermic coma and died. The many tests and lab diagnoses revealed no abnormalities. The autopsy could pinpoint no reason for her rapid demise.

In the United States, any unexplainable—and therefore potentially communicable—incidence of disease is by law reported to the Centers for Disease Control (CDC) in Atlanta, Georgia. On August 19, 2007, the CDC received from Corvallis, Oregon, and from Bellingham, Washington, separate death reports that read almost identically. Dr. Howard Mathers, Assistant Director for the CDC's Initial Investigation Department, relates the Centers' reaction to these reports:

"Normally, we would have played these reports a bit skeptically and made telephone calls to acquire information. From such an initial inquiry we determine if adequate reason exists to investigate more deeply. But that same week reports began filtering into the Center from London, Paris, Buenos Aires, Mexico City and several other world locations . . . reports of individual deaths that formed exact prototypes of what was now being chronicled on the West Coast. We initiated instant action. We sent investigators to Corvallis and Bellingham."

Dr. Mathers concludes by running his hand through his hair in frustration. "As you well know, we needn't have bothered. It was going to show up at our own back door soon enough."

One month after the CDC received the first reports on the appearance of the new malady, the world seemed to explode into the ALLIS age. Day after day, from every state, from cities large and small, from all around the world, accounts poured into the Center. While CDC investigators rummaged through the Bellingham hospital's files, medical centers in both Atlanta and nearby Warner Robins, Georgia, documented cases of a fatal sickness that dramatically lowered the patients' body temperatures, sapped them of strength, and soon killed them.

The CDC found itself walking a tightrope. By October 2007, every state in the union, every province in Canada, every nation in the world had experienced an instance of this new and deadly disease. Yet the CDC did not release an official report on the disease until weeks later.

Dr. John Carwin currently heads the CDC's newly formed ALLIS Research and Investigation Team. "We had to balk for a long time after this thing hit. We had to keep our information away from the press for a while. We needed time to get a solid finger on ALLIS so as to not send the world population into hysterics."

That finger, exposed in a press conference at the CDC, proved to be connected to a fairly shaky hand. Statistics compiled by the Centers' data banks showed that this alien disease had, by October 1, 2007, claimed over 9,000 lives worldwide.

"But you must consider," declares Dr. Carwin, "that this number was dispersed over the nearly 200 countries in the world. That means out to about fifty deaths per country, the larger nations tallying more, the smaller ones less. The United States reported fewer than a hundred deaths. That's less than two per state."

"This is what we had to determine," says Carwin. "A hundred deaths in a large nation is not a plague. The people of New York or LA don't have to panic. The facts reveal ALLIS to be a very rare disease with a statistically nil chance of any particular person acquiring it. We didn't want panic buttons pushed, and so we held our information until we had some real facts on the subject."

Those practical facts currently represent the only positive news concerning ALLIS. Between the CDC's October report and an unofficial, preliminary listing of figures for mid-December, ALLIS-caused deaths have tripled in number worldwide. Everyone still remains a statistical improbability for contracting ALLIS. But any disease that has freely penetrated every corner of the Earth, and that triples its casualties in two months, and that has no cure, rides in the foreground of scientific and lay minds alike.

As one CDC researcher humorously stated: "You'll soon be able to recognize CDCers by their balding noodles, because we are all the time scratching our heads about this one."

. . . . .

ALLIS, THE DISEASE NO ONE UNDERSTANDS

Scratching heads seems to be all researchers trying to penetrate the mysteries of ALLIS are doing these days. *Newstime* launched a worldwide search for authorities on the subject of ALLIS and discovered that there are none.

The facts known about ALLIS are indeed few. In early August of 2007 a minute number of people—yet a scattering of people from all over the world—began contracting an unknown disease. Five months later, the incidence of the disease rapidly increased and continues to defy logical distribution patterns. Researchers currently discount the idea that ALLIS is a contagious disease. Rural settings seem as vulnerable to its touch as the densest population centers. Arctic Eskimos living in antiseptic environments and nomadic African tribesmen who rarely contact outsiders have also experienced "a new kind of dying." Meanwhile, there presently are no reported cases of a mate, a family member, or a close-contact friend of an ALLIS victim also contracting ALLIS. This fact alone eliminates contagion theories.

The other certainty medical science can affix to ALLIS is the uniform manner in which it affects its victims. Without exception, those who have died of ALLIS experience deep and uncontrollable chills accompanied by a sudden loss of muscular strength. The 98.6 degree Fahrenheit body temperature considered normal takes a 2.0 to 4.5 degree dip and never rises again. Doctors' single diagnostic tool in determining ALLIS contagion occurs when the patient's temperature remains below normal for five days and can by no means—natural or artificial—be elevated. In certain illnesses, and in incidences of hypothermia, a person's basal body temperature does drop for a time. But when the person is treated, the temperature returns to normal. If that core temperature fails to rise after five days, probabilities dictate that the person has ALLIS. Approximately five more days of chills and slowly decreasing body temperature follow before the person slips into a hypothermic coma, caused by a body temperature that is too low to support life. Two to three days after entering this coma, the person painlessly fades into death. No person afflicted with ALLIS has lived more than fourteen days after its initial manifestations.

These two short paragraphs summarize all anyone knows about ALLIS. The mysteries to be solved and the questions to be answered concerning the disease are innumerable.

What causes it? Virus? Bacteria? Heavy metal poisoning? Depletion of the ozone layer combined with the dangers of acid rain that we studied for so long and did so little about? No one knows. No cause has been isolated. There's no common ground for researchers to use as a beginning. There's no environmental accident, no initial starting point that the illness spread out from. There's no pool of common genes it attacks, no habits such as drug use or sexual promiscuity it attaches itself to. So far, no laboratory value, x-ray or diagnostic imaging reveals any trace of an unusual bodily condition.

What spreads or transmits this disease? No one knows. There's no pattern, no predictable process, no conformation to any of the set rules of contagious and degenerative disease.

What cures it? Nothing to date. No medicine, no drugs, no radiation treatments, no diet, vitamins, minerals, hot springs, etc. have even slowed its progress. No one knows.

As of press time, scientists and medical researchers worldwide have begun an all-out assault on the riddle of ALLIS. Government funding and private endowments are currently contributing millions to universities, laboratories, and medical think tanks to pursue any course of action that may lead to a cure or at least to an understanding of the disease.

Beginning research into ALLIS is taking many directions. One of the more promising approaches in attempting to trace the disease follows a theory propounded by Dr. Edward Ming of the University of California at Davis Medical Center. Dr. Ming is surgically extracting thyroid tissue from ALLIS patients and implanting this tissue into the thyroids of various primates. His theory, one that guides many researchers, states that because the thyroid gland is the body's control center for metabolism, and because ALLIS by all appearances is a metabolic disease (Rapidly Declining Metabolic Syndrome—RDMS—is the official nomenclature of ALLIS), discovering how the body acquires the disease will lead to a cure. When asked if any of his monkeys had yet contracted ALLIS, Dr. Ming stated: "Not yet. But we have great hope."

Other researchers are diligently looking for a new and as yet unidentified form of life—perhaps something smaller and deadlier than a virus. There is growing speculation that a new, super-killer bacteria or virus has escaped from the U.S. Army's biological warfare center or from one of its many contracted university labs (see accompanying story). Two private research firms are exploring the possibilities of the Earth having been contaminated with alien microbes from recent NASA space flights.

As the beginnings of deliberate and methodical scientific research settle into place, two fundamental facts surface. The bad news is that no one yet knows anything concrete about the deadly disease called ALLIS. The good news is that the sharpest of minds, the finest of resources, the best of science and medicine, and the prayers of the people are all focusing their attentions on understanding and curing ALLIS. At no time in history have these forces been vigorously activated and left us with an empty hand.

· · · · ·

ALLIS, IT'S JUST A NAME

ALLIS, the common name for the disease called Rapidly Declining Metabolic Syndrome (RDMS), had its origin first in coincidence and then in euphemism. The first two persons to die of the disease in America were both named Alice, Alice Cherskin of Sweet Home, Oregon, and Alice Whitaker of Bellingham, Washington. A correlative report from England had simultaneously reached the Centers for Disease Control (CDC) in Atlanta, Georgia, informing them of a strange manner of death affecting a Bristol woman named Alice Snodder. Although ALLIS has since proven its ability to affect anyone with any name, the original CDC investigators needed an appellative for this undefined condition. Because the first three reports of the event contained similar victim names, they initially designated it "The Alice Disease."

As information on the disease accumulated, CDC clerks felt that the name "The Alice Disease" might be taken too personally, especially by the tens of thousands of Alices in the world. They substituted the euphemism "ALLIS" on the file titles, thinking it would be but a temporary naming. RDMS has since been identified and officially named, but the eponym ALLIS has stuck like glue.

· · · · ·

ALLIS: DON'T BLAME ME.
An interview with Jim Bowerns, FDA
Investigations Director.

Jim Bowerns boasts an impressive track record. The suave and uncompromising director of the Food and Drug Administration's

Fraudulent Practice Investigations Division has a charming and continuous way of quelling the rising anxieties of both press and public. Not for the first time has the nation's entire media armada marched to his door hungry for answers and assurance and left replete with both.

Today's interview specifically dealt with an underlying possibility that the worldwide ALLIS outbreak may have found its birth in the union of technology and warfare. With no solid understanding of the disease, many researchers are asking the United States Army what connection its Biological Warfare branch may have to the outbreak of this new pandemic. Did the Army, in its quest for lethal organisms, create and release a new breed of death on the world? If so, please let science know so constructive reaction can begin. Other than categorically denying any such event, the Army, until this interview, has remained silent on the growing questions.

"I have personally spoken with the commander of the Fort Detrick biological facility," boomed Bowerns in his robust voice. "I have even been given access to a review of their top secret records, and both General Jenkins' testimony and the facility's own records prove what we already knew. The Army has done nothing, has no knowledge of anything along the lines of the ALLIS disease. More than that, there has never been an accident; there has never been a release of organisms from the grounds. The security at that place is incredible, and the safety procedures infallible."

Several reporters raised their hands to ask questions, but Bowerns shook them aside.

"What I say to you, what I challenge you and anyone spouting this Army 'foul play' nonsense to do is present proof—proper and adequate proof—that such an occurrence has happened. Newspeople, be responsible. Don't jump on unfounded rumors. We're awfully busy in all departments of the government these days, trying to get a hold on the ALLIS progression. I, and all the officials, have to ask you to not panic the public and to not repeatedly bother us with every rabid and unproven rumor that surfaces. Sure, if I were a Friends of the Earther or a Sierra Clubber, I might take an unexplainable event like this and use it to help my cause. But this situation is too serious for anyone to take to pushing panic buttons when they don't know what they're talking about. I have access to the facts, and the facts are that the

Army biological warfare research has nothing to do with the ALLIS disease. We don't know if the Arabs in their research may have unleashed such a beast . . . but like I say, let's not start any rumors."

Bowerns then reported on how much time, effort, money, and material the United States and other governments of the world are expending on ALLIS research.

"You the populace have to realize that this one is getting all the attention, all the efforts and top priorities. Unofficially, no less than five separate research facilities have reported to us that they are nearing vital and important breakthroughs. I can assure you that the clouds are lifting and the sun is about to rise on this one. Please offer the listening public the truth, not a bunch of rumors."

Bowerns then opened to questions from the reporters. A reporter from *Mother Jones Magazine* asked when he had read the Fort Detrick top secret papers, because the reporter had been at the FDA offices for two months and hadn't known Bowerns to take a trip to Maryland. Bowerns frowned, then stated that this was living proof of what he was saying about rumors from alarmists distorting the facts. He asked rhetorically if Mother Jones had ever heard of the U.S. Postal Service.

Later, another alternative magazine journalist questioned Fort Detrick's "supposedly infallible safety procedures," citing past workers' exposure to a deadly pathogen and past public testimony on Fort Detrick's massive safety problems and missing vials of various viruses and super-flus. Bowerns then called the press conference to an end. Leaving the room, he advised the "real reporters" to print the truth, publish the positive news, and ignore these "living examples of rumor-rats."

With the biological warfare question put to rest, the quest for a cure for ALLIS has one less false direction to follow. If science cannot find an antidote via the normal course of experimentation, perhaps it can stumble onto one through a path of elimination.

◆ 5 ◆
Environmentalist

January 5, 2008, 7:30 A.M. A country farmhouse, north of Boulder, Colorado.

"The environmental movement is dead!"

Absolute silence answered this early morning call, as the voiceless dawn greets a rooster's first crow.

Jeez. She must have not heard.

The rooster cackled again, louder this time. "The environmental movement is dead!"

A muffled voice did respond from the bathroom. "What's that, hon?"

The crower gave it his all this time, yelling at the top of his voice. "I said that the environmental movement in this country is dead! Kaput. *Finis.* It's gasped its last breath."

Jenny Willox, working her long graying-brown hair into braids, rounded the kitchen corner, strode over to a cluttered countertop and began slapping together a peanut butter and mayonnaise sandwich for her sack lunch. "Why is that, Jerry?"

"Because I quit. I've plain ol' had it. I'm leaving."

Jenny smiled to herself and looked at her brooding husband. "Oh Jerry dear, dear Jerry. Again?"

"I'm more than serious this time, Jenny. I've been stewing about it for weeks. More than thirty years on the ecology front lines, and I don't feel like I've won one battle. Nothing's changed. Nobody's become enlightened. The Earth is ever closer to terminal, man-caused decay. And it seems that fewer people than ever even care, at least actively."

Jenny threw an apple into her lunch sack and searched the disordered room for her coat. "Posh! You've done more to make this world a livable place than any other ten men . . . and more than any hundred Congressmen. And you know it."

Jenny Willox stared for a moment at her overemotional, over-worked, overcaring and loving husband of fifteen years. "Now listen, sweetie of mine. Don't you go making any rash decisions on your future until we air things out tonight. I'm late for work and gotta dash. There's warm cereal on the stove top, and the shopping list is on the refrigerator door for when you go to the store. Oh, and keep an extra close eye on Johnny. He started crying last night, a different kind of cry. I don't like it. It feels strange. But he doesn't have a fever and he's sleeping comfortably now."

She smiled and blew him a smooch. "I love you, sweetie."

"I love you, Jenny. So much."

Jerry and Jenny Willox kissed each other goodbye for the day. Jerry watched his wife hurry out the door, and there he remained, standing and staring at the closed doorway long after she had caught a ride with the local car pool.

And there you have a fair part of the problem, Jenny my love, my love. For thirty-plus years I've wandered from courtroom to Senate hearing to Forest Service and BLM office, from nuclear power plant site to peace march to "save the whales" and "quit clubbing the baby seals" protest rallies. Thirty years it's been, and man, I've organized, defended, fought, argued, spoken to crowds, led groups, received a few minor awards, all in the name of maybe keeping this Earth a livable and beautiful place. And for what? My lady still has to go out and work at some shit job, answering telephones so we can make ends meet, when I know she'd rather be home with our new babe. Thirty years of environmental lobbying, and I still can't buy us a decent house or a reliable vehicle.

He turned from the closed door and wandered into the kitchen. *I could handle that, dear Jenny. And you've told me many times that the lack of things doesn't matter to you as long as I'm following my heart. Oh what a support you are, girl. 'Cause you know my heart just disintegrates whenever a river dies under a chemical spill, whenever a bomb or a power plant destroys a landscape, whenever an entire species of life disappears from existence or a mountain is left void of life and beauty because it fed a developmental appetite that can never be satiated. I guess I could handle the material lack, IF all these years of effort had done anything to really stem the tide of environmental destruction.*

Willox ignored the pot of simmering oatmeal and poured himself a glass of milk and grabbed a handful of homemade cookies. He shuffled into the living room of their small, extremely "lived-in" house. He wandered over to a corner of this room that was screened off to form a tiny, cluttered business office. On a desk, one dwarfed by a perpetual pile of environmental alerts, speaking invitations, anti-nuclear protest rally schedules, and massive Environmental Impact Statements for proposed developments, there rested three picture frames containing the diamonds of three decades of Green labor. Recognition certificates from a dozen conservation groups were bunched together in one frame. A couple of tributes from national academies occupied another. A third, larger frame held a fading picture of a much younger, sparsely bearded Jerry Willox proudly displaying a "Love Your Mother" Earth flag at the 1970 Earth Day rally in Washington, D.C. Willox gazed at the picture while out of habit he stroked his bushy and graying beard.

The first Earth Day. We were going to give the world a needed facelift then. For a while "pollution" was an evil, and everyone had had enough of it. For a while environment wasn't something "out there" but became known as an inseparable part of existence. Effective control laws were passed, wilderness was saved in quantity, rivers were actually cleaned up; the Earth was being given a chance because the people cared. En masse they cared, and en masse they put that caring into demonstrable action. As the man said, if the people lead, the leaders will have to follow.

The contemporary face of Willox stared at the younger version in the photograph and sighed.

For a while, that is.

Willox then reread a recent newspaper article on his desk, one about the current President's latest nomination for Secretary of Interior. Willox also stared at the alerts from various environmental groups, all of them stating that this potential secretary was no more qualified to administer the nation's vast wealth of public lands than Genghis Khan was to run a day care center. The results, the alerts asserted, would be the same. They noted that the potential secretary owned vast ranch holdings and was vocally sympathetic to the cattle and sheep industries; that he had private interests in various mining operations that were flagrantly lax in meeting reclamation standards; that he couldn't possibly be knowledgeable in dealing with National Parks or unbiased when it came to wilderness classification.

Willox then stared at his feet, sadly, knowing well that the standard environmental groups would hotly contest this appointment, and that the President would just as hotly support it, and that Congress would probably approve it in the end. Most of all, he knew that the people—the public to be affected by the decision—would be lost in their own day-to-day living and not know or even care what the outcome would be.

What I can't understand, what I internally scream about again and again, is how mass breakdown into apathy occurs. Polls repeatedly show that people express a desire for environmental protection. Seventy percent want our air to be clean. More say they are concerned about this nation running out of safe drinking water. And God only knows that all of them, if they'd take two minutes to think about it, realize that a nation can't lose 200,000 acres of topsoil a year to erosion and stay healthy. But then in the elections they vote in these same lawmakers who attack the Earth while ignoring un-ignorable signs of decay. That's what I can't understand.

A typical day in the life of environmentalist Jerry Willox was unfolding. He paced the house's small living room, leaving a trail of cookie crumbs down his beard and on the carpet.

Even my friends, the ones who marched with me on Earth Day and worked through the '70s for the environment. They got into families, and then into houses and cars, and then into jobs to keep the houses and feed the families, which of course is all right and just and proper and helpful. But how can they so easily forget that every time they and a million others leave every light in the house on, the need for a nuclear power plant draws closer? How did they forget that if everybody demanded—would buy only—a vehicle that got fifty or sixty miles to the gallon, the auto industry would have to supply such a car? Why has it become easier to let the industry dictate the popular monsters of the day and their feeble mpg limits of twenty to thirty? The sink drain becomes the place to throw poisons because it's a hassle to take them to a reclamation center. When did they forget the river that drain empties into? I'll never understand—how did they get into the space where they vote conservative because consciously or subconsciously they're scared that in protecting the environment they may have to give up having more . . . and more . . . and more?

You're right, Jenny, I've gone through this debate on quitting many times before. But this time I really am a shish-ka-bobbed and totally burned-out environmentalist. I simply can no longer ignore how little active caring the majority of the people today display, and—

Something resembling a banshee howl forced Willox to drop all thoughts and two halves of cookies and dash around a corner and into the bedroom. He stooped to gently pick up a squirming bundle of blankets and spoke in soothing tones. "Hey, Johnny, Johnny, my boy. That's no way greet the morning, crying like a wailing wind. Let's get you changed and some of Mom's fresh-pumped milk warmed up and put down your gullet. That'll make the day seem better."

Willox was an expert parent by now. Cloth diapers flew, preboiled glass nursing bottles were filled, all-cotton pajamas were exchanged, and breast milk was warmed to just the right temperature.

After the bustle of helping nine-month-old Johnny Willox meet the day, Willox paused and treasured a moment of watching his son. "Hey, big guy. What's up? You're not nursing with your usual vigor."

Willox, propping Johnny in his elbow and angling the bottle toward his tiny mouth, resumed pacing the room. "Anyway, Johnny ol' buddy. You get to listen here to your pop's problems. I can't let Jenny come home and talk me back into my life's work. She's just too good at making me and my dreams feel like they're worthwhile. I want out of this for once and for all."

Willox looked lovingly and long into the half-focused eyes of the child in his arms.

"Ah, my son, will you still love me if I discard my 'Live Simply So That Others Can Simply Live' T-shirt and don the business suit of the working world? I mean, it's not too late for me to become a spokesman for the foreign fishing industry. I could put together quite a case for the fact that limiting a fleet's use of twenty-mile-long line nets is a ridiculous profit-cutting practice, that to stay financially viable we absolutely need to net and kill every bit of life in our path. Why, with the salary I'd make, we could buy your mother a . . . a fur coat! She could join the ranks of the thousands of middle-class women who are individually contributing to the steel-jawed trap mutilation and prolonged deaths of thirty or more animals per coat. And then I could enlist my services—"

The milk bottle crashed to the floor as tiny arms flailed the air and baby screams rose to new crescendos. Willox paced in small circles, patting his son's back and realigning his thoughts.

Who am I trying to kid? Even as a joke it makes my heart do its disintegrating act. And Johnny must have tuned into the bad energy, because he's really crying now.

Willox walked and rocked and patted and embraced and spoke to his child. "Hey, Jocko, easy here . . . Jenny was right. This crying doesn't sound normal. But you don't have a fever, guy. You're kind of cool if anything. Let's see if—"

God Almighty.

The environmentalist paled, then vigorously shook his own head from side to side.

What a flash of terror! C'mon Willox, don't freak out. The news commentator just last night said that the statistical probability of it happening to any individual was less than one in two hundred thousand.

Willox gazed intently at his crying baby. "Listen, kid. Don't you dare get ALLIS on us. Because of my beliefs about population control, we waited until the eleventh hour and the fifty-ninth minute to have you. You get ALLIS, and it would kill your mother and me. It would kill you, too, even worse, and a lot quicker. Let's not even think about that kind of stuff. Okay?"

♣ 6 ♣
Cure

January 6, 2008, 1:00 P.M. A small mountain cabin near Canyon Creek Summit, south of the town of John Day, Oregon.

The reclusive herbalist named Gurner peered from behind a pine tree and looked into a secluded clearing that sheltered the two-room log cabin he called home. He was playing woods-sleuth because he wanted a sneak preview of what awaited him before he openly revealed his presence.

Not so bad, God. Not so doggone bad. Only one car and two people. I expected about twenty people to be camped at my door. I guess disappearing for a while has its advantages. It lets people think you're a rumor instead of a reality.

Gurner left the forest and walked toward his cabin. A distraught man emerged from a small Subaru and ran to meet him. Gurner warily greeted him. "Howdy, can I help you?"

"Mr. Gurner. You're back in time. Thank heavens."

"What's happening here? You look as shook up as a hound-treed cat."

The slender man answered Gurner's question in an excited voice. "My name is Brian Johnson. My wife—Mary—in the car. She's got ALLIS. She's going to die. I . . . we . . . you . . . You've cured some other people. Can you help her?!"

Gurner closed his eyes for a moment. *Good grief, God. You're not even giving me a little time to put this theory together on paper. It's suddenly "jump-right-in-and-begin-round-two."*

The healer opened his eyes and assessed the man in front of him. He was a small man, dapperly dressed, and obviously distressed. Gurner pointed to the cabin. "First thing we do is get you and your wife into the cabin, build a hot fire, and then make you up a cup of herbal nervine tea to ease the shaking of your hands. Take some breaths, calm down a little, and help me get her out of the car. You're sure it's ALLIS? How long has she had the symptoms?"

The two men eased the blanket-wrapped and shivering woman from the car and guided her toward the cabin door.

"Eight days, Mr. Gurner, almost nine now. Her temperature is four and a half degrees below normal, and she has no strength. It can't be anything else. I drove here practically nonstop from Washington, D.C., and have been waiting here for a day and a half, hoping against hope that you would return."

Gurner leaned against the cabin door and it swung open. *Holy Hannah, what an incredible situation. This man is putting his whole and only hope into my hands. Well, I'm doing the same, putting my whole hope into Yours, God. You led me to this cure idea. Now it will either work or it won't.*

Gurner turned on a light and began searching for paper and kindling. Billows of frosty breath rose from the three persons. "Lay her down on the couch there, Brian. Sorry this place is such a mess. Some . . . uh, pranksters broke in just before I left and scattered everything. I didn't have time to clean it up properly."

After the wood stove fire was crackling, Gurner lit a propane burner and placed a small pot of water over the flame. Within minutes the water boiled, and he lowered the flame, adding some nondescript leaves to the simmering liquid. Minutes later he brought Johnson a steaming cup of bitter-smelling tea.

"Now, you drink this. It might make you sleepy, but mostly it should relax you a bit. While I attend your wife, you can sit and watch, or snoop around the cabin, or do whatever you want. But to work on Mary I've got to have time and silence. You won't see any tools or tests so common with regular doctors. It's in my inner mind that I try and tune in to what's happening with her."

Johnson grimaced at the taste of the tea. "Of course I'd like to watch you, Mr. Gurner. I'd even take notes, if you don't mind."

"Be my guest. You won't understand much of what's happening. Just don't ask questions until later. Then I'll try and explain. But do understand this. I can't promise you anything. I'm going into this pretty blind myself. If your entire world depends on me finding a cure for Mary, your entire world may have chosen the wrong guy."

"You've cured at least three other people with the disease."

"That's rumor. The *truth* is, a few ALLIS people I worked on lived. The facts are I did something different on each of them, and everything I did was pure guesswork. I think I recently stumbled on a common thread in the treatments. Mary will be the first person I try this idea on. Do you understand that? Your wife will be the very first statistic in a life-or-death experiment. I'm not even sure I want to take on that responsibility. How can you?"

"Nothing else anyone anywhere has done has had success. Go for it, Mr. Gurner. If Mary dies, I'm not sure I'll have a reason left to live."

Look at his hands shake. Go for it, he says. Oh please, God my Friend, don't let this woman die under my hands. "Have another cup of that tea, Brian. We'll be with you in a couple of hours."

The healer positioned himself at the head of the supine woman. He closed his eyes and lightly rubbed his hands together for several moments, exhaling a long, audible sigh. Then he gently cupped her head in his hands.

Hello, Mary. Not feeling so hot, are you? Shaking like a leaf, in fact. Let me just put my hands under your neck and tune into your vibrations . . . let me sense the vibrations of your body's working . . .

Brain feels fine. Pituitary strong. Thyroid OK. Can't understand this. A metabolic disease and not one thyroid I've felt on an ALLIS victim seems to be off. Heart . . . lungs . . . stomach fine, perhaps a little shy on digestive acids, though whose isn't in this nutrition-less, stress-filled country? Pancreas feels a mite weak. Bet you're hypoglycemic . . . yeah, because also on the down side are the adrenals. Liver . . . spleen . . . intestines and colon feel good . . . reproductive system is fine.

Gurner, never opening his eyes, leaned his body closer to Mary's.

OK. Saved you for last. Let's see if part one of a two-part ALLIS bonding theory also holds true in this person . . .

Yes! Sure enough! There it is again. Weaker than a cut flower. I'll be able to pay attention to this facet now that I know. Let me tune into it a little deeper . . .

Yes! That's it! It feels like a top spinning the wrong way. Not only spinning backwards but also in that wobble a top goes into just before it falls down.

Gurner filed this present information, glanced at Johnson, whose head was bobbing as he tried to stay awake against the tea's soporific effects, and moved deeper into his intuitive inquiry.

Feels like you're lacking in some nutrition, Mary . . . vitamin A. OK. The B's. Down that long list. C and bioflavinoids. D, E, F, and G. Good. K, and T. Also good. Calcium is adequate. Zinc seems lacking . . . often part of the game with hypoglycemia. Chromium deficient, too. Don't sense much else. A little too much aluminum . . . you must be a soda pop drinker.

Well, Mary. If ALLIS weren't taking such precedence here, we could tackle this hypoglycemia and give you more energy and health than you've felt in a while. Agrimony and juniper berries for the pancreas, add some licorice root and goldenseal for the adrenals; get you to supplement the minerals until things balance out. Also get you off that damn sugar and onto some whole foods . . . there. There's that internal sigh in me that says it's the proper route for this particular body. But first we've got to get you beyond the ALLIS.

Gurner, without opening his eyes or breaking his concentration, moved his forehead closer to Mary Johnson's forehead.

So now the big one. Will this herb that I haven't even classified yet . . . will this herb give me that same deep and harmonious click inside when I tune into it and then mentally inject that tuning-in into this woman's ALLIS? Will it, oh dear God, will it? Is this plant the second part of the answer?

Yes! . . . Are you sure? . . . Yes! Try a few of the other herbs that I gave to the other people . . . No, no there's nothing there. No internal, intuitive click of rightness. Try this herb again . . . Yes! Yes! Oh God, yes!

As Gurner looked up at a deeply snoozing Brian Johnson, his mind retreated to a recent back-country, herb-gathering expedition. *Found this herb on a trip last summer and was intensely attracted to it. Brought some home, dried it, and promptly forgot about it. When the ALLIS-stricken people came, every time I went into the drying room to put together some herbs for them, I sprinkled a small amount of this herb into the mixture. Did it almost unconsciously. As it stands now, the one man who didn't take this herb died, and the four persons who did lived.*

Out of habit, the herbalist almost shouted to the cabin's ceiling, but managed to check his enthusiasm before waking Johnson from his slumber. He spoke in a whisper. "Easy, Gurner. Push back this rising scream that wants to shout that there is a cure for ALLIS, and let's just wait for the proof to happen. But dear Mary. I honestly feel you're going to make it. And any more, these feelings don't seem to come just from me."

· 7 ·
Denial

January 12, 2008, 3:04 P.M. Jim Bowerns' office, FDA headquarters.

Jim Bowerns, advised over the intercom by his secretary, opened the office door just as his agent raised a hand to knock. Bowerns' voice carried an uncommon exuberance.

"Johnson! Come on in, my boy. Good to see you. I was just thinking of you and wondering what's the latest news on your case."

Brian Johnson entered the room and looked dubiously around, first at his supervisor and then at a handsome young woman seated in front of the chief's desk.

Bowerns played host. "Brian Johnson, I'd like you to meet Dr. Stephanie Peters, recently graduated from our neighboring Baltimore medical school. Dr. Peters, Brian Johnson, a finest and foremost agent, a man who was instrumental in closing several of the cases I was just telling you about."

The two strangers formally shook hands and then lapsed into silence. Bowerns kept the conversation alive.

"Brian, several of Dr. Peters' colleagues suggested to her that she come and interview me. She's investigating the potential of alternative healing, and they wanted her to have access to the entire story and not just the fairy tales a bunch of nutritionists and herbalists babble out."

Bowerns did not notice the flash of interest light up Johnson's eyes, nor did he catch the slight blush that coursed over Dr. Peters' face.

"You can well imagine that I've been filling her in on some of the grim facts and quack realities out there in the real world. We've covered everything from radionics hokum to faith-healing bunkery. In fact, I was just about to mention Gurner and use him as my final example. Your timing is perfect! You can not only fill me in on what I hope is a final chapter on the man, but also allow this young lady to attain a sense of our work when we get on the trail of a medical phony."

Johnson's face congealed into strained expression. "Mr. Bowerns, I, ah, think I'd better talk to you about Mr. Gurner alone."

"Nonsense. No, sit down, Dr. Peters, please. I insist that you stay. I would really like you to hear about this Gurner person, a man who is using the ALLIS terror to aggrandize his own name and gains. All under the auspices of 'natural healing.' I feel you need a thorough exposure to this side of the story."

Bowerns turned his attention to Johnson. "Now, Brian, your wife, what was her name?"

"Mary. Look Mr. B—"

"Yes, Mary. You thought she had contracted ALLIS. Did this prove to be so?"

"Yes, doctor confirmed. Look, Mr. Bowerns, I—"

"I'm sorry to hear that, Brian. But you did then take her to Gurner to be . . . uh . . . 'healed,' like we talked about?"

Johnson's face suddenly set itself in stone. *OK, Bowerns. O-doggone-K. I'll play your sick game here. For just a few moments.*

"Yes. Yes, I did."

"Excellent, Brian. And he did try and treat her?"

"Yes, he put his all into it."

"How far into the disease was Mary?

"She was just about to slip into the coma."

"Excellent! Er, ah, that is . . . what did Gurner do?"

"He spent over two hours in total silence with his eyes closed and his hands cupping the back of her neck. And then he spent two days gently pouring an herbal tea down her throat."

Jim Bowerns clapped his hands together in elation. "And you were there the whole time, witnessing him doing this?!"

Johnson offered his boss a cold stare and an affirmative nod. "The whole time."

The branching vein on Jim Bowerns' forehead began to throb. "That's great! This cinches the case. And Mary is now . . .? Go ahead and say it son; we all have to face this sometime."

"Mary is right now attending a surprise birthday party for her mother."

At least sixty seconds of uncomprehending silence and occasional, uncontrollable face-twitching followed Johnson's statement. Stephanie Peters watched with fascination as the two men exchanged eye fireworks with each other. Finally, the chief of Investigations forced a crooked but not-too-happy smile.

"Ha ha, Johnson."

Johnson shook his head and blew out a long and labored sigh. His spare body arched into a Goliath-battling stance. "Ha ha, yourself, Mr. Bowerns. Now you just shut up and listen. And listen without bias, if you can. Because of your insistence, we now have a witness to this next speech, and that may be for the better." Johnson shot the visitor a fair imitation of a stern glance. "No, Dr. Peters. Sit down. Please.

"Mary was dying, and most of me was dying with her. I did take her to Mr. Gurner, but not because of your sick suggestion to frame him through her. I was hoping for a cure. But even then some kind of God-awful loyalty to this wretched work had me acting as an undercover information gatherer."

Johnson shook his head again and looked as if he was going to spit. "Well, here's the information. Mary is alive, and the thanks for that belongs wholly to Mr. Gurner and a herbal remedy."

Bowerns, forehead vein swelling like a pair of inflating forked balloons, drew a breath and opened his mouth to speak. Johnson slammed his fist on the boss's desk and cut him off. "No! You just keep quiet and listen to this whole story. And you . . . sit down . . . please, Dr. Peters.

"He, Mr. Gurner, said he had found an herb that may have saved the other ALLIS victims he worked on. He said that we were going to give that herb to Mary in full dosage. Every two hours he brewed some of this strange-smelling plant into a tea and teaspoon by teaspoon he placed the liquid into Mary's mouth, urging her—forcing her—to swallow it. All day and all night he did this. And all the while he was talking, praying to God as if God were sitting on the couch right next to him.

"Twenty-four hours later, Mary came back to her senses. Do you hear that? She slipped from the grasp of the coma that to our knowledge has let *no one* go. We took her temperature, and it was only one degree below normal. Up three and a half degrees. Do you hear that? One more day on the tea and Mary, though still weak, was strong enough to walk to the car and talk in full sentences. Her temperature was totally on the mark: ninety-eight point six. Two days more and not a soul could tell she had been so close to death."

Bowerns again inhaled, fiercely, but Johnson again cut him off. "No, you just listen to one more thing. Sir, hear this, so you know that Mr. Gurner is not the glory-grabbing opportunist of your views. We were leaving, Mary and I, and I asked the healer how much I owed him. He said that he worked on her for a total of four or five hours, how about a hundred bucks? I couldn't believe it. A hundred dollars? I said, 'You kept her here for two days. God almighty, you *healed* her. You could charge $5,000. Even more.' He said that he didn't heal her. He said that he really didn't know what he did, and that if he were the kind of person that charged $5,000 for a gift from God, then he probably wouldn't have been given an insight into that herb in the first place."

Johnson lapsed into silence. The two FDA men stared at each other in a contest similar to a blazing sun shining onto a mammoth glacier. Stephanie Peters, like the seed of a spring flower, sat motionless off to the side, waiting to see which force—summer or winter—ruled.

Winter rallied. "If you are quite finished, *Mister* Johnson. I can't believe this. I cannot believe my ears. This Gurner must be a hypnotist as well as a phony. He's obviously got you under his spell."

Summer held its ground. "Hypnotism hasn't done a thing for ALLIS, try as the best hypnotists in the world might."

"She obviously never had ALLIS."

"Tell that to Mary, who spent nine days feeling herself fade away. Tell that to the doctors who examined her, six days into the disease and again after we returned from the healer's cabin. They're literally shaking me by the collar, trying to get me to tell them what we did. But Mr. Gurner didn't want to generate a mountain of false hopes. He insisted that I make no public statement until he has a chance to prove the efficacy of this herb. That's the only reason I didn't get on the phone right away calling every newspaper in the country. But as soon as he tells me it's okay, that's exactly what I'm going to do."

Reason was not aiding Winter in its battle. Winter resorted to cold authority. "Johnson, you'll do no such thing. You have a job to do, and an obligation to the principles of this organization. This story will *not* leave this room, or . . ." Bowerns glanced sharply at Dr. Peters, "heads will roll. You're damn near out of a job anyway, man, and one foolish move will push you over the line."

Summer was at its height. "Mr. Bowerns, my resignation will be in the minute I leave this room. I've had too much time to think this over, and it's become terribly obvious that we and the AMA, in trying to maintain complete control over the health practices of people, are going the wrong direction in a blind alley. If we just went after the real quacks it would be one thing. But I can no longer set up alternative practitioners or in any way help the medical establishment crush new shoots of wisdom simply to maintain a position of control."

"Then what the hell are you even doing here?"

"Quite simply, a disease that defies all logic and description is in the beginning stages of ravishing this world. A miracle has happened, and in it lies the hope to avoid the massive grief and terror that is looming ahead. You know the potential course this ALLIS thing is taking. You are one of the most influential men in top government today. Your opinions dictate directions. You could easily direct some government ALLIS research moneys into studying this herb, isolating whatever chemical or component in it that is effective on ALLIS, and then synthesizing it into an available vaccine for the masses. I'm here because I think your help is the fastest way to avert calamity. Mr. Gurner is all for it. He'll help all he can."

Summer ended its speech and looked long and hard at Winter. Summer could see, judging from the protruding, pulsating vein on Winter's forehead, that a severe tempest was mounting in Winter's thoughts. Summer tried one last flower bouquet as an offering. "Sir, at least talk to Mr. Gurner. See for yourself."

Winter blew, screaming like a raging snowstorm. "I'll be talking to him and damn soon for sure! At the gallows! Even without your feeble help, Johnson, we've got his number pegged. We've got proof that a man died whom he treated for ALLIS. And murder, even if it's herbal murder, that's enough by any court's book."

Summer realized that it also owned a scream, like the mid-July sun screaming at a desert land. "Now *I* can't believe my ears! Hope is injected into the hopeless, and you tell me you're going to hang the man who discovered it?"

"And you too if you don't goddamn get on the ball and add your testimony against him."

"Like holy hell I will."

"That's right. You holy hell will. You will be called to court, will be under oath—"

"While some neon-mouthed prosecuting lawyers ask the questions in such a way that the information will come out condemning Mr. Gurner. I'll contempt first."

"Good. You belong in jail."

"And you belong in front of a mirror. Have you ever taken the time to see what kind of creature exists beneath that 'exemplary' exterior of yours?"

Jim Bowerns strode over to the office door and jerked it open. "Good day, ex-agent Johnson."

Johnson gaped in disbelief for a second. Then he stormed through the doorway without another word.

The office door efficiently clicked shut behind the retreating man's footsteps. Jim Bowerns stood by that closed door for a minute as various shudders coursed through his body and his forehead vein. By the desk, the Spring flower seed decided that she didn't like glaciers all that much, and that the Summer sunshine seemed to be getting away. She gingerly stood up, trying to be as inconspicuous as possible.

"Excuse me, Mr. Bowerns. I'd . . . I'd better be leaving."

"Wha—? Oh, Dr. Peters. I'm so sorry you had to witness such an irresponsible display. I assure you that this department does not—"

"Yessir. Excuse me, but I have to run."

"I hope you don't think—"

"Excuse me. I have to run." *If I don't run now, I'm afraid I may be running the rest of my life.*

Dr. Peters slipped out the door and ran, along the building halls and past astonished employees. She peered into every open doorway on her route, and then dashed across the main lobby and out into the parking lot.

Oh please don't let me have missed him. I can't have missed him. Oh, If I missed h— Oh yea, there he is.

Johnson was in process of unlocking his car door. "Mr. Johnson! Mr. Johnson! Please wait a minute. I need to talk to you." She sprinted across the parking lot. "I need . . . would you . . . I ask you to tell me how to get in touch with this Mr. Gurner."

Johnson cocked his head and looked askance at her.

"Look, Mr. Johnson. It sounded like you just had an experience that offered you insights and changed the course of your life. Well, I've spent twelve years pursuing my medical diploma, but it doesn't seem to be sitting on a complete foundation. When I heard you talking about this healer, something in my heart said that he might be my best chance of filling in the missing pieces. I have just got to talk to him."

Johnson thought for a moment, then pulled a notepad from his car and began writing on it. "Dr. Peters, it sounds like your meeting Gurner would be a good thing for you, a good thing for me, and even a good thing for him. His phone has been disconnected. Small wonder, what with the number of kooky calls he was getting in those two days I was there. He lives in Oregon. It's a long way from this end of the continent. But I could really use a messenger to deliver him a note as quickly as possible. If you want to make that trip, I'll give you directions, if you'll promise to head right there and also promise to immediately give him this letter. If you will do that, I can get going on informing the media that there is an ALLIS cure."

"I thought you said Mr. Gurner didn't want publicity."

"He doesn't. But that's what's going to save his neck—if anything still can."

Dr. Peters didn't hesitate. "Count on me, Mr. Johnson. I'm a free woman, just out of school yet with no practice of my own. Plus, it feels really right that I meet him."

Johnson smiled a relieved smile. "Great! And maybe, hopefully, both our actions will prevent Bowerns' trap from springing shut and whacking off the head this world desperately needs right now."

· 8 ·
Newstime

January 23, 2008. Excerpts from *Newstime* magazine.

Never in the publication history of *Newstime* magazine has a feature article netted such copious mail response. The questions, fears, and lack of answers concerning the ALLIS disease have deeply penetrated the reading public's thoughts. To date, our editorial department has received more than 200,000 letters from readers worldwide. Some of the correspondence did accuse us of "jumping the gun" and reporting the newsy side of a story before any conclusive evidence could be cited. Other letters praised us highly for offering the public the hard facts.

Though the letters are too numerous and varied to publish, the editors did notice, in reading every response in this mammoth pile of mail, an oft-repeated question: "Aren't there more positive hopes concerning this disease?"

Newstime continues its quality networking in search of answers for this query. In this issue, we examine the various paths researchers are pursuing in the quest of an ALLIS cure.

· · · · ·

ALLIS: A FACTS UPDATE

Three weeks in the life span of a disease is not a long period of time. By rights, no significant statistical change should occur in so short a span. But the recent and deadly malady named ALLIS proves itself a rule breaker. Three weeks ago, statistics cited a two-month tripling of the worldwide death numbers attributed to the illness. The latest ALLIS fatality figures released from the Centers for Disease Control (CDC) in Atlanta, Georgia, have nearly doubled. By mid December 2007, verified ALLIS-caused deaths had reached 27,000 persons worldwide. Planetary figures compiled by the CDC as of January 18, 2008, reveal that more than 50,000 people have now died from the disease.

It doesn't require a professional statistician to calculate that if such a logarithmic base became the trend of this disease—a doubling of expiration figures every two to three weeks—the Earth's population of 6.6 billion people would no longer exist after 34 to 50 weeks.

Dr. John Carwin of the CDC's ALLIS Research and Investigation Team laughs at this worst-case scenario. States Carwin, "There you reporters again blow a simple statistic out of proportion. Allowing this 50,000 number to stand by itself without explanation is like condemning a pregnant cow to slaughter because her milk production has slowed without considering that a cow always dries up a few months before she calves."

Dr. Carwin continues: "Our analysis states that most of the 23,000 new deaths in these recent figures are not—I repeat, are *not*—an uncontrolled explosion of ALLIS but are—I repeat, *are*—a compilation of numbers from earlier deaths that were not attributed to ALLIS. In other words, this is such a new disease that many parts of the world could not ascertain the real cause behind their unexplainable deaths. In time, media coverage and medical reporting made this knowledge available to smaller, primitive-type clinics. This new number is simply a flood of old numbers catching up. We at the Center confidently expect these figures to soon level off and assume more predictable proportions."

Other update information on ALLIS remains the same. The disease still strikes without warning, without boundaries, without rhyme or reason. A person's class, age, sex, geographic location, life style, and present state of health seem to have no bearing on the distribution or occurrence of ALLIS. The disease is centralized nowhere; it's been identified in every corner of the world. It always commences with a lowering of the body temperature and a sudden loss of strength. The course of the disease continues for eight to ten days before its victim slips into a coma. Approximately three days later, the victim dies. With but one current exception [see accompanying article], no one has survived verified ALLIS for more than fourteen days. No science yet claims any knowledge as to the cause or cure for this virulent and vague affliction.

When Dr. Carwin's rational explanation of the ALLIS statistics is placed on the dissection table, one discerns that the ALLIS fatality numbers didn't triple over the two-month period from October to December. They almost sextupled. That may be reason enough to slaughter the cow. If only we knew how.

. . . . .

ALLIS: THE ASSAULT ON MANY FRONTS

The poster is a catchy one. A young man is supporting his blanket-enveloped, shivering and obviously ALLIS-afflicted wife; his wallet lies empty at his feet; a bottle of some kind of questionable potion with a skull-and-crossbones label rests on a nearby table. The husband is desperately trying to spoon this mixture into his love's mouth while a dark-clothed and antithetical character slips out the back door. The shady personality clutches a handful of money, presumably from the wallet and paid in exchange for the ominous healing potion. Beneath this diabolical scene are the words: "Heard of a good ALLIS cure? Please help us look into it before cure becomes kill." A Food and Drug Administration toll-free 800 number is then listed.

"When science is temporarily unable to answer a scary question, superstition often begins to surface. And unfortunately, a lot of opportunists prey on people's mythological fears." With these words, John McComb, M.D., commissioner of the federal Food and Drug Administration, opened a press conference announcing the FDA's new campaign against unproven and potentially dangerous black-market cures for the disease called ALLIS.

The United States Food and Drug Administration carries the enormous responsibility of assuring quality standard controls be applied to the innumerable foods, beverages, and medicines consumed in this country. In light of the thousands of new foods and chemicals introduced into the market every year, this considerable task becomes an increasingly difficult accomplishment. When a "wasp in the beehive" such as ALLIS enters the scene, a predictable onslaught of "Gramma Somebody's Cure-alls" invariably follows. The FDA then finds its limited resources further taxed.

Dr. McComb: "I remember the arthritis potions of the '50s; poisons at best. I remember the cancer cure quacks in the '60s and '70s; coffee enema addicts is what they were. Along with the American Medical Association, the FDA fights a continuous battle

to keep naturopaths and chiropractors and nutritionists and herbalists and other uneducated know-alls from misleading a gullible
and too-willing-to-listen public.

"And now we have ALLIS," continues Dr. McComb. "With it
we face another influx of hotshot cures. I have in my office a
bottle of some concoction called 'Goodbye ALLIS,' a formula
'guaranteed' to counter the disease's temperature-lowering effects.
It contains, in a concentrated alcohol base, coal tar and cayenne
pepper. This formula consists of an irritant—and a poisonous one
at that—a stimulant, and a vaso-dilating depressant in one dose.
One shot of that stuff would make you forget you had anything
. . . for the moment. Do you know what this 750 milliliter bottle
of seventy-five cents worth of ingredients is selling for on the
streets? Fifty dollars! Need I even mention how ineffective it is
on the disease itself?"

This latest educational awareness program from the FDA is
Fraudulent Practice Investigations head Jim Bowerns' newest
brainchild. Says Bowerns: "We're seeing, purported as ALLIS
cures, wonder salves and mineral cure-all creams, electro-crystal
vibrators, and wild rituals that amount to voodoo dances around
the old oak tree. Before things get out of hand, we want to inject
some sanity into the situation. Thus the hot line number. When
someone deliberately plays on the terror of the ALLIS victims by
promising them that an herbal tea will heal their ills [see accompanying article], we want to be able to act. We're asking people
who are approached by street vendors purporting ALLIS cures to
phone the information into our center. Help us look into it. Help
us to determine the validity or the fraudulence of a specified
remedy, before its lack of effectiveness and its potential deadliness
are discovered the hard way."

Medical science to date has not been able to produce one drug
or therapy that counters ALLIS. Governments and private endowments around the world are contributing increasing amounts of
money, manpower, and materials to scientific research on ALLIS.
Almost any think tank, university, or science foundation with a
feasible research proposal on the cause or cure of ALLIS can
easily acquire funding from several sources.

One of the more promising research projects was that of Dr.
Edward Ming of the University of California at Davis Medical
Center. Unfortunately, his injections of ALLIS-victim thyroid
gland tissue into healthy primates has been temporarily suspended.

After weeks of unsuccessful attempts to induce the disease in monkeys and chimpanzees, Dr. Ming grabbed a lab rifle and shot and killed fifteen primates involved in his experiment. U of C Davis' only comment on the incident was an anonymous spokesperson noting: "This shows how seriously we take our research here."

Humans appear to be the only animal on Earth susceptible to the ALLIS plague. Laboratories have tried to induce the disease in lower life forms—dogs, cats, mice, etc.—with no reported success. Similarly, no one has yet been able to successfully induce ALLIS in humans. Experimenters reason that understanding how humans contract the disease would offer a strong starting point. This knowledge, like the disease, remains a mystery. No artificial attempts to transfer the disease from one person to another—including blood transfusion from ALLIS victims to healthy individuals—has increased the incidence of disease beyond what normal statistics dictate.

Hospitals around the world have attempted to artificially elevate the body temperature of persons after they acquire ALLIS. Patients are wrapped in electric blankets or placed in hot baths and sauna-like rooms for long periods of time. An elevation in body temperature does occur in these situations, but it is only a temporary warming. Even volunteers who permanently reside in heated rooms or pools still slip into the coma nine to eleven days after contracting ALLIS. No one has recovered the lost muscular strength.

Many investigators are attempting to discover sub-microscopic forms of life—disease organisms smaller than viruses—that may be the cause of ALLIS. Despite an array of remarkable technological aids, no success has been reported.

The thyroid gland finds itself under intense research these days. Due to assiduous scrutiny, several exciting breakthroughs have been made concerning this master of the body's metabolism. Observations from several researchers reveal that the addition of chlorine and fluoride to drinking water may inhibit the thyroid's immune and antibacterial capacities. While endocrinologists find reason to rejoice over these new discoveries, nothing concrete has yet established a link between the thyroid gland and the ALLIS disease.

In the short history of ALLIS, but one variation on the disease has occurred. A baby boy in Boulder, Colorado, contracted ALLIS more than seventeen days ago. Although quite deep in the hypothermic coma of the last stages of ALLIS, the child is still alive. Johnny Willox, nine-month-old son of Jerry Willox, a renowned and outspoken environmentalist, is now the longest-living victim of ALLIS.

Medical researchers are excited. This single baby presents a strong potential in a world weak on needed facts. If science can determine what it is in the baby's body that allowed it to survive beyond the normal ALLIS life expectancy of twelve to fourteen days, they may discover a factor that will be transferable to other humans. The parents, Jerry and Jenny Willox, have indicated that they will donate their boy's body to research immediately after he dies. The parents did demand that they be left alone with the baby until this last moment.

The hope of scientific success in mitigating the ever-growing ALLIS threat appears bleak at this moment. But again, things must be put into perspective. Many research projects have only begun to accumulate data. Many theories are in their crude and beginning stages. Educated and technological minds from around the world are in the first degrees of focusing on the problem. Unlimited material resources are being made available to these searching minds.

Dr. McComb of the FDA again reminds readers that science is working hard to find a cure for ALLIS. He states that the public must be careful not to turn its common sense aside and grasp at unproven, unscientific treatments and purported cures. "Trust," says Dr. McComb, "in that precise medical and scientific system which has guided mankind to where we are now in this modern world. Trust not in the coarse guesswork of mental haploids claiming to be healers."

· · · · ·

THE EXISTENCE OF HAPLOID HEALERS: POINT/COUNTERPOINT

Brian Johnson emphatically states that he is not a crazy man. He then metaphorically puts his foot into his mouth and declares that there is an efficient and effective cure for ALLIS. He says that a man whose only known name is Gurner has discovered an herb that relieves and permanently reverses the symptoms and final consequences of this new disease. Finally, Johnson asserts that the United States Government, specifically its Food and Drug Administration, is deliberately attempting to both conceal and obliterate this fact.

Such a statement would normally be regarded as incredible. But this particular speaker carries two incontestable credentials that lend credence to his testimony. Johnson, for more than fifteen years and until recently, was an agent of the FDA's Fraudulent Practice Investigations Division. This means that he has been a prominent person in the government's inquiries concerning illegal and phony healing claims. If anyone would know about the effectiveness of purported cures, Johnson does.

Johnson's second recommendation stands beside him in the form of a pretty and petite brunette. His wife Mary holds in her hand two medical diagnostic reports. One states that she was four days into suspected contagion of the disease ALLIS. Another is dated two days later and proclaims she was six days confirmed into the disease and not expected to live another week. Both reports accurately list Mary Johnson's display of standard ALLIS symptoms and disease procedure. Both reports are signed and dated by Dr. Abram Jensons of the Potomac Medical Clinic in Washington, D.C.

While Mary looks on, Johnson relates what he claims to be a true tale. He talks of the six months he spent gathering prosecution information on an effective healer from Oregon named Gurner. He tells of the arguments he found himself involved in, first with himself and later with his boss, Jim Bowerns, as his investigation revealed more truth and less fraud behind the healer's many purported cures. He mentions four persons Gurner supposedly cured of ALLIS. As an inspector, Johnson eventually determined that these persons were indeed bona fide ALLIS victims, and that true healings were associated with this man named Gurner. Eventually, Johnson was forced to put Gurner to the test. Mary, a day before slipping into the hypothermic-like coma of the final stages of ALLIS, was brought by her husband to the healer's door.

Two days later, after repeatedly drinking a tea made from an unidentified herb, Mary walked away.

Johnson: "Only don't think, America, that you can now look up 'Gurner' in the phone book, drive your dying loved one to his door, and find the same kind of treatment. As soon as I reported what happened with Mary to my FDA superiors, they closed their minds. Three days later they attempted to apprehend him. Luckily, somebody must have warned Mr. Gurner. It looks like he disappeared a few hours before federal agents came to arrest him."

Jim Bowerns, chief of the FDA's Fraudulent Practice Investigations and Johnson's former boss, paints an entirely different picture of this story.

"We don't really know what happened to Brian [Johnson]. One day he was wrapping up an investigation on one of the phoniest opportunists this department has ever encountered. The next day he one hundred and eighties, starts glorifying this same man, and begins waging an unjust word-war on the FDA. I don't know what happened to Brian. But I would like to state a few things:

"This Gurner character is the number one worst shark I've ever encountered. I'm afraid he's but a forerunner of what will be an unending stream of hokeys trying to capitalize on the ALLIS disease. Look, the very fact that he vanished just as some of our investigators were approaching him for an interview indicates the worth of the man and his cures."

On the question of Mary Johnson and her miraculous reversal of verified ALLIS, Bowerns states that the Potomac Medical Clinic is currently under investigation by the AMA for slipshod medical practices. Bowerns also notes that the attending physician, Abram Jensons, recently had his medical license suspended by the Washington, D.C., licensing board of the AMA. Dr. Jensons, in an interview with the Washington Post, notes that this suspension occurred but two days ago and insisted that his diagnosis on the woman was as accurate as possible considering the present state of ALLIS knowledge.

Jim Bowerns states that no one is more anxious about finding a cure for this disease than the U.S. Government, the FDA, and the AMA. Johnson just as emphatically says that the cure is here, and that the above three actively form the major blockade to its being publicly revealed. He asserts that Gurner wants to share his herb discovery with scientists so they can analyze it and determine its medicinal properties. "But that," says Johnson, "will not happen if the man can't show his face without encountering arrest. He knows that if he is arrested, his discovery will never be tested."

An interesting corollary has surfaced at the newly established ALLIS Worldwide Watch Institute (AWWI) in Detroit, Michigan. The AWWI is an information and clearing center that compiles facts, statistics and stories pertaining to the ALLIS disease. AWWI has recently received three individual reports from varied locations in the northwestern United States that follow a similar theme: someone was mortally stricken with ALLIS; a stranger with no name happened by and gave friends or relatives a small portion of a dried herb with instructions to brew it into a tea and feed this tea to the victim; within two to three days, those ALLIS victims claimed complete recovery.

The FDA says it places no credence in these reports and is investigating.

♦9♦
Payback

January 24, 2008, 6:30 A.M. A country farmhouse outside of Boulder, Colorado.

Jerry Willox's mornings had always involved a lot of back-and-forth pacing. He generally ate an on-the-move cookie and milk breakfast while plotting solutions to the day's problems. But now, for over two weeks, although his pacing and thinking were as intense as ever, pressing ecological necessities never entered the environmentalist's mind. Nor were there any homemade cookies to eat.

So, now I know. Numbers are just numbers until someone you love becomes one of them.

Willox walked briskly to the living room window and stared out at the dark winter morning.

How many times have I wished for some kind of disaster to smack this civilization alongside the head and knock off about a quarter of the people so the Earth could be given a breather from overpopulation? How many times?

Willox reversed direction, rounded a corner, and strode into the kitchen.

Ain't it a different tune when one of your family gets tagged as the answer to your wish?

Willox paused his pacing and listened, afraid he'd again hear muffled sobs coming from the bedroom.

Oh Jenny, dear Jenny, will you ever smile again? You comfort and reassure me, and then walk around like a zombie who has no more tears to shed yet can't stop shedding tears.

Over eighteen days. Why does that boy keep hanging on? For the love of Peter, Paul, and Mary, it's to the point that it will be a relief when it's finally over. And yet . . . now that it's about over, I mean, now that his breath is almost nonexistent, I just can't stand the idea. I . . .

Willox wept again, in exhaustion, as he stepped over to a crib and for the thousandth time in eighteen days picked up his blanket-swathed, pale, and unconscious son.

Oh Johnny, if there were just a way. You're half of all the happiness I've ever known with people. You and Jenny and the wild, beautiful world are my nurturers. I don't know if anything will be the same without you.

Still cradling the baby, and out of habit, the tired environmentalist resumed his pacing.

I always figured if you or Jenny or I died, we'd have our ashes scattered from a towering, wilderness-encompassed peak on a windy day, so a piece of us could rest on that which gave us definition in life. But now . . . I had to do it, Johnny. I had to agree to give you to those scientists. I'd live in guilt if there were a cure in you and I prevented the world from having it. It makes me sick, to think that they'll dissect and discombobulate you until you're nothing but a bunch of serums and slide samples. Dammit, Johnny. For all the people in the world who are crying for their loved ones as Jenny and I are for you, let one of those slides show a researcher something that—

A loud and demanding knock sounded from the back door. Willox's pacing halted.

At the back door, now? And who in the hell this time?

Willox replaced his inert son in the crib and walked toward the door, yelling angrily, "Hey, whoever you are, go away. Can't you read the sign on the front door? We want to be left alone."

A cautious voice called back from behind the locked door. "Jerry Willox? Open up. Is your baby still alive?"

"You research bastards! I told you I'd call you when he died. Now leave us alone until that happens."

The hidden voice pressed into the room with greater urgency. "If that means your son is still alive, then for God's sake open this door before it's too late to save his life."

Jenny joined her husband and the Willoxes looked at each other with incredulity. Willox moved to the door and cautiously slid open the dead bolt. A total stranger, a tall man dressed in well-worn clothes and sporting a week's worth of unshaven beard, barged into the room. Without acknowledging the Willoxes, he began shouting orders to a more dapperly dressed woman who, in obvious embarrassment, followed him into the house.

"Stephanie, get some water boiling, fast. Get the tea steeping. Be sure you don't boil the leaves."

Willox walked up to the curious stranger and stared him down. "Who in the hell are you?"

The stranger stared back. "You're Jerry Willox."

"Thanks. I needed to hear that. I repeat. Who in the hell are you?"

"I just read about you in that series of articles on ALLIS in *Newstime*. If you read them too, then you read a bit about me."

"Jeez-zus! You're that Gurner fellow?"

The stranger offered a slight bow. "The one. The criminal, wanted by the FDA, the AMA, and possibly now by the FBI because I've crossed some state lines hiding from everybody else. The very culprit whom the head of the FDA says is going to poison your loved ones and take all your money in the process. Do you mind if I have a look at your baby?"

Jerry and Jenny exchanged another disbelieving glance and then led Gurner to the crib. The healer's facial expression softened and his eyes closed as he picked up the barely-breathing body and held it close to his face.

Oh dear God. Couldn't You have let me find out about this kid twenty hours sooner? There's darned near nothing left in this body for the herb to work on.

Gurner opened his eyes and faced them. "How long?"

Willox's suspicions began to grow. "Eighteen and three-quarters days. Look, er, ah, we don't really want—"

Gurner held up his hand for silence, placed Johnny near his forehead and closed his eyes again.

You know, God, this kid is pretty far gone. I'm not sure the herb will do the trick. Can't We take a faster route? Couldn't I just once lay my hands on a body and have Your . . . power flow through me and heal? C'mon, Let's try it, God. Let's do it!

Never opening his eyes, Gurner knelt to the floor. He cradled the baby firmly in his hands and slipped into a deep meditation. The Willoxes stared in disbelief. Moments passed.

Think of nothing here. Think only of God . . . only of Light.

More moments passed. Jerry and Jenny fidgeted in unison.

Gurner's face contorted as he focused his attention to more

inward realms. *Go deeper, Gurner, damn-it-all. I will with all my will which is Thy will. Go deeper.*

More time passed. Jenny and Jerry's fidgeting grew into physical impatience. Stephanie Peters finished clattering pots in the kitchen and paused to watch the scene.

Gurner finally shook his head in disgust. He looked to the ceiling and loudly uttered his displeasure. "SHOOT, God! The puny tingle I feel in my hands wouldn't illumine a night-light, much less get Lazarus to sit up. And I don't think this kid owns enough future breaths for amateur healers to be trial-and-erroring on him. We've got to move into the field I do know, and We've got to move *now.*"

Jenny's eyes pleaded with her husband to free their lives from this character. But as Willox opened his mouth to serve eviction, Gurner, still cradling the baby, rose to his feet, breezed past the parents and yelled into the kitchen. "Stephanie. Quickly. Where's that tea?" The doctor, carrying a pot of simmering liquid, hurried into the living room. Gurner motioned Dr. Peters to sit on the couch beside him. He then gave the flabbergasted parents a slight smile. "Jerry Willox. Meet Stephanie Peters."

Stephanie offered the house owner a wan, apologetic shrug.

Gurner positioned Johnny on his lap while looking at Jenny. "Hi. You must be Mrs. Willox. I'm Gurner."

Jenny swallowed and simply stared in dismay.

Gurner took the pot of liquid from Dr. Peters. "Great, Stef, thanks. It looks just right." He again spoke to the parents. "Have you guys got a long eyedropper? Would you get it, please?"

Willox, confused beyond speech, disappeared into the bathroom and returned with the requested item.

As Gurner situated the inert baby in his arm, he began filling the eyedropper with a greenish tea. Then, looking at the appalled parents, the herbalist spoke in a gentle tone. "Now, Jerry and Jenny Willox. I need your permission to use this herb on Johnny. And I need it real quick, simply because there is no time left for you to think about it."

The couple looked at each other, but neither knew what to say.

Gurner's voice grew more imperative. "Look. Stephanie is Dr. Stephanie Peters, an M.D. She delivered me a message from Brian Johnson, whom you read about in *Newstime,* warning me of the FDA's imminent crackdown on me. This herb did save Johnson's wife's life. And Dr. Peters has in the last week witnessed four other ALLIS goners do a reversal, thanks to the herb. I can't promise you Johnny's life; he's deeper into ALLIS than anyone I've tried this stuff on. But for the love of God and your baby, give me a yes and let me try."

Jerry and Jenny glanced from Gurner to Dr. Peters, the doctor nodding her head in encouragement. Jenny burst into tears and words: "Yes, please, Gurn . . . er, Mr. Gurner, try it. Try anything."

Her husband dubiously agreed. "Even chasing a rainbow at the last minute has to be better than doing nothing."

Gurner nodded a slight thank you to the parents and immediately withdrew into himself. *Well, they said yes. OK, God. We're on.*

Gurner took a deep breath, eyed the dropper full of liquid and the comatose baby, and realized he had no idea how to combine the two. He offered them both to the M.D. "Stephanie, you're the doctor. Are you up on your skills at slipping liquid down a comatose baby's throat?"

Dr. Peters took the tea-filled eyedropper and made a few practice runs in her mind. Gurner used the moments to fade into himself. *God. We're going to need every Angel You can spare. There's no life force left in this little guy. Wish I could believe more in this herb. And yet, again, it feels right. It simply feels true inside me . . . wish I could trust my feelings more.*

Gurner left his prayer and spoke to the parents and the doctor. "OK. Our whole goal in life here, my new friends, is to every little while—in the beginning every five or so minutes—to slip a teaspoon or so of this tea into Johnny. We'll also have him inhale some of the herb's steamy vapors between dosages. I can't say how long we'll be doing this. Until something happens, one way or the other."

The caring and efficient doctor in Dr. Peters surfaced and pushed aside her situational silence. "Jenny. Hi. I'm Stephanie. Do you know Johnny's current temperature?"

"Er, yes. The research group, the one going to study him when he . . . when he dies, wanted meds in here monitoring everything. We wouldn't let them. So they asked us to keep an accurate record of his vital signs every fifteen minutes. Just before you came in, let's see, his temperature was just below 94 degrees; respiration rate was 25, though very shallow; blood pressure, 75 over 50; eye pupils not dilated or constricted; and heartbeat steady at 80. We also in intervals put a drop of his blood on a slide and dip that into some solution they gave us."

Dr. Peters' trained mind ran the a mental comparison on the statistics. *What a weird disease. Everything but the temperature reads half of normal, and yet this baby is all but gone.* She cradled the baby and positioned his tongue so the eyedropper could follow its curve to the esophagus.

"OK, sweet Johnny. Bottoms up."

· · · · ·

7:58 A.M.

Gurner was sipping a cup of tea in the Willoxes' kitchen while Dr. Peters ministered to the baby. Willox, who hadn't said a word since the tea party began, now approached the healer with a major question in mind.

"Gurn . . . er, Mr. Gurner. How is it that you're . . . what are you doing . . . why are you here?"

"I read about you and Jenny and Johnny in *Newstime*."

"That means you also read about 50,000 other ALLIS victims. Why did you come to us?"

"On a very deep level, I felt that I owed you a debt."

Willox pondered the healer's statement. *This guy really is strange. I can't believe I've been letting him work on my boy for the last hour and a half.* "I've never met you, Gurner. I don't understand your statement at all."

Gurner gestured for Willox to take a chair beside him. "In the late '70s, I was a normal college freshman thinking beer drinking was cool and pot smoking cooler. My life was shaping up pretty bland: a degree and a career, lots of book learning and intellectual knowledge. I'm sure I was on the path to getting a loan and a car, probably a house, maybe even a marriage before I had a chance to find out who I was. Perhaps the Army would have claimed some of my time and some of my mind, because I'm sure at that period of life I wouldn't have had enough sagacity to ask if Vietnam was a good, bad, or indifferent cause.

"You came to the campus and gave a slide show and lecture to the school's mountaineering club. And as you were talking about your pictures—I think they were of a month-long solo you took in the High Sierras—you shone with a confidence and a *power* that literally shattered the dreary foundations I was then laying. Perhaps it wasn't you shining so much as it was those wild mountains speaking through you. They gave you something,

something I've decades later come to realize can be described as 'knowing a piece of your soul.' Thanks to you, Jerry Willox, my common complacency was broken, and I wanted that something too."

Gurner paused and peeked around the corner to see how Dr. Peters and Johnny were faring. He then returned attention to Willox.

"After that, the wilderness—mountains, deserts, oceans, and prairies—became my obsession. Nature became first my partner, then my friend. Sometimes She was my greatest tormenter, but that only happened when She was being my greatest teacher. For a while She even became my God. But Nature doesn't allow someone to cling to incomplete concepts. She moved me onward and inward to searching for the God that's beyond even Her.

"I don't know that these last twenty-five years would have been . . . heh, such a struggle, such a fulfilling, glorious struggle if I hadn't felt that compelling voice of Nature reflected through you that day. Following that inner voice has never been the easiest of routes. But at least it has been the most alive."

Gurner looked deeply into Willox's eyes.

"You've done more than just turn me on to a 'natural' high, Willox. As you well know, time spent in wilderness amounts to a lot more than mere time spent in wilderness. I've been out there finding my Self, finding my happiness, my Path, and evolving into my destiny. Sometimes I think that's becoming a healer . . . often I don't think that. The point is, through Nature, I'm moving toward Me.

"But you, you who love the wilderness so, you actively commit yourself to working in this 'other reality' that controls the destiny of wilderness. Your preservation work gives back to the Nature that gave to you. I'm a typical, sideline, send-a-check, write-an-occasional-letter environmentalist. You're a front-line warrior, barricading the former Rocky Flats nuclear warhead gate, actively protesting the incredible boobery of Forest Service planning, fighting for reasonable wilderness and clean air and against the current policies that are turning this planet into a ecological time bomb.

"So why am I here, Jerry Willox? I guess to say 'thank you.' For everything. I really hope this works for Johnny."

Willox said nothing more. He silently stood up and walked to his desk, picked up the 1970 Earth Day picture and stared at it, wondering if perhaps the last thirty-odd years had indeed been worth it. Jenny, who had been listening to the conversation while she and Dr. Peters dosed Johnny with the strongly scented tea, gazed at him with pure pride in her eyes.

. . . . .

10:02 A.M.

"Gurner."

"What is it, Stephanie?"

"This baby's temperature is up."

"Up! Holy God! How much?"

"A tenth of a degree."

Crash. "One tenth of one degree? Shoot, Stephanie, that might just be a normal variation."

"I don't think so. Johnny's pre-tea temperature chart shows an unfailingly steady decline. After we started the tea, the temp leveled out. Three and a half hours later, this is a first and definite rise."

"Well, let's shoot for a continuum of that rising before we crack the champagne, OK?"

Oh God. Look at the hope in those parents' faces. You really wouldn't raise their hopes and spirits only to let them fall and crash, would You?

Would You?

. . . . .

12:02 P.M.

The phone jangled loudly. Willox left his lunch and rushed over to answer it.

"Hello . . . who? . . . no, Johnny is not dead yet. I said I'd call you the minute it happened. Now back off, you gosh-damned wolves . . . I know it's of ultimate importance the body be delivered to you immediately upon death. I said I would. I will . . . yes, we are totally faithful in saving the urine and taking the blood and vital signs . . . no. Hell no. You can't come up and check. You'll let us be alone with our son during these last hours or the whole deal of giving him to science is off . . . I told you, I'll call you immediately."

Willox slammed the receiver down, unplugged the phone, and walked over to look out the living room window.

"They're hovering out there like vultures. An ambulance is ready to roar Johnny's body to the nearest park where a helicopter will then blast him to the CU Medical Center where they'll turn him into scientific pulp and data. Looks like about thirty reporters are lurking outside, greedy to capitalize on the emotions of the parents of the longest surviving ALLIS victim. I swear, if they ask how good it feels to have donated my boy's body for such a worthy cause, I'll punch them."

Willox whirled and faced the healer.

"Gurner. Along with all the other reasons I want Johnny to live, I really hope your tea works, so these bloodsuckers have nothing to drink."

· · · · ·

2:35 P.M.

Willox was napping, reclined on the couch. Dr. Peters continued to feed baby Johnny a dose of herbal tea, now in fifteen-minute intervals on directions from Gurner. The healer had isolated himself in a corner of Willox's cluttered office space. He appeared to be in deep meditation, but inwardly his thoughts, never inclined toward relaxation, were involved in a one-sided conversation.

God. It's weird. For over eight hours we've been pouring herb tea into that baby's body. He's now in a state of continuous urination. In goes the tea; out comes the pee. Meanwhile, he's got it the easiest of anyone here. He doesn't know what's happening. The rest of us, especially the Willoxes, have to live every minute, every eternal minute, in an agonizing state of despairing hope.

Gurner heard someone lightly step to the office screen and pause, as if peering in at him. He said nothing and neither did the person. The footsteps receded.

In eight hours we've gained three tenths of a degree body temperature on that baby. His breathing seems a tiniest shade deeper. I guess that is incredible. I guess that means the herb is working.

Working, but shoot. What a game it's been. Because the researchers don't believe the kid is still alive and are demanding to see the body, Jerry has had to threaten to shoot anyone who comes though the door. Jenny's eighteen days of grieving finally caught up to her when the hope that he might live let her relax a little. She's now sicker than heck, and I don't have any herbs to ease the headache. Good ol' aspirin at such a time. Stephanie Peters turned out to be a remarkable soldier, though. Delivered Johnson's warning about that Bowerns guy. They would have confiscated my herbs. Probably added a few lethal ones as evidence. Good thing I'm free to split on a moment's notice. I would have bolted into the forest, if this lady doctor hadn't insisted on me going with her. Wants to learn my methods so she could compare them with her schooling!

I guess that was a real blessing, though. If we hadn't left in her car, if I had simply run out the back door the way I wanted to, probably they would have nabbed me. We weren't ten miles down the highway when we saw the cars coming and I had to duck to the floorboard. Three carloads of federal agents. Well, they ambushed an empty cabin, but I'm sure they scoured those woods. They would have had me sure.

Gurner looked up at the ceiling. "Great way to live, God. Spent over a week in terror, suspicious of every person we met."

I finally couldn't take it any longer and opted to vanish into the wilderness around the Salmon River. Stephanie, crazy woman, insisted on coming with me. Said she was learning and didn't want to quit. Heh, but medical school does not train their students for campfire cooking, freezing temperatures, and primitive winter living. Her nature is definitely not one that can rough it . . . and enjoy it.

Gurner opened his eyes and peered for a long time at the woman doctor who was busily coddling Johnny.

I'm a loner, God. Alone with You. Always have been. I don't think You'd want me to change that now. I don't think Stephanie understands, but she can't come into the middle of a man's inward calling and expect much of an outward response from him for her. I hope she'll soon realize that taking a fancy to me would be a dead end road for both of us.

Gurner closed his eyes, redirecting their focus inward.

But . . . she is a beautiful woman. And not just physically. Over eight hours she's nursed one hopeless patient on an unproven remedy. Which means she's saying nix to the money she could have made as a regular doctor, and she's saying hello to prosecution when the AMA discovers what she did. There's a doctor like this world just doesn't experience any more.

Gurner paused in his endless thought processes and for a few more moments simply watched Dr. Stephanie Peters care for Johnny Willox. He then walked over to the couch and sat beside her.

"You look exhausted, Stephanie. Let me take over here while you catch a snooze. Just show me the trick of getting the tea down the right tube."

The healer cradled Johnny and silently tuned in to the child's progress.

Oh my. This baby is going to make it. I can sense it. I can feel an internal energy in him that says "I'm a-gonna be A-OK." He's back in balance in that one area where every ALLIS victim has been off. When this Johnny-chapter is over, I've got to glean an understanding of why that area goes weak and how this herb works to rebalance it.

I also feel, awfully strongly, that I'd better be getting out of here. All the FDA's number one most wanted criminal herbalist needs is to have the CU medical personnel come crashing in and recognize him. And the way the crazy laws of this country work, keeping this baby alive with an unapproved herb tea might be a greater crime than having let him die.

· · · · ·

January 25, 2008, 4:30 A.M.

At Willox-baby-teatime plus twenty-two hours, three of the four adults in the room were playing cribbage while the fourth, the doctor, again checked the baby's vital signs.

Gurner said in one breath, "Fifteen two, fifteen four, and a pair is six, what's Johnny's temperature now, Stephanie?"

"It's starting to climb in leaps and bounds. Right now it's . . . ninety seven point three. Up almost half a degree in the last hour."

As if that statement formed his long-awaited cue, Johnny James Willox emitted a thin wail of an attempted baby-cry and began thrashing at the blanket that encompassed him. Cards and cribbage point-pegs flew as parents and healer threw chairs aside and raced across the room to join the doctor in staring at the phenomenon of reawakening life. The baby's lungs, unsure of themselves at first, soon found a firmer footing and let the world know that they were *not* as pleased with life as was everyone else who stood around with fulsome grins lining their faces.

Dr. Peters carefully handed the crying baby to the Willoxes.

"Uh, crumb, you who are his natural parents ought to hold him here, you know."

Shortly, all five people in the room were crying.

Suddenly, Willox grabbed Gurner's hand with both of his hands and began shaking it violently. "Gurner . . . Mr. Gurner. You did it! He's alive! You and Dr. Peters. Jeez! You did it! If Jenny and I can ever do anything for you to repay . . ."

Gurner clasped Willox by the arms to lessen the shock of his excited handshaking motions. "Whoa, whoa, whoa, Jerry. First of all, I didn't do anything but share a gift that had been given to me. And second, I think in a very short while you are going to be asked to do a lot, for me and maybe everyone else in this world."

Gurner glanced at the front door, expecting an armed SWAT team to any minute barge in. "Look. I've got to split. No, listen, all three of you. There are people lurking outside your door whose beliefs are quite set on the outcome of this event. Hearing a baby crying from this house is not going to compute with them. You're not going to be able to keep them out. And I can't be discovered, not yet. I'm a man wanted by the wrong people for the wrong reasons.

"For weeks I've been doing deep prayers and meditations on this ALLIS plague that's biting the world. The further my intuition probes into it, the bigger, blacker, and more gruesome a monster I sense. Something is wrong, something is terribly out of balance with this world, and ALLIS is either a manifestation of or a capitalization on that situation. I don't know yet what it is. And I don't yet know why this herb counters it.

"But I do know that if I get caught now, there's going to be no hope of knowing. I've been close to some of the holistic M.D.s squished by the AMA and FDA. The mega-controllers are so darned scared that they might lose their power-hold on the masses that they destroy people who counter the restrictive guidelines they dictate. And they don't just ax the aberrant healers. They also ruin those persons' years of research and work."

Gurner continued talking as he gathered his winter jacket and mittens. "For reasons beyond comprehension, I'm a threat to certain people. Having been, as far as I know, the only person shown the gift of this herb, I'm not yet in a position to trust myself to the internal workings of this system."

Willox helped the healer put on his coat. "So Gurner. You said Jenny and I could help. How do you mean?"

"I hope I'm wrong, but I'm a-feared I'm not. I don't think ALLIS has even stretched its little finger, much less raised its entire body into being. You just get a sense for these things in the work I do and the way I do it.

"If you guys would . . . first buy me some time to fade away. Even a half an hour will be enough. Then let the meds in. And make triple-sure the reporters accompany them. Then Jenny, nurse your living baby in front of them. And tell them the whole truth and nothing but. Tell them all that happened here."

Gurner continued talking as he slipped on his overboots. "Stephanie, you're the doctor who's witnessed all this. Don't speak to the reporters like a recent graduate, but in the tone of a full-fledged physician. Tell them everything just as it happened."

Dr. Peters opened her mouth in protest, but Gurner had anticipated her statements. "No, no, listen, it would be crazy for you to come with me. If you were uncomfortable in the gentle, woodsy outdoors where we've been, you'll croak in the place I'm now going. No, if you choose to, we need your authority here. If you choose to, I say. I know you know that the same thing that happened to Mary Johnson's doctor will happen to you. You'll very likely be hung on some wild charges."

Gurner gently pulled the four persons in the room into a goodbye embrace. He lowered his voice, as if disclosing a valuable secret. "Here's what we're trying to pull. ALLIS is rising, and science is helpless. In the midst of such a situation enters this Lone Ranger healing herb. But if the masked plant is going to have a chance in hell, Tonto here has got to for now keep it out of the hands of the Powers That Be. Meanwhile, via media coverage of examples like yours, the public must be shown that this cure exists. Knowing it exists, they will demand access to it, and hopefully that demand will force the various administrations to back off and let me—a free me—give it to the proper researchers who will publicly isolate the curative in it.

"Jerry, you know how impossible it is to jack up the apathetic masses. But I've a hunch dying family members will prove to be a much greater impetus than dying landscapes . . . even though the latter eventually leads to the former.

"So you guys tell them all that I've said, and all that has happened here with Johnny. Don't tell them this, but somehow I'll be in touch with Brian Johnson, and will speak through him if necessary. Just make this point clear. Johnny and some others are alive because there is a cure for ALLIS. I'm not hiding it, or keeping it to myself. But I've got to have an irretractable public promise from the FDA that I'm an exonerated and free agent. No prosecution, of any kind whatsoever."

Gurner relaxed his hold on his four friends and prepared for departure. Dr. Peters, not happy about being left behind but aware of the logic behind that decision, asked the question on everyone's mind. "Well crumb, Gurner, just what is this herb? That's the question we'll be pummeled with. What did you give Johnny and those others?"

"I don't know. I haven't been able to find it in any classification book anywhere. Chances are it's one of the many plants that mankind hasn't yet tagged. I've only seen it in one isolated spot and have a hunch it's a rare and unknown species. And of course, I can't reveal that location, because the panicking masses and the scientific masses and the profiteering masses would all converge on that one spot, and everything within its boundaries would quickly be obliterated."

Hands were warmly shaken. And hugs all around were given. Gurner went back to the back door and pointed to the line of bushes that followed an irrigation ditch. "There's my escape route. Same way in, same way out. I hope." Gurner took a step out the door and then turned and faced his friends again.

"I guess among friends I can also say that part of my need to hide is the simple fact that I'm deeply scared of legal systems. Many of my heroes—some of the original herbalists—spent a fair portion of their lives in jail . . . simply because they gave all they could of themselves, trying to ease the pains of someone else. But even with that as an ideal, too much of me would wither and die like a plant ripped up by the roots if I weren't free."

The three adults looked at Gurner in silence.

"Just didn't want you to think that I'm some prophet or some invincible seer. I'm actually running mighty scared here."

The party suddenly grew aware that a lot of noise was trying to intrude on their adieus. Gurner lifted his hand in a goodbye wave. "Anyway, there you go. The phone ringing, knocks on the door, and the baby crying, to boot. I gotta go. This is soon going to be too hot a spot."

End of Book I

BOOK II

DECISIONS

◆ 10 ◆
Loggers

May 3, 2008, 5:14 P.M. On the Squanni Hill clear-cut job site, in the Willamette National Forest, east of Eugene, Oregon.

Ernie Slate could rightly be described as a big and burly logger. But whenever he stood near his friend and fellow lumberjack Joe Simpson, even Slate felt like a dwarf. Simpson should have been playing guard and tackle for the Seattle Seahawks—both positions simultaneously. The giant of a man stood alone in a corner of the clear-cut, mechanically cleaning and oiling his tools. Anyone could see that his mind was elsewhere. Slate knew that his own information was worth interrupting Simpson's thoughts. He walked up behind the big logger and wasted no time in getting to the crux.

"Hey, Joe. The boys figure about Friday night those fruits will be out of the trees. And that's when we plan on coming up and finishing the job."

Simpson jumped and looked around, half startled. "Wha— Friday? . . . Job?"

"Hey, Joe, where the hell's your mind these days? Even the boss has noticed you spend more time staring into space than running a saw. I better warn you, he's not too pleased."

Slate pointed to a small stand of old and tall trees. "Now you know we been talking for a week about zipping down those trees that the eco-creeps have been camped in. You know, we'll both finish this cut up right and play a nasty on them for being such a bother to this job."

Simpson shuffled his massive body from side to side in a display of nervousness, an action Slate had never known him to perform. "I don't know, Ernie. You better count me out on this one. It just doesn't feel right."

This statement further amazed Slate. "What! This can't be Joe

Simpson talking. The Joe who I've seen a dozen times shove Sahara Clubbers into a corner and pound on 'em a little until their true colors shone yellow instead of green. The Joe who cranked up a D9 cat and ran it a quarter mile into that Three Sisters country as a protest against them adding more wilderness to it. Shit, Joe. You're a loggerman's logger and a hero for that. What do you mean, it doesn't feel right? Those B-turds tied this cut up in court for months. When we finally did get an OK to move in, first thing Tom Hokum did was run his saw into a spike. We had to use metal detectors on every damned tree. When those five Greenpissers roped themselves into the tops of the taller firs, the boss said, 'Cut the seventy-nine and a half acres around them, and leave just that half acre standing.' Gave 'em a box-office seat to watch their precious virgin forest bow to a clear-cut.

"Now it's done. We made good money from this stand despite the Greenies' protests. And Harry and Sam and me and a few other of the long-timers want to level that token stand after the buttercups leave. Just to show 'em we're not going to stand by and take their crap. You ought to join us, Joe. You need to be with us. This is your life and livelihood as much as it is anyone's."

Simpson did not believe that Slate was the understanding and compassionate soul he needed to talk to right at this moment. But for the past three months extraordinary and totally incomprehensible emotions had been fermenting his insides. With the conclusion of this personally grueling logging operation, he needed to either express these agitations—air them openly and try and sort them out—or explode from the internal pressure. Talking more to himself than his companion, Simpson began piecing together the jigsaw puzzle of his recent mental earthquake.

"Ernie, for thirty-five years I've roamed this Cascade country with a saw and a skidding rig. And I've done good by it, too. Jean and I have a fine house, and we can afford to send all the kids to school if they want to go. And for thirty-five years I never questioned what I was doing. I just did what I had to do to stay alive and out of the poor house.

"Until about twenty years ago, that was fairly easy. Work was plentiful; money was good. Then the environmentalists started screaming at us: what we were doing was silting up the creeks and killing the fish; what we were doing was destroying habitat for endangered species; what we were doing looked ugly and was wiping out our national heritage. Hell, all that we were doing was what we had always done—feeding our families and making an honest dollar.

"You know the story. It got harder and harder to move into a section of forest for a cut. A thousand pages of paperwork every time. All these new regulations. Lots of small firms went under 'cause it was just too expensive. And I got madder and more bitter every time, just like most everybody else. I wanted to fight back at those backpacking imbeciles, not only because they were threatening my livelihood, but also because they were painting such a damned false picture of me. I'm a not half-crazed, frothing-from-the-mouth maniac sawing down everything in his path. I'm a man doing a man's job, a hard and dangerous job. I'm a father of five kids who haven't been starved or abused, and I'm a human who has a lot of friends he'd help on a moment's notice. I piss and spit and shit just the same as they do, and I also laugh and play and enjoy quiet times."

Simpson noticed Slate shifting his weight from one foot to another.

"Sit down, Ernie, dammit."

Simpson was a huge man, built like the ancient tree trunks that gave him a living. Even seated on a freshly-cut stump, he appeared larger and stockier than most men would standing straight.

"It was the court hearing on this Squanni Hill cut. Something started churning in my gut . . . something I haven't been able to control. Remember the hearing? We were all there in protest, ready to explode if the judge went in favor of the environmentalists. Hell, half of the fellows hadn't worked for months, and eighty acres of this kind of original timber is a big job these days. Well, in his closing statement, the Sahara Club lawyer made a remark that hit me like a punch in the gut. I can remember the words exactly, Ernie. He said, 'Put things in perspective with this fact. Outside of the National Parks and the protected wilderness areas, only 5 per cent of the virgin forests are left in the Northwest. Five percent in an entire region. And you want to clear-cut a large chunk of that?' He went on to talk about the probabilities of destroying rare and endangered ecosystems and things like that. I don't know what else he said; I didn't listen to much more. I couldn't get that '5 per cent is all that's left' out of my mind."

Slate opened his mouth to speak, but Simpson cut him off. "I know, Ernie, I know. Don't even say it. Why in the hell should that bother me? A simple solution would be to declassify some of the wilderness. That would up the statistics nicely . . . and give us more work, too."

Simpson paused a long time, and said, almost painfully, "But I see now that we'd soon be back to the 5 per cent mark and we'd have even less forest left." He shook his head vigorously to throw that thought away.

"Anyway, I lay awake at nights—first time ever in my life—thinking about it. It just wouldn't leave me at peace.

"Well, a week later we moved onto this Squanni Hill. God, I was excited, Ernie. These were huge trees, like we cut in the old days. A mountain full of brush needed clearing, and then we faced tree trunks that even our largest saws had to make two and three cuts to fall. Soon the hills were full of hard and good men, working good and hard. That felt good." He shook his head again. "But it didn't last long."

"I know. The flower brigade climbed up in the trees and put a damper on everything."

"No . . . shut your trap and listen. I'm talking more for my sake than yours, here, but just let me talk it out, OK?

"I mean, if 5,000 or more people had come out and each shimmied up a tree, we'd have been helpless. But five of 'em was all, and they were easy to work around. Hard to ignore, but easy to work around.

"No, it wasn't them, Ernie. The uneasiness was all inside of me. The very first time I ran my skidder up a slope to retrieve some logs, I started feeling this queasiness inside my gut. Not a physical sickness. I've never been healthier. Remember when you had to get up before the EIS hearing on this cut and give a little speech in favor of logging it? You were complaining about the somersaults your guts were doing having to face a microphone and an audience. It was like that, that same kind of nervous feeling just roiled in my bowels."

Simpson eased himself off the stump and sat on the ground, using the tree trunk as a backrest. He still appeared larger than most men.

"Once, when we were kids, my brothers and I raided an old, backwoods moonshiner's still, thinking we'd get the whiskey and make some easy money selling it to the other guys at school. From the minute we started for the still, all the way through stealing of the booze, all the way home, and even during the selling it to friends, some voice inside of me was screaming at me, 'This is wrong; we should not be doing this.' I figured it was just a fear of being caught, either by the moonshiner or our folks, so I ignored it."

"Did they—?"

"Ernie, dammit. If you don't quit interrupting . . ."

"Sorry. I was just curious if you got caught."

"No. We didn't get caught, exactly. But it turned out that the brew was a bad batch, and seven teenage boys were hospitalized, almost poisoned to death because of what we sold them. That was more trouble than if we *had* been caught.

"Anyway, that same exact inside-screaming has been racking my insides since day one on this job. Every time I ran a cat or skidded a log over this land, my head and heart and belly were just screaming at me, saying 'This is wrong; we should not be doing this.' And the scary thing is, the last and only other time I felt such an inside warning, I almost killed seven people. This time, the screaming was louder."

Simpson gazed at the big diesels loading the last of the huge tree trunks onto trucks destined to transport them to the various mills. A few big bulldozers piled the slash into manageable, burnable piles, further gouging an already shredded topsoil and landscape.

"I got to where I didn't understand anything that was happening. My insides were screaming, but my mind kept saying that those feelings were crazy. And then this nutsy idea popped into my head that not only was something bad happening here, but that I should try and put a stop to it."

"You didn't say—"

"Of course I didn't say anything. Logic kept my mouth shut. I knew that forty men and millions of dollars worth of equipment were not going to stop good-paying, deadline-meeting work just because one veteran logger suddenly lost the brain beneath his hard hat. Of course I kept my mouth shut."

The big logger ran his fingers through his hair. "Well, that's all past now, Ernie."

"I'm certainly gl-"

"When the operation rolled into its last phases, everything shut down. My guts quit churning, the voices quit. All's quiet on the brain front now. *Too* quiet, Ernie. Too damned quiet. Now it feels like something is missing. Not the voices. I'm thankful they're gone. But it's a feeling like . . . like as would happen if a beautiful woman vanished just as your arms were about to gather her in. It's like something is telling me, 'Something good was here, and now it's gone, gone, gone.'"

Simpson looked into his companion's eyes. He noticed Slate's facial lines portraying a serious skepticism, but he still said, almost pleadingly, "That's what I've been living with for the past months: voices saying what we're doing here is wrong, and now voices saying nothing, and saying nothing so powerful it scares me. Does any of it make any sense to you at all?"

Slate stiffly stood up, looked at his watch, and turned to face Simpson.

"Well, ol' buddy. I don't know. You're tired, probably. Maybe you got the flu. Hell, maybe you got ALLIS. Oops. Sorry. That thing ain't much of a joke any more. But listen. You go and have yourself about ten stiff drinks. Really tie one on. Then go and get a good lay from your old lady. Might just solve all your problems. The boys and I will take care of those standing trees, and we'll still get you credit for helping."

Slate patted Simpson on the shoulder and lazily walked away. As Simpson watched him leave, another inner voice offered a thought: *Christ, Ernie. Your advice feels about as wrong as clearing this mountainside did.*

• 11 •
Alone

May 5, 2008, 6:00 P.M. Wenatchee National Forest, in the Glacier Peak Wilderness area, near Lake Chelan, Washington.

The healer Gurner sat alone on a rock outcropping overlooking an unnamed mountain canyon that emptied into spectacular Lake Chelan. His sparse beard was quite long; his face, tanned and weathered, glowed. But his mind, far from being at peace in the restful country, was engaged in a gripe session.

Oh, God. It's just too hard. Do You hear me? It's just too doggone taxing. Ignoble Saul became enlightened Paul in a matter of days. Why does it take years and maybe lifetimes for the rest of us to even approach that state?

Gurner's habit of voicing his opinions aloud to the listening universe had grown during the past three months of isolation. He now yelled loudly, across the small canyon and toward the lake far below. "It's just too hard! Too hard to be half-a-Buddha. It's no fun!"

Buddha, the compassionate One. When the sufferings of the populace are presented to Him, He both shares the pain and has the power to relieve those throes. But half-a-Buddha? Half-a-Buddha is certainly able to feel the pain of another person, yet he hasn't advanced far enough to ease that suffering. His blessings are hopeful yet impotent words. The blind and lame come to the full Buddha and find a love that's powerful enough to wash away the darkness and smooth the limp. But if they unfortunately find their way to half-a-Buddha, the only thing they encounter that's powerful is a wish to be able to do the same.

Gurner shifted his sitting position on the rock and faced the forest behind him.

It's awful, God, to be developing this intuitive empathy yet not be able to tap into the grace that eases the burden of others.

It's really hard for those of us only halfway along the road to You. At such a place, we know what can be, and that makes us all the more aware of what currently ain't.

· · · · ·

May 7, 2008, 1:23 P.M.

Gurner's beard was two days longer, and his face two days more weathered. But his thoughts were by no means two days more peaceful.

Shoot, I don't have much of this herb left. But what am I supposed to do? Everywhere I go I meet somebody on the way to kicking the ALLIS bucket. Everywhere someone is crying because a loved one is suddenly and rapidly fading away. I can't pass them by, knowing that in my pack rides the key to their very lives.

You're going to get caught doing this, Gurner. Caught and hung. That head guy at the FDA, Brian said last time I called him, has promoted me to number one most wanted in the U. S. of A. Brian thinks it's a good sign because it means that Bowerns is facing pressure to abandon the charges and solicit my help in combating ALLIS. He says that the Willox baby stories have sent ripples all over the world. He also says to continue giving the tea to occasional ALLIS victims because that is creating a profound and cumulative effect on shaping support for me. Brian says my mysteriousness and popularity with the public is increasing logarithmically.

Gurner turned toward an easterly direction, as if hoping his vocalization would reach Washington, D.C. "Brian, I don't want popularity. I honestly don't want any part of this show."

Anyway, the herb has healed fifteen people since I left Boulder . . . goodness, over three months ago. Shoot, through those healings I've got to be painting a blazing trail for the FBI to follow. And I'll bet that you, Brian my friend, have no idea what it's like, day after day, to feel that surge of inner fear whenever some stranger looks at me with a curious eye, or that terror of being caught whenever a patrol car passes by. I'm ready to permanently disappear, to become a resident cave-monk. And that may not be such a bad idea because this whole expo may be futile. The FDA still adamantly denies this "unscientific" cure, and most people choose to believe what authority dictates.

. . . . .

May 8, 2008, 11:07 A.M. Near Lake Chelan.

You know, God, this is all right. Really, it is. I mean, I sometimes get to the point where hugging a friend or just warmly shaking a hand would be different. But in overall terms, for months it's been just You and me, in the wilderness and alone. And I can feel how much I've grown from this time of intense meditation on and prayer with You.

"And how, oh Gurner my boy, have you grown?"

Oh no! Maybe I have been out here too long. Now I'm starting to carry His side of the conversation . . .

Well, in answer, a few direct benefits seem to be happening as a consequence of these months of silent communion. My intuition, my inner knowing, seems to have grown in leaps and bounds. I always had an ability to tune into a person, to read deeper feelings behind the face mask. That inner perceptivity naturally flowed into healing work, perceiving the balances and imbalances of a person's body. Then it expanded a bit more, into the plant kingdom and the subtle energies offered by the various herbs. But lately, these last couple weeks or so, I'm beginning to think a piece of Omniscience has entered my being.

"Don't go into Chelan today," said an innermost voice. I listened and didn't. Three days later when I ventured to the little burg, the townsfolk talk still centered around the team of government agents combing the area for information on me.

I guess I have left too obvious a Gurner-trail to this part of the country. But apparently the Feds received a report that someone was boasting an ALLIS cure near Oroville, and they dashed off toward the border, probably afraid I'll go international.

Gurner smiled sadly as he informed the nearby rocks of his predicament. "Still, my picture—before the beard—smiles from the post office cork board, and probably from every newspaper in the state. Reward offered for information leading to the arrest of yours truly."

But You know, there's more than accurate, inner-warning voices that I'm experiencing here. For one, answers to questions come to mind more easily. If I put my mind to a problem after I've touched a piece of the Peace that follows time spent in Silence, solutions are just there. Often times the explanation is simply

"Wait." But that answer, which used to drive me crazy, suddenly feels right, and I'm content with it.

And I also . . . Gurner paused a moment and reflected on his thoughts. He glanced into the faultless blue sky. "Look, God. I'll shut up in a minute and try and get back to that Silence I'm so highly praising. But a whole bunch of me is still human, and that human part really yearns for some conversation. Even if it is only with myself."

I'm also sensing an expanded awareness of all that is around me. The plants of the forest tell their secrets a bit louder these days. It's as if my consciousness has extended itself so as to accommodate and interpret more space and events at one time.

It's really amazing. And it's really scary. To be tuning into a greater mode of perception, to be sensing an awareness more vast than normal . . . that idea excites me to the marrow. A part of me cries to get on with it and follow it all the way.

But, shoot. Another part of me wonders if my "expanded consciousness" syndrome is simply the imaginings of a lone fugitive and gradually maturing madman. I might be making all this up in my own mind; there's sure no one here to contradict me. That idea gets real lonely.

Gurner again cast his gaze over the mountain lake. "If I could just talk to some illumined sage, he or she might reassure me in this . . . except I'd probably end up questioning the sage's sanity, and then be even more confused."

· · · · ·

May 8, 2008, 1:30 P.M.

Holy Hannah Almighty God anyway! That may be it! That just may be the answer! I think I may have an idea of what this ALLIS disease is about.

It has to be. I need to research this, but it . . . it must be. And if so, that would be why this herb works in curing it.

"Thank You, God. This is one hell of a moment of inspiration."
Oh my. Who in this world is ever going to believe this?

• 12 •
Newstime

May 15, 2008. Excerpts from *Newstime* magazine.

WHAT'S NEW WITH ALLIS?

The statistics read somewhat like an adept extortionist's mounting Swiss bank account:

• December 11, 2007	27,000
• January 1, 2008	50,000
• January 26	77,000
• February 16	112,000
• March 9	240,000
• April 6	535,000
• April 21	870,000
• May 12	1,320,000

Unfortunately, these figures do not count out as dollars stashed in an overseas vault. The numbers represent lives—lost lives—a swelling compilation of worldwide human deaths attributed to the deadly affliction called ALLIS.

On May 3, 2008, ALLIS global fatality figures topped the one million mark. One week later another 300,000 lives were added to that list. In less than ten months the ALLIS plague has, in a world of over six and a half billion inhabitants, killed one of every 5,000 persons.

An overview of official government statements, released in chronological correspondence with the above dates and tallies, presents a pattern of the evolving feelings associated with the ALLIS disease.

• The CDC expressed relief over the January 26 count of 77,000

ALLIS victims. They noted that the death percentage had decreased from the previous tally.

• On February 16, death figures topped the 100,000 mark. While admitting concern, government officials noted that the number was not a significant statistical increase.

• Less than one month later this number more than doubled. Official spokespersons stated that their interpretations of the figures warranted further investigation.

• By April, ALLIS again almost doubled its toll. At this juncture, the CDC repeated an oft-presented promise, declaring an imminent cure.

• Two weeks and more than 300,000 additional lost lives later, people stopped believing government statements. A continuous lack of concrete information on and solutions to the ALLIS problem contributed to the public's anger.

• On May 12, after more than a million deaths, the government responded to the threat of ALLIS in the same manner as the people. That is, basically, it panicked.

Organized by the United Nations, an emergency meeting of world leaders has been called. In two days—a record for worldwide response—scientists and political heads from nearly every nation on Earth will assemble in New York to discuss the potentialities of ALLIS. Finding an ALLIS cure at all costs will be the focus of the assembly.

"There's not a country on this planet unaffected, and there's not a person in this world free from the fear of ALLIS," says Robin Debonce, U.S. Ambassador to the United Nations. "I believe every nation will donate resources—monetary, educational, scientific, and religious—to the common cause of eradicating this disease."

Congress has been formulating its own contributions to the ALLIS war. The House and Senate, both Democratically controlled, handily passed a much debated De-ALLIS Bill, and have sent this emergency measure to President Robert Wolfe for final approval. This bill opens the U.S. Treasury for unlimited funding to any research facility that can prove it has a viable ALLIS cause or cure proposal. Republican President Wolfe, noting that all funding will be gleaned from the military budget, has vowed to veto the De-ALLIS Bill. But congressional leaders feel the bill is already law. House Majority Speaker Dwayne Ross states: "If the President unwisely vetoes this bill, we will override him. If this disease continues its current course, who's going to need a military?"

Congress willing to rob the inviolable war machine for funding; the world's divided nations merging together in comradeship to do battle with a common enemy; scientists should be residing on Cloud Nine. Rarely do researchers experience a no-holds-barred go-ahead for their experiments. But unabated joy is not the case. In major research facilities across the nation, an overriding sense of investigator frustration permeates the air.

"One main reason for this [frustration]," notes Dr. Samuel Reese, director of the National Academy of the Sciences, "is the simple fact that the best brains in the country have done about all they can do. We have been focusing energies on ALLIS for months. We have yet to score a point for the good guys."

While ALLIS death figures rocket skyward, solid data on probable causes and effective cures have yet to find a footing. A medical report written six months ago listing causes and possible cures reads the same as a similar paper written today. No one yet knows why the disease is, what the disease is, how a person contracts the disease, or how said person can counter the disease once it strikes.

ALLIS has claimed more than a million lives. Yet the disease continues to display a remarkably even distribution pattern throughout the world. No one nation or area of a country shows a greater population percentage of ALLIS victims than any other nation or area.

ALLIS is both ubiquitous and relentless. It never varies in its deadly program of loss of muscular strength and core temperature decrease. No branch of science has yet pointed to any cure that reverses or halts the progress of these symptoms. [See accompanying story.]

The concentrated attention of the researching world now focuses on ALLIS. As scientists delve deeper into their experiments, they know they have the support of the entire world.

· · · · ·

ALLIS ON MY MIND

It's becoming a frequent scene in cities across the world. A vacant building is renovated into a modern care facility. Brightly painted walls line the rooms, and curtain-less windows allow as much sun as possible to shine inside. Cheerful posters decorate the walls. Casually dressed volunteer and professional care-givers stroll from one bed patient to another. It's a quiet, almost soundless scene, and an uninformed observer would never guess the terrible reason behind the building's silence, nor guess the grim sadness those painted walls and bright colors are trying to lessen.

In large urban areas the alarming 1-in-5,000 death rate of the ALLIS disease has created a critical need for facilities where people afflicted with the sickness can find a supportive environment. Inside these "ALLIS foster homes," disease victims experience a caring and comfortable environment. Here they await a gentle but rapid death.

Such centers are badly needed. With 12 million inhabitants, New York City and suburbs have experienced approximately 2,400 ALLIS deaths. Potential exponential growth of the disease indicates that the contagion rate will continue at increased levels.

Dr. Andrew Mason used to devote his psychology and M.D. energies to counseling and treating terminal cancer patients at Miami Mercy Hospital's Center For Ennobled Dying. Dr. Mason now works in a similar position at the new ALLIS Evanesce Shelter, a combined effort of Palm Beach, Broward, and Dade Counties, a 200-bed home-care facility where people diagnosed with ALLIS retire to spend the last days of their lives. Says Dr. Mason: "We've had more than a thousand people succumb to ALLIS in this southeastern Florida population strip. These people, one day alive and the next day sentenced to a two-week life span, desperately need professional counseling and a supportive environment to help them face the changes—the rapid changes—ahead."

ALLIS is known for its complete lack of discrimination. The Prime Minister of Belgium died from the disease; a Congressman from Rhode Island is also an ALLIS fatality; an aged and unknown diabetic street person contracted the illness; so did a twenty-six-year-old super-athlete in the prime of his career. When San Francisco 49ers star quarterback Mike Ross began fumbling the football in preseason training, no one could have believed someone in his physically prime condition could twelve days later helplessly slip from life. In life as well as in dying, Mike Ross gave his all. Before consciousness left him, Ross liquidated his estate and donated the proceeds—over three million dollars—to the United Way Organization with instructions to build and maintain a compassionate dying center for other ALLIS victims in the Bay Area. Ross stated: "It's too damn scary, on such sudden notice, to be cut from the team of the living. I decided all my material gains were worth a hoot only if they could help other sufferers make the passage a little easier."

Ross was given a hero's funeral by the city of San Francisco.

More than 60,000 other Americans have died from the same disease that killed the football star. ALLIS has surpassed the fatality count of the Vietnam War. As in that war, the listing of ruined lives does not end at the death count. Immediate families and friends experience the pain associated with suddenly and meaninglessly losing someone they love. Unlimited funding may be available for scientific research on ALLIS, but bereavement counseling for the hundreds of thousands of immediate family survivors is practically unobtainable. Twenty-eight years of unrelenting budget cuts in the social services sector of the government have left but a skeleton of a national social program, and it cannot begin to deal with the numbers currently in need of professional help.

"Not only is there a total lack of available counseling for families suddenly facing the deaths of loved ones, there are many more needless deaths occurring because of no accessible psychology-comfort services for those people who live in dread fear of contracting the disease themselves," according to Henry Simblers, Ph.D., who donates two days a week of his private counseling service to the Tarrant County Social Services Division in Fort Worth, Texas. He cites a growing number of suicides in the Dallas-Fort Worth area, many of them attributable to the person's fear of contracting ALLIS.

Says Simblers: "There's a new kind of mental anguish happening everywhere. The supermarkets can't keep fever thermometers on the shelves. We're becoming a nation of neurotic temperature takers. Anybody who wakes up with a chill freaks out, thinking they have ALLIS. People cannot handle the idea that they might have but two weeks to live. Suicide rates are, percentage-wise, climbing in proportion to the ALLIS death rate."

In a confusing, beset-by-ALLIS world where science is, so far, helpless, and government tells a different story every time it opens its mouth, people are turning in increasing numbers to what one philosopher called the "opiate of the masses." Worldwide, religions cite a considerable surge in membership. Leaders of standard and newly formed religions around the world conduct hourly prayer services directed toward invoking God (and/or the gods) to help mankind overcome this current ALLIS predicament.

But some of the "ministries" add more confusion to the picture. Henry Simblers relates relevant examples from his counseling experiences: "You have one house telling people that this disease is Almighty God's retribution upon the terrible sinners of the world. A family may believe that explanation. Then their mother, who has basically been an angel ministering to the masses, dies of ALLIS. The family now compounds its grief with confusion and a questioning of their faith. You have another house just as vehemently telling people that God is perfect love and is taking care of everything, and then their only child dies of the disease. These people are left not believing in either life or love. You also have a noticeable return to cult worship practices—especially that of animal sacrifice ceremonies. Any psychologist can tell you of the scrambled brain and reasoning decay possessed by people who practice those observances."

Simblers continues: "I don't think God is the answer to this disease. But time will prove that thought right or wrong."

Time is what all eyes now watch. If ALLIS continues to double its death figures every three or four weeks, time will become quite limited for researching minds to put together an effective solution.

· · · · ·

ALLIS—POSSIBLE CURE OR DESPERATE HOPE

It may be his first name, his last name, or his only name, but the man called Gurner is currently the world's most talked about, most speculated upon, and most wanted person. And he is wanted on many levels.

The FDA wants him on several counts of practicing medicine without a license, selling and profiteering potentially dangerous drugs, and resisting arrest. The FBI wants him for interstate flight and suspected interstate drug distribution. The AMA wants him canned because of his reputation as a successful and unorthodox healer. And the IRS wants him for an audit because they do not believe the meager earnings he reports on his tax forms.

Forces more benign also want to talk to this man. There isn't a scientist who wouldn't pay dearly for the chance of open discussion with Gurner. Researchers of every specialty would love to extract information from him. Other nations have promised him amnesty should he decide to make an appearance at their embassies. Mostly, the people of the world want him. And they are beginning to loudly raise their voices in support of a man they know almost nothing about.

Nine months ago Gurner was an unknown, living in the mountains near the small town of John Day, Oregon. Where he came from, no one knows. He rented a primitive cabin from Grant County Commissioner Harry Smith. From this nestled spot near Canyon Creek Summit on U.S. Highway 395, Gurner began an arcane herbal medicine practice.

Silas Parkins of John Day claims to have been one of Gurner's first clients. "I was getting real crippled with arthritis, and real pissed off at doctors and their endless drugs that cost me dear yet didn't do anything for the aches. I was bellyaching about it, and this young fella comes up and says to let him have a look at the bad joints. I said, 'OK, got nothing to lose,' and met him at Smith's cabin. He mostly put his hands on me and closed his eyes and didn't do anything for a long time. Then he told me my kidneys were shot and my stomach wasn't doing something right, and because of that I wasn't getting the minerals I needed. He also said I had a system full of toxins from the bad kidneys. He gave me a bunch of herbs to take, advised me to make some big changes in my diet, and said good luck. Well, I tell you, sir, those herbs were the most God-awful thing this boy ever tasted. And having to give up meat and coffee about drove me crazy. But something about that Gurner fella's sincerity kept me at it, and damned if in three or four weeks this old body didn't start to loosen up. By God, I kept up with that program, and now the wife and I can go dancing. I'm also back at mechanicking. The doctors are saying it was their medicines that eased the arthritis."

Via several such instances, and through word of mouth, Gurner developed a minor reputation throughout the John Day River Valley. "That crazy but effective healer up in the woods" became his local appellation. He's credited with curing everything from backaches to headaches to allergies and skin rashes. His methodology follows the extraordinary pattern of laying his hands on a person, engaging in a lengthy, talking-to-himself meditation, and then suggesting diet changes, vitamin and mineral supplements, and various herbal remedies. Those interviewed who did employ his services note that he never charges more than twenty or thirty dollars for a couple of hours of consultation time. These same people quickly mentioned that this was many times less than the cost of a visit to a doctor.

But Gurner's efficacy may have prompted his downfall. Local physicians cited him to the AMA, who referred him to the FDA, who began gathering information on the man.

Meanwhile, Gurner's growing renown led a California man, one of the first persons in this country to contract ALLIS, to seek out the healer's services. John Slamder of Sacramento, seven days into the ALLIS condition, asked relatives to hustle him to Gurner's door. He was subjected to the hands-on meditation and soliloquy of the healer, and was given several herbs to drink in a tea with no promise that they could help. John Slamder: "I thought, 'What the hell, got nothing else to try,' and drank this tea. My temperature immediately ceased falling, and within a day and a half it began climbing. The chills left within two days. I am now living proof that the man our asinine government has persecuted into hiding has the key to save millions of lives."

Gurner is credited with saving additional ALLIS victim's lives. One of those resurrections is Mary Johnson, wife of Brian Johnson, former FDA investigative agent assigned to Gurner's case. Johnson now heads the self-appointed force working for the dropping of all charges against Gurner.

On January 15, 2008, federal marshals raided Gurner's residence, confiscating a variety of dried and fresh herbs. But they missed capturing the main root, Gurner himself. The healer disappeared, and massive federal search efforts have failed to track him. Occasionally Gurner has made his presence known. When this happens, earthquakes don't cause the repercussions that he does.

On January 30, 2008, *Newstime* carried the heartwarming story of Johnny Willox, now known as the ALLIS Wonder Baby. For over eighteen days Johnny lay dying of ALLIS. His parents tell of how, during what should have been the last minutes of their son's life, a stranger—positively identified as Gurner—came to their Boulder, Colorado, house and with the aid of a recently graduated medical doctor, Ms. Stephanie Peters, began a drop-by-drop feeding of an herbal tea into the baby. No picture has ever touched the world as did *Newstime*'s photograph of the smiling, tearful parents holding up a very alive infant while medical workers stand in the background and stare in utter disbelief.

Since then a trail of at least ten confirmable instances have occurred where ALLIS victims have been given an unknown herb by a stranger later identified as Gurner. After drinking a tea made from this herb, the persons afflicted with ALLIS survived. Government agents following Gurner's "miracle trail" of healings currently believe he has fled from Washington state into Canada.

This small synopsis of "Gurner's Travels" creates a few glaring questions. As the only person in the world who has a possible way to counter the nightmare of ALLIS, why is he playing hide and seek at such a time of world need? A simple rearranging of words asks a different question. Why are some of the biggest guns in the government pursuing that person with a list of charges that will place him behind bars until the ALLIS crisis—one way or the other—passes? Why aren't they devoting this energy to soliciting the herbalist to help? The first question asks what Gurner has to hide. The second two questions ask what kind of game the government is playing.

Johnson notes that he thought he was overworked as an FDA agent. Since his wife's purported resurrection from ALLIS by the healer Gurner, he has spent long hours trying to convince government heads that they need to acknowledge that the man does possess an ALLIS cure—perhaps the only cure. Johnson adamantly contends that the healer does desire to offer this cure to the world's scientists, and that the only thing he wants in return is a total dismissal of charges against him. "Charges," says Johnson, "that have been trumped-up. I know. I was involved in the trumping-up process."

In answer to the "Why is Gurner running?" question, Johnson notes that the healer wants his God-given cure to be just that. Johnson: "He [Gurner] says that too many people will needlessly die while the government tests, regulates, and controls the product. He states that it [the government] is famous for allowing something deadly on the market while perpetually withholding approval on more natural substances [herbs] that work as well. He says it would not be right for a major drug company to develop and patent the cure, and thus be able to squeeze large sums of money out of a population that had no choice but to buy their [the drug company's] product. Mostly, he says that a sure cure for ALLIS is going to be an incredible power source, and that no government in history has ever shown much benevolence to certain other governments when it solely owned and controlled that much power."

Johnson concludes answering the "Why run, Gurner?" question by saying, "Gurner, besides needing to be a free man, simply wants a fair deal for everyone concerned . . . which happens to be the entire population of the world."

Representatives of the varying agencies tracking Gurner were asked the "Why?" questions concerning this unique manhunt, and answered with a standard: "It's our job." Jim Bowerns, head of the Investigative Division of the FDA and a man who some say seems to carry a vendetta against the healer, simply stated that Gurner has violated the law and it is his duty to apprehend him.

But Johnson thinks that due process of the law is about to bend in its unwavering course. Says Johnson, "My job is done. Every day members of Congress receive thousands of letters demanding that charges against Gurner be dropped. So does the President. I think government representatives felt that immediate directives from the people were dogs long dead. But this particular pooch now weighs about 900 pounds and is ready to snap off the head of anyone who resists it. Our lawmakers are going to have to follow what is becoming a unified voice of the people and invite Gurner to the crossroads."

♣ 13 ♣
Planning

May 22, 2008, 5:05 P.M. A public telephone booth, inside the Martin Luther King, Jr. Library, Washington, D.C.

Brian Johnson placed his hand over the receiver as he stuck his head out of the phone booth. He shook his head from side to side and said a short sentence to a young woman standing near the booth. The woman reacted quite vehemently to that sentence.

"No! He said no? He can't say no. Let me have that receiver, Brian. I've got to talk to him."

Stephanie Peters grabbed the receiver as she stepped into the booth. Agitation blanketed her face. *Living alone in the woods all these months without a woman must have addled his brain.*

"Gurner. This is Stephanie. Whaddaya mean no? You can't— . . . I'm fine, thanks. Whaddaya mean you can't accept the President's offer. He gives you total amnesty. I thought that's what you wanted . . . Of course it's a political ploy on his part. Anyone with one-third normal brain power knows that he's grown real unpopular since vetoing that De-ALLIS Bill. Anyone who looks can see that adding your ALLIS cure to his bag of tricks will immediately reinstate him with the public. But listen, Gurner. In less than two weeks' time almost 700,000 *more* people have died from ALLIS. It's about to hit the two million mark. And the point here is that while you're lollygagging around waiting for the world to lay itself at your feet, hundreds of thousands more people may die. That doesn't sound like the actions of a true healer to me."

Dr. Peters leaned her head out of the phone booth. "He wants me to read him the President's compromise message. Brian, hand me that *Newstime*. Thanks.

"Let's see. President announced . . . 'In the midst of despair, we now have a hope' . . . Here it is. Are you ready? 'As President of the United States, I gladly offer Mr. Gurner complete amnesty from any criminal charges. He may rest assured that any illegal actions concerning his practice of prescribing herbs will in no way be held against him' . . . Gurner, let him verbally convict you all he wants. We're talking about saving lives. This disease is beginning to make world wars look like tiddly-winks games . . . Yes, I'll continue. 'If Mr. Gurner will simply appear at any police or federal office in any state, proper messages will be relayed to the Centers for Disease Control in Atlanta. The government will immediately jet Mr. Gurner to the CDC where he can share his most valuable information with a waiting team of experts. The CDC will immediately began analysis on this herb to discover its role as a cure for the ALLIS disease.' Wolfe blathers on about the great gift he and you are providing for humanity.

" . . . You're paranoid, Gurner. Whaddaya mean your herb will never be seen again? . . . You want me to do what? Gurner, playing games at a time like this is . . . All right, all right. I'll pretend for a moment . . .

"I'm pretending. I'm pretending I'm a big and powerful nation with several other nations as enemies. OK . . . And I as this powerful nation discover the cure for a terrible worldwide disease. OK. . . . Would I willingly and openly and freely offer that cure to the little Central American or Asian or Middle East nations that are my sworn enemies? Well, I personally would, but that's not what you're asking. Well no, as a nation stuck in old ways of thinking, I would not, but Gurner—

" . . . Would I lovingly give my hard-earned cure to an opposing nuclear power nation without demanding something from them they may not be willing or able to give? Crumb, Gurner, this is a rough class you teach . . . Well, yes, you're probably right. If denied access to the cure, those nations might nuke me off the face of the Earth, simply because they would be doomed to die anyway, and I, their supposed enemy, might as well join them—"

Dr. Peters sighed. "You're right. It's the same thing we would do to them if the cards were reversed. But what the hell are we going to do? Sounds like it's 'die if you do and die if you don't' with this herb. But damn it, Gurner, if you don't get it out into everyone's view, it's definitely going to be *die* . . . "

Dr. Peters again leaned out the phone booth. "Brian, have you got a pen? He's going to dictate to me a list of events that must happen for this healing herb to be made public. And he says he has a plan that will help that happen. Thanks.

"Go ahead Gurner. I'm ready to write . . . yeah . . . yeah . . . got that . . . um hum . . . you don't want much. You want it all. And now what's your plan? . . . I see . . . we can do that . . . You gotta be kidding! . . . OK . . . Gurner, you're nuts! . . . OK. We'll try . . . "

I don't believe I'm in the middle of this. I'm already ass-deep in muddy waters, and he wants to blow up the dam.

. . . Ohhhh. You and your damned intuition. "No, I'm doing fine. I don't know why you think my voice has a down tone to it."

. . . This guy might as well have a crystal ball. No. No, I haven't started my practice. I . . . I don't have a license anymore. It's like you said would happen. Two days after the Willox baby story hit the papers, they jerked my M.D. status. I 'knowingly administered unsafe and unproven medicines,' among other atrocities . . . Oh, don't be stupid, Gurner! Look. You talk to Brian. I gotta think over the hows of this list you just laid on me.

"Here, Brian."

Dr. Peters handed the receiver back to Johnson and dashed from the public phone booth. She then raced through several circles around the reference book shelves.

"Hey, Gurner. This is Brian again. . . . Oh, you know, Stephanie has had to temporarily sacrifice her dreams to work for what she believes in. It's not an easy time. . . . What does she believe in? I've never met anyone quite like her. She believes in the human race. You happen to be pretty important to it right now, so she currently believes in helping you. But I think she would do that anyway, because you by yourself are pretty important to her. . . . Yeah, well, we're talking heart here. That's not so easy. I doubt I can point out to her all the 'insurmountable' differences that stand between you two.

"Look, Gurner, it sounds like you gave her a lot of heavy information, and that we'd better get on it. And I get uncomfortable when we talk on a phone for more than five minutes. We've come too far in this game to have them trace you now, so why don't we hang up. I'll take my stroll at the normal times past a phone booth with this number: 202-555-4443. Call if anything comes up or changes. . . . Yeah, Stephanie has your demands written down, all across the face of the President delivering his 'Gurner come home' speech on the new *Newstime*'s cover picture. . . . OK, my friend. Stay well hidden, hopefully for just a little while longer. Mary says hi. And I say bye."

Johnson placed the pay phone receiver back in its cradle and walked to a nearby library table where Stephanie was intently transcribing her hasty shorthand onto a legal pad. "Are you OK?"

"Yeah." Dr. Peters looked up at Johnson and smiled. "All better."

"Well, hearing one side of that conversation was very intriguing. I'm a bundle of curiosity to know what he told you."

"He's a nut, Brian. He's an extreme, on the far end of the idealistic pendulum, nut. And that's probably the kind of 'nuts enough' it'll take to pull this off. Here's the list of demands everyone must publicly agree to before he'll come out of hiding. You read it, and I'll finish translating his plan of action that might just allow it to happen."

Johnson slowly read Gurner's list of demands. "Hum. Well, that about covers things, doesn't it? And we, I take it, have a role to play to help convince our government to do something it's never done before?"

"You got it. In a day or two, Brian, you're going to receive a small package in the mail, or via UPS, or somehow. That package will contain enough of Gurner's herb to treat two ALLIS victims. We're to line up two positively diagnosed ALLIS victim volunteers to publicly drink the tea. 'Publicly' is the key word here. Gurner's idea is that every reporter of every imaginable media scrutinize this event. He's confident that the two people will be cured. And when they are cured, you know, in live action, right before the world's watching eyes, there's a good chance that the public will then be amenable to be presented Gurner's list of demands. With them, he's telling the people of the world to claim the herb by making the government do what they want it to do . . . which hopefully includes exonerating him and following that list of guidelines."

Johnson skimmed over the demand list again. "Indeed. Immediately responding to the people's dictates. That truly is getting the government to do something it's never done before. And you know, Stephanie. This list of Gurner's wants. I don't see a one of them that could be called selfish."

"Yeah. I guess not."

"So what's your problem with it?"

Does everybody have an intuition that won't let me keep my feelings my own? "Sometimes I wonder if he's not kind of enjoying having the world so manipulable under this special discovery of his. And if he's not just experimenting, trying to do something no one has done before.

"But these doubts are probably just my thoughts. You know, me who would share everything with everyone immediately. When I think of some of the ideas he espoused as we traveled together those couple weeks, I have to admit that the man's inner vision has grown too big to reduce itself to self-indulgent games." Dr. Peters sighed. "Of any kind."

Johnson gently grabbed Dr. Peters by her arm and helped her stand up. "So then, Stephanie. Let's formulate a plan of action to help instigate the plan of action. We probably ought not to solicit volunteers until I get the herbs. Don't want the package intercepted in the mail. Then, let's not call the reporters until the day of the tea-drinking party. I'm sure it could be interrupted by the powers that be. I don't imagine that finding a couple of ALLIS sufferers willing to offer their swallowing services will be difficult."

"Gurner had a suggestion. He said he read that the fellow who replaced you at the FDA has contracted ALLIS. He wondered if you were good enough friends with that man to approach him with the idea."

Johnson laughed out loud. "Oh, what a good one. Dan Crimsom. We're good friends. He's six days into ALLIS and scared beyond comprehension. He also hates Jim Bowerns' guts. For the sake of balance, let's have a woman be the other person. Mary was talking the other day of a good friend of a good friend not having long to live due to the disease."

"Don't get someone on their death's bed, Brian. The herb has to heal them. If it doesn't, we'll never have another chance and both be in jail besides."

"Dear one. We may be in jail anyway for this. But I've got to do it."

"Me too. Crumb, me too."

Johnson, still holding Dr. Peters' arm, walked toward the library exit. "Who's going to give the herbs to the volunteers? We should have a doctor . . . er, a licensed doctor, I'm sorry to say. One who doesn't mind getting hung."

"Hey, leave that one to me. Gurner wanted me to do it, but you're right, we need current credibility here. However, there's a growing contingent of medical professionals joining the rising voice of folks demanding to learn of this herb at all costs. I have several friends from med school among this list. I'm sure I can get half a dozen certified docs from all kinds of specialties to medically administer—I love it—a cup of tea."

Johnson held the library door open for his companion. "All right, Stephanie. Onward, I guess."

Dr. Peters paused in the vestibule. "It feels like we ought to propose a toast."

"We don't have any liquid. Or glasses."

"Let's pretend, Brian."

Johnson and Dr. Peters paused in the middle of the busy entrance to the library. Johnson smiled as he faced the doctor. "All right, Stephanie. What would you propose a toast to?"

"To the end of ALLIS."

"To the end of ALLIS. Yes. And to the beginning of fulfillment of dreams—yours, mine, Gurner's, everyone's."

Well, Gurner's dreams about me and my dreams about Gurner might clash. But . . . "I'll drink to that."

They clinked fingers, took an imaginary sip, emptied the remaining invisible liquid on each other, and moved into the next phase of planning.

· 14 ·
Reaction

May 28, 2008, 1:15 P.M. FDA headquarters, office of the
Chief of Fraudulent Practices Investigations.

Dan Crimsom hated his present situation. He hated his job,
and he hated his boss. He had always heard that life took a better
course for those who returned to it from near-death experiences.
But everything here and now seemed terribly the same to him.

"Come on, Mr. Bowerns. You know you've got to sign it, and
you might as well sign it now as later. First, the President has
basically ordered you to. Second, if this is the worst list of demands
you ever have to accede to, life will have been mighty kind to
you."

Bowerns' blistering glare, for instance. That hadn't changed a
bit. "Are you enjoying yourself, Crimsom, watching me be forced
to consent to something I know is wrong? You're quite a 'notable'
now, with your tea-sipping face plastered all over *Newstime*. I
still can't believe you did that. When I moved you to Johnson's
position, I thought I had chosen a man of character, one who
believed in his job . . . one who wasn't a drop-of-the-hat turncoat."

"A character whose funeral you would have attended about
two days ago. You might have even shed a perfunctory tear or
two. Doesn't it mean anything to you that I and that Johanson
woman would be additional death statistics if we hadn't drunk
that healing herb tea? Doesn't it touch you anywhere to know
that someone has discovered a cure for the biggest nightmare to
strike the world?"

And Bowerns' bellowing voice. If anything, it had gained
power. "At the exorbitant price of an anarchist dictating his values
to our free government?!"

"That's not the case."

"Yes it is, Crimsom."

"No, Mr. Bowerns. Before I consented to being the guinea pig in this unusual experiment; before Sara Johanson agreed; before those seven doctors put themselves on the line and acquiesced to administer the tea; we all read and re-read Gurner's list of demands. And we all agreed this was not an oddball or an anarchist talking, but a man of prophetic vision." *And yes, speaking of things being the same; there it is, that protruding, branching, expanding vein on Bowerns' forehead.*

"Oh Jesus! Now we've got vision involved. First he raises people from the dead. Now he's got visions. Next he'll come riding into the streets of Washington, D.C. on an ass while the people scatter palms and petunias before his path."

Bowerns projected at Crimsom his most menacing stare and pregnant silence. He then spoke to the agent with a precisely calculated cutting edge to his voice. "But I can promise you, Crimsom, that before our latest godling claims his throne in the White House, there's going to be a heavy cross fall upon his shoulders."

Dan Crimsom quit biting his inner cheek and dropped his jaw a bit in disbelief. *For the love of . . . This isn't a normal thinking man. This is a madman.* "Is that what you think? That Gurner has power as his goal? And wants to be hero-ized into the Presidency? Mr. Bowerns, have you even analyzed this list of his demands?"

Bowerns, when not in the public eye, easily crossed the fine line of his control. He jumped up and bellowed across the desk at Dan Crimsom. "Demands from madmen are just that! Goddamn demands! And, Crimsom, I'm not acting as head of this busy office so I can spend my time wrangling with subordinates!"

Crimsom retreated into subservient sarcasm. "Then, *Mr.* Bowerns. I, as your humble lesser, do dutifully suggest that you sign the paper that exonerates Mr. Gurner of all FDA charges against him. It's due at the President's office for his scheduled news conference. All the other needed forgiveness papers have been signed and delivered, and quite frankly, *Sir,* your ass will be grass if you're the hold-up."

Bowerns wearily plunked himself down on his desk chair and placed his head between his hands, letting a long sigh escape as he mused to himself. *I'll get you for this, Gurner. I swear, I'll tie you to a caduceus stake and light a fire around you . . . a fire fed by fuel made from your goddamn herb.*

Without looking at his agent, Bowerns spoke in a disgusted voice. "Read me that list, Crimsom. Out loud. Start with demand number one. I'm wasting time because I want it to be known that at least Jim Bowerns resisted the magician's spell until the last minute."

Dan Crimsom picked up the papers from Bowerns' desk. Contempt flickered from his face. *Maybe we could cast a spell on you and make your hemorrhoids pop.* "Gurner's demands, number one: 'I must have total dismissal of all federal and other criminal charges against me, as the President has promised. The IRS can audit all they want; there's nothing to hide.'"

Bowerns lifted his head from his hands. His voice regained its power. "I never thought I'd see the day a Republican President would buckle like that. But you got it, Gurner." Bowerns' voice carried an undertone of wickedness to it. "For now."

Crimsom winced inside. *Oh God no, Bowerns, don't make me suffer through your running philosophical commentaries on every one of these.* "Demand number two states: 'All knowledge of the herb or of any synthetics or derivatives from the herb must be shared with every nation, people, or person on this planet. To insure this is so, and since this herb grows in the United States, I'm asking:

- That every nation, but especially the United States (since the herb is here), open the research facilities studying the herb to teams of scientists from every country.
- That the news media be involved every step of the way. Through this, may nothing concerning an ALLIS cure be kept hidden from the public.'"

Crimsom looked up from the paper and smiled hopefully at his boss. "That sounds good, doesn't it? He's leaving no opportunity for the Russians to say to the Chinese, 'Tough titty, Charlie, no cure for you.'"

"He's saying that he doesn't have any love, respect, or trust for this country, you yahoo. He's saying that he's a Communist."

Crimsom cringed. *If he were saying that, you retard, he'd be in Cuba now and leaving us all to die. Damn, I wish I had the guts Brian does. I'd up and quit and leave this monkey pulling his own tail.* "Gurner's third demand states: 'I also ask a public promise that no patent on this herb or any product synthesized from this herb be claimed. It and any of its offspring compounds must be available so no monopoly on the product can form. Also, the cost of its manufacture must be public knowledge, so a fair price can be charged and the world isn't beset with another rich man's cure.'"

Bowerns, unable to remain seated, bolted up, gesticulating. "I've never heard such hogwash in all my life! The man is cutting down everything this country stands for: free enterprise, capitalism, economics that work, and proper payment for those who have the capabilities to accomplish what's needed."

Crimsom suddenly realized that he was beginning to enjoy this reading session. *Oh, go sit on a hot stovepipe and hold your breath for an hour.* "Finally, Gurner states, 'I must ask for the protection of an exceptionally beautiful piece of this country's wild heritage. I've found this herb in but one area, on one remote hillside. It may be the only area the plant grows. Federal troops of some sort must be stationed around the area to protect it from the inevitable ecological plunder that would follow once its location is revealed . . .'"

Bowerns slightly eased his disgust. "Now that's finally making some sense. Get the Marines around it and seal it off and let our—"

"Gurner goes on to add, sir: 'Reporters, scientists, researchers, etc. from the world over will not be banned from the area. Walk gently and don't clear-cut every stalk of the herb for the laboratory. If nothing curative can be synthesized, this plant may have to be farmed.'

"Gurner then says: 'When this list, made known to all, is publicly approved, I'll head for the nearest newspaper office. From there *we* will call the government for the promised and speedy action to seriously begin the ALLIS cure study. The *we* I refer to are the reporters who will at all times accompany me. There will be no secret interviews or closed-door questioning sessions with Gurner.'"

Bowerns shook his head from side to side. "There he goes with the damned reporters again. Crimsom, no government, good or bad, would survive if they were to tell the public everything. If he thinks he can undo decades of subterfuge and covert—" Bowerns stopped in mid-sentence and looked at Crimsom. "Well, er, never mind, but mark my words, he can't, and no good will come from his trying."

Crimsom tried not to stare at his boss. *Whoa. What did he say?*

There's something more to this guy than FDA. I wonder if he's Trilateral or Giant or Illuminati . . . or whatever those guys call themselves.

"Well, don't just stare into space, Crimsom. Is there anything else?"

Crimsom returned to his papers. "Gurner concludes: 'To the peoples and the governments of the world. The ALLIS disease is more deadly and dangerous—'"

"Agh. Never mind. I don't want to hear his pettifogging plea."

"'. . . and dangerous than the wildest imagination can conceive. If you the people feel this is so; if you the people also feel that the above demands come from someone who is honestly trying—'"

"I said that's enough, Crimsom."

"'. . . honestly trying to offer a proven cure to the entire world and not just a selected few, then you the people must and must rapidly—'"

"I said that's goddamn *enough!*"

"'. . . must rapidly and via democratic, nonviolent process pressure your elected officials into complying with them. God has given a cure for ALLIS, and I want nothing more than to offer the world what He's shown me. The same direction that led me to the cure now leads me to seeking—'"

"You're way overstepping your boundaries, bud!"

"'. . . to seeking assurance that all will receive it. If you believe what I say, you've got to act, because ALLIS is just about at everyone's door.'"

Dan Crimsom looked up from the paper he was reading and mockingly smiled. "The end."

Bowerns' menacing glare attained staggering proportions. "Crimsom, when you come up for your evaluation next month, your rating is going to be so low a dung beetle won't be able to find it. If you think you can—"

"Excuse me, but if you're going to berate me, sir, you better do it in the next minute, and do it while you're signing those papers. I've got half an hour to get them to the White House, and it's a twenty-five-minute drive if the traffic's good."

Bowerns snarled, scrawled his signature onto the papers that would, for now, place the healer Gurner out of his reach, and threw the document at Crimsom. The latter bowed very sightly and exited, letting the office door close itself with an efficient click.

As was his habit, Bowerns walked over to the full-length mirror in a corner of his office. He stared at the discontented person reflecting his image in the glass. His mind immediately posed the tentative question, asking him if those demands weren't more fair than he was allowing. But these inner mental queries never gained acknowledgement, much less an honest answer. All thoughts in Bowerns' mind were drowned under the angry ruminations of: *I'll get you for this, Gurner. I swear, I'll monkey wrench you somehow.*

◆ 15 ◆
Destiny

June 6, 2008, 11:45 A.M. Anacostia River Park, near the National Arboretum, Washington, D.C.

The healer Gurner never felt less at home in his life. He habitually looked to the horizon for the inspiration of snow-capped mountains, but murky haze and endless buildings were what the skyline offered. He strained to hear some yearned-for silence, but the busy city had long ago laid that delicate concept to rest. With less outside beauty to hold his attention, Gurner's mind retreated more inside itself.

I want to go back. That's it in a nutshell. I want to go back into the woods and forget this last week ever existed.

And if You're going to take me back, let's go back far enough to where I can ignore both that herb and the instinctive feeling I had to gather it when I passed through its habitat.

Gurner turned from his inner workings for a moment and gazed at the surrounding crowd of reporters and curiosity seekers who perpetually attached themselves to his presence. He sighed, shook his head, and spoke in a voice loud enough for all to hear.

"Look, people . . . all you multitudes of people. There is a tree over there by the river. A shady, isolated and all-alone tree. I'm going over to that tree—*alone*—and sit there—*undisturbed*—for as long as I need to. Don't anybody follow me; don't anybody come over and interrupt me. Harold, do me a big favor. Explain to these well-meaning folks the value of solitude."

Gurner abruptly walked away from the crowd. His thoughts anticipated their reaction: *And with that, amidst dozens of cries of protest, he gracelessly stomped off to enjoy some solitude and to talk to a tree.*

Beneath breeze-clattering maple leaves, fifteen minutes passed, a quarter of an hour in which no wayward thoughts entered the healer's mind. A gradual peace both relaxed Gurner's tensions and turned his mind to a mental review of the past days.

Holy bananas. For a week I haven't had moment one to let my thoughts return to their Center. Not since the President said—was forced to say—"Yes, Gurner, we need your help." Such a compassionate President we have. It took three and a half million ALLIS deaths and the people threatening to impeach him to get him to respond to their wishes.

Shoot, that was awful. After I mailed those herbs to Brian, there were two more weeks of ALLIS fatality figures doubling. Me with a cure . . . and me also with an inner voice dictating that I stay hidden until that list of terms was met. It's no wonder that nationwide editorials were questioning how I ever got the title "healer" attached to my name. Editorial cartoons showed me as a caricature herb putting a hammerlock on the world.

Gurner gazed up and into the tree branches, speaking aloud, directing his voice to the sky beyond the leaves. "Why is it the louder one hears Your voice, the harder everything fights one as he tries to follow that voice?"

Gurner attempted to return to silence, but his thought process was too much in motion. *So, three hours after the President satellited his Gurner-sanction around the world, Medford, Oregon, became the most focused-upon spot on Earth. I wandered into the local newspaper office and asked if I could call Washington, D.C., on their phone. Heh, guess I should have identified myself first. They were ready to toss me out as a kook until the sports editor put together who I was. Then did they bend over backwards. Too far backwards, God Almighty. Not only was Washington, D.C., called, but they also notified every radio, press association, magazine, and neighboring newspaper.*

It took about fifteen minutes for that newspaper building to jam with wall-to-wall people. And it took about five minutes more for me to realize that I made a big, big mistake. Curiosity seekers swarmed in. Reporters of every sort began a deluge of questions that hasn't ended since. Worst of all were the people there whose relatives had just contracted ALLIS. They began screaming for the herb, begging me to save them, reacting angrily when I said I didn't have the herb with me. Then someone yelled out that his brother had died of ALLIS while I was hiding in the woods. Others started calling me names, telling me how I had let their loved ones die. All the time an increasing number of persons screamed at me to save them from ALLIS. I think it was a classic example of uncontrolled panic behavior in crowds. But all psychology aside, this herbalist was about to season a sacrificial stew.

Gurner again looked to the heavens. "You know, God. All these years I've prayed to You to help me be a healer who could lay his hands on people and cure anyone of anything. But maybe You've been most merciful—to me anyway—by not answering that prayer. In that crowd, I felt like a cob of corn tossed into a gathering of starving pigs. People would eat alive any man who sported a regenerative power like that . . . and bury him in the mud if he ever failed."

A shudder coursed through Gurner's body as he returned to his inner narrative. *Yeah for timely entrances by police.*

Now I had a uniformed wall between me and a crowd that somehow reasoned it could kill ALLIS by killing me. But nothing abated the machine gun fire of questions, questions, questions from growing numbers of reporters. It was: "Lights! Camera! Action! This is station KZZZ bringing you the area's most complete and live coverage. Today we have as our guest Mr. er, ah, Gurner. Say something profound for our audience, Mr. er, ah, Gurner." A dozen microphones got jammed under my nose, and two dozen flash bulbs simultaneously flared inches from my unsuspecting eyeballs. I was left blinded, unable to speak and wondering if World War Three had started. "Thank you, Mr. er, ah, Gurner. Station KZZZ, folks. We'll return to our interview after this important advertisement, and after we figure out what kind of speech impediment Mr. er, ah, Gurner has."

I wanted to leap out the window and run away . . . a feeling that hasn't left since.

Then the federal helicopters roared into town. I randomly picked two reporters to accompany me, and via those choppers we raced to the nearest military reservation, there to jet to Washington, D.C.

Another big mistake. I reemerged in Oregon because that's where the herb is. That's where I want to begin. They told me the President and Congress insist that I come to D.C. Shoot, wasting time to travel across the continent while ALLIS is growing is too much like entering a boxing ring blindfolded. I just wasn't adamant enough.

Gurner looked up again, and then around and over the murky

river waters, and then at nothing in particular. "God. These days have been long. I need a five-minute nap here. Just You and me and the sun and the wavelets lapping onto the shore. Let them focus their telephotos on 'Sleeping Beauty.' Tomorrow's papers will headline: 'Gurner sleeps while ALLIS spreads.'"

Seven minutes later Gurner awoke. His mind automatically continued its narrative.

Wasting time while ALLIS grows. That's what's happening. I've wasted nearly a week in this blasted capital city, entangled in the complex web of a crazy government that's evolved from a curator of freedom to a pomp-and-circumstance theatrical. Meanwhile, ALLIS, in this week, has snatched another 150,000 souls. Gurner, ol' buddy, unless you grab on to the bull and guide this journey where it needs to go, this bureaucratic snail of a government is going to ceremony, debate, and show-and-tell its way to world oblivion.

The healer glanced toward the congregation of people he had recently abandoned. He could tell that their collective being wanted to steamroll over and invade his location. He also watched a motley-dressed, exceptionally skinny individual serving as impromptu crowd control coordinator. Gurner smiled in gratitude.

It's incredible here. All I've been to are parties and dinners. Senator So-and-So's snippety wife simply "MUSSST" have a "PAR-TY" in my honor. Then there's the honor banquets, because I've made such a wonderful discovery. And then I "absolutely have to" meet and chat with the ambassadors of the world's countries. On and on it goes. One thing like that after another after another.

Gurner didn't look up, but opted to yell to the river. "God, We've got to take some positive steps. What am I going to do about moving beyond this stagnation?"

Ah! That story about India's Mother Teresa. An honoring ceremony was initiated to commemorate her achievements for helping the poor and homeless and dying. Walking over to the party, she passed someone poor and homeless and dying on the street. While the many officials hosted a reception praising her efforts, she remained out on the street, giving to that poor, helpless and dying human.

It's that simple, Gurner. You do what you know you need to do.

The tree trunk bore the brunt of the healer's directional gaze.

"OK. We figured out the government easy enough. But tell me now, God, what are We going to do about those reporters?"

I mean, this is really a lesson for the learning. I'm the one who insisted on having the press involved in everything. Now I'm the one who has had an ass full of them and their incessant questions. One asks a question, then another ten repeat. Then they print an answer that doesn't resemble what I said. I turn around to a hundred cameras focusing on my nose. Every word I say is public domain. Every time I piss I wonder if they're watching me. What we need to do now is not jabber endlessly over every detail of the story but get out there and put that plant to use. ALLIS is on the verge of ruining this human world. But when I try to tell them that, they can't accept how I'm sure of such a thing. Intuition isn't part of a reporter's vocabulary.

Shoot. I can't yet explain what this disease is about. I know what's causing it. But my ideas would fall short if I tried to publicly map them out. I've got to dig up a little scientific background knowledge before I propose these kinds of theories. Even with documentable backing, it'll be hard to not have this idea sound like lunacy.

So, I end up with almost nothing to say to the press. Because of that, they get offended. And because of that, I end up in print sounding like a mute joker with an IQ of 14.

"So, what to do to get this media gorilla off my back?"

Finally the answer came.

Harold Reeves! Of course! My "crowd control manager" over there. Only real friend I've made since I came out of the woods and into the big city. Harold Reeves, thirty-five-year veteran news cor-respondent, now working for Newstime. *Physically, he's almost an insult to look at, with his 1930's straw hat and checkered jacket, with his lanky, angular body that could be a tinkertoy triangle that collapsed on itself. Verbally, he can drive you crazy in five minutes, always repeating himself, stuttering. But man, is he a breed apart from the reporting cast I've met. He knows how to wait. He lets every one else prattle their surface questions and then he asks what needs to be asked. When I first faced that mob of big-time nationwide reporters, Harold was the one who took me aside and explained that I didn't have to answer every question I was asked. He said I was in control, not the microphone in front of me.*

Blacklisted, always-in-trouble Harold Reeves. A lot of the current politicians won't let him talk to them because he insists on asking embarrassing and therefore relevant questions. Been shot at and run off the road for uncovering too much on somebody. Harold Reeves, the lone reporter who had the balls to actively protest the government's control of news releases back during the Iraqi war. He tried to initiate a reporters' revolt. Tried to get every news agency in the world to refuse covering the war if they wouldn't let coverage be open and honest. No one followed Harold's suit, of course. The media sucked up and spewed out the military-censored news like an over-revved vacuum cleaner. And Harold accomplished as much as any one-man protest ever accomplishes. Nothing. Freedom of the press now knows smaller boundaries, and Harold got fired from the network he worked for.

Harold Reeves. He'll agree. He'll help me get this idea moving, Harold will.

Gurner tossed a twig into the river's murky waters. "God. The first plan will have every bureaucrat in office pissed at me, and this idea will ignite the reporting world into a rage."

The only substantial news in the past week is . . . I had in my possession enough of the herb for three more doses. With the entire press watching, I gave the plant to the government and told them to make sure that it is what it's claimed to be. Now three more people, including a primary aide to a Congressman, join the tiny number of ALLIS survivors. That's why everyone is being so good to me. I got the key.

But the key holder needs to leave this peacockery behind and get on to opening the door.

Gurner stood up, and one last time gazed to the heavens. "Well, thanks for the time, and—are You ready, God? Guess You and I should saunter back into the mainstream crowd. They're already convinced that I'm a fruit loop, and taking this much time alone and by myself only adds fuel to the fire."

The healer watched the stick float out of sight. "But, oh God of mine, I guess We're now going to toss a gasoline bomb onto that fire . . . and simply piss everybody off."

. . . . .

June 7, 2008, 5:30 A.M. On a military jet transport, direct flight from Washington, D.C. to Eugene, Oregon.

Gurner sat cross-legged and barefoot on an airplane seat that was made for neither. He kept to his private thoughts, and the Air Force crew members did not interact with him.

Well, We did it, God. You'll be happy to know that now everyone in Washington, D.C., is pissed at me. If I weren't such a national asset, I'd surely be in a national sepulcher. They're mad at me from the top all the way down.

Gurner leaned back into the stiff seat and closed his eyes.

I announced to all present in the park that we were in a major press conference. I noted that while officials wined and dined me and courted promotional photographs of me shaking their hands, millions of people were dying from ALLIS, and that it was time to get this cure quest moving. I demanded that the authorized agencies get me out of this place and to the herb site by tomorrow.

Wow. You could just feel the smirking and the derogations ripple through the crowd: "You bet. This witless stranger thinks he can come into town and get the square ball rolling uphill. You bet."

I stood paralyzed for an eternal minute at their reaction, but good ol' Harold Reeves opened a way for me. Let's see, he said: "Gurner, you, you are aware that in four days the President is planing a banquet to honor you and the scientists who will be studying your healing herb?"

I could only stare in disbelief and say, "Four days from now?"

"Four, four days, yessir," was all he said, but his eyes were blazing at me, screaming, "C'mon, get it, get it."

And I finally got it. "Mr. Reeves," I said, "tell me. With your vast knowledge in statistics. At the current death rate of ALLIS, how many additional people will die if a cure is delayed four or more days?"

That afforded a teeny smile on his lips that no one else noticed, and he said, "There will be, be approximately 100,000 to 200,000 more deaths."

I told the press to thank the President for me. I told them the Mother Teresa story. I told them that I could tell there was no getting Washington to move faster than its accustomed pace, and that was fine, that I'd meet everyone out west when they were ready. And I took off down the road, thumb extended and legs walking faster than any of those camera carriers could.

His eyes still closed, a smile spread over the healer's face. When a loud chuckle erupted from him, suspicious stares emanated from nearby Air Force personnel.

You know, God, it would have been fun to have a little

omniscience during those next couple of hours. Right away a battered old car with some obviously drugged-up kids in it pulled over, and I climbed in, and we sped off into the distance. Harold, when I called and asked him to accompany me on this plane, said Nagasaki didn't buzz from the atomic blast like the D.C. communications network did when that speech and car-pickup scene were aired over worldwide TV.

Several hours later some federal officers found me hitchhiking in Virginia. Told me to come on back. Everything was arranged for a morning Air Force flight to wherever I wanted to go. Why? Because people swamped the telephone and telegraph circuits to the Capital, demanding it.

Gurner looked up at the aircraft ceiling. "So it worked. But have You an idea what it means for a single citizen to publicly embarrass a President like that?"

The healer suddenly remembered that he was not in an isolated wilderness setting. He sheepishly met the stares of the plane crew members. "Sorry. But you all are going to have to get used to me talking to myself." Gurner retreated into his chair and mind.

There You have it, God. The look those officers gave me is identical to the disapproving glances and vindictive stares I've been receiving since I reentered the modern world—and especially since my departure announcement made the President look like he was the one holding everything up.

And now I've also made every reporter in the world irate. All but one.

Gurner looked across the isle at gangling Harold Reeves, who was engrossed in editing transcripts for his next news report. The healer straightened his stare and whispered softly so no one else could hear. "It would be a big and lonely world without You to talk to, God."

At the press conference, before we boarded this jet this morning, I publicly made one more demand. Without explaining why, simply saying this is the way it is going to be, I am now accompanied by one reporter only: Harold Reeves. Harold has agreed to be the newsman, photographer, and my personal press agent. He's promised to give all information and relevant stories to everyone. The needed communication to the world will still be there. And I'll know a lot more peace.

As the protesting howl rose, Harold and I slipped into the plane. The door closed; I'm free from the media, and they have nothing more to say about it. Shoot, the press should be used to that kind of treatment. The Government does it to them all the time. But I'd hate to read this evening's editorials.

Gurner gazed out the small aircraft windows. *Wow. That looks like the Three Sisters down below, which means Eugene and landing isn't too far away.*

With this new chapter on ALLIS happening here, what do We currently have? We have a world dying of a disease that it may have brought on itself. We also have a world whose survival hopes are tied to one person, a person they've been forced into depending on, and a person they generally do not like. What ever can you say to that? . . . No, I better not say that . . . Oh go ahead, Gurner. Say it. Say it out loud and say it loudly.

"AMEN. So be it."

. . . . .

2:01 P.M. Western central Oregon.

An uncomfortable Gurner sat in the back of a government motor pool vehicle, one that led a caravan of public and private cars eastward, out of the city of Eugene and into the Willamette National Forest. The healer's thoughts reeled with recent events.

Wait-a-minnit. Wait a doggone minute here. This is not good, at all.

I mean, I expected a bit of a crowd to be at the airport. With the renegade herbalist leading the world to his ALLIS-curing herb and coming to Eugene to do it, this is a big-time event. One could rightly expect a crowd to show up.

But that wasn't a mere crowd. That looked like half the population of the Earth gathered around the air field. Miles of people and cars, a spectacle of mass humanity that was. And that crowd wasn't there to applaud science or well-wish the persons now facing long hours in labs. They were there simply and wholly to behold me . . . me!

And I do not like the manner in which I was being beheld.

Gurner stuck his head over the car's front seat and pointed a direction to the driver. "There. Take a right at this road, and a few miles past Fall Creek you'll take a left on a paved road that heads east and past Fall Creek Reservoir." He then resumed his back-seat isolationism.

Dear God. Those masses of people were looking upon me as

a savior of some kind. Dear God. I don't want to be savior . . . of any kind.

I can't believe this is possible. But those banners . . . "Thanks for saving us Gurner." And those Gurner T-shirts, of all the crazy crap. And there was this undeniable general feeling that I was being held in some kind of awe or reverence. Somehow, I've been elevated to a sort of Christ status. And I got a hunch that it doesn't matter too much that I'm without a corresponding Christ Consciousness to accompany that status.

I'd like to think that if I'm popular it's because I defied the law for a just cause—healing. If I'm a hero, I'd like it to be because I helped rally them into realizing that they really do have control over their government.

But I'm in demand because they're scared of dying, scared of facing an unexplainable and quite efficient death march. Scared, because before a "danse macabre" like ALLIS, human history, human achievements, and even humans themselves all crumble.

I really want to heal ALLIS . . . and the cause of ALLIS. But surely I don't have to acquire savior status to accomplish that.

Somewhere, sometime, Jesus himself had to end up saying: "How in the hell did this happen?"

Well, the path to take here is plain and simple. I'll show everyone the herb and its location, and then do a complete disappearing act. Go back into isolation and the nameless woods where I belong. Once they've got the plant, they won't need me any more anyway.

All right. Thanks, God. It's a good way for me to get out of this mess and still have done my part.

"OK, Mr. Driver, take another right here on this dirt road. It's about four or five miles from this crossroad."

· · · · ·

4:00 P.M.

Gurner stood at the head of a long procession of a varied assortment of the world's leading citizens. Comprising his impromptu retinue were scientists of all degrees, agriculturalists, botanists, medical doctors, fifty lightly-armed Marine guards, and one skinny newsman, Harold Reeves, laden with notepads, several cameras, and a selection of two-way radios to transmit information back to a centralized mob of other reporters. The healer raised his voice so all could hear.

"So, if everyone will sort of walk gently and follow me. We have to climb this one hill. Be careful. It is steep. When we get to the top we'll have a good view of the north-facing slope of the next mountain where the herb grows."

Gurner turned and began hiking up the mountain slope. The followers formed a snakelike file and attempted to imitate his sure footsteps.

God . . . hello, God . . . are You there, God? SOS from Gurner . . . please come in.

Please, please tell me . . . what is happening here? Something is wrong. Something is WRONG! Every cell in my body just throbs with an almost sick feeling. I feel empty, void, like a river without water. Every step I take up this hill puts more and more goose bumps on my spine.

Gurner spoke to his feet as he moved up the slope. "Breathe, Gurner, take some deeper breaths. What the hell is the matter with you?"

Bad medicine. Those are the words that keep sounding in my ear. Bad, bad stuff.

God, I can't believe this feeling means You're trying to tell me to not take these people to the herb site. Shoot, this is what these past months of adventure and game playing have led to. Besides, I already told them it's just over the hill.

The healer paused and for a long time intuitively scanned the surrounding countryside. The people stalled behind him began expressing disapproval of the delay before he came out of his reverie and resumed the uphill hike.

This place has changed since I was here over a year ago. Where we parked used to be the end of the road. Now it continues, freshly cut into the mountain's side. Wonder how much further it goes. And that road up there on the mountain to the south. That wasn't there either. Probably logging roads. SHOOT! I hope they haven't stuck too many roads in here. Roads automatically turn beautiful hillsides into ATV playgrounds. I remember this place as being especially peaceful and powerful. It'd be a shame to see it become just another motorized run.

But something else is happening here. Something powerful, in a negative way. What is it? I almost feel sick.

Gurner stopped again and yelled to the crowd. "Folks, let's pause for a breather before we top the ridge."

Gurner waited until a puffing line of people had all assembled in a small clearing. He spoke a final time to the troupe. "So, folks, listen. Just over this ridge there's a gentle and open south-sloping hill. And across its little valley a thickly and majestically wooded north-facing mountain holds an abundant supply of the herb you all are so interested in. Everyone has got to tread this land lightly. I've hiked all over this area in my herb-gathering quests. I've never seen this plant anywhere else. In Washington, D.C., I leafed through every classification book, and this herb was listed nowhere. For safety's sake, let's assume that this is an undiscovered species of plant life, and that this is its only known habitat . . . and that it doesn't like being stepped on."

Gurner ended his speech by closing his eyes and shaking his head. *Ahhh, shoot. These people are going to do what they want to do anyway. Their auras just vibrate with an oh-shut-up-and-let's-get-it-on agitation.*

Well, it's out of my hands now. I'm about ten minutes away from slipping onto that hidden game trail and following it all the way to wherever it leads and freedom.

"Everybody ready for the last leg? Hi ho."

God. I might as well have about a thousand pounds on my back. I feel like a turtle who one morning awoke to find its protective shell gone. WHAT IS HAPPENING HERE?

The earthscape changed from vertical to horizontal. Gurner faced his flock one last time. "OK, folks. This is the top, and that over there is the other mountain top. You'll get a good view of the whole of it down by these rocks."

Let me just race a few steps ahead here, so I get a last view of this wonderful area before it perpetually swarms with people. Thank you, hillside, for all you've given me, and—

For the first time in his life, Gurner's body, mind, and soul experienced complete silence. Then the healer's knees buckled as he howled to the void in front of him.

"OH MY GREAT LIVING GOD ALMIGHTY! NO!"

٭ 16 ٭
Loggers, II

June 9, 2008, 1:00 P.M. Inside the Crosscut Affair, a popular loggerman's bar in Oakridge, Oregon.

The four loggers—Ernie Slate, Sam Braxton, Harry Meers, and Winston Stacey—idly sat around an old, cigarette-and-bottle-bottom scarred table inside the smoky room. Each had a mug of beer in hand, and each vented several gripes about the fact that they were in this bar on a working day rather than in the forest cutting. A sudden presence filled the establishment's entrance, forcing them to look toward the door.

"Hey look! There's Joe."

Slate yelled out loud: "Hey, Joe! Joe Simpson! Over here. Harry, move over. Make some room for Joe."

Meers' chair grated across the worn wooden floor as he called to the newcomer, "Howdy, Joe. Come on and have a seat with the rest of us unemployed bastards."

Braxton yelled an order to the barkeeper. "Hey, Arnold! Another round for us, including Joe."

The four loggers cleared a space at their table that was big enough for two men. Joe Simpson's bulk easily filled that gap.

"Hey yourself, Ernie. Hi, Harry; Sam. How ya doing, Winston?"

"Well, I'd complain, Joe, but I think it's a gonna get worse before it gets better. So I'll just save the griping till later."

Slate gulped a portion of his beer. "Winston's playing the philosopher, as usual, Joe. But Harry and Sam and I are fed up with this whole damned deal."

"Why's that, Ernie?"

"Why's that, you ask. Joe, you gotta be in the same sinking boat as us. Logging's our livelihood. It keeps the cupboards stocked and the banker's repossession papers unsigned. And now all logging activity in the entire state of Oregon has been, and I quote: 'temporarily discontinued while government officials search the remaining old-growth forests for establishments of the AC herb.' Don't these jokers realize that people can die of starvation as well as they can of ALLIS?"

Braxton wiped some beer foam off the corner of his mouth. "What's 'AC' stand for, Ernie?"

"Who knows, Sam? Scientists gotta label everything."

Simpson received his beer, took a tiny sip as a primer tasting, and answered the question for all. "It's the nickname of the herb that Gurner fellow was leading the researchers to. It's the unofficial name of the herb we apparently wiped out when we cut that Squanni Hill site. 'AC' stands for ALLIS-CURE."

Slate looked painfully at his friend. "Ah, Joe. Not you too. Every newspaper and TV in the country is now bad-mouthing loggers. It's like the public needs somebody to blame, and we're the handy suckers. Harry here has had his car damaged by rocks. My kids came home from school crying 'cause their friends turned on them. Tell him your story, Sam."

Braxton placed his mug on the table. "Hell, besides being glared at—angry, hateful stares, Joe, everywhere I go—yesterday evening this woman comes up to me on the street and starts pounding on me with her fists, screaming at me that I killed her husband. I guess he died of ALLIS. I mean, if a man did that to me, he'd wake up in the hospital with his jaw rearranged. But what do you do to a woman? Especially when she's half your size and must be nuts. Meanwhile, a crowd had gathered around us, and man, their mutterings were not kind."

"What'd you do?"

"All I could do was brush the woman aside and hop in my truck and drive off."

Simpson turned to the philosopher. "How about you, Winston? Is your life the same?"

"Well, Joe, all I know is that we logger people were the most respected group in this valley until a few days ago. Hell, we're its economy and mainstay. But after that Gurner guy was seen on TV, tears running down his face, saying how Americans cut and develop first and then worry later . . . well, it's got rough. Ever since Gurner held up that old dead thing of a plant and said here's what's left of the cure for ALLIS, and that it can now be renamed 'The Loggerman's Disease' . . . well, I don't know if I want to admit that I'm a logger."

Meers scratched his head in distant thought. "I remember that plant. It was all over the hill, growing wild under the big trees of the Squanni cut. An artist put a picture of it together from Gurner's description. Its poster is being circulated all over the Northwest."

Simpson suddenly grew excited, so excited he half stood up and almost upset the table. "Have you seen that plant anywhere else, Harry? Can you remember seeing it at any other cut, anywhere?"

"If I could, Joe, I'd be claiming the reward the government is offering for anyone locating it."

Simpson sighed, long and hard, and repositioned himself in his chair. He stared at his beer.

Slate took a long gulp of liquid and slammed his mug on the table. "Well, I think the whole thing is goddamned unfair. We're not botanists. We're loggers, and we were simply doing our job. That Gurner turd and everyone else has no right blaming us just because a stray plant decided it had to grow on a forested hillside we needed to cut. We didn't do anything wrong."

Simpson looked up from his beer-gazing, and his eyes narrowed into a malevolent stare. "Ernie, I'll bet you haven't read this morning's paper, have you?"

"No, Joe. Why?"

"There's an article there might just interest you. And you other guys too. It seems that not only could this AC plant *not* stand bulldozers and skidding rigs and logs rolling over it, it also turns out that the plant couldn't survive in direct sunlight either. It needed the shade of the forest. According to the article"— Simpson's eyes grew icy—"that half-acre of trees left standing due to the Greenpeacers and Earth First!ers sitting in them, it supported a fair stand of the AC plant under its bower."

Simpson's voice began to rise in volume. "And then, according to the article, some unknown persons moved in one night and leveled the remaining half acre of standing trees."

Simpson's voice also began to increase in intensity. "The researchers found these remaining AC plants between the fallen logs, still rooted in the ground, but yellowed and dying. Beyond recovery. From exposure to direct sunlight."

Simpson stood up again. "They figured that if that half an acre had been left alone, maybe there was enough AC plants to start science on its way to an ALLIS cure! As it stands now, thanks to you three sons of bitches, ALLIS has topped five million deaths and nobody in the world has a leg to stand on how to stop it!"

Simpson towered over the seated men, his face red, his massive fists clenched, and his huge body trembling in anger.

Slate, looking quite pale, spoke for the accused. "Ah, Joe."

Winston Stacey touched the huge man's sleeve. "Joe. Joe, listen. Unclench your fists and listen to the philosopher for a moment. This is bad news, but I can't completely understand why it's upsetting you this much. You're a logger, and you darned well know how loggers have been shoved into corners and have to fight back out of desperation. I know you know, what with your bulldozing the wilderness that time and the many protests you've initiated. Sometimes this is how we make a statement. This is what you've done yourself. It was a big mistake in this case, obviously, but why should you take it so personal?"

Simpson's energy faded completely. He slumped back into the bar chair and placed his head between his immense hands. His uncontrollable shaking acquired a different aspect, and he choked as he spoke. "M . . . Myra has ALLIS."

"Myra is—?"

"My second kid . . . my oldest daughter. My . . . she always was daddy's tomboy, and . . ." Tears began to trickle down the huge man's face.

Sympathetic groans and pats of comfort from around the table were extended to Simpson. Braxton called to the bar: "Arnold! Bring us a big shot of whiskey."

Slate placed his hand on Simpson's massive shoulders. "You sure about this, Joe? I read where thousands of people may have killed themselves thinking they had ALLIS when all they had were some flu chills."

"Too sure, Ernie. Doctor's sure. Jean's sure. I'm sure. And even Myra is sure."

Another stream of tears tumbled down Simpson's now-rosy cheeks.

"Ah, Joe."

Stacey's appellation as the philosopher wasn't for naught. "Well, what are you going to do now, Joe? I know you're not the type to sit around and weep. How you going to move on here?"

Simpson straightened his massive posture and placed a huge fist in a huge palm. "I know, Winston. Dammit, I gotta do something. But how do you punch back at a virus or an alien germ or . . . or the wrath of God? Under a fallen log this Gurner fellow found an AC plant, one that was pretty yellowed and mostly dead. Under his supervision—he said he felt some life in it, whatever the hell that means—they tried it on an ALLIS person. The newsman said that person hasn't recovered yet like the others did, but that his temperature has quit falling. When I heard that, I thought maybe I'd take Myra to Squanni Hill and see if I could try the dead plants on her. If I could—"

Slate chimed a negation. "They'd never let you in. They got that place guarded like a Fort Knox."

Stacey said, "Ernie, your optimism would sink a battleship. Let's not throw roadblocks across Joe's path here."

Simpson continued. "Thanks, Winston. And don't interrupt me, all right, Ernie? If I thought it would work, I'd have to try it no matter the odds and official orders. But now the news says that was the *only* half-alive plant they could find, and that the tea has no effect on curing ALLIS if the AC plant is dead."

Simpson looked at Slate, at Braxton, and at Meers, and again began to show anger. He immediately checked himself and continued talking. "And they're all dead. We were too damned efficient, boys."

"So where are you at for a thing to do?"

"The only thing I can come up with . . . the idea keeps popping into my head to get hold of this Gurner and see if he can help. He's tromping up and down the Willamette looking for more herb. I'm going to catch him and see if he can suggest anything. Anything at all."

Slate, as soon as he was certain that Simpson had ended his sentence, presented another counterpoint. "Hey, I've already been accused of being a pessimist here, but I don't want to see my buddy flying kites only to have them run into power lines. When Gurner went to Washington, D.C., he publicly gave over what he said were his last three doses of the herb. And I don't recall reading about him healing anybody since then."

Meers sided with Slate. "Ernie's right, Joe. And besides Gurner, about 50,000 other people are combing those woods. I'll betcha they're killing off a hundred other plant species in the process of looking for that one. You'll be another body in a mass of bodies in the woods."

Simpson nodded. "You guys make too much sense. But I gotta

do something, and I feel I got to do this. I'm gonna follow my feelings for once. I wanted to protest our work on that Squanni cut, and I didn't. I felt it was wrong for you guys to cut that last half acre of trees, but I didn't do anything to stop you. I've got this gut notion to approach Gurner, and for a change I'm going to follow it, even if it's hopeless."

"Well, Joe, you won't have trouble locating him. Reporters keep a close watch on everything he does. But you better hurry. I heard a rumor that he doesn't think there are any more AC plants, and he's about to wander off and search for different plants in different pastures."

"Thanks, Winston. I didn't know that."

Simpson drained his remaining beer in a single gulp. "So I better be on my quest. Thank you, gentlemen, for the drinks and the company."

"See ya, Joe."

"Good luck, Joe."

"Catch ya on a job sometime, Joe."

The logger paused a moment over this last statement. "Maybe."

Simpson stood up, accomplishing what he always accomplished when he stood up, amazing the people near him by his enormous size. He gave the whiskey to Braxton, and moved for the exit.

"Hey, Joe."

"Yeah, Ernie?"

"Do me one small favor, will ya?"

"Mmmmm?"

"If you run into Gurner, just kinda beat the shit out of him, just a little bit. For that Loggerman's Disease remark he made."

Simpson turned and squarely faced his friend. "Ernie, if beating the shit out of anyone could save Myra, you all would be a pile of blood and bones right now. But it won't. It won't do any good. I'm beginning to see that quite a few of our old ways won't do anybody any good anymore. And I reckon that includes logging merely to make a living today instead of living for our kids too."

"Ah, Joe."

End of Book II

BOOK III

SEARCHING

♦ 17 ♦
Gurner's Gang

June 10, 2008, 7:30 A.M. Inside Jerry Willox's house, outside of Boulder, Colorado.

Jenny Willox created a whirlwind of kitchen activity, baking cookies—five dozen, three varieties—for her husband. She didn't know when she would have another chance to satisfy one of his precious-to-her habits. Jerry Willox paced around the bedroom, nosing through dresser drawers and closets, occasionally tossing an article into an open backpack. He also did not know when he would again enjoy a favorite pastime of his: spending time with his wife and son.

This is really great, in quite a few ways.

. . . And this is really pretty sad, in quite a few ways.

God knows we need the money. Johnny being the longest living victim of ALLIS, and then a miraculous survivor, may have been good publicity, but it didn't do a thing toward paying the bills. First those tertiary-brained hospitals run all kinds of tests on Johnny, trying to determine if had developed any auto-immunities against ALLIS. Useless tests, because all that equipment didn't find a thing. And then they send me a bill for $7,000 for lab tests and hospital stay! I guess by now they know where they can shove that bill, and how far.

Oh well, at least now money isn't going to be a problem, thanks to Gurner.

Willox knew he might be hiking in the back country for a long time. He stuffed eight pairs of socks, five T-shirts, five handkerchiefs, three pairs of pants, two sweaters, and a wind/rain parka into his pack. Something was missing. What was it? Thinking hard, he remembered, and pulled one pair of extra underwear from a drawer and shoved it into a side pocket.

Of course, money only lasts as long as the society that values it. If Gurner's plan doesn't bear fruit. . . .

Man oh man, that image of Gurner still shines in my mind. I mean, the Newstime *cover photograph of Jenny and me holding up a healthy Johnny-baby was mighty depictive. But I don't think it holds a candle to the Reeves' picture of Gurner incredulously staring at the clear-cut, cleaned-out mountain in front of him, like Moses after all those years in the desert finally leading his people to the Promise Land and finding out it's a nuclear proving ground.*

A tent and a sleeping bag, an air mattress (because wilderness lovers do grow older), water bottles, a first aid kit, a flashlight, and an assortment of personal items found their way into or onto the expanding pack. Willox crammed the last tail of a ground cloth into the side pocket with his underwear and cinched the tie-downs tight, just as Jenny yelled from the kitchen, "Don't forget to leave room for cookies."

So, two days after the world watched Gurner weep and maniacally beat his fists on a bulldozed Earth . . . two days after AC herb-doomsday, he called me and said the plant is extinct. Said he's walked everywhere, meditated long and hard, and can't feel its vibrations anymore.

Willox puzzled over that idea a moment, then continued packing.

Let the questions go, Willox. You don't have to understand. Feeling vibrations is how the guy works. That was how he healed Johnny. Besides, something tells me he's right.

So he says, there's no more AC herb, no more simple cure, but he has an idea. Wow, quite an idea! Could easily be no more than a grab in the dark. Anyway, Congress is now scared enough to act immediately. ALLIS has taken almost one of every thousand people on this Earth, including one Senator and one Congressman, a few of their immediate families, and some wealthy constituents. Gurner's plan could be the only way to remanufacture a key to the cure-door.

Willox hefted his pack to his shoulders and grimaced, both from the weight of the pack and from the knowledge that such weight had never before fazed him.

So now the money used to buy the fin of one guided missile will finance a certain unusual expedition. They should have used this kind of money earlier, for biological diversity studies, so we could have preserved things we don't yet know we need. Then maybe the world wouldn't be in the unhealthy situation of calling five maniacs its only hope.

. . . And yet, it's kind of fun, to be one of those five.

· · · · ·

> June 11, 2008, 3:33 P.M. Inside a small buffet apartment overlooking the Jones Falls Expressway, Baltimore, Maryland.

Stephanie Peters knew it was summer, but she also knew from recent experience that wilderness gets terribly cold. She was not going to be caught unprepared this time. Polypropylene long johns and wool pants and sweaters were neatly folded and precisely placed into her suitcase.

That reporter said, "Thank you, DOCTOR Peters, you've been most helpful."

DOCTOR Peters. I didn't realize how much that title meant to me, or how much I missed it until I got it back.

So now I'm a doctor, an official M.D. again. But for how long? You can twist people's arms until they yell "uncle"—or in this case "doctor"—but it doesn't mean that they mean it.

But golly. Enjoy it while it lasts. For now, it's DOCTOR Peters.

Dr. Peters realized she could be in wild country for a long time. She methodically packed eight pairs of underwear into her suitcase, thought a moment, then added four more pairs.

Gurner, you're sure a strange character to come into my life. Into anybody's life for that matter. You seem to be somebody who would be happy to be forever sitting on top of a mountain, communing with plants and with the Maker of plants. And you probably could, if you didn't spend all your time talking to God. You must be driving Him crazy with your constant chatter. He HAS to send you into the world just to shut you up for a while.

Dr. Peters looked longingly at her closet full of dresses. She sighed, and moved to a drawer of work clothes.

Now, Stephanie. Just because he would rather meditate than respond to your advances. Just because almost everything about him seems to turn you on, and most everything about you doesn't seem to move his heart or hormones at all. Just because . . . well, don't get on the high horse here . . . but crumb anyway.

What a character. Sometimes you think you've met a prophet. Sometimes you know you've met a loony. Sometimes you wonder if there's a difference.

Well, I get to now observe him a bit more. And I've got my doctor's standing back. I'll be getting some fair pay and lots of adventure besides.

Dr. Peters pictured the adventure she might soon be having. She shuddered, made a note to buy more mosquito repellent and skin lotion, and put two more pairs of underwear into her suitcase.

So, Gurner called me from Oregon, wants me to join his little . . . well, not so little; in fact, I'd call it colossal . . . wants me to join his colossal, chimerical undertaking. Said he very much needs a doctor to administer the herbs and handle medical emergencies.

I said sorry, but I'm not a doctor.

He said yes you are.

I figured his loony side was edging over to the prophet side, and said, "What?"

He said some of the figures in Congress liked his idea. And that they (directed by him) called the AMA board that suspended my license and explained this new proposal of his. They explained that as it stands now, his idea is the only hope to combat ALLIS. They explained that he wants me as the licensed doctor on the trip.

He said the AMA board was quite firm in the conviction that I was no longer a licensed physician.

He said his callers again repeated their explanations, this time not as an option.

He said the AMA board said some nasty things.

He said his callers said some nastier things and threatened investigating the way the AMA handles aberrant doctors.

He said there was quite a bit of fussing and double talk from the AMA end of the line.

He said his Congressional callers stated they had no time to waste talking on the phone, that there were investigations to begin.

He said that the AMA board said my recertification would be mailed that day.

I said thanks, but I prefer to earn my own stripes.

He said that takes time, and that ALLIS may well kill everybody off by then.

I said that's true, but why would he choose me as the doctor for this proposal.

He said because I was the most experienced doctor in curing someone of ALLIS.

I didn't say it, but crumb, I really wished there had been a few other reasons besides that one.

Dr. Peters automatically packed three tiny containers of perfume. She reflected a moment and realized that no one in this crew would give a snoodle about how she smelled. She placed the bottles back on the shelf.

And so, without further ado, Mr . . . er, Gurner, DOCTOR Peters joins you and the others tomorrow. And the next step of this adventure begins.

. . . Though it really doesn't seem like there's a lot of hope for it to succeed.

. . . I wonder if I should start talking to God.

· · · · ·

June 12, 2008, 12:00 P.M. On United Airlines Flight 6234 en route from Washington, D.C. to Eugene, Oregon.

Brian Johnson checked the magazine pouch on the back of the seat in front of him, wanting to be certain it contained *all* the essentials. Seeing two plastic-lined disposable bags, he returned to reading a letter he had just written.

So, how does it sound? I always get so darned queasy, riding on a plane. Better make sure it's readable.

"My dearest Mary,

"Four hours since the plane left D.C., and already I miss you. I know I've said it until you must be sick of hearing it. But since your recovery from ALLIS, I just don't have many moments when I don't feel like saying how much I love you."

Johnson stared at the letter and shook his head. *Good grief. Since when have I started using double negatives to express love for my wife?*

"This has been the most efficient flight I've ever experienced. No lines, no delays, no hassles. I thought the modern world had long ago extinguished the incredible courtesy everyone extends me. Of course, having the media report on what Gurner and we others are doing, I guess that does make me kind of an instant celebrity. It's quite a feeling, Mary, knowing that wherever you go you'll be helped by everyone in any way you deem necessary. It's funny how the threat of death brings the world closer to a sort of 'utopia'; more so than uninterrupted life ever did."

The flight attendant's voice crackled over the loudspeaker. Johnson was a strange passenger: he listened.

Descent to Eugene about to begin? Already? I suppose the rest of "Gurner's Gang," as the press is now dubbing us, will be there already. Let's see, this letter . . .

"I really don't know why Gurner wants me as part of this group, Mary. He said he needed me because I am an articulate speaker and knowledgeable of the workings of governments. He figures that communication, especially with localized groups, may prove to be a key element in this project. But I suspect a good part of the reason I'm with him is that he knows our current situation—yours and mine. Everybody may admire people who quit their job-secure futures rather than do what they no longer believe in. But as we immediately learned, such an action in no way gets AT&T and the power company and the bank to pop the hero's name out of the payment-due computer. Now, thanks to Gurner, we don't have to worry about money shortages for a while.

"I have to admit, it is kind of exciting, to be a member of a 'Gang' on whom the world is depending. But the more I review what Gurner said we were going to be doing, the more I realize such excitement will be short-lived. Especially if things drag out over long periods of time. That's another reason he chose me and the others. He said we're 'stick-with-it' people. Send some prayers my way, Mary, so I can live up to those expectations.

"So, lover, I'm running out of paper and things to say. But do let me one more time note how much I miss you and . . ."

Johnson lowered his head between his legs and deepened his breathing.

Urrrg. I never could read while in motion. Airplane landings are the worst. I better seal this letter and keep breathing deep. Because all the watching, hopeful public needs to see is a "Gang" member—the articulate, communicative, stick-with-it one—get off the plane pale and sweaty and holding a vomit bag in his hand.

· · · · ·

June 12, 2008, 4:20 P.M. In the FDA headquarters, Investigative Division offices, Washington, D.C.

Jim Bowerns sat at his desk, and he was laughing.

Oh ho and ah ha ha! This is wonderful. Great! Just great! Bowerns, if you'd been a hippie years ago you might even exclaim something more profound like . . . like "far out"!

I haven't felt this good since Johnson fell under the medicine man's spell. But now the healing gander seems to be turning on the gas and stepping through the oven door. "Right on!" I think they used to say.

Bowerns picked up a new government-issue pencil.

You know, this is the lesson we have learned. And here it is, working for us again. We don't have to eliminate these people. There's no need to outright kill them. In fact, that action only surfaces others, and then we're in worse shape than before. No, no need for violence, albeit justified . . . unless there's absolutely no other course. It seems to be a law that with enough rope and enough time, they hang themselves.

And now Gurner proves he's no exception to the rule.

And I love it.

Bowerns rhythmically bounced the pencil eraser on the hard desk top. *I mean, just to observe the absurdity here, let's analyze things:*

—ALLIS has the potential to cause utter pandemonium before it ends all human life. No one can deny that the disease is "bad news." (There's another one.)

—With all our science and knowledge, we do not have any immediate means of preventing or curing the disease. That's a simple fact.

—Another fact—although I hate to admit it—is that this self-proclaimed healer really does know of a cure for the disease. Crimsom and that Johanson woman proved that well enough. When Gurner gave the scientists his "last three doses" of the healing herb, and those ALLIS victims were cured, even I had to believe he found something.

Bowerns rolled the pencil between his thumb and index finger.

Oh, you're very crafty, Gurner. You're a madman, but you're an intelligent one. Publicly give your "last little bit" of the herb over to science. You sure sucked the world in on that one.

The pencil snapped into two pieces.

—Then, refusing to do what any true philanthropist should do, Gurner withholds this valuable knowledge and goes into hiding while millions die like flies.

—In his wanderings he comes across a clear-cut—a controversial one at that, all the better suited for his purposes.

—Aided by Johnson and that goddamned environmentalist, he makes a public name for himself. He even comes across as a savior—The ALLIS Savior. When I saw that Oregon crowd ogling him, I almost puked.

—With his newfound power, he barges into Washington. Being the only person in the world with a cure for that cruel disease, he could dictate terms. And dictate he did. He proved that he could tell the President what to do, that he could insult anyone in any way he wanted.

Bowerns rolled the pencil halves—one in each hand—between his thumbs and forefingers.

—Then, when the fancy suited him, he led the hopeful world to the clear-cut. Put on an incredible and convincing act—A-plus for acting—that left everyone believing lack of environmental caring has doomed the world.

You have to admit. It resembles genius.

Both pencil halves broke.

—Finally, "Wait," says Gurner. "Now that you are despondent, I've got this wonderful plan that might save you. Tell you what. You put the world at MY disposal—fly me wherever I want to go, open every door to me—and just maybe somewhere I can find another herb that will work on the disease. And after another ten or so million of you have died, and all hope has been abandoned, and the world teeters on the brink of total chaos, I'll find the magic herb (which will really be an herb I've already found and am keeping secret). ALLIS will be conquered. AND, of course, I will be the hero of heroes and possibly become the first world leader."

Bowerns rolled a pencil quarter between each forefinger and thumb.

He's accomplishing what Hitler couldn't accomplish with military force, and he's doing it with herbs and treachery.

One pencil quarter broke; the other ran a sliver into the director's fingertip.

I get so mad I could spit venom, knowing that people are being duped by this . . . this right-brained dipshit.

Bowerns angrily brushed all the pencil pieces off his desk.

But. Mr. . . . er, ah, Gurner. Methinks . . . hell, me knows . . . that you can't see what I can. Your power has peaked, buddy, and it's downhill from here.

Take this current showy plan of yours. It's a Gurner death knell. I mean, you had it all going your way, forcing Congress and the President to back you going on a worldwide search for another herb with ALLIS-healing capacities. The governments and businesses of the world have all agreed to help you in any way imaginable—transportation, lodging, food, salary for you and your crew; help of every kind will be given you in your "valiant" search. You now have a top-priority, globally-accepted, unlimited credit card with your name on it.

But if you're going to conquer the world, geek, you have to be more careful who you choose as associates.

Jim Bowerns leaned back in his chair, trying to remove the sliver in his finger by picking at it with his teeth.

I have to laugh. Here this guy gets the entire world to sing his tune, and then he appoints circus clowns as his top advisors. We now have, as the "Gurner Gang" of shining knights against ALLIS, a leader who talks to plants, a certified fruitcake of an environmental fanatic, a totally inexperienced doctor-in-name-only, a former petty bureaucrat, and the goddamnest son-of-a-bitch of a reporter, Harold Reeves, who can't print an honest story and who everyone from the President down to me refuses to deal with.

Gurner, if I didn't think that you already had an ALLIS cure, I would be really worried that there IS no cure. Because this group of sick hobos will never accomplish anything.

I can just picture it. And won't it be fun. Willox should die of malaria in a swamp. That Peters girl looks about as wilderness-oriented as a newborn baby. She'll probably go from dehydration in some desert. Then Johnson-the-two-faced. He deserves a pit viper in his sleeping bag. Reeves, for you slow-acting quicksand would be too good. All that's left is Prince Gurner. When you come out of the hinterland and reveal your "newly discovered" wonder herb, when a cure for ALLIS is a sure thing . . . Mister, what you're going to experience will make the Wrath of God seem like peace. We have so many ways to get you. We will so destroy your credibility that you won't dare show your face. The people who will testify that your herbs caused them irreparable harm. The taxes you've evaded. On and on, Gurner. Your kingdom will topple, and the world will forget you even existed.

. . . And, if that doesn't work, we can always create an accident and kill you.

Hey man, I mean, that's like, "good shit." Ya dig?

• 18 •
Newstime

June 26, 2008. Excerpts from *Newstime* Magazine

A LETTER FROM RODNEY MALSON, *NEWSTIME* MAGAZINE'S NEW MANAGING EDITOR:

It is with immense sadness that I and all the staff of *Newstime* use this column to say goodbye to a superior editor, a good man, and a dear friend. On June 23, Miles Lotter, 52, passed away, another victim of the ever-increasing swath of death the ALLIS disease is inflicting upon this planet.

Miles formed a sort of anomaly in the journalistic world. For the past eight years he was managing editor of the world's largest news magazine; yet anyone describing Miles usually noted that he was a man of few words. His taciturn yet frank guidance of junior writers helped many budding journalists become seasoned reporters.

I should know. Miles placed me, a verbose and grammar-less fledgling writer, under his disciplinary wing and transformed me into a core reporter. Miles' definition of "reporter" meant a newsman who was human enough to shed tears of grief or joy while being professional enough to buck out all sides of the story.

Before Miles slipped into the hypothermic coma that precedes death-by-ALLIS, he shared a few words that I would here pass on. They were typical Miles Lotter statements—terse, profound, filled with courage. He said: "Rodney, if you take over [editorship of *Newstime*], whatever you do, don't balk. If you feel too satisfied for too long, know that you're missing something somewhere."

It is becoming more difficult to report on the worldwide ALLIS pandemic. Difficult in the sense of reader discouragement. Every report of ALLIS jacks up the death statistics in an exponential fashion while repetitively acknowledging the helplessness of re-search science. Readers write, saying, "Please say no more about ALLIS until you have something hopeful to offer."

To respond to news in such a manner would be to balk. From the beginning, Miles taught his charges to dig hard and uncover every scrap of information concerning a story. When the going seemed hopeless, he showed us how to dig deeper. For in carefully uncovering every grain of sand, the anthropologist finds the fossil revealing the missing link of a complex theory. A story, even one so repetitive as ALLIS, does not change for the better by ignoring the facts.

Miles Lotter died of ALLIS. But his searching and valiant spirit lives on at *Newstime* magazine. In that spirit I would note . . . may it never happen . . . that even if the worst scenario comes to pass, and a cure never is found for ALLIS, we as a news-reporting journal, to the last person, will not balk.

Sincerely, Rodney Malson

. . . . .

ALLIS: THE UPDATE

The facts are grim, and that's the grim fact of things.

ALLIS, in less than one year's time, has claimed nearly 15 million lives. Current statistical releases from the Centers for Disease Control (CDC) in Atlanta place the worldwide ALLIS death figure at 14,900,000 people. People of all ages, all gender, of every health consideration; people of every locality; persons of wealth, poverty, and the many monetary lines between; people of all professions; people who try to hide from the disease and people who flaunt their indifference by manning the front lines, working with other ALLIS victims; the Loggerman's Disease has proven itself nondiscriminatory and totally ruthless. Three out of every 1300 people in this world have succumbed to death by ALLIS.

Wars always offer safe areas to which people can flee. With a disease like AIDS, there are specified behaviors to which one can adhere and thus avoid contagion. But with ALLIS so unex-plainable, so unpreventable, so capable of striking anyone every-where, its only mercy seems to be the fact that it hasn't yet struck "you." "Yet" forms the predominant idea racing through every person's mind.

Three people dying of ALLIS in the town of Green Lake, Wisconsin (population 1,400) can seem like an insignificant number. More persons are subject to cancer and heart disease deaths. Approximately 9,000 ALLIS deaths in Los Angeles (population over four million) gives the picture a more realistic perspective. Considering that nearly 750,000 persons in the United States (population 300,000,000) have succumbed to the disease, one begins to understand the scope of the calamity. These straight-across-the-board, three thirteenths of a percent death-rate figures hold true for every location on this planet. Never in history has a pestilence been so utterly mechanical and unerring in its distribution. Says Dr. William Abrams of the CDC Special ALLIS Investigative Division: "ALLIS is worldwide, in equal percentages everywhere. Somewhere in this unalterable aspect lies a clue to understanding the disease. We're on overtime trying to find that clue."

The nature of ALLIS also spawns several sidelight stories. U.S. Census Bureau figures show a 30-percent decline in the number of babies being conceived. Couples feel there is little reason to bring a child into the world until the prospect of life for both child and parents is more assured.

Paralleling the dropping birth rate, the suicide rate of every country of the world is skyrocketing. Statistics show a 25-percent increase in suicide-related death attempts. Dr. Robert Midler, clinical psychiatrist and head of Boston University's Psychology Department, states that most people, while able to cope with the idea of dying, are terrified of dying from an unknown, unknowable cause. [See accompanying story.]

Drug abuse and alcoholism are on an upswing. People aren't seeking kicks; they're seeking escape. Crisis hotlines and toll-free help numbers are in continual overload. Police and fire departments perpetually dole out calming lectures to frightened citizens who call their offices in need of reassurance.

Aware of growing citizen reaction to the mounting ALLIS figures, the U.S. Government has begun an advertising campaign geared to promote calmness and patience as an alternative to fearful reflex action. Media advertisements noting the seriousness of the ALLIS plague yet calling for the need to face the crisis with equanimity circulate throughout the country.

Dr. William Hogan, retired U.S. Army general and current assistant to the U.S. surgeon general, states the message more briskly and, according to results, more effectively. In a nationwide interview, Dr. Hogan "took command" of the situation: "C'mon America. If you start killing yourself and hiding behind drugs when only three of every thousand persons has died, what the hell will you be like if it gets worse? We'll become a nation of impotent boobies, and impotent boobies are the last kind of troops we'll be able to defeat this thing with. We're the powerful country we are because we face challenges, not hide from them. Let's get with it and be the distinguished soldiers we need to be to win this battle."

Positive reactions to the ALLIS plague occasionally surface. Historic violence has tapered off in several of the world's traditional hot spots. The Catholics, Protestants, Irish Republic Army and the British have again reached a truce in northern Ireland. Similarly, throughout the Middle East, adversary countries have tentatively agreed to initiate joint ALLIS research ventures. Nations that formerly stockpiled military might now consign much of their war-chest moneys to ALLIS research and ALLIS-victim care. Cooperative teams of scientists from nearly every nation now band together and explore the little remaining wild habitats of the various countries of the world. [See accompanying story.] Most are searching for a plant or animal species that may contain the key to finding an ALLIS cure.

"The statistics and the future prospects of the ALLIS disease are rough, no doubt about that," comments noted sociologist and Harvard professor Willard Duncun. "But we are also observing an unprecedented spirit of cooperation developing among the world's peoples. When they give up war, and use those moneys to explore and preserve natural land habitats, you know a higher evolution in thinking is taking place."

Perhaps, when the cure is found, and ALLIS is a nightmare of the past, this mutual spirit of cooperation will remain throughout the world.

· · · · ·

ALLIS: A GROWING BATTLE OF MANY FRONTS

These days, every scientist, research worker, and scholar in the world, professional or amateur, with access to a test tube, microscope, and dissection kit—of the most modern or the most primitive kind—is funneling energies into one of two ALLIS-related research categories. The quest to discover either a cause behind or a cure for the ALLIS disease has anyone with a hypothesis working to unlock the hidden secrets of an unknown shadow. Certainly, the research facility and persons that crack the iron door of ALLIS are guaranteed fame, fortune, admiration, and every scientist's cherished dream, one or more of the coveted Nobel Prizes.

Thousands of theories and millions of hours of experimentation have passed since the first ALLIS cases were reported less than a year ago. To date no one has been able to claim that promised celebrity. A Stanford University researcher's conclusion forms the applicable epitaph to the many hypotheses that have been pursued over the past months: "We've mutilated so many monkey thyroids trying to find a clue; we've injected so much ALLIS-victim serum into so many living creatures trying to induce the disease; we've dissected and reduced victim corpses to the primal elements of the chemistry chart; and we're still treading water, with no solid footing in sight."

Three main ALLIS theories tend to dominate current solution-finding directions. One is based on scientific hypothesis, one on guesswork, and the third is based in religious desperation.

Most scientific experts agree that ALLIS has to be caused by an as-yet-undiscovered virus or supervirus-type life form. Supervirus is defined as a smaller-than-viral, deadly-to-human, quasi-infectious agent. Nearly all experiments and research at the modern, more complex laboratories focus on trying to discover this tiniest-of-tiny life form that is causing so much grief in the human world.

This sub-virus theory, although plausible, has yielded no breakthrough into the ALLIS mystery. A growing number of scientists are again voicing the opinion that such a supervirus could only have originated from the military's biological warfare and genetic manipulations research. More than 1,000 leading university research scientists recently formed a petition coalition asking Congress to mandate the U.S. Defense Department to allow access to all biological warfare data files. Dr. J.G. Handles, co-chairman of the newly formed Scientists Wanting Access to Army Bugs (SWAAB), states his organization's case: "We face perpetual dead ends in our research. ALLIS has the potential to sterilize the Earth of humans if its death rate continues. The Army has who-knows-how-many and who-knows-what-kind-of mycotoxins and pathogenic agents brewing at a hundred labs around the country. More and more reports of safety problems and exposed workers and missing vials of viruses are being made public. What are we to conclude but that the ALLIS supervirus is a big mistake either they or another military counterpart has made? And how are they going to rectify this mess if they don't allow access to information that might lead to a cure?"

The Army categorically denies any association between ALLIS and its biotechnology research. It also denies access to its files. SWAAB doesn't carry the persuasive force that the healer named Gurner did. But a growing number of voices are being added to SWAAB's demands for information access. If enough people stand behind the mandate, perhaps the Army will have to yield.

The second "why-ALLIS" theory posits extraterrestrials. Every conceivable concept has been proposed, from Martian invaders systematically zapping increasing numbers of people with a lethal, ALLIS-causing energy, to a space-bacteria life form having found entry to Earth via the many space shuttles. These ET proposals do not have a large following, but they claim a continuous retinue and are regularly investigated. Samples of "air" from space, the moon rocks returned from the Apollo space missions, meteorites that have fallen to Earth, all are being analyzed for a hidden and virulent life form.

Finally, there is the simple and extremely commanding idea that ALLIS constitutes the wrath of God upon a sinful Earth. Scientists tend to defer comment on this proposal, for it is a difficult theory to document. But the peoples around the Earth have brought a thousand manifestations of the concept into being. Endless gloom-and-doomsday preachers have risen to immediate heights by extolling the numerous sins of mankind and their own prescriptions to salvation. Jesuit Father and noted Christian philosopher Frank Diller, S.J., comments on the surge of new religions that have gained notoriety in the past six months:

"Talk about the deceptive powers of Baal. An electric-voiced preacher and a dread of the unknown seem to be the ingredients for mankind's return to barbarism. There are new sects and even some weird Christian cults that are sacrificing animals—even humans, I'm told—as appeasements, if you can believe this, to the God of Love. Any hellfire and damnation character who can shout finds himself commanding people's fears. A lot of confused, desperate people are being sucked into giving up everything they own to various organizations as a way of being spared from ALLIS.

"Point A:" continues Father Diller, "if God did inflict ALLIS on the Earth—and I highly doubt He had a hand in it—it's about the most benign death one can be given. It's rather quick and painless, and leaves no doubt as to cause. And point B: these overnight 'faiths' miss the central theme of what religion is about. They tend to center around ALLIS; true religions focus on God."

Whether God-caused or not, ALLIS has sent the world's population into prayer. Around-the-clock prayer services have been initiated by every religion in the world.

Hope does spring eternal. An unidentified Methodist minister is quoted as saying: "There is a God. Don't doubt that for a minute. And He has got to hear this massive plea from His children, and lead us to a cure."

· · · · ·

ALLIS VS. GURNER'S GANG

No one any longer doubts that there once was a cure for ALLIS. That cure, a previously unidentified and rare plant nicknamed AC Herb, no longer exists. It and the one location in which it thrived in Oregon's Cascade Mountain Range were obliterated by a controversial logging operation. No single incident has so magnified how little knowledge mankind has of the intricacies of the Earth's environment he is so rapidly changing.

The man who discovered this priceless and hitherto unknown plant, an obscure and enigmatic healer from central Oregon named Gurner, metaphorically moved bureaucratic mountains to lead the world to the site of the AC Herb. Once it became known that salvation had been demolished by bulldozer and chain saw, the contrary healer again rallied his energies. Through the amazing means of unifying public demand, he has successfully solicited the aid of every private, commercial, and governmental agency in the world to help him and his by-all-standards unqualified team attempt to find another plant that could counter the Loggerman's Disease.

Since the untimely demise of the AC herb, scores of research teams have begun scouring the world's environments. Botanists have classified many new species of plants, and scientists have brewed endless teas from endless leaves and roots, trying to find a similar cure for ALLIS. Persons who have had contact with Gurner proclaim that he does not run his plant-search program on blind hope and luck.

Gurner apparently possesses a unique and accurate intuition concerning medicinal plants. Modey Swanson, a carpenter from Libby, Montana, claims Gurner helped cure him of kidney failure. Swanson says that the healer once told him he had developed a meditative ability to both sense the cause of a disease and listen to the particular plants that positively respond to healing that disease. This idea leaves rational researchers shaking their heads in disbelief. But the proof in the pudding also leaves rational researchers batting zero, whereas Gurner has sixteen verified ALLIS cures under his belt.

For the past two weeks Gurner, along with former FDA investigative agent Brian Johnson (whose wife Gurner cured of ALLIS), environmentalist Jerry Willox (whose child Gurner cured of ALLIS), newly graduated medical doctor Stephanie Peters (who administered the herbal cure to Johnny Willox), and *Newstime* special correspondent Harold Reeves have been tromping the western United States, seeking, as so many now do, another plant that combats ALLIS.

Johnson acts as the liaison of the group. He arranges, for example, the Idaho National Guard helicopters that transport the group—labeled "Gurner's Gang"—and their supplies into the various wilderness and roadless areas of that state. He talks to the Arizona land and ranch owners, obtaining permission for the group to explore their properties. He secures the needed supplies, transportation, and permissions that allow the five to venture into the areas that Gurner's roving senses dictate they should explore.

When the Gang heads into a specific area, such as the barren and isolated Cortez Mountains of central Nevada, Gurner and Jerry Willox spend several days trekking the terrain. They often trudge into base camp long past dark and rise again before dawn's first light. Gurner and Willox will cover between twenty and thirty miles a day, gathering and labeling the various plants that Gurner feels should be tested. Willox has said: "It's like following a chlorophyll bloodhound. Gurner has an ability to sense and find weeds that I wouldn't even notice. He sits by these discoveries for a time in closed-eye silence. Then we either gather a few specimens, noting their location and abundance, or move on to a new locale and a new species. I serve as his pack mule, toting the species take of the day and carrying lunch, allowing him to put his full concentration into his work."

Once Gurner has gathered plants that he feels might have

ALLIS-curing potential, he and Dr. Peters are flown to the nearest large population center, there to test the herb's effectiveness. Johnson, in the meantime, will have acquired a roster of ALLIS victims in that city. Johnson has no problem finding ready volunteers willing to try anything anyone may offer as a hope. At a central location, usually a hospital or medical center, Dr. Peters, who also serves as camp cook, takes charge. Along with Gurner and the hospital medical staff, she administers infusions and tinctures of the herbs to the ailing people. Everyone involved hopes to find that one plant that means success.

Newstime reporter Reeves is the link to the public in this strange-bedfellows adventure. He's the only reporter allowed on the scene and the only media person with whom Gurner communicates. Reeves has quoted Gurner as explaining: "If talking helped cure ALLIS, I'd blabber nonstop. But the current need calls for silent concentration and uninterrupted effort. Harold *is an excellent reporter* [emphasis is Reeves'] and respects my need for space and silence." Reeves' *tireless, thankless, and demanding job* [emphasis is Reeves'] is to disseminate important information, interesting discoveries or relevant stories to the worldwide press network.

Two weeks of the Gurner Gang exploring vast stretches of western land, funded by government De-ALLIS bill money, following the dictates of the healer's intuitive guidance, rounding up the ailing masses and conducting unapproved experiments that the AMA and the FDA continually denounce as potentially fatal—what has all this yielded in concrete results? The answer lies in two categories.

One is statistics. Aside from the AC Herb, Gurner's efforts have found no other potential ALLIS cure. The Gurner Gang has not fared as well as a less renowned research team also scrutinizing the plant kingdom.

Near Manaus, Brazil, a French research team claims to have located a rare species of rain forest orchid that effectively halted the physical decline of ALLIS. Unfortunately, the French team boasted of their discovery, affording the public a description and location of the plant. Immediately, most of the population of Manaus, Brasilia, and the wealthier population of Rio De Janeiro stormed into the area and eliminated both the orchid and any chance of scientific follow-up.

Should Gurner make such a discovery, notes reporter Reeves,

the healer plans to keep such plants and locations a strictly guarded secret, revealing them only to an international team of ALLIS research scientists, and only after a United Nations armed intervention team has been dispatched to protect the area.

Gurner's second category of results lies in the delicate field of human hope. The healer, via his first plant discovery and via his sure-footed, take-charge actions, has given a frightened world population hope that somewhere a second chance does exist.

By all rights, offering the masses hope for the seemingly hopeless should elevate Gurner to worldwide hero status. Indeed, that seemed to be his destiny the day he led the watching world to Eugene, Oregon. But now, although every news-conscious individual follows Reeves' field reports of the Gurner Gang with a tremendous fervor, Gurner himself is hardly mentioned.

Dr. John Johnstone, head psychiatrist at the New York University Medical Center in New York City, explains why, in one easy step, Gurner moved from highest prominence to a ghost no one wants to acknowledge:

"Psychology students are currently going ape over this new mass psychology syndrome named the Gurner Complex. Gurner, through no fault of his own, is ignored in the subconscious sphere of a person's mind because he represents a contradictory dichotomy. In other words, he's not admired by people because, while being their only real hope for an ALLIS cure, he also serves as a constant reminder that they were given one very big chance (the AC Herb) and they, as stewards of the Earth, blew it."

The healer also draws resentment because he, like no other person in history, successfully dictated to the entire government. Says Dr. Johnstone, "You have a needed 'hero' who is mistrusted and disliked by most, and outright hated by the very powerful."

Reeves reports that Gurner is happier being left alone than being idolized as something he is not. "He's enjoying the solitude," says our reporter.

Reeves also comments on the incredible amount of cooperation Gurner manages to generate among the peoples with whom he and his group deal. Reeves: "Day after day, sixteen to eighteen and more hours a day, these four work to find an ALLIS cure. They also inwardly and outwardly display the ideals of truly wanting to help cure ALLIS—with no attached thought of personal gain. That attitude spreads a kind of rich halo around them, and everyone seems to tune into it and catch the giving spirit. Cooperation naturally follows, and impossible tasks naturally get accomplished."

Reeves concludes his report by editorializing: "Witnessing such agreement and fraternity does leave me thinking, wishing that even a few of the leaders of the nations of this world were so selfless and could foster such constructive cooperation."

◆ 19 ◆
Intuition

July 3, 2008, 4:14 P.M. Central California.

The Owens Valley, thousands of feet below and many miles to the east, lay hidden behind a sullen smoke screen. The Inyo Mountains—the land horizon east of the Owens—with their early July forest fires, seemed to breathe out a resinous haze that gradually drifted westward and deposited itself onto the lower lands, obscuring the Owens Valley. For Willox and Gurner, standing on a rock outcropping at over 12,000 feet elevation near Kearsarge Pass by Kings Canyon Nation Park, the smudgy curtain draping the distant valley simply served the purpose of obliterating all signs of human life. U.S. Highway 395, the tiny town of Independence, the scenic road leading from that burg toward the pass, all remained smoke-enshrouded, out of sight and therefore out of mind. The High Sierras, including California's tallest, Mt. Whitney, penetrated the crystal-blue summer sky with a luster and a clarity and a massiveness that left the human viewer aching— beautifully aching, unexplainably aching, burning inside with a kind of lustful religious joy.

Willox finally had to place some words onto the ineffable beauty. "Man oh man oh man, will you look at that view? Makes you kind of forget what we're here for. Makes you forget everything you don't like to remember."

Gurner, poised like an Olympic high-dive finalist on the naked rocks, could only agree. "And remember everything you wish you'd never forgotten. Let's grab some lunch here, Jerry. My mind's kind of played out. This feels like the perfect place to recharge."

Willox watched the healer scout out the most comfortable spot amid the rocky terrain. *I should say "played out"! Jeez-louise,*

Gurner, you've been going nonstop for almost three weeks now. Up early to pray or meditate or converse—whatever it is you do; then off at dawn's first shimmer, you and me foot-trucking over miles of landscapes, investigating the plant life. I catch some catnaps when you do your thing and tune into a species. But you, you're always thinking, always probing into the depths behind life in a manner that most of us can't grasp. If we find a few plant candidates, you then whisk off to some city, there to test, test, test its value. So far nothing has struck gold. So you race back, and we're off again, in an even more fevered pace, exploring new plant biota and pitting your intuition against this time bomb of a disease.

Stephanie's about to have a shit fit. She told me that if you lose any more weight, she's going to play doctor and ORDER you to take a week's break. I said that an obese probability is all she'd have, trying to get Gurner to adhere to that. She said she was also reading a book on aikido and would put a wrist lock on you while I pumped sleeping pills down your gullet. At least we got a good laugh out of—

Gurner's voice interrupted Willox's thoughts. "You're looking kind of wan, Jerry. If you need a couple of days off to relax, don't be afraid to take them."

Willox stuttered as his inner thoughts and outer vocalizations competed for the same space. *I do not believe the insight of this man.* "Gurner! I . . . you . . . you're the one who needs . . ."

Gurner laughed out loud, something Willox hadn't seen him do for weeks. "From the solicitous way you were staring at me, I knew you were taking to heart Stephanie's doctrine that a person isn't healthy unless he's adequately plump and sleeps one third of his life away. I'm doing fine, Jerry."

Willox wasn't convinced. "Are you, Gurner? Physically . . . and mentally?"

"I am. Things are in a whirlwind, but that doesn't mean life is out of control."

"I've got another question, Gurner. Are you a mind reader? I mean, did you tune into my thoughts then? Can you do that . . . read a person's mind?"

Gurner paused, as if weighing his words. "No. Guaranteed your thoughts are your private domain. Lately, I seem to be able to sense a person's feelings more keenly. In your case just now I picked up on heavy concern. I'm getting to where I can usually read a person's subtle nuances. But for sure, the specifics of a person's thoughts I can neither hear nor understand. . . . Good God, nor would I ever want access to such a talent."

An almost imperceptible breeze began fanning the ridge top, motioning the multi-colored collection of alpine flowers into a serene flutter-dance. The two men padded their backs against the rocks with packs and shirts and settled in for a relaxing lunch break. They rarely talked, Willox and Gurner, mainly because they never found time for conversation. But after three weeks and nearly 400 miles of wild turf covered together on foot, with a silent sharing of amazing polychrome sunsets and mellow sunrises over every kind of landscape, by mutually discovering micro biota and environments of every precious description, and by being comrades in the emergency situation of the world's need for their undertaking to succeed, these two men had developed a bond of friendship that could otherwise have required a lifetime to cultivate.

Willox peeked over to see if Gurner was napping, half hoping the man was asleep, half hoping the healer wasn't so he could ask a long-standing question.

"Gurner, I've gotta ask you something."

"What's that, Jerry?"

"Three weeks ago, in Oregon, right after you faced that clear-cut, and you were tromping around the nearby hills and woods looking for some more of the AC herb? And I had gotten there a couple of days earlier than the others, and joined you, and we were out hiking the country around the Middle Fork of the Willamette? Remember? And Joe Simpson, that big burly logger fellow, came crashing through the forest and intercepted us, and told you his daughter was dying of ALLIS and asked you if you could do anything? Remember that?"

Gurner nodded. "Quite clearly."

"Did you know that he was not only one of the loggers that cut Squanni Hill, but was also a main energy behind opening the place to logging in the first place?"

"Yes, I knew that."

"And do you know who he is? He's one of the boldest and most brazen anti-environmentalists in this area! He acquired some notoriety when he drove a bulldozer into a classified wilderness area. He's organized protests against sound forest planning. And he's known to use his bulk to bully conservation workers."

Gurner again nodded. "Yeah. I had read about him."

These casual affirmations confused the environmentalist. "Then Gurner. What am I missing here? You didn't tell the media the whole truth. You did have a few leaves of that healing herb left. Enough for us gang members to secretly have a solid dose, as a 'vaccine' against ALLIS. Beyond that, you had a couple more leaves. One more dose. Of the millions succumbing to ALLIS, why Simpson, who perhaps more than any other man is the reason there is no cure for the disease? Why did you give him the last leaves of the only viable treatment?"

Gurner stared at the open sky for so long that Willox began to wonder if the man hadn't fallen asleep with his eyes open. Finally the healer softly spoke. "Would it make any sense, Jerry, if I said that Simpson helped me to at last be at peace with my destiny?"

"Um, not very much."

Gurner repositioned his hips on the rocks. "Okay. Let's see if I can explain. I remember that monster of a man, charging through the forest like a grizzly, yelling 'Hey, I gotta talk to you.' You recognized him right away and bristled up like a hound about to face a bear."

"I thought we were going to be fighting for our lives."

"Well, between your reaction and him stomping up to me, I didn't know what was about to happen. Then he started talking of his daughter, ALLIS-stricken, six days to live, could I help, for the love of God could I in any way help?

"I realized who he was, and I have to admit, my gut reaction was, 'Where in the hell does this guy get off, asking for a cure?' But I also noticed tears in the corners of his eyes as he talked about his dying daughter."

"How does that make him different than anyone else?"

Gurner paused a moment to consider Willox's question. "Well, although Simpson didn't exhibit the most gracious mien, he also wasn't throwing commands at me from a body thrice my bulk. With this perceptive ability of mine, I was able to tune into him. And Jerry, that next moment allowed me to feel like I found the one piece of a jigsaw puzzle that lets you know the rest of the picture is going to fall together."

Gurner's hips didn't like their new rock acquaintances. He jostled into a new position. "Before me, in the form of Joe Simpson, stood a representative of every concerned father of every dying child, everywhere. In that man I suddenly beheld the part of every man who would do anything—including cut down forests as a job—for the family he loves. It struck me with a moment of intense compassion that I can only call Divine. Simpson asking 'Can you help her?' triggered a reaction and a voice in my head that screamed: 'Of course I can help. *I'm a healer!*'"

Both men leaned their heads against the mountainside boulders and watched a bit more of the motionless day pass before their view. Gurner appeared contented and complacent. Willox looked totally confused. Gurner again seemed to read his mind.

"Jerry, you probably need a little history to understand the implications of that internal scream."

"Only if it feels right to share."

"I'd love to talk it out." Gurner cast a withering glance up and into the alpine sky. "You don't know how nice it is to share my deeper feelings with someone who talks back.

"About twenty years ago I started dabbling in the alternative healing arts. Most of those beginnings stemmed from a motive based on the fact that my body was hell-bent on a disease course. Let's make it succinct here. Thanks to a few opportune and resourceful natural healing practitioners—and no thanks to an array of M.D.s that I visited—I currently am not arthritic, am not diabetic, and a life-long sinus infection is now manageable.

"But the people who helped my physical body, they weren't put-the-poultice-on-and-leave type herbalists. They were healers, Jerry. True healers."

Willox silently wished he had let this man sleep. His friend needed rest, not heavy-duty philosophizing. Gurner smiled, as if acknowledging that thought, stared fixedly at a distant cluster of mountain peaks, and began talking, it seemed, to the sky.

"This world is filled with endless models of health professionals. Good, skilled, long-suffering and hard-working health workers of all kinds. But so few are genuine healers."

Gurner wrinkled his brow and concentrated his thoughts, looking for a wording, needing to properly express this for himself more than needing to have Willox understand it.

"Let me tell you a quick story, Jerry, about one of the herbalists I studied under. This man—Dr. Malbott—was supposed to die at age seventeen from all kinds of degenerative diseases, and yet he outlived the five doctors who gave him that cheerful prognosis. This healer spent large amounts of his life incarcerated in slimy jail cells because he had dared to treat people—and oftentimes successfully treat people—who the medical establishment had either written off as incurable or sidestepped because they couldn't pay the costs."

A sudden impulse forced Jerry Willox to look over at Gurner. The healer's eyes, still gazing at the distant peaks, were candid reflectors of a mind that no longer seemed to be bound to the sphere of the physical body. On other occasions Willox had witnessed Gurner in this noumenal state. When the healer fixed his total attention onto—or into—a single species of plant life, Willox could tell that an extraordinary interchange was occurring between life forms. During those communicative moments, Gurner remained in silence. Here, although the man was obviously distant and immeasurable, he continued talking aloud and in normal tones.

"That man, that true healer, told me about an experience he gained in one of those jail cells. The floor, the bed, the walls, everything in the prison was caked in unwashed filth. He had been abused, falsified, lied about, tossed in prison with no due process or moral justification—just a bunch of AMA-directed laws that stated if you weren't AMA, you weren't. Every belief he owned concerning good and right and justice had been cracked, and every conviction that his calling was valid and honorable had been blasted. He said he lay on the floor, praying and praying, on the verge of breaking, of giving up. And right then—it was night—a shaft of light descended from a barred window high up on the cell wall. This light surrounded him, warmed him through and through, and, most importantly, it filled him with a knowing that what he was doing in the world was good and righteous. And God-blessed."

Gurner's eyes intensified their distant focus. His voice quickened by several degrees. "There are true healers in this world. They're few and far between. That's because true healers, like true prophets, have somehow, in some way, been irreversibly touched by God. They may or may not display a special gift. But for sure they are consciously or unconsciously in tune with Spirit's grace directing their actions. Because of this directing, they are selfless givers. Because of this giving, they don't simply do what they've been trained to do and make a living at it. They also have the ability to touch . . . they also *have to* touch the lives and the hearts of the people they meet. . . . Touch them for the better, touch them with beauty . . . touch them with Love."

Gurner shifted his gaze toward Willox, and the healer's eyes slowly refocused to the physical realm. His voice leveled off.

"I so wanted to be a healer, like Dr. Malbott. And for the longest time I sported this notion that the only way it could happen was for God to zap me with lightning and fill me with the same kind of miraculous healing power Christ displayed. The all-or-nothing syndrome. With that as a guiding idea, I've ignored and belittled the very gift of intuition God has helped me develop to answer my prayer to be a true healer."

Gurner's gaze returned to the faultless sky. "Strange as it seems, Jerry, it was that moment in the woods with Joe Simpson that opened a door. This simple gift of intuition somehow manages to blend people's ailing bodies and the healing plant world into a useful combination. It can be the gift of a healer. And right at that moment of 'Joe-contact' I realized another quality of a true healer, an essential attribute. I know dear ol' Dr. Malbott would agree. I understood that healers do not refuse their help to anyone life directs to them. That's an intense statement. In an extreme realm, it means that if Squanni Hill loggers or even the infamous U.S. Presidents of the '80s—the guys who did more to degrade the Earth's environment than anything since the Ice Age—even if they and a bunch of those Idaho and Utah and Wyoming senators who have never been able to conceive that human life really does depend on a livable environment; even if *they* came to me with an environmentally caused disease, and I could help them, I would."

Willox, who understood little of Gurner's narrative, focused on his last statement. "You *must* be a healer. That's more than *I* could do."

"Well, heh, *I* could never testify again and again before a bunch of subcommittees and slow-moving bureaucratic land directors without screaming at their ignorance of the simple fact of 'no living Earth, no people.' Yet you keep your calm so a careless insult doesn't alienate them and blow a vital bill or project."

After a pause, Gurner again chuckled, a small laugh that crossed between grimness and reassurance: "At least I seem to boast a few healer qualifications. I do have a special gift—intuition. And for doggone sure, like most alternative healers, I'm being persecuted by the narrow minds that have nosed their way into power."

Willox repositioned his rock-numb posterior and faced his friend. "And how about that Touch, Gurner? Like your Dr. Malbott, have you seen that Light, or heard that Voice, or felt that Hand?

The Sight or Sound or Feel that fills you with knowing you're right, is it yours?"

As if intuition were catching, Willox could feel Gurner's aura alter itself from an outwardly radiating quiescence to an inner wrestling match with agony. Gurner finally answered in a shy tone. "I . . . I guess saying 'almost' is the same as saying 'no.' No, I have not. Not to the depth of being able to know I know I know."

Willox pondered Gurner's answer. "Hmmm. You sure do make it sound like an all-or-nothing-at-all affair."

"Welcome to the hell and the hope of the potential prophet, or healer, or whatever, the man called by God."

"Well, as witnessed by you."

Gurner dropped his head to his chest for a moment. "You're right, Jerry. God, you are absolutely right. Stephanie is a healer, as are the people all over the world selflessly working to counter this disease. Perhaps they more so than I. Stephanie helps and gives her all; she heals; she loves the people she contacts; and the idea of God isn't an Armageddon raising continuous chaos in her mind. You don't know how often I envy her."

The rocks were winning the Willox's-behind-vs-the-rocks-battle. He again shifted. "Speaking of Stephanie . . . one more question, Gurner. Can you handle one more?"

"I don't know. Your whole energy just changed from curiosity to devil's advocate."

This guy has to be a mind reader. "Well, I'm gonna ask it anyway. What about Stephanie? What does she mean to you? You know, if ALLIS wins the battle, there're going to be damned few people around to play Adam and Eve. It will be up to Brian and his wife, my Johnny and perhaps that young girl you saved, and maybe you and Stef."

Gurner sputtered something unintelligible, stopped in midsentence, and then vividly blushed. Willox had never seen his friend so visibly embarrassed or at such a loss.

"Gurner. What's up? She's certainly good looking."

Gurner nodded. "Yes. Beautiful inside and out."

"And she's certainly attracted to you."

"Yes. One doesn't need super-intuition to know that."

"So, what's the deal? You've no feelings for her? You . . . you lose your potency by experimenting with some herbs that didn't do what they were supposed to?"

Gurner could not force a smile at Willox's joke. "Jerry, all I can say is that the last fifteen years of my life I've chased thoughts and ideals that haven't allowed any standard definitions of relationship. Asceticism and aloneness have been the major keys to my path. And I know I'll never give up flying those kinds of kites. Now someone like Stephanie enters my sphere, and feelings I've never acknowledged are screaming at me. But then my mind, which seems to be the greatest part of my being, kicks in and realizes that over the longer course of time those yearnings will subside."

Gurner now produced a grim smile. "And the fiery lady named Stephanie Peters, M.D., would not be one to flow with the idea of 'God first' in her man's mind. Frankly, I think God would buckle under the competition."

Willox agreed. "That's probably true. Well, Gurner, whatever you know you gotta do, you gotta do."

"Yeah. If I should become famous and Hollywood tries to make a movie out of it, it won't be very exciting. No sex scenes."

The environmentalist winked at the healer. "Not to worry. They'd totally lie about it and transform you and Stef into the hottest and juiciest lovers of the new century."

Both men laughed and then enjoyed a few moments of the calm that laughter brings to an earnest conversation. Finally Gurner yawned, stretched his muscles, and popped about seventeen body joints in the process of standing up. "We better wander, Jerry. Let's check this ridge out for a few miles and then head back to camp. Harold must be going nuts by now, afraid the big discovery will happen and he won't be there. He would blow that weedy body of his to pieces if it meant following a news story."

Willox's body also required several joint rearrangements when standing. "Yeah. Poor guy. Huffs and puffs and sweats and works so hard all day to keep up with us and then sprains his ankle going to the john at night."

"Guaranteed that comfrey poultice will have him bounding like a gazelle in a few days." Gurner again grew serious. "But I don't think we're going to be doing that much hiking any more."

"Oh?"

"This isn't working, Jerry. It's too slow. We trot all over the landscape and we're wearing ourselves raw. So far we haven't found a single plant that buffers ALLIS. Meanwhile, ALLIS soars past 30 million worldwide dead. Another doubling of figures. If this keeps up, in less than twenty-five weeks human life will be kaput. I'm pulled to leave the United States and explore other countries. Also, I strongly feel that we're not going to make it if we hike every single ridge top and gully. So we'll do more flying over the countryside, and not physically explore the land unless my internal intuitive pull is intense, meaning a real hummer of an anti-ALLIS plant. We've got to find a big one and find it fast."

Willox swung his backpack onto his shoulders. "Everybody in the Gang could use a breather."

"Then let's move on. I can't help but wonder how many more people died of ALLIS while we took this break."

· 20 ·
Flower Talk

July 7, 2008, 8:55 A.M. The Bitter Root River Valley, Montana.

Gurner sat cross-legged on the ground, surrounded by over-grown, weedy chaos in an abandoned yard in the center of this picturesque Montana mountain valley. His attention focused solely on the plant in front of his face.

Hello. Hello little Arctium lappa, hiding under the branches of this willow tree. You with the composite purple flowers and elongated, heart-shaped leaves on a stout stalk. We've already met, years ago, when I learned about your arthritis- and fever-curing abilities. But I sensed some deeper energies as we flew over in the plane, and now I have to ask you some deeper questions. Do you have other arcane secrets, something that will be beneficial to mankind in this time of need? If you don't mind, I'll sit by your side awhile, and hopefully you and I will have a talk.

Gurner's eyes closed as his mind centered on the leafy life form.

Silence, Gurner. Silence. Even before mentally reaching out to the plant; even before praying for help to be an open receiver; first you must attain a complete silence. It's getting easier, but God, sometimes I still have to sit for long bouts of time, fighting down my mind, listening, listening for nothing but nothing. Only in the nothingness of silence do I truly hear. So be silent . . .

Shush mind. Silence is not thinking about how silent I'm being. Silence is not thinking. Shush . . .

Peace, my thoughts. Silence forces nothing into being. Silence simply lets prayers be answered. Peace. Peace . . .

. . . Now, oh God, in this time of inner harmony, talk to me. You are the hidden energy behind the voice of Arctium lappa; I

am the listening universe. Speak, for Your servant truly does listen . . .

My plant kingdom friend. I reach out to you. Arctium lappa mankind calls you. But I call you friend. For when we become Essence touching Essence, there is no separation. We are One in the Creator. And in this Oneness I learn your gifts. What healing have you to offer the human body and mind? What are the reasons you've been made sacred in creation?

Wordless moments blended and passed as Gurner sat suspended in silent communication. Finally, subtle twinges coursed across the healer's serene face.

Words. Words are returning. Mind is refocusing. No ALLIS-curing qualities in the realm of this fine plant. But if I ever get back to practicing herbology on a general basis, it's going to be exciting to use this as a lymphatic cleanser.

Thank you, my friend. May your seeds be well scattered, whether mankind appreciates your sticky burrs or not.

Gurner stood up, stretched, gazed a few moments at the gorgeous valley setting, then walked toward the waiting Highway Patrol vehicle that had brought him here from the local airfield.

God, my Friend. We must be getting better at this. That analysis only took about thirty minutes. I wonder where the rest of the world disappears to when I enter that communicative space?

You know, God, You have got to finagle some things so I can further decrease the amount of time it takes to plant-commune. Even if thirty minutes becomes normal, there's not going to be enough time to check out everything before ALLIS completes its deadly cycle.

· · · · ·

July 8, 2008, 7:00 A.M. Inside a twin engine Otter aeroplane, above the mountain ranges of central British Columbia.

The five Gurner Gang members sat in various states of discomfort on the Spartan seats of an older bush aircraft supplied by the Canadian Government. Gurner, in usual form, perched on his seat cross-legged, barefooted, eyes closed and deep in mental directions.

Silence, Gurner. Silence. It's no different a couple thousand feet above the ground in a plane with hundreds of square miles of British Columbia mountains below. It's no different than sitting before a lone plant on the noiseless desert sands. If I'm not successful at silence, nothing will be heard; if I enter my space of true silence, nothing will remain hidden. Silence, Gurner. Go for silence . . .

No, mind, no. Ignore the stereo drone of these twin engines. Ignore Harold snoring and Stephanie humming. Ignore Brian hovering over his air sickness bag. Go beyond. Go beyond it all . . .

. . . Beyond. Go beyond all form and all thought. Silence.

Now, oh One, let omnipresence flow through me. What are ten thousand square miles to the mind that hears the One Voice? Grant that that Voice speak to me as the energies of any life forms having the curative aspects we're seeking. Grant that I may feel the call of any such plant . . .

Hello my friend, the expansive acreage of land below us. Hello Nechako Range and the many pathless valleys you shield. Have you a secret helper hidden in your forests? Does a side streamlet support a life form on its banks that signals the end of the Loggerman's Disease?

As if dispelling bothersome gnats, Gurner rapidly shook his head from side to side.

Lots of little energies here. Lots of the kind of mini-tugs that Jerry and I have spent the last month delving into. Hard to ignore them. Got to ignore them. Got to find a plant that works in a big way.

Call again. Got to keep calling. Is there anyone . . . ?

Whoa! What is this? Gurner unfolded from his seat and strode to the plane's fore to stand behind the controls.

"Pilot. Er, Mr. Jenkins. Er, Ken. Please veer to the west, about 45 degrees."

The healer again closed his eyes. *Who are you? Where are you? Please call again. I listen in silence. Please let me feel you again.*

"More to the west. A little more. Good. Hold this course."

There! God Almighty. There it is. It doesn't have the oomph of the AC herb, but this is the most powerful ALLIS-healing energy I've felt since the Oregon clear-cut.

Gurner opened his eyes and spoke to the pilot. "Ken, please, on your navigational chart. Mark a circle around the eastern slope of that ridge. Yeah, that one there, with the old forest fire on its upper flank. We'll be coming back to it in a helicopter soon."

Gurner forced himself to maintain inner poise as he returned to his seat. *Back, Gurner. Back. Don't lose the silence in the excitement of a potential find. Don't stop listening. We've got to feel out the rest of this country. You might miss something bigger if you don't . . .*

Hello. Hello big country, my friend. Is there anyone else out there . . . ?

. . . . .

July 8th, 2008, 2:20 P.M. On an unnamed ridge top, in the wilds of British Columbia.

The two Canadian Air Force jet helicopters barely fit in the natural clearing high on the precipitous mountain ridge inside north-central British Columbia's remote Fawnie Mountain Range. While its crew members secured one of the copters to the landscape, the other metal bird revved up for an imminent departure. Gurner had to shout his last-minute instructions over the noise of the chopper.

"Ok, Brian. That's the plan. You and Stephanie and the CAF pilot buzz to Vancouver and arrange things at the hospital there for testing this herb on ALLIS victims. Jerry and I and ol' Hollerin' Harold should locate this plant before dark. Soon as we do and get back here with it, this other copter will jet us to the city."

Reeves, whose lean-cheeked face always portrayed agony whenever he had to yell, was forced to yell. "You're a bit, bit more than excited about this one, aren't you, Gurner?"

"You said it, Harold. I feel like I've been swinging a heavy hammer for weeks but barely been hitting the nail. Until today. When we flew over this country, I sensed that we may find a large piece of the missing ring."

Dr. Peters, like Reeves, was frowning. Her attention was fixed on the surrounding country, with its devil's club, nettle, dense vegetation and impossible bushwhacking. The wilderness scene caused her to shudder. "Fawnie Nose Mountain. Headwaters of the Nechako River. This country wasn't created to be hiked. It's here simply to grant definition to the word 'impenetrable.'"

Gurner's lips formed a slight smile, and he winked at the other men. "Gosh, Stephanie. I know it's rough to be the one who has to return to the big city when before you lies a paradise of untracked bramble and cliff. But Brian really needs you to help set things up because we want this herb tested in record time."

Willox added, straight-faced, "Stef, we promise you priority exploration rights when we reach the jungles of the Congo.

Dr. Peters shuddered again. "Blugggh. This forest is a nothing but a thorny labyrinth atop a seventy-degree mossy rockslide. You wouldn't catch me vanishing into it if . . . if the single cure for all the world's diseases were found here and only here."

The other four Gang members faces indicated curiosity, for such an uncompromising statement did not sound like the caring Stephanie Peters they had come to know. Dr. Peters directed an equally sly and much more defiant stare back at her male companions. "So don't any of you woodland morons get lost or hurt in this joyless jungle. Because if Brian and I have to rally to the rescue, we're so tuned into hiking, we'll first set the forest on fire so it'll be easier to travel through."

The men knew they were one-bettered. Willox scuffed the ground with his foot and looked up sheepishly. "OK, boss."

Johnson, faceless until now, added his ever-practical wisdom to the scene. "Really, you guys. Be more than cautious. This isn't the open Nevada mountains. There's a reason people don't vacation here."

Gurner glanced at the chopper pilot who nodded an affirmative. "Gotcha, Brian. This Gang goes one safe step at a time. Personally, I don't think we've got that far to travel. Make sure the Canadian Government seals off and protects this area, *and* that they call in an international observation team."

"OK, Gurner."

"OK, Brian. OK, Stephanie. Rendezvous with you guys soon."

Johnson and Dr. Peters boarded the waiting helicopter and belted their safety harnesses. The doctor smiled and waved goodbye as the chopper rose in takeoff. Johnson's eyes closed and his mouth curved downward as Earth and helicopter parted ways.

Gurner turned to the Canadian Government officials who had accompanied him to the mountain site. "You guys hang back here. It's just Jerry and Harold and me. We have the two-way if we need help. But try not to call us until we call you. I simply cannot be disturbed while looking for this plant."

The representatives protested, wanting to be a part of the potential discovery. But their orders were to do as Gurner asked. All the Canadians could do was glower at the healer.

Gurner ignored them. "Ready, Harold? You sure your ankle is strong enough?"

"When this ALLIS thing, thing is done, I swear, Gurner, I'm going to fill media pages with articles on the value of comfrey."

Gurner smiled, nodded to Willox who nodded back, and the three men began a slow, weaving traverse along a jutting mountainside. So thickly entangled in plant overgrowth was the land, and so steep were the slopes, that progress immediately assumed a turtle pace. Gurner led the way. Willox and Reeves, in accustomed fashion, dropped behind several paces. The healer half closed his eyes, leaving but a modicum of attention directed toward his footsteps.

Silence, Gurner, silence. It doesn't matter an iota that you're walking or slipping or sometimes barely able to keep upright on this mountain slope. Silence is the key. You've got to listen. Let your feet and legs become automatic, but give your mind to silence . . .

Deeper. Deeper, man, go deeper into your Self. A branch slaps your face; ignore it. You slip; let it happen but don't stop penetrating silence. And especially ignore all the voices of all the other plants, calling, calling to be touched and known. Today we've got to find that one. Go deeper . . .

More. C'mon. Just a little bit more. I can feel it coming . . .

Oh my Friend. I pray to be an open channel. Your wisdom becomes mine. Your Voice becomes my answered question. Grant me the ear to hear, the inner quiet to listen. And speak through this plant to me . . .

Hello, my plant friend. Whatever your name may be, I call you friend. You have an energy in your being. I have a receptivity in mine. Dear friend, you signaled to me today. Please break your silence again and I will listen . . .

Gurner's body rotated like a radar antennae. He yelled to his companions. "This way, Jerry. We've got to cut out of these woods and head north for these cliffs."

The trio emerged onto an open rockslide laced with whitish-flowering plants. Gurner squatted on a rock and continued his meditation before these plants.

Is this it? This is it! Thank you for talking. And oh, what a voice. What a power. Let me sit by your side and listen. Let me hear what you have to say . . .

Words. Words are returning, refocusing. When the plants speak, there are no words, just a merging where all information is exchanged in silence. And I leave that silence knowing, aware that in my consciousness the answers now exist. Then I can put them into action . . . and into words. Thank you, my friend, for the exchange.

Gurner excitedly waved to his cohorts. "Harold! Jerry! This is the one! God, this is great! The whole mountainside is covered with it. Have you got those identification books in your pack?"

Willox handed Gurner a thick, biological keying book. The healer began leafing through the pages. *Ugg, I resist this part. I do not enjoy breaking things down into components for tagging. The true energy lies behind the whole, not in the piecing and labeling.*

Let's see, long base-clustered stalks; cluster flower, white to greenish white; five petals; five stamens; five round calyx lobes; hmmmm, I get it belonging to the Malvaceae family. What? This isn't a Mallow. But let's see if the habitat checks: "Grows throughout Northern Mexico and into Southern Arizona on gravelly, well-drained southern slopes."

Gurner slammed the book shut and tossed it back to his companion. "Jerry, I'm a healer, not a scientist. Would you give me that Audubon wild flower field guide. The one that breaks the flowers down into colors and gives all these pictures to look at instead of this classification gibberish. . . . Thanks."

This is more like it. White flowers. White elongated clusters. That's the category. Man, look at all these beautiful plants and flowers. I don't have enough lifetimes to personally get to know all these guys. . . . Here. This looks close. Rose family. Partridge Foot? Not quite. The leaves are different. . . . Here. This is the one. It even gives me that inside click that says it's the one.

Smiling broadly, Gurner yelled to the lurking reporter. "Harold! Get your camera. You've been documenting every flower I pluck. I think this one is going to be worth plucking. Jerry, let's fill the carrying sacks with it, and preserve several of them in the press."

Reeves hobbled over and knelt beside Gurner. "What specifically, specifically is it, Gurner? Unlike you, the readers want to know names."

"As far as I can tell, call it Alumroot, of the Saxifrage family. Heuchera . . . spelled H-E-U-C-H-E-R-A . . . is the genus. I can't give you species names, as these guys hybridize a lot. An accurate identification needs someone more botanically competent than I."

Reeves scribbled feverishly on to his notepad. "You're pretty keen, pretty keen on this . . . this Alum being a potential cure for

ALLIS. I do not want to offer any false hopes to the world. But people could really use a healthy shot of hope right now."

"Then Harold, simply note that Alum is known for its astringent and antiseptic properties and don't promise anything until we test it on the battlefield. But right now, off the record and between you and me, this little beauty has a lot to offer."

Reeves clicked three quick pictures of the healer staring at the Alum. "Your facial expression, expression is saying 'but.'"

"Indeed, but. But I don't know if it has *enough* to offer. It doesn't have the power of the AC plant. It just doesn't feel like anything will be that simple again."

For the thousandth time, Gurner forced mankind's environmental follies out of his mind and focused on the immediate course of action. "So, call the copter on the two-way, Jerry. Maybe they can pick us up in that open area above these cliffs. That will save us an hour walking. Brian and Stephanie will have about a three-hour head start on us. That should be enough time to have things in Vancouver lined up."

While Willox radioed the Canadian Air Force personnel and Reeves expended roles of film capturing the Heuchera at every angle, Gurner again focused his thoughts into the small, mountain plant.

Hey, God. What is this complete yet incomplete feeling inside of me? This plant is the answer, and yet it isn't. What does that mean?

. . . C'mon, God. You could answer me openly. Just once . . .

Oh well. Harold, ol' buddy. In a day or two you may have your hope-filled story.

. . . And, you may not.

· · · · ·

6:06 P.M. On the CAF jet helicopter flying full speed toward Vancouver, British Columbia.

Silence, Gurner. Got to enter into silence. You're getting better and quicker at this. But the bottom line is shutting the mind down . . . completely. Even now, when I'm not diving into the realm of a particular plant species, or not flying over an endless landscape, searching, searching, I've got to be especially quiet now, when simply meditating, simply praying, simply trying to expand the inner horizons . . .

Silence. Peace. Silence. Peace . . .

No words. Be still and know. No prayers. Be still and know. No questions. Be still and know, know, know. No searching. Just listening. Just being. Just letting what comes happen as it will. Just nothing . . .

Words. Returning. Kind of like awakening.

How long a time has passed? I never know till I ask someone with a watch. What did I learn? I never realize until it's suddenly there, presented to me in my thoughts or speech or actions. Where do I go? Nowhere, I think. Yet it also seems like I journey into a bit of everywhere. Am I really but a madman off on a weird trip? Yes, of course; when can I go again?

. . . God. There's one thing We got to talk about. It's about these voices I keep hearing. Not voices. Whispers. Whispers of voices that aren't.

Gurner gazed through a helicopter window and spoke aloud. "It's a good thing You're God and You know what I'm talking about. Explain that statement to Harold and the news media."

Voices that were but aren't anymore. I keep hearing them, tasting their vibrations on the fringe of my consciousness. But I'm unable to focus them, to clarify them. They're like ghosts. Ghosts of . . . Christmas past? Past? Past is the word . . .

Of course! I mean, just remember where I heard them, these broken whispers. Southern Nevada. Very strong there, especially over the Nellis military proving grounds. Southern Idaho, especially along that Snake River route that has transformed every square inch of habitable land into a plowed field. In the National Forests, especially in the massive acreage clear-cuts of Washington and Oregon. In cities, especially near the monster cities . . . Phoenix, and that front range mess in Colorado, along most of the west coast of this country. Of course. It makes sense . . . actually, it makes no sense.

We humans barreled in and took eighty acres out of the side of a small Oregon hill and lost forever the AC plant that could have cradled the world in the palm of its frond. Without mandatory biological diversity studies—before development, that is—what's going to happen to similar unknown species? Hundreds of square miles of land get paved and concreted, or leveled and plowed, or bombed and nuked into moonscapes. What do we risk losing, each time? You gave me the ability to tune into the energies of plants. Now I'm feeling—as whispers—the energies of the plant species that are no longer with us. What they had to offer, we'll never know. Maybe a cure for MS? Perhaps something that would heal the severest burns? We'll never receive their gifts now. You didn't put those plants here without a purpose. And yet, now, wherever this Gang travels, I'm picking up on a hell of a lot of whispers of energies that are no more.

. . . Plant species going extinct. Several per day, they say. What do We do about this problem, God?

. . . Silence, Gurner, silence. Let's see if there're any answers . . .

. . . Silence. Gotta find an answer. Silence . . .

Nothing, God? Flat out nothing whatsoever? Maybe this isn't the problem You want me to handle . . .

Sure hope You direct somebody to handle it sometime soon . . .

Sure wish somebody would have handled it before ALLIS roared into being.

♣ 21 ♣
Committee

July 9, 2008, 8:01 A.M. In a plush, private conference room, 45th floor of the Chrysler Building, New York City.

With no formalities or table-rapping announcements, the meeting came to order. Ron Harrison simply looked at his watch and stood up, and everyone in the room quieted and eased into a listening position. Harrison, tall, well-dressed and obviously a sure-footed personality, served as the co-president of a small, very closed, hardly known and rarely mentioned fraternity of social, financial, and influential giants from around the globe. The speaker moved right to the point.

"Well, Bowerns, since you're the person most concerned with this guy, why don't we begin with your update? About a month ago you signaled an alert to this committee. Since then, I've closely scrutinized the actions and characterizations of this Gurner, and, to be honest, I disagree with your evaluation. The facts show a definite humanitarian working his living ass off in an attempt to salvage mankind's existence. It seems to me that preventing mankind's demise translates to saving both us and our little 'enterprise.'"

A murmur of thirty consenting voices reverberated through the room. Jim Bowerns strode to the head of the lavish meeting room, reviewing the faces before him. Powerful, confidence-exuding faces they were, all focused on him, focused and intense in their listening ability. Bowerns set himself to match this audience's faculties.

"Thank you, Ron. Where's DuPont? He ought to hear this."

"Our friend Jacques is currently . . . ah . . . residing in a Paris hospital."

"Oh oh. Nothing serious, I hope?"

"Serious? He has about four days to live."

"Four days?! Is it—?"

Harrison cut Bowerns off. "This is why we're more than keen to hear what you have to say, Bowerns. In the final analysis, our little group is dependent on this Gurner fellow too, just like everyone else in the world. Jacques has ALLIS. Not only that, Doobie's son in Queensland just died of it. This is one thing this group is not used to. Until now we've been safe. Revolutions and wars really can't hurt us. We're too powerful, and of course we know about them long before they begin and therefore know where not to be. Old age is about the only disease we have to fear, and when you know how, and can afford it, even that can be staved off.

"But now that goddamned ALLIS has tossed us all onto a different boat. So Bowerns, I and all the gents and ladies here are extremely interested in why you think we should hamper Gurner instead of placing a billion dollars in his pocket as an incentive to keep him going full steam on what he's doing."

Ceding the podium to Bowerns, Harrison took his seat, joining the others in giving him their undivided attention. Bowerns nominally adjusted some papers while he organized his thoughts.

I'm going to have to change my ploy here. They're on his side already. Gurner's got to be axed . . . what to do? What to do? . . . Gurner's simply got to be axed. Okay, that's it. I'll use what I have to arouse suspicions. Plant a little seed, feed their misgivings over time.

"Well, gentlemen and gentle ladies." *Must look unassuming here.* "To begin with, I must confess that I bounded off on a wrong path when I first started following Gurner's tracks as an FDA investigator. At that time I thought—and quite erroneously— that we were facing another get-rich-quick schemer capitalizing on the latest agony afflicting mankind. In investigating him, we followed procedures aimed at exposing someone presenting serious threats to citizens via unsubstantiated claims of cure." *Look a little apologetic.* "But now—and you know the story as well as I— ALLIS did not prove to be a simple mudpie disease, and Gurner is not a phony when it comes to that one point of having discovered an effective cure for an awful malady. However . . ." *Get more serious now.* ". . . from the beginning something about the nature of this Gurner aroused every suspicion in my old bones. I've made it a personal affair to closely monitor his actions. And I think . . ."

Need a suggestive pause here. ". . . I *strongly* think you'll be amazed by some of the observations I've gathered."

Good time to take a small sip of water . . .

"Take a minute here, my friends. Simply take a short minute and reflect on the known history—not on the potential and hoped-for history—but the known history of this man. Until six months ago he was an absolute nobody, a vagabond running around the mountains and not making enough to have to pay taxes. I realize that the media currently plays him up as some kind of efficacious herbal healer. I also understand that various persons are trying to enhance their own names by telling stories about how Gurner healed them of gout or ended their bout with arthritis or . . . or cured them of decapitation." *Good, got a chuckle. They're with me.* "But I can assure you, we at the FDA have investigated these claims to the full extent of our powers. And this is the final word. Most of these stories are simply that: stories. Unsubstantiated, unprovable. Prattling fairy tales. Everyone in this room is keenly aware of how easy it is to ignite the emotionalism of the masses. We ourselves occasionally provoke entrenched national temperaments, from mere sentimentality to outright hysteria. Be aware that the media and the populace are playing Gurner for more than he is and more than he deserves.

"Now . . ." *Pull on the mustache, look like you're thinking deep.* ". . . manufactured hero or not, that does not deny the fact that Gurner has cured sixteen ALLIS cases with an herb while all of modern science scratches its collective head and can't produce a flake of curative dandruff. But, if I may be so bold as to say this to you competent persons . . . I do not believe the handy chain of events that have accompanied Gurner. The clear-cut and the consequential demise of the AC herb—I do not believe this has happened as it's been chronicled. And you shouldn't either." *A few brows wrinkled on that one. Push this idea further.* "Let me offer you a list of questions."

Bowerns paused for another sip of water. *I do love it when minds open, and I'm the one who gets to fill them.*

"Compadres, just ask yourself:

"First, why is Gurner so secretive about his whole operation? He won't tell anybody anything. We don't know who he is; we don't have an idea what he stands for. Before leading those scientists on that hike to the clear-cut, he refused to answer any of our questions concerning the AC herb. Now he continues his evasions and won't talk to the reporters he once was so keen on acquiring. Look, I'm talking to the world's leading experts on working behind the scenes. Have you ever known anyone shrouded in such secrecy to *not* be up to something?"

Don't give 'em time to answer that. Move on quickly.

"Second, ask yourselves, as I have many times asked myself, why didn't he tell us—why didn't he tell anyone—about this herb *before* the clear-cut happened, before the loggers moved into that area? He obviously had discovered the herb before the area was cut. Either he's a complete idiot, or . . ." *OR—the magic word when used at the perfect time and left with a pregnant pause after it* ". . . or something has been preplanned. Something big."

Don't give 'em time to think.

"Next, ask yourselves this. This man, this one-named magician, what does his success ultimately portend for us? I offer you these considerations. For one, the fact that Gurner, after making a show of relinquishing his last three doses of the AC herb to government scientists, did in fact give more of the herb to a man named Joe Simpson. In itself that proves him a liar. But get this. Simpson was one of the loggers who fought for the Squanni Hill clear-cut, and who worked from day alpha until day omega cutting down that plant-protecting forest . . ." *Good. Suspicions. Gently plant suspicions.* ". . . You know, that just smacks of conspiracy. The herb of life given to the man who caused its death? Sounds like an agreed-upon payment. Payment for what, is what I'm asking."

I better wind this up. Short and sweet is a much better seller. But let's do put some real passion into my voice and gesticulations.

"Let me point out something of more practical concern to us. Even if Gurner and everything he does in his search for an ALLIS cure is bona fide . . ." *Emphasis here. Talk boldly.* ". . . we need to be very aware of the danger of this man. Beware and be aware of his proven ability"—Bowerns held up one finger—"to rally the people, the general masses, into an action mode . . . a mode supportive of him and *his* wishes."

Bowerns held up two fingers. "Beware of his proven ability to transcend 'due process,' as he did in forcing the government to concur with *his* plans and wishes. As you know . . ." *A grin here would be appropriate.* ". . . 'due process' in a government is always slow, which of course offers time to manipulate its out-come."

Bowerns held up three fingers. "And finally, be aware of his proven ability to garner the governments *of the world* into complete cooperation. Even God doesn't seem to be able to do that.

"Folks. That's a hell of a lot of power for one man. One unknown man who has no association with us. How much more power will he gain if he's successful in finding a world cure for ALLIS? How much more renown will he acquire if he's proclaimed far and near as a world hero? How much more influence will he wield if he wins a Nobel Prize for his efforts? On how firm a footing will our economic control and manipulation of the world stand if a Christ, or at least a perceived Christ, comes along?"

Bowerns again surveyed the attentive faces. *Feels pretty complete, Jimmy. Now end it both humanly and effectively . . . while inserting more suspicions.*

"Obviously, we need Gurner. I need him. Hell, I've no desire to watch a lifetime of dreams, work, and ambition wither away in twelve cold days. But I am saying, I am putting out, that we've got to stay on top of him with a steady and suspicious eye. We've got to have some plans to damp this guy, or he may explode into a chimney fire of a new leader. And then what of our own world vision?"

Take a bow. Just a slight bow. "Thank you. Thank you all so very much for listening."

Harrison, applauding, as were most others in the room, reclaimed the speaker's position. Bowerns slowly returned to his seat, carefully noting those who were not clapping.

Harrison spoke. "Thank you, Bowerns. Frankly, I think the one we have to watch out for is you. You could talk smoke into going down a chimney instead of up. I think everyone here will actively mull over what you've said."

Bowerns again stood up. "Thank you, sir. If I may . . . I forgot to mention. This is as hot off the line as it comes. It seems that Gurner has discovered or"—Bowerns held up four fingers, two on each hand—"quote, 'discovered,' if you're a person of my aroused suspicions—an herb in Canada that is apparently effective on the ALLIS disease in some way."

A minor, vocal uproar, something resembling a cheer, broke from the room's occupants. Bowerns waved the outbreak down.

Cripes, they're just like the common plebe. All they want to do is save their skin, even if it means forgetting everything I just said. I've got to remind them of what I just said. "That's all I know. Whether or not it's a cure, I can't tell you. I'm sure tomorrow's papers will bristle with the news. But part of sharing this information with you is to let you know that we may be facing 'Gurnermania,' and all of its implications, real soon. So . . . please, mull over what I've said. Rapidly, if you will."

Harrison said, "Thank you, Bowerns. You all have heard, and I expect commentaries by this afternoon. Now we need to turn our attention toward the main reason for this meeting. As you all know, due to ALLIS, no wars are being waged anywhere in the world, and therefore economic indices are declining across all the major markets. Economics is the nose-ring by which the world is guided. We need to think about how to keep a grasp on that ring when the economic mainstay of warfare gets put aside and nobody fights."

♦ 22 ♦
Education

July 10, 2008, 6:20 P.M. Main Street, Oakridge, Oregon.

The two burly men, dressed in plaid flannel shirts, elastic suspenders, and steel-toed logging boots, paused by the hardware building as one of them, Harry Meers, pointed across the street.

"Over there. In front of the drug store. It's Joe."

Ernie Slate called out loudly. "Joe! Hey Joe Simpson! Wait up. Kee-rist, we haven't seen you for a coon's age. Where ya been hiding?"

The huge man turned and smiled as his workmates strode across the highway and toward him. "Howdy yourself, Ernie. Hi, Harry. What're you two ol' hogs up to these days?"

Slate answered the question. "Same as usual, Joe. We're back cutting, in the Umpqua this time. That Gurner guy finally got his ass out of the state of Oregon, and the government decided it's really hurting from lack of timber revenue. So they opened up some sales in a few places they know they're not going to lose any precious plants. We're damned lucky to be there, 'cause a lot of communities haven't let logging pick back up yet.

"But what about you, Joe? Why aren't you with us? How come you're dressed like you're going to church? Where's your logging boots?"

Simpson smiled again as he adjusted his huge body inside the dress slacks and shirt. "Ernie, you might say I'm on a sabbatical."

"What the hell's that?"

"Call it a vacation. A pause from the logging world. Jean and the kids and I are moving up to Corvallis. And I, my dear gentlemen, am going to get educated."

"*What!*"

"That means I'm going to school, Ernie."

"What!"

Meers edged into the conversation. "You hurt your back, Joe? After thirty-five years of logging, your vertebrae petered out, and you need to do something to make ends meet?"

"That's not it at all, Harry. I'm registered as a student at Oregon State. Begin classes in a couple of weeks. And it's all voluntary on my part."

"WHAT!"

Simpson smiled one last time. "Ernie, your vocabulary is astounding. But do you know any other words at all?"

"Wha . . . *why?"*

"That's better. If you gents will buy me a farewell beer, I may just answer both of Ernie's one-word . . . profun . . . profundities."

. . . . .

6:30 P.M. Inside the Crosscut Affair Bar, Oakridge, Oregon.

Joe Simpson called out an order to the barkeeper as he placed his bulk onto a protesting chair. "Three of your biggest and most expensive beers, Arnold. Thank you kindly." He turned and faced his friend. "Now, you had a question, Ernie?"

"Joe, what the hell are you doing? Pressed pants and words nobody can make sense out of. Going to school? At your age? You're a stud work horse, Joe, not some fancy gelding like those college kids. What . . . are you doing?"

"I'm adding some new dimensions to an old game, Ernie."

"What? You gotta talk American. Simple American."

"OK. And you gotta listen up."

Simpson blew aside the foam and took a tiny taste of his brew.

"You know a little of the story, ol' buddy. You know how all during the Squanni Hill cut my conscience was screaming at me to stop that logging operation. You—"

"Yeah, you told me. I still think you were overworked and just needing a rest."

"Let me continue. You know how I ignored that voice, didn't speak out. And you know the results of my silence. We creamed the only cure for ALLIS. A—"

"Hey, we couldn't have known that. There's no way we could have known that would happen."

Simpson scowled at Meers. "Yeah, Harry. Let me continue. And you know my daughter Myra got ALLIS. And Gurner told me to not to tell anybody, but people pretty much figured out that he gave me some AC herb to cure her. T—"

"Yeah. Boy, why would the man who called ALLIS The Loggerman's Disease give a Squanni Hill logger the last of the plant? Just the other day me and Harry heard—"

Two massive fists crashed into the table. "*Goddammit* to Holy Hell! If you two jackasses don't quit interrupting me, I'm going to show you how much of a logger I still am! Now shut up and listen."

Simpson's voice was as big as his body. His two friends meekly looked into their beer glasses.

"All right!" Simpson gulped a big swallow of beer. "Now, what you and most everyone else don't know, but what I live with every minute of my life, are the pangs of guilt that rise up inside of me every time I hear an update on the ALLIS death count. Forty million, the news said this morning. Forty goddamn million. Ever felt 40 million pangs of guilt, Ernie?"

"I, ah . . . "

"Don't answer that. Don't answer nothing."

Simpson continued after a pause. "Anyway, I listen to the news and I feel guilty. I read the paper and I feel guilty. I attend the funeral of a friend who died of ALLIS and I feel especially guilty. And I'm not going to spend my whole damned life feeling guilty. So the next question that comes up is, 'Well, what're you going to do? How're you going to change all this?'"

Simpson took a long and slow pull at his drink and then continued, staring into the half-empty glass. "First I had the idea that I ought to say logging is wrong. I mean, look where it's gotten us now. We never took the time to care about the world and so we never knew what it had to offer us. Suddenly I could see myself . . . Joe Simpson, reformed logger turned environmentalist, chaining himself to a tree and daring another logger to touch it—"

At the garbled sound, Simpson looked up from his beer glass. "Don't choke, Ernie. That idea lasted about as long as it took to think a new thought. You don't get the hamburger grilled by dousing the fire. Logging is part of my fire. But maybe the fuel is smoky and just not doing as good a job as it could. Maybe it's even ruining the meat. Maybe we even need a different kind of wood to burn."

Two more contemplative sips lowered the beverage in Simpson's glass by another third.

"ALLIS, and me and my life's work being part of its present rampage, and my Myra nearly dying because of it, these have all shown me a few things about logging and mining and about every other kind of operation like that. I think it's just like they say. We're at the limit of this world's ability to give. We can't just keep on falling trees, loading them up, and hauling them to the mill. We can't keep on just ripping a big hole in the land and using poison to leach what we want out of it. Fishing can't be mile-long nets that catch everything and kill everything they catch. Not anymore. Those days aren't practical any more. There's not enough of the world left.

"But dammit. We still need logging. And fishing. And mining. So there's *got* to be ways that work can be done, and that jobs can be had, and that disasters like the AC herb wipe-out can be avoided. There's just got to be some compromise."

Simpson left one last swallow of beer in the bottom of his container and begin swirling it around and around in the glass.

"That's why I'm off into a new world, guys. Me? In school? College? Christ, I'll be like a banana trying to keep up on a downhill roll with a bunch of apples. But it's the only answer I've got to that nagging question of what am I gonna do about what's been done. I know logging, and I know loggers and what they do. If I can learn about the Earth, and what it needs, maybe I can help figure out how the two can be put together. But before that can happen, I've got to learn about—check these words— ecological interactions and interdependencies."

Simpson paused and spent a moment attempting to read the expressions in his companions' eyes, looking for any sign of support or understanding from them. "Anyway, that's what I gotta try. I gotta try it.

"Probably I wouldn't really have done it, it would have been just one of those thoughts that come and then they're gone, but then these government FDA characters came to the house and grilled me on Myra's ALLIS recovery."

Slate looked at Meers and Meers looked at Slate and then both stared at Simpson, but neither dared to ask a question.

"I think the government is out to rake Gurner over the coals. Those SOBs. They showed me their IDs and then interrogated me like Gestapo lawyers. I told them how I approached Gurner in the woods one day and asked for help, and how he opened his pack and gave me—gave me, the logger—for Myra, the very last bit of AC herb. I mean, Ernie and Harry, you gotta understand, when Gurner gave me that herb, there was a feeling of peace in the air that I can only describe as religious. He told me I could sell that little bit of herb for a whole lot. Hell, he could have done the same thing too. But he gave it to me, for Myra. But shit, by the time those feds got done twisting the story, it sounded like Gurner had a whole stash of the plant and was purposely hiding it from the world. That pissed me off, and I told them to beat it." Simpson stopped swirling the foaming drink and chuckled. "Heh. Those government guys can move pretty fast when they think they're going to get their necks broken.

"Anyway, I gotta do what I can now, to help him—Gurner, that is. And to help loggers. Goddammit. Herb finders and tree harvesters are both needed."

Simpson sloshed the last bit of beer down his throat, checked his watch, and stood and stretched his giant frame. "Well, right or totally wrong, there you have it, gents."

The monstrous man looked at his two logger friends. Something deep in him was almost begging for understanding from them. But should they mock his ideas, Simpson had determined to wade the swamp alone.

"Joe, am I free to say something now?"

"Heh, sure Ernie."

"Joe, you're craz . . . you're nu . . . you're . . . er . . . good luck, Joe. Dammit-to-hell. Good goddamned luck to you." Slate took Simpson's hand and shook it vigorously.

"Why . . . why, thanks, Ernie. Thanks a great big bunch. I really appreciate that."

Simpson nodded and, feeling surprised and pleased, he strode toward the bar door. Slate and Meers watched him barely fit between the doorjambs and then pass into the street. They stared at their mostly empty glasses for several moments.

Meers finally broke the silence. "Well, Ernie, wha-da-ya think of that?"

"Harry, by God, Joe's not the only one who can philosophize. Frankly, I think he's a sorry dreamer. Listen, it's a good idea. It's probably even a needed idea. But practical? That it's not. What logging company is ever gonna go along with that kind of idea? Someone like an educated Joe comes up with a half-good idea, it's still going to cost profits. And what Greenie group is gonna agree to letting the other side have half say? You and I both know people are mainly interested in 'our side only.' The Forest Service needs another middleman like it needs another hole in its head, and they most of all listen to nobody but themselves. Simpson can become a goddamn Pee-H-Dee, but he'll still be pissing into the wind, 'cause people don't wanna compromise."

Slate ceased swirling the ale in his glass and let a little of the beverage slide into his mouth as he thoughtfully stared across the room.

"Look, put it on a more common level. Your old lady and my old lady and most everybody's old lady ain't gonna buy a dollar-nine-cent can of tuna when right next to it they can buy a sixty-nine-cent can of tuna. It doesn't matter a tittleshit how many dolphins the dollar-nine-cent can saves or how many the sixty-nine-cent can creams. People forget ecology when it comes to the wallet, Harry."

Slate swallowed a tad more of the now-warm liquid.

"Besides. I think Joe's too late. 'Interaction' and 'interdependency' studies should have been done long ago. They weren't, and Gurner ain't gonna find a cure for ALLIS. We already blew it beyond return."

Meers paled just a bit. "You really think so, Ernie? I mean, I hate to think man's allowed to blow it once and then that's it."

Slate held his glass of brew up to the ceiling and stared at the overhead light through the remaining amber liquid.

"You bet I do, Harry. Look at Winston. If ALLIS got him, it'll get everybody."

"Yeah, but—"

"No buts, Harry. ALLIS is doubling every two weeks. Five or six more months and there simply ain't gonna be anybody left. So you might as well grab all you can while you can. That's the way most of mankind has always lived, and that's why we ain't got no future."

And with that, Slate drained his glass.

◆ 23 ◆
Newstime

July 13, 2008. Excerpts from *Newstime* magazine.

ALLIS: A RAY OF HOPE

Wall Street gaining ten thousand points in one day's trading. A remedy for the rapidly deteriorating ozone layer discovered. A delicious form of manna falling from the heavens. None of these desirable yet improbable circumstances, even if they occurred together, could have engendered the waves of joy produced by a single, verifiable piece of news announced at the General Medical Center of Vancouver, British Columbia, Canada. Evidence suggests that for the first time since the untimely disappearance of the Oregon AC herb, mankind has a hope in combatting the plague called ALLIS.

The celebrated healer named Gurner and his "Gurner's Gang" have discovered a new plant that does counter ALLIS. At least, the plant acts upon the disease's most serious complication. In a yet-to-be-discovered manner, this herb delays the final stage of ALLIS—the death stage.

"We don't know what [the herb] does or how it manages to postpone death by ALLIS," notes Dr. Isaac Keens, immunological specialist at General Medical. "It's too early. We're only five days into administering the plant on a test basis. All we can truthfully say is that of the thirty-three ALLIS victim volunteers to whom we have dispensed a tea preparation of this plant, only one has died. Twenty-three of these cases were in or near the final comatose state of the disease. And none—*none*—of these persons, although all are comatose, none is dead. Normal ALLIS statistics would have two thirds of them dead. We're all questions and no answers at this point. But it's a beginning. How truly wonderful to have a beginning."

Indeed how "truly wonderful" to attain a focus in the fight against ALLIS. Scientists and researchers from around the world are now converging on Vancouver. The fact of another plant effective in halting the disease's progress becomes the focal point of every eye.

"Now we can move." David Instler of the National Academies of Sciences voices the sentiments rippling throughout the scientific community. "Science can analyze anything. Having something to work with, we can figure out what makes it tick. I predict the beginnings of an ALLIS cure in a very short time."

There is more good news. The Oregon AC herb was a rare and undiscovered species of plant that thrived in a single location. This new herb—tentatively labeled "AH"—a member of the Saxifrage Family, covers a vast area of the western North American continent. Nonetheless, a large detachment of United Nations forces and Canadian Army reserve troops have been dispatched around the wild Fawnie, Itcha, and Nechako Ranges of Central British Columbia where Gurner located the herb. This action will insure protection of the plant and its habitat in case the particular Alumroot plant is a rarer subspecies that thrives only at the discovery location.

Good news is a welcome breeze in this ALLIS-plagued world. But experts still face many questions concerning humanity's future.

Gurner's latest discovery does not of itself cure ALLIS. Initial findings indicate that an infusion of the plant merely delays the disease victim's death; for how long has yet to be ascertained. AH does not prevent the disease's loss of muscular strength, nor does it counter the lowering of a person's body temperature. It also does not halt the progression of the disease-stricken person to the hypothermic-like coma. Only at this stage does the AH herb—and its unknown properties—come into play. Persons given the herb remain in a slightly less intense coma, but in a coma they do remain.

Questions do arise. Have we been offered not an ALLIS cure but a mere delay in its final effects? Will those kept alive but in a coma by AH become addicts in a sense, dependent on a daily dosage of herbal tea to keep them alive while science searches for a permanent cure? And the major question: is this one herb going to be enough, in time, to allow science the course of discovering a cure? At present the only answer comes as a reflection of Dr. Keens' statement.

At least we have a beginning.

· · · · ·

ALLIS AND THE ENEMY OF ALLIS

Scientists and researchers from around the world now zero in on Vancouver like hungry bees drawn to a lone flower blossom. Meanwhile, the man whose abilities brought all this attention to the Canadian port city and to a mountain Saxifrage flower now nicknamed the AH herb has skipped town. Not only town. Gurner (never one to stay where the crowds gather) and his self-appointed research committee of four have left town, the country, and the continent.

Four days after transporting AH to Vancouver's General Medical Center for experimental testing on ALLIS patients, Gurner again took to the air in search of other herbs that will counter the ALLIS plague. In a rare and short interview with reporters at Vancouver International Airport, an exhausted-looking Gurner shared a modicum of personal information concerning his next steps.

Why such a rapid disappearance from the scene that finally offers hope? "Science can handle this herb from here. I'd simply be in the way. Plus, I don't feel that this one plant is the whole answer. Plus, it is now mid-July, and many plants have completed their seasonal cycle. We need to check out the globe's northern climates before the rest fade into autumn."

This intriguing group of people who dedicate their time and energy to exploring the mere hunches of a bizarre man, where are they now bound? "We're on our way to London via Greenland and Iceland. After the British Isles, we plan to scour the European countryside. Beyond that, I imagine Russia will be a next step."

Is there anything we the watching public can do to help speed things along? "The best aid anyone can give us now is to stay out of our way. Everyone seems to know of a plant they feel I need to investigate. It's all very nice, but it costs time we don't have."

How does he find the plants? How does he so magically know which plants do combat ALLIS and which plants do not? "I don't know how to answer that. It's a gift I have that I can't explain."

What does he think is the cause behind ALLIS? "I can't answer that right now either. There's not enough time. Right now, finding a cure is the only hope."

Gurner then concluded the interview. "Thank you, but Brian [Johnson] is already in Europe, arranging transportation and interpreters. The rest of us have to get moving."

With those intriguing yet inadequate snatches of information, Gurner boarded a nonstop jet flight to Greenland.

Who is this question mark of a mystery man, this man who has captured all the world's hopes? Gurner, he calls himself, and no one seems able to trace a different or a second name to him. From 1990 through 2007 he filed taxes under the single name "Gurner." He has no record of taxes or a social security number before that time. His declared earnings during those years never topped $8,000 per year. Samuel Jackson of the Internal Revenue Service in Portland describes Gurner as "one of the thousands of unknown individuals who never fit into society, who by choice remain anonymous and out of the picture." Jackson hypothesizes that Gurner began earning money in his healing work, and being honest he also began to report taxes. Jackson states that the amounts were so piddling, the IRS never investigated.

We know his name is Gurner. We know that no school—herbal, medical or naturopathic—can claim having Gurner as a former student. We know he was an herbal healing practitioner outside the city of John Day, Oregon, and, according to the local populace, was successful in his work. We know he discovered an effective herbal cure for the disease ALLIS. The Food and Drug Administration and the American Medical Association attacked him and he fled into hiding. Months later, in the face of the seeming omnipotence of ALLIS, Gurner emerged from seclusion, forcing the United States government to bend to his demands. After the demise of the AC herb by a contested logging operation, this man managed to bring every government of the world into accord, agreeing to help him in his search for another ALLIS cure.

Does this very simplified account sound like the makings of a new world dictator endowed with incredible power? Some, including Jim Bowerns of the FDA, believe that to be the case.

Since Gurner first entered the ALLIS limelight, our readers have sent us varying opinions and scratches of information on him. Following are a few examples:

• About eight years ago, in Columbia Falls, Montana, this fellow that sure looks like the Gurner pictured in the papers heard me coughing and asked if he could help. I said it'd be nice, nobody else has been able to. After thirty minutes of sitting beside me in a silence where I'd thought he'd fallen asleep, he gave me some herbs to take over the next couple of months. Be doggone if the coughs didn't lessen and finally disappear. —S. Lewis, Whitefish, MT

• Gurner has to be God's gift to this Earth in its time of need. No one else can help us. —J. Sherton, Pascagoula, MI

• Let there be no doubt. This Gurner is Satan Incarnate. He talks (sacrilegiously, I might add) of God but never mentions Jesus' name. Who else but the devil himself would have the power to convert so many minds to his wishes? —Rev. O. Oddsgood, New York, NY

• Gurner for Prime Minister (or President). Wouldn't it be unique if elected officials had that kind of insight and intuition, and used it in such a caring manner? —S. Sunya, Montreal, Quebec, Canada

• Frankly, I mistrust him with every fiber of my (still alive) being. —H. Honer, San Diego, CA

• Doesn't it say somewhere that the meek shall inherit the Earth? Maybe they'll save it, too. —B. Burns, Lorain, OH

• What is he ultimately up to? That is what I ask. Does anyone else sense that with Gurner we've got an over-ambitious monarch in the making? —J. Bowerns, Washington, D.C.

Harold Reeves, *Newstime* reporter, member of the Gurner Gang, and the one representative of the media allowed to document Gurner and his group's activities first-hand, sends us his observations of the man. Gurner, notes Reeves, is mostly silent, mostly internalized, and totally dedicated to his task. He rarely talks superfluously and never talks of his past except to relate stories about the healing power of plants and other natural therapies. He is, states Reeves, an excellent healer. Reeves suffered what he himself labels a "compound, super-severely-sprained ankle with terrible complications and intolerable pain." Gurner, according to Reeves, wrapped the ankle in comfrey leaves, and that *incredible, miraculous plant* [emphasis is Reeves'] healed the "incurable" [quotations are Reeves'] in two days. Once, in northern Idaho, Stephanie Peters was bitten by a spider and suffered a severe allergic reaction. Gurner, says Reeves, disappeared into the woods and after a while returned with some herbs, one for a poultice, one for a tea that he brewed. Within fifteen minutes Dr. Peters' swelling reversed itself and her strained breathing began to ease.

Reeves states: "I can't fully offer an in-depth on Gurner. Gurner is half a mystery even to us continually stationed with him. I can give a few observations.

"He's very devoted to a communion with God, but it is definitely an individually cultivated communion. He's interesting to be with when he centers his attention outwardly, but in the next moment he can be somewhere far away inside of himself. He meditates often and thinks continually. He talks to himself, and he talks to his God, both aloud and freely. Personally, I've never met anyone whose actions showed more caring for others—or who talked less about it."

Who is the Gurner who holds the life of every individual on the contingency of his continuing benevolence and his ultimate success? Answers to these questions remain, like Gurner, aloof. As one reader, M. Haily of Dunnellon, FL, so aptly states: "Obviously, I need him. But he can't be my hero. Because I just don't know anything about him."

· · · · ·

ALLIS: YET ANOTHER UPDATE

The numbers are growing quite large. The numbers are growing too fast to accurately keep tabs on. And some of the highly trained statisticians who so adeptly handle numbers are now themselves a part of the numbers.

The numbers are quite scary. The numbers exceed the entire death toll of any war ever fought in all history.

The numbers continue to almost double every two weeks.

Worldwide, approximately one in every 120 people has died of the ALLIS disease. Fifty-five million casualties. If current doubling rates continue, in fourteen to sixteen weeks human life on Earth will be gone.

The numbers are as cold and ruthless as ALLIS itself.

The numbers are beginning to demonstrate their wearing ability. For three weeks the stock listings of every major world broker have declined in proportion to ALLIS' increasing increments. On July 8, the day the AH herb discovery emerged from General Medical in British Columbia, the stock market rallied over 300 points. Otherwise, there has been a steady decrease in trading and an average daily decline in share value of almost 20 points.

Governments are feeling an "ALLIS squeeze." Local, state and the many federal accounts report decreases in revenue. With fewer people, fewer taxes are being paid.

Some businesses boom. The undertaking and medical/health professions now deal with record numbers of clients. But nationwide, almost all retail businesses, from automobile sales to gift shops, report decreases in sales.

Dr. William Hogan, assistant to the U.S. surgeon general, once again reminds Americans to stress the positive side of this nightmare. Referring to the AH herb, Hogan states: "All right, America. We've hung in there, and now we've got a beginning. Don't jump the ship of hope just as the leak is about to be repaired. Pitch in with a positive attitude and a fair amount of patience, and we'll keep this vessel afloat."

We at *Newstime* send our encouragement and prayers to the scientists in British Columbia and to Gurner's Gang, somewhere in the skies over Europe.

· 24 ·
Conflict

July 19, 2008, 10:45 P.M. In the air, 2,000 feet above the dusk-colored hills of Northern England.

A twin-engine Otter droned slowly and lowly over the rolling, sunset-brushed Cheviot Hills that nominally separate Scotland from England. Back and forth the plane sailed, back and forth above the cultivated lands like a remote-control broom being swept first in one direction and then the other. The plane never covered the same territory twice. It gradually expanded its northerly east-west sweeping motion until the entire land mass between Kirkcudbright and Berwick-upon-Tweed had been touched by both its engine monotone and the closed eyes inside the plane viewing it. Having covered this swath of land, the plane then swung northward to the Southern Uplands, to once again systematically zigzag the island land mass between the North Channel and the North Sea.

Inside the plane, a woman's voice made no attempt to hide its irritability. "Gurner! Crumb! It's nighttime. It's dark. Goddammit, take a rest!"

Another just-as-perturbed voice testily yelled back. "Stephanie, back off my case. If we don't find something soon, there won't be enough scientists around to make anything we find later viable!"

The first voice was not going to be outdone, in loudness or in irritability. "You idiot! If you drop from adrenal exhaustion or your brain waves short out from no sleep, you won't be able to find anything for the scientists or anyone else!"

A third voice, equally out of humor, joined the contest. "Hey, you two chumps. Pipe down! Jeez, all this expedition needs right now is for you blokes to start fighting."

The first voice sallied. "Oh for crumb's sake, Willox. One day over the English landscape in a plane, and you're trying to sound like a native. Why don't you put your energies to better use and help me convince our moron leader that he's pushing himself and us too far?"

The second voice did not retreat. "You want to go to sleep, Peters, go to sleep. And I'm sure as hell not your leader, so quit thinking of yourself as an oppressed follower!"

The third voice changed its attack plans. "No, jeez, she's right, Gurner. *You* go 200 percent all the time; *we* go 200 percent all the time. It's the nature of this unit we've created. Trouble is, none of us have 200 percent left in them, including you. Frankly, you look like shit. We all look like shit. Tired, frustrated shit."

A fourth voice, less troubled, tried to soothe them. "Okay, friends. Let's all calm down. Why don't we try a different approach. We can . . . we can vote on whether or not to quit now."

Dr. Peters, the original voice, crisply counted all parley attempts. "Brian, why don't you take your democratic approach and shove it all the way up your—"

Something resembling lightning flashed through the plane's quarters. All four voices suspended for a moment.

Willox's voice—the third voice—now gained a deeper irritation. "Jeez, Harold! Now is not the goddamn time to be taking goddamn pictures."

Reeves proffered his winning-est smile, which resembled a starved scarecrow displaying ill-fitting dentures. "News is, is news, Jerry. No matter what its face."

Gurner resumed the conversation, raising its tone several decibels. "Look. There're blankets overhead. There's plenty of floor space in this plane. Why don't you whiners just sack out for a while. You can't help me scan the country anyway. I'll wake you if—"

The first voice exploded. *"Whiners?* Damn you, Gurner! Life gives you an extra piece of extrasensory cake, and you think that bequeaths you the right to do it all! When your ass cracks from fatigue, buddy, we'll see who's the whin—"

Willox did not let the tone or the intensity of the debate decline. "I've seen pigs in pig sties act better than this crew! And they didn't look like shit! Tired, fatigued sh—!"

"All I'm trying to say . . ." Nothing soothing was left in Johnson's voice. In fact, it carried through the plane louder than the rest. ". . . is that there's a better way to handle things! And what the hell do you mean, shove it—"

FLASH—

Four voices, in unison, bellowed at the reporter. "*Goddammit,
Harold! Not now! No goddamn pictures now!*"

Reeves merely returned an indifferent shrug of his bony shoulders.

Suddenly Gurner was crouched atop the plane seat, pointing
his fingers at the others, yelling. "Whiners! Whiners and weepers!
Whiners and weepers!"

The volume of the original voice equalled his. "Heroes! Goddamned crummy self-appointed heroes! Macho, mortal, maniacal,
moronic males, all of you!"

The body belonging to the third voice began jumping up and
down and shouting till its face turned bluish. "Shit! Nothing but
shit! Tired, fatigued shit, shit, shit!"

The one-time soothing and democratic voice was *not* going to
be outdone. "All the way up! Shove it all the way up yours too!
All the way up!"

The four voices embarked on a maximum-pitch yelling match.
Apt and not-so-apt body pantomiming simultaneously and naturally
occurred. And then, suddenly, they were all laughing. "Sorry
Whiners! . . . Worthless Heroes! . . . Shit! . . . Unending shit!
. . . All the way! . . . All the way Up! . . . Up! . . . Shit! . . .
Heroes! . . . Whiners!"

Finally, all the actors in this melee grabbed hands and screamed
together at the top of their voices.

"YAAAAAAAAAHHHHHHHH!!"

FLASH—

. . . . .

11:10 P.M.

Peace had returned to the interior of the Otter aeroplane.

*Oh my great goodness. My sides hurt. We must have been
helpless for ten minutes, laughing, laughing so wonderfully. I've
been chronicling this journey to Mary, but this episode, I doubt
I'll be able to convey its depth to her. And how badly we needed
it. I feel like I'm starting anew. . . . I wonder if old Jim Bowerns
has ever experienced free craziness and the open laughter of
release like that? . . . I wonder why he popped into my mind just
now?*

·····

Jeez. Did we need that. If I could ever get a bunch of hard-core environmentalists and hard-core developers into that mode of nuttiness at a conference table . . . it would do everyone's soul good, sharing a hollering session and a laugh like that . . .

Hmmm. 'Cept they'd all probably take it too seriously, and it'd end up in a great big fistfight. . . . But now it feels like we've got the energy to continue. And continue we gotta. Every day when I call home, I'm so scared Jenny'll say she's got ALLIS. Wish there was more I could do to help Gurner speed things along.

·····

Crap anyway. I can't, can't believe it! I cannot believe this. Twenty years in photography. Awards and more awards. And I goddamn didn't catch the film tail on the roller, and the film didn't advance and catch those pictures. Crap. That one of them all yelling and hugging together could have made the National Geographic cover. Well, at least the National Enquirer . . . I'm sure glad the crew is back on the wavelength again. It was getting too scattered here.

·····

Oh crumb. I can't stop laughing even yet. And my ribs are killing me. Stop now, Stephanie! Everyone else is in control. Oh, those poor pilots. What that must have looked like to them, the world saviors losing their marbles. Aboard THEIR airplane. Oh ha ha ah ha ha ha stop Stephanie, you've got to stop . . . how many people would you cure, and how many doctors would you help if you could get patient and physician to laugh together like that? Did Gurner lead us to that, or did it just happen? It all felt too natural to be a ploy. And when we hugged afterwards . . . we might as well have been baptized. Everything feels charged now, ready to fight another round . . . crumb. There was that hug with Gurner. Oh I wish I weren't so attracted to that man. He sure isn't attracted to me. But hell, he isn't attracted to anyone. Never seen a man so totally oblivious. Look at him now. Back to work. Reading the landscape at night from a plane window. Trying to save a dying world. Probably in deep communion with his

Creator and experiencing all kinds of major revelations and visionary insights.

. . . . .

God, ol' Buddy. That was great. We do need a break. Maybe when we land in Glasgow we can get a Scottish pizza and catch some kind of a late show. Let's keep the lightness going just a little longer.

End of Book III

BOOK IV

RESPONSIBILITY

♦ 25 ♦
Earthview

August 2, 2008, 7:03 P.M. Fifty-five thousand feet elevation, over central Europe; course due north.

B-1B bombers were not designed for sightseeing. Human passengers who felt that amenities like large windows would be nice were quite out of luck. Gurner made do as best he could, perched on one of the aircraft's co-pilot seats and staring through a cubby window at an Earth so far below it held no recognizable shapes. His thoughts focused on that delicate Earth, so far below.

My God. What have we done to Your world? Omniscience is supposedly one of Your stronger points, but . . . how long has it been since You cast an inspecting eye toward this planet and observed what teeming mankind has left of Your original work? How long, oh God, since You've tallied what we've left, both for You and for our own future generations?

Maybe You have. Maybe You've given the place a rigid inspection, saw what I'm now seeing. And fled in disgust and disbelief. Maybe You are even now reconsidering bestowing free will on whatever creatures inhabit the next rare and living world You create in the middle of dead space. Free will has proven itself to be kind of an accursed gift down here, especially when by a vote of about four to one the inhabitants of this terrene, through their actions, opt for desertification, deforestation, declimatization, toxification, and over-population of a quite finite resource.

Gurner cocked his head upward and tried to peer at the sky above the plane. He whispered, softly, so the pilots wouldn't suffer through more of his one-on-None dialogues. "Ahhhh, what the hell do I know about purposes behind Divine gifts?"

The healer, as glum as a skyline in a stage III pollution alert, pressed his nose against the plastic window. *But it's pretty bad, pretty sad what we've done to Your once-in-an-eternity work of art called Earth.* He silently reviewed the past several weeks' course of events.

Shoot, it's amazing, the tracks this journey is taking. Puddling around in a propeller plane was not getting the land masses of this planet examined in ALLIS' limited time schedule. So now— believe it or not—the Gang and I are soaring at 50,000 feet over vast territories in a B-1B bomber . . . one quite reluctantly "volunteered" by the U.S. Air Force.

I had to come out of "seclusion" and create a hot and heavy press conference. So precious time wouldn't be wasted haggling over authorizing civilian usage of a military machine, I had to play on people's fears via the news media again.

Gurner sighed, started to speak aloud, thought a moment and then redirected his thoughts to his mind. *People are scared. Real scared. And once again, real scared people forced the government to act. Then the government made the military cooperate, so now I've got a state-of-the-art aircraft—minus bombs—and proportionately more enemies.*

Gurner glanced at a particular button on the instrument panel, labeled with a piece of tape stating "Bombs Away." *How ironic, that part of the cause of ALLIS may speed the finding of a cure.*

The healer sank deeper into the co-pilot seat as he returned his nose to the window.

Somehow, God, for some reason, my perceptive abilities have again increased. From this incalculable distance in the air, I can intuitively scan an entire small country and read the patterns and hear the whispers from the energies of the plant biota below. It's amazing, to somewhere in my head be able to discern which of these many, many voices may be beneficial for the ALLIS disease. Harold insists that I explain how I accomplish this. I keep having to say, "It just happens, that's all I know." Harold grumbles a lot about inadequate answers.

So, when I feel a promising energy pull from a place, like the Adriatic coast of Northern Italy, this supersonic jet heads for the nearest airport that can accommodate it. From there, jet helicopters race us to the general land location, and we zero in on what is hopefully a deadly thorn in the side of ALLIS.

Gurner sighed again, wearily leaned back in his seat, and forgot about his attempts to remain silent. "As Harold would say, 'crap anyway, crap anyway.'"

For some reason, at this altitude I can feel the vibrations of the plant life below, but I can't distinguish between present, living-now species and the endless array of voices from the plants of the past. I keep hearing distant voices of the plant species that are no more. They plague my mind wherever I go. I thought the States were bad, with their overgrazing and clear-cuts and urban sprawl. But shoot, this European-Mediterranean-Western Russian quadrant of the world sounds more dead than alive. It reverberates more from the what-once-was side of life than it does from the what-is-now-alive sector.

One could never guess that the face of Gurner had ever smiled. *Indeed, dear God. What have we done to Your world?*

—In Southern Greece I sensed a plant that would have countered ALLIS. My whole being tingled inside, sure that the long search was over. But the sheep and goats had left nothing under seven feet tall alive on that hillside. Whoever that plant was, it's now a voice from the past.

—There once was a forest outside of Frankfurt. There once was an herb that You placed in that forest just in case a disease like ALLIS got manufactured. Unfortunately, that herb grew in part of the 80 percent of the German forest that is dying because of acid rain and industrial pollutants. And that herb is 100 percent dead. It's another voice from the past.

—The Baltic Sea coast of Poland. Must have been a beautiful spot once upon a dream. Must have also held a rare species that cured weird twenty-first-century diseases. I felt it there when we explored, a voice that now could only say "I was" instead of "I am." In fact, this whole block of Eastern European countries is trashed beyond description. Ecologically, it's nearly vibrationless.

—Israel's come a long way, "baby." They've converted the desert into an agricultural paradise. But ALLIS also chooses the chosen ones, especially when you consider that they didn't choose to do a biological diversity study before converting all those acres to croplands. Some unsung species used to live in those tilled acres that, considering present circumstances, would have been better than manna.

—Once upon a time there was the world's fourth largest inland body of water called the Aral Sea. But the Soviets diverted so much of the waters that fed it that the sea has dropped forty feet elevation and sixty miles from its original shorelines. Where lack of water doesn't kill the coastline plants of this now SIXTH largest

inland water body, the salt and dust storms off the dry sea beds do. It killed forever some ex-plant that called to me, one wanting to help fight ALLIS.

Gurner, eyes closed, drooped so far into the co-pilot seat that he about fell out of it. *Oh, what have we done to Your world, God? ALLIS isn't a plague sent by big You to punish little us. But we humans have sure chopped the heads off these saving-grace plants before they've had a chance to speak. What hasn't been Chernobyled has been flooded by dams; what hasn't been dammed has been shredded under tank tracks or artillery shell explosions. Rome and Paris and Istanbul and Birmingham spread their boundaries into the countryside and no one ever asked what they were destroying in the process. If my inner readings are correct, each one of those cities destroyed an unknown species of some rare plant that I know to my depths would have helped the world.*

I'd weep, like Jerry does when he witnesses such mindless destruction. But the void inside is too much to even let tears flow.

Gurner bowed his head forward. *A void. On an etheric and physical level, our blue-green Earth is beginning to feel like a colorless void.*

His shoulders sagged under the weight of his thoughts. *And soon we head over the Third World countries, the monstrous populations of Asia and Africa.*

His back slouched, and his head slowly moved from side to side. *And I don't know how many more voices from the past I can bear to listen to.*

In his seat, the healer sat scrunched into a curled fetal position. *Help, God. Help me hear a few laughing plant intonations that are presently alive, and who speak of an ability to stunt ALLIS. And if You want to throw some more time in, that'd be great. Because at the present rate, we're not going to make it in time.*

Hear my prayers for effective, live plants and for time. Hear my prayers, because I not only hear the cries of the dying plants and animals of Earth. I hear the cries of the dying people.

Gurner shook his head and struggled to regain an upright sitting position. He spoke aloud, again forgetting Air Force pilots beside him. "No quick and easy answer, huh? Just silence again, huh? Oh well, I'm getting used to it."

The healer again gazed out the window. *Well, onward, I guess. First we land this bird in Stockholm and then jaunt up to the northern corner of Sweden. Somebody of the plant kingdom is—or was—there, and needs to be investigated. Shoot. I suppose England's industrial wastes, blowing across the North Sea, have smothered this one too.*

I'm so doggone ready to have this expedition over with and just go wandering again, alone, into some last, untouched forest . . .

. . . before it, too, disappears.

. . . . .

7:04 P.M.

The crew compartments of the B-1B equaled the flight cabin in austerity. The four other members of the Gurner Gang had to settle themselves into the odd corners and positions and make the best of day-by-day life on a warplane. One member no longer griped about the lack of view and windows. He didn't want to see any more.

Jeez, I don't think I can continue as part of this outfit any longer. I don't think I can witness any more of what a purposeless catastrophe the ecology of this Earth has become. If what we've seen and experienced so far represents the fruits of the more "civilized and intelligent" societies of Earth . . . man, my heart just ain't gonna make it through the Third World. I don't think a committed environmentalist can survive a scenic trip like this one.

Jerry Willox, staring listlessly at a metal wall and ceiling, lay on a mat on the plane's floor.

Ohhh, I wish that every Senator and Congressperson, President and Interior Department official that ever hatcheted a land, air, or water protection initiative could be forced to take this trip. Fly the northern corner of Africa along the thirtieth latitude. See desertification in its greatest magnitude. Listen to that old Algerian guide talk about how at one time grasslands used to cover so much more of the now lifeless desert. Maybe they'd understand that nobody thought such a land disaster could occur, and occur so rapidly. And realize that in their positions they hold the key to prevent America from slipping into the same dying path.

I wish that every Forest Service and BLM permanent employee, especially the higher-ups, could be required to spend time touring what's left of the European forests. And study on what stretches of beauty they used to be. SEE what pitiful, dying, minuscule souvenirs they are now. Maybe they'd get a perspective on what rare treasures they're responsible for protecting at home.

I wish that every board member of every industry with a smokestack had to live a month in smog-dead Krakow. And every miner had to spend a stint in "metal-fever" Glogow. I don't think they'd object to added environmental protection costs if they had to inhale a bit of Poland's "Environment is the price of progress" reality.

Every American who tours the world comes home full of appreciation for the freedom of life in the United States. I can't understand why they're not filled with a religious fervor to protect its ecosystems. We've still got a lot of what most of the rest of the world has lost.

Willox closed his eyes and reviewed some of the images he'd recently observed.

But I've had my tour. And I'm thinking I gotta leave. Enough pain is enough.

The environmentalist's eyelids jolted open.

Hmmmm. Can't take it? What I would force every other American to experience? But jeez, dead rivers and dying seas, air that doesn't even contain enough oxygen for breathing, whole forests whose browning foliage looks like a delicate garden after a hard frost smears it . . . it all hits like an arrow through the middle of my heart.

And Gurner, damn him, leading us on all these hopeful explorations to plants that don't exist any more. What the hell is he doing? It's hard enough having to tune into what's VISIBLE, without also being shown the extinction processes we can't see.

Willox uncrossed his arms and repositioned them with hands folded behind his head. His eyes again closed. *So quit, Jerry. Quit and split. Go home. Hug my Jenny and be with my Johnny. Watch Gurner's progress from a Channel 7 news report rather than be part of the personal agony that happens every time he discovers something that's not there anymore.*

Why don't I just quit and doggone go home?

Willox suddenly sat himself upright and stared straight into the cabin wall. *"Daddy, I just learned in history class. You were once part of the team that found the cure for ALLIS, weren't you?"*

"Why yes, Johnny, I was."

"Were you the one who quit, Daddy?"

"Well, er, yes, I guess I was that too."

"Why, Daddy?"

"Well, son, I think it was because I loved this Earth so much

that I couldn't stand seeing any more rivers polluted until they were without life. Nor could I any longer touch land that once supported animals and people but had turned to desert. I just cried over the various plants and animals that had disappeared from the planet altogether. Especially the living things that disappeared from life forever, Johnny, that was the hardest of all to be around."

"Gee, Daddy, do you think that some of those plants and animals would have made it if you hadn't quit?"

Willox's head slowly bent forward until it rested against the wall in front of him.

So I'll continue as long as this crew continues. What has kept me going, and working, and clawing for tiny handholds on a glass wall of greedy indifference for thirty-plus years—future generations—now has the face of my son . . .

. . . Future generations and my son. Even if we do successfully counter ALLIS, they and he still inherit our woebegone Earth. They still have no easy time ahead of them.

·····

7:05 P.M.

Harold Reeves crumpled another piece of paper and tossed it by his feet, where it joined a growing pile of crumpled papers.

Crap anyway. I can't send in this report. Too touchy. Too easily misinterpreted. Too subject to media aggrandizement. Too much truth in it.

I mean, sure, this gang is in a morale slump, but who wouldn't be when the human species you work night and day to save has guillotined the cure, many times over, in a few polluting decades.

But if I send a communiqué to the networks about our low spirits, sure as hell headlines will sprout up all over the world: "Gurner's Gang ready to give up search."

Reeves rapidly scribbled a few ideas onto a clean sheet of paper.

My job is to report. I've always done just that. But I know that the hopes of the human species are dangling on the thread of this group of searchers. People hate Gurner a lot more than they love him. But if they think he's failed them, if they think he's quit on them, they'll kill first him and then themselves. The morale of mankind is just too low at this point for that kind of disappointment.

That sheet of paper joined and topped the crumple pile.

What we need is a great big success. Or at least something significant. Something to kick us in the pants. But crap, other than immediately finding a cure, I can't think of what it would be.

· · · · ·

7:06 P.M.

They didn't teach us about this in medical school.

Dr. Peters sat straight in her seat. Her jaws were clenched, her facial expression as rigid as her spine. *Crumb, I must have repeated that statement three hundred times since this Gurner Gang journey began.*

I can tentatively diagnose just about anything in anybody. I can insert any number of remarkable instruments into any orifice the body offers. And if that's not enough, I can cut a few of my own openings. I can mend, replace, or remove a whole gamut of human parts and appliances. I can dispense an array of chemicals that'll force the body to do just about everything, including sometimes heal itself.

Dr. Peters' sigh was her only bodily motion.

But they never taught me how to inject positive attitudes into overwhelmed minds.

Crumb, I'm glad I'm not so uncommonly intuitive like Gurner. Knowing what isn't there any more, that can't be an easy gift to bear.

And I'm glad I don't have such an intense love affair with this planet, like Jerry. This journey, for him, must be like watching his beloved die of Lou Gehrig's disease . . . cell by cell atrophy . . . irreversible . . . incurable.

The doctor's two hands suddenly clenched shut into fists.

But right now, how do I say it to them? I want to grab 'em by something that dangles, shake 'em good and hard, and yell at 'em:

"Hey, you morbid, morose prophet. Cheer up. I thought the nature of the God you talk to is joy. You're about as radiant as burnt toast!

"Hey, you pitiable, long-faced ecologist. Lighten up. Nobody's going to want to fight for the Earth if they see that losing a few rounds leaves their leader looking like a walking funeral.

"Hey, you pensive, double-talking reporter. How about some

cheer? If you can't write happy lines with your pencils, at least draw some smiling faces.

"*Hey, you careworn characters. Get with it here. ALL IS NOT GLOOM AND DOOM, for crumb's sake.*"

. . . Well, that's what I want to do.

Dr. Peters' fists unclenched.

I'm not so blind that I can't see how bad it really is on this modern-day industrial and military Earth. You get so high up in one of these planes and see how limited the planet really is. You carry with you the realities of the environmental degradation we've encountered. You can't help but realize that the limit has been exceeded.

But Gurner and Jerry dwell on it. That's their problem. They can't just shrug it off and let things go until the time is right to deal with it. They CANNOT do anything about the dying planet RIGHT NOW. People dying from ALLIS have priority. It's that simple.

Her body slowly relaxed its tensions as she turned to face the cockpit. *Rx for Gurner and Willox, by S. Peters, attending physician: QUIT THINKING. GET ON WITH THE WORK AT HAND.*

. . . And that's what they're going to do, if I have to perform a couple of lobotomies to get it done.

. . . . .

7:36 P.M.

"*Dear Mary,*

"*It's been a few days now since I last wrote. As always, even more so since Gurner secured this high-flying monster, we've been busy beyond belief. Plus, the attitudes of this crew have been in the dumps. I thought I'd write when spirits elevated themselves again.*

"*Well, I guess one could say that in the last half an hour, spirits have elevated. Been placed on a burner turned to high heat forms a better description.*

"*Briefly, we were all sinking deeper and deeper into a slump. This inch by inch touring of the planet has shown us what Jerry and other environmentalists already knew. Day after day, we witness biota destroyed by pollution and population and unfettered development. Then, to further the fun, for some reason Gurner, in his wondrous way, started tuning into plant species that are no longer living. That are extinct. I don't understand, but for some reason his perceptions now often lead us on plant treasure hunts to lands that are just gruesome with filth and pollution and whose herbal gem is . . . no more. Each time our quest of finding a cure for ALLIS is thwarted by an environmental degradation that could have been prevented, the general cheer of this group plummets. Mind you, this sequence has been happening for weeks. Until about thirty minutes ago, we were in a slump about as benumbing as some of the soul-less pieces of land we've recently visited."*

Johnson adjusted his seat belt. He was the only person on the jet wearing one.

"And then . . . Mary, it was exquisite. Gurner was perched in the cockpit with the pilots. He hadn't smiled for days. Jerry Willox sat in a corner by himself, brooding. Harold endlessly crumpled his notes and continually swore to himself. Suddenly, Stephanie jumped out of her seat, forcefully strode toward the cockpit, snagged by the coat collar a very surprised Jerry Willox and hauled him along, and together they charged into the cockpit. Jerry looked like a feeble bird following a bolt of lightning.

"I had an eagle's-eye view from my crew seat. I've never witnessed anything quite like this.

"Gurner looked up in wonder as she burst into the little quarter. That was surely the least graphic expression his face would portray for the next ten minutes. She began at about three-quarters volume, calling them—Gurner and Willox—the dumbest, most bleating, dull-eyed, inconsistent jackasses she had ever met. Gurner's face went from surprise to shock. So did Jerry's, and the two Air Force pilots. Her list of adjectives grew, and so did her volume, and she began covering the gamut of human idiocies, from insensitive to self-centered to impractical. She said Gurner and Jerry might as well be baby brats in diapers, considering the lack of character they've displayed these last couple of weeks.

"I watched their faces—especially Jerry's—go from astonishment to anger. A heck of a fight was portending. But she let no one interrupt her and poured out volume and words at full throttle, letting them know that they in no way lived up to the ideals that God, Nature, or anything else they held sacred offered them. She told them that by being such morose, ungrateful, unpleasant, and moody sourpusses they were in effect nullifying everyone's efforts, AND being fools and hypocrites besides.

"I saw Jerry take in a sharp breath, about to explode. But right then he noticed that a broad grin was sprouting on Gurner's face. A grin of recognition and acknowledgement. A grin of agreement. I think Stephanie knew then that she had won the battle, but she didn't stop yelling. She told them to get with the program, to quit being such self-pitying, senseless egotists and to turn this morbid energy into positive work toward healing ALLIS.

"And then she stomped out of the cockpit. Jerry still looked a bit shocked, but Gurner was beginning to laugh in a big way. Harold also started laughing and began writing one of his never-ending reports. As Stephanie passed me, I thought she might spend the rest of her whirlwind force on me. But I smiled—a big, toothful, exaggerated grin—and she nodded and sailed past.

"Mary, she knew what was needed. The air is lighter now. It feels like we passed a crisis and can focus on our task. I don't know if the poor pilots caught in the middle of this will ever understand. But I hear Gurner directing them toward Sweden with more enthusiasm than he's displayed for a long while."

Johnson tilted his head back and took three full breaths.

"So my darling, I better close this letter. With practice I'm getting better at controlling my airsickness. But a limit still does exist.

"I love you. So much."

✦ 26 ✦
Newstime

August 7, 2008. Excerpts from *Newstime* magazine.

LOOK OUT ALLIS, HERE WE COME

Scene one. Kiruna, Sweden.

Question: Where in the world is Kebnekaise?

Answer: It's that 7,000-foot, highest-in-the-nation mountain peak South of Abisko, west of Jikkasjärvi, and forming the head waters of the Kalixälven River.

Question: Say what?

While the geography of northwest Sweden may not be familiar to most readers, a simple, timely, and most welcome two-word phrase now being broadcast from this nearly uninhabited portion of the globe is forming a song of hope the entire world understands.

Those words are: ALLIS CURE!

That is to say, another *potential* ALLIS cure has been discovered.

The renowned assemblage of five known as the Gurner Gang has again presented a gift more precious than all monies combined. After two weeks of error-ridden attempts to discover an ALLIS-beneficial medicinal plant, Gurner and his associates have zeroed in on a Scandinavian tundra plant. The world's focus now centers upon a species of alpine moss that abounds in the above-timberline environment of the mountains along the northern Sweden-Norway border.

On August 3, Gurner's B-1B bomber landed in Sweden's capital city of Stockholm. He and environmentalist Jerry Willox and *Newstime* correspondent Harold Reeves then traveled in Swedish Air Force F-14 jets to the isolated burg of Kiruna, a small city 100 miles north of the Arctic circle. From here, waiting helicopters transported them to the barren slopes of Kebnekaise Mountain.

Newstime correspondent Reeves notes Gurner's excitement as he began exploring the mountainside. His eagerness increased as he studied—in his own internal and mysterious manner—a small mountain moss. Finally Gurner yelled, "Jerry, this is another one, I'm sure of it!" He and Willox gathered large quantities of the abundant herb. The Air Force escort and the three "Gang" members raced back to the nearby town. From Kiruna, the Gang immediately flew to Stockholm, where Brian Johnson and Dr. Stephanie Peters were recruiting ALLIS victim volunteers for testing at central medical facilities. Initial testing procedures on this new plant soon began.

Initial testing via the Gurner method leaves most researchers shaking their heads. Gurner's procedure is quite simple. No blood or other laboratory tests are required; no expensive and complicated machinery is called into use. Gurner places his hands on the ALLIS volunteer and settles into a state of closed-eye meditation. The healer and Dr. Peters then offer the person a strongly brewed cup of herbal tea. The tea, in this present case, is brewed from the foliage and flowers of the Kebnekaise moss (tentatively called the AK herb). Gurner then directs the attending hospital staff to administer this same tea to the patient every so often, depending upon the information his meditation offered him.

Twenty-five ALLIS victims in various stages of the disease received AK herb tea. And the waiting began.

Results from less than one week of tests are too tentative to allow solid conclusions. But two patterns from the initial experiments have been indicated. One, sadly, is that AK does *not* have the capacity of AC to be the cure-all herb for ALLIS. This herb does not seem able to stop the progression of ALLIS. The hopeful news from Stockholm is that the Kebnekaise moss reverses one of ALLIS' primary effects, the lowering of the body's core temperature. Persons not yet in the coma stage of the disease who were given AK regained near-normal core temperatures. People inflicted with ALLIS and given AK do continue to experience a loss of muscular strength and do continue to slip into a comatose state before dying of the disease. But one might say, at the risk of sounding callous, at least they die warm.

Researchers now have another clue to follow, another potential to investigate. That the ALLIS coma may not be induced by hypothermia opens a new line of thought. Since the tiniest clue could advance a cure, Gurner's efforts have given science another avenue to explore.

Scientists from around the world are journeying to the Mount Kebnekaise site. By Gurner's request, a United Nations contingent of armed police has been stationed on the mountain. "Mainly," says the healer, "to enforce protection of the fragile tundra environment." Quantities of the one other plant species known to have a halting effect on ALLIS—AH from British Columbia, Canada—are being flown to Stockholm. Scientists hope to determine what effects a combined mixture of AH and AK will have on ALLIS-stricken persons.

The wilds of Oregon. The wilds of British Columbia. And now the wilds of Sweden. Correspondent Reeves quoting enviornmentalist Willox: "I hope people are beginning to notice that it's plants coming from the country they've left wild that may just save their asses."

Question number two: And the man who forms the centerpiece of these ass-saving, optimism-bestowing discoveries, where is he during the hubbub of activity now occurring in Sweden?

Answer: Gurner? Why, he's in South America, of course.

Question: Say what?

Scene two. Mirante de Serra, Rondonia, Brazil.

It has often been proven that overpopulation and the massive raw-material needs of twenty-first-century humankind destroy biosystems before these unique parcels of variegated life can be fully studied and appreciated. Nowhere on Earth is ecological rack and ruin more evident and more potentially ominous than in the tropical rain forest regions of the Earth. Oregon, British Columbia, Sweden, and now the upper Amazon. Once again, a parcel of the wildland that has been preserved may offer humans a key to the locked door of ALLIS.

Rondonia is a jungled sub-state of Western Brazil, bordered on the west by Bolivia. It's an unknown land, isolated and containing a treasure chest of primal rain forest biota. At least, such was the case until the mid 1970s when World Bank loans financed Brazilian government colonization plans and paved the passage for settlement and population migration to the area. Since then, Rondonia has played host to an incalculable number of migrants. These land-hungry, mostly poor settlers have roaded, deforested, mined, and burned close to 60 percent of the Brazilian Northwest Region frontier rain forest.

In the late '80s, under sharp criticism for its development-only policies, the World Bank placed a hold on loans to Brazil until several environmental assurances and aboriginal Indian protection clauses were met. Thanks to this economic pressure, one of the small corners of the Brazilian jungle now declared inviolate is the Urueu-Wau-Wau Indian Reserve. No longer—on paper and in theory anyway—can slash-and-burn farmers and dig-and-desert miners lay waste a pristine portion of forest that housed an innocent tribe of native forest gatherers.

Presently, on a worldwide basis, it appears that that particular action was a damned lucky piece of preservation.

His name is Ianiá. He claims to be a Urueu-Wau-Wau tribal chieftain. On August 5, Ianiá and seven warriors approached the FUNAI outpost of Alta Lídia in Rondonia. (FUNAI is Brazil's National Foundation for the Native Indian.) Luckily for the small staff of FUNAI representatives, Ianiá offered signs of peace. After appropriate greeting and gift exchanges, Ianiá asked to speak to "the man who talks to plants." No one at Alta Lídia had an inkling what the Indian chieftain meant, and they expressed their confusion. A complex verbal communications effort ensued. Finally, what Chief Ianiá wanted, and what he offered, became electrically clear.

Four months earlier, to the north and east of Rondonia, a French biological research team discovered a rare species of jungle orchid they claimed exhibited curative effects on the ALLIS disease (*Newstime*, June 26, 2008). These hopeful statements were never proved because, after the French boasted of their find, multitudes from the city of Manaus flocked to the discovery sight, uprooting and devastating the plant they thought might save them from disease. That was a single-site species of orchid.

The French research team, led by internationally renowned biologist Dr. Jeane Lamour, resumed its quest for a biological ALLIS cure, investigating the rain forests surrounding the Medeira River, a large tributary of the upper Amazon. This tiring foot journey eventually led them into the jungles of Rondonia. They investigated the Pacaas' Novos National Park, an untouched preserve of forest that lies in the middle of the Urueu-Wau-Wau Indian Reserve. FUNAI arranged for native Urueu-Wau-Wau guides to accompany the team, both to serve as knowledgeable scouts and to prevent the medicine necklaces of the warlike Urueu-Wau-Wau from becoming adorned with French teeth. Two of Chief Ianiá's tribesmen were in this guiding party.

The French biologists did not have the healer Gurner's intuitive ability to listen to the medicinal offerings of plants. Finding nothing, they eventually left the Indian reserve. But what they lacked in perception, the French made up in words. Nighttime campfire stories centered on the ALLIS disease, and on the quests of Gurner and the latest news from wherever in the wide world he was traveling. Through the French, Ianiá's men learned the cause of the unexplainable deaths of some of their tribesmembers. They also heard stories of an uncharacteristic white man who was presently searching the world for an herbal cure for the disease . . . a man who could listen to the plants. From these Urueu-Wau-Wau guides, Ianiá and his tribespeople heard these stories.

Selected members of the Urueu-Wau-Wau tribe have long practiced the applications of medicinal herbs. With the manifestation of this new disease, the tribe's healers plied their skills and eventually focused on a plant that does have a curative effect on ALLIS. When asked to reveal the plant, Ianiá emphatically stated that he would reveal it to no one but "the man who talks to plants."

Someone at Alta Lídia that day was thinking. Someone did not do what was expected of him and radio this incredible news to the government of Brazil. Someone at Alta Lídia deserves a hero's medal, because that day, via short-wave radio, he contacted a United Nations relief team in Brasilia and relayed this amazing news to them. The Brazilia UN official phoned the New York UN office, which transmitted the news to Sweden and to the officials in touch with Gurner. Gurner, having just finished his initial tests on the newly discovered AK herb, received this news with irrepressible elation. He was quoted as saying, "C'mon Brian, if we split right now we won't have to listen to Stephanie lecture us on why we need sleep." Johnson and Gurner immediately taxied to the Stockholm airport, where they boarded the waiting B-1B. Reeves, with several cameras hanging from his neck and loose notepaper scattering in every direction, ran up the boarding platform, banged on the aircraft door, and was admitted. In an unprecedented display of international cooperation via radio communications, the B-1B flew directly to Rio de Janeiro, Brazil. Gurner, Johnson, and Reeves were greeted by Brazilian officials, and all immediately jetted to Porto Velho. From there they were helicoptered to the patch of cleared ground in a sea of jungle named Alta Lídia.

At this issue's press time, all that is known is that Gurner, Johnson, Reeves, and two long-time members of FUNAI are in the Rondonian jungle with Chief Ianiá and his tribe's people. An assortment of quite miffed Brazilian officials were, at the chief's and Gurner's insistence, left behind at Alta Lídia.

Gurner apparently holds high hopes—or perhaps great intuitive expectations—for this site. He does not want a repeat of the French Orchid Disaster. Reeves' last report stated the healer's instructions for a large force of international military to be immediately placed around the Urueu-Wau-Wau reserve borders. A large contingent of military personnel from seventeen countries is currently en route to the Amazon.

Scene Three: The Census Bureau.

For nearly eleven months, ALLIS death statistics have shown an uncanny and relentless ability to approximately double numbers every two to three weeks. The July 13th tally, as listed by the U.S. Census Bureau, placed the mounting death toll at over 55 million persons. If the disease's nonwavering patterns had continued, the most recent ALLIS death update would have claimed over 100 million persons. But something has gone wonderfully awry. The August 5th weekly ALLIS tally released by the Census Bureau lists worldwide ALLIS deaths at 86 million persons.

"These statistics form the most accurate, most up-to-date compilation of figures in the world," says Henry Avins, acting director of the ALLIS Statistical Evaluation Office of the Census Bureau. "This is not a government manipulation of figures. These are the bona-fide numbers, carefully researched and documented. In this last two-week period, although total numbers are still increasing, the death rate of ALLIS, for the first time, has dropped."

Hopefully, this good news will continue. Hopefully, the death rate decrease isn't simply a one-time fluke. Thirty million persons dying in a two-week period is hardly reason for celebration. But if the ALLIS death rate continues to decrease, it may signify that the disease could eventually level off. Perhaps humankind is developing an immunity toward the disease, however undetectably.

All of science, all of humanity, is voicing a unified "I hope so."

Scene four: Vancouver, British Columbia.

The disease named ALLIS suddenly finds itself counterattacked from Sweden and Brazil. The number of fatalities appears to be declining. Unfortunately, the primary battle line, led by the AH herb of Northern British Columbia, has stalled.

Two and a half weeks ago Gurner presented science with an herb, labeled AH, that delayed the final stage—the dying stage—of ALLIS. No one at that time knew why or how this plant worked. It temporarily kept the ALLIS-comatose person from dying. It has offered from seven to twelve days of continued life for a person in the ALLIS coma.

Now, two and a half weeks later—$300 million later, a severe taxing of some of the greatest scientific minds and pieces of equipment later—no one yet knows why or how the AH herb works on ALLIS, only that it does.

Dr. Immanuel Gonzales of Spain's Madrid University and one of nine international researchers coordinating AH investigative efforts, notes that lack of funding, poor equipment, incomplete cooperation and feeble efforts have *not* been the reasons AH remains elusive. "Never have I seen people from of all over the world working together like a precision clock. Never before have all the governments of all the nations walked so hand in hand trying to solve a problem."

Amid such unprecedented international synergy, AH—the ALLIS Hopeful herb—has been analyzed to its tiniest physical components. Every fragment of plant material has been synthesized in the chemical laboratory, and every particular has been tested on hundreds of ALLIS patients in an effort to determine what in the plant halts the disease's progress. Dr. Gonzales shakes his head and voices the burning frustration of every scientist: "The AH herb in natural state, it works. Single laboratory parts of the herb, they don't work. Mixing every part of the plant back together via the laboratory, that doesn't work. Only the leaves and flowers of the original plant work. Why? We don't know. Goddammit to hell, we don't know."

Frightening ramifications surround the inability to isolate and synthesize the active principle of the AH herb. The foremost consideration is that ALLIS, although slowed slightly according to the latest death-rate statistics, imposes a quite limited deadline. More immediately, freezing temperatures and winter can move into the British Columbia mountains within a month. Massive quantities of AH are being gathered and dried. Every researcher and scientist desperately hopes to isolate the curative principle of the plant while a fresh supply is available.

Perhaps the AK herb of Sweden or the latest plant dubbed AR of Rondonia, Brazil, will hold the clue that decodes the AH herb in British Columbia. That's the hope. That's the fervent prayer. But a nightmare rears its head: the idea that none of the plants will have an ingredient that science can isolate and synthesize in time. Dr. Gonzales, speaking for his world colleagues and for the hundreds of researchers working under him, feels that this will not happen. "By God, an answer does exist. We will find it. Even if we have to approach this problem at a different, unscientific level."

• 27 •
Experience

August 14, 2008, 8:45 P.M. In the heaven-reaching mountains south of the Chinese border, north of the capital city of Thimphu, Bhutan.

Four male voices, voices not tuned to the same key, sang, croaked, rasped, and tremoloed in fair unison through the crisp and silent mountain air:

"So put another log o-on the fire, *Doctor*,
And come and tell me why you're leaving me!"

Stephanie Peters laughed—maliciously—as she placed a blackened pot on the grate above the open fire. "You crummy simians think you're hot stuff, don't you, having an M.D. serving as your campfire cook? But I've been meaning to tell you. For the last two weeks I've been lacing these meals with heavy doses of gonadotropin, steroids, and rat crap. In about three days, your nuts are gonna drop off."

Willox looked aghast as he spoke. "Jeez! That's why Harold looks like he's growing breasts. I couldn't tell for sure under all those cameras."

The inimitable reporter quickly glanced down the front of his shirt as he answered. "And, and you, Jerry. The woodsman's voice is beginning to sound like a piccolo when it calls through the forest."

Gurner said, "My God. All this time I thought it was the herbs I'm having us drink that give us energy and stamina. And here it's due to—"

Four voices called out in unison. "Rat shit!"

Gurner admitted to the obvious. "Ah ha ha ha ha. I guess so. Rat shit, a panacea nobody could have ever guessed."

Brian Johnson's psychological makeup forced him to inject something conciliatory into the conversation. "Don't take us seriously, Stephanie. The food you're putting together is both appreciated and . . . er . . . [Brian's makeup also made him tell the truth, or at least choke if he lied.] . . . delicious. Anyway, I gather you've come a long way in the art of woods cooking compared to the parboiling attempts when you guys first split from the feds and hid in the wilderness."

"Why thank you, Brian. They didn't teach us much about nutrition in med school, much less vegetarianism, much less how to properly cook anything. But I know if somebody didn't bend a back over the campfire—well, you characters get so wrapped up in your work, you'd forget to eat."

The mysterious mountains of the unknown Asian country of Bhutan. They had projected an indefinable calling to the five Gang members as they flew over Southeastern Asia. When the Air Force bomber was forced to land in Katmandu for repair, Gurner secretly used his influence to have his crew transported to the fairy tale "Land of the Dragon" for an overnight "day off." The exotic countryside immediately diffused its peacefulness and openness into the tired explorers. Conversation readily flowed around the campfire.

"Stephanie, I'll bet, bet you're learning a lot of ideas that no med school classes communicated."

"Oh, Harold. 'A lot' is quite an understatement. So many potentially powerful healing concepts were never even mentioned there; others were just outright condemned."

Dr. Peters stirred her pots. "We—the established American medical profession—are a self-created, self-sustaining organism that has walled itself off from the rest of the universe. In that tiny space, we've become all-pervasive and all-persuasive, and we don't allow room for other healing ways and means. We who call ourselves medical healers don't recognize other forms of healing if they fall outside our given boundaries. That those alternative means may really work is unimportant. And, as you all know, our self-protecting fortress reigns pretty supreme these days. So Gurner and other herbalists, naturopaths, nutritionists, kinesiologists, are labeled 'false,' branded as quacks, and persecuted."

Dr. Peters paused to dip a spoon into one of the pots and taste her spaghetti sauce. "Understand. I'm a medical doctor, and I always will be . . . as long as I can. And as long as medicine accomplishes so much good and offers so much relief and succor for so many people. But crumb. What a closed mind orthodox medicine displays toward anything that doesn't fit its rules.

"Now, after I have watched Gurner use herbs to reverse the course of all kinds of minor and major bodily infirmities, I feel as though all twelve years of med school has taught me is how to play the basic, major chords of a piano. And that it's time to start learning some real music . . . and the heart behind the music."

The spaghetti sauce bubbled over the pot just as she finished talking. The four hungry men shot glances at each other, but no one voiced his fear that tonight's dinner would be another "learning experience."

Johnson spoke, continuing her line of thought. "Well, er, a-hem, I can say . . . that, because of 'Me,' there's not much of a chance you'll become a musician of the heart, Stephanie. Not with that kind of liberal attitude. Who am I? You identified yourself as the medical profession. I—I guess after working with them for over twenty years, I'll always think myself part of them—I . . . I am the FDA. I am in charge, I am the sole proprietor, the undisputed overseer of what is allowed and what is not allowed in this country when it comes to what we drink and eat, what we take as medicine . . . and what choices we're allowed to make concerning those actions.

"Understand. I started out as a superb idea. Food, drink, chemicals, and drugs, all had to pass standards of safety so Americans would be protected from poor quality and contamination. A beautiful philosophy. But I lost sight of my human role and became overly engrossed in my self-defined protection role. I closed my eyes to the many alternative directions evolving around me and focused on a few set and proven ways—ways now directed by our rigid standards. And believe me, the FDA is *not* comprised of liberal thinkers like Bernie Siegel or O. Carl Simonton, much less of alternatives like John Christopher and Stan Malstrom. My decision makers are products of the same 'One way, my way' school that your professors and overseers are."

Johnson pointed a stern finger at the cook. "And you, little doctor, you want to learn how to play an alternative waltz when standard marches are what have my approval? Honey, *I don't like your music!* And I've got the power—and I employ it readily—to make you either play a march or give up piano lessons altogether."

Johnson reclaimed his log seat. Gurner, in tune with the evening's flow, stood up.

"Great analogy, Brian. It's a shame the FDA and AMA board members can't hear it. Maybe ol' Harold the reporter is a means for us to bridge that span. Anyway, I can add some specifics to your generalities."

Gurner glanced at Dr. Peters to see if he had enough time for a speech. The doctor munched on a strand of pasty pasta and nodded affirmative.

"Before I developed—before I was somehow given—the gift of sensing the energies behind herbs, and thus began gathering them on my own, I used to go to herbal pharmacies and health food stores to acquire these medicines. But over time, as I went into these 'original' drug stores, the FDA had forced more and more herbs and supplements off the shelf by making them illegal to sell. There never seemed to be any comprehensive testing carried out on the purported offenders. They were merely 'banned by the FDA.' The bugaboo here was that these mandatory deletions were *always* the most effective herbs, the herbs that really worked.

"The FDA, and its zygomorphic equivalent, the AMA, under the guise of saving the public from 'perceived dangers,' are in a frenzy to make unavailable the gifts of the Creator that were meant for healing. Remember a few years ago when the FDA worked overtime to pass laws that classified herbs and nutritional supplements as drugs and made them available only by a doctor's prescription? Mind you, we're talking doctors who have no training in nutrition or herbs. Besides blatantly ignoring centuries of amazing health qualities attributed to plants, nobody at the FDA works to stop the promotion of nutritionless junk food. Additives long suspected of being carcinogenic are still allowed in foods.

"I quote . . ." Gurner spoke in a baritone monotone: "'We ah . . . definitely suspect this plant of something terrible, like efficacy. Malign it. Ban it. Kill it.'"

Gurner now voiced a philosophical alto. "'Ah yes, there is scientific evidence that nitrate preservatives do change to nitrosamines and that nitrosamines do promote cancer, but . . . what the hell? Hot dogs made out of ground up cow lips got to be preserved.'"

This was a lifelong battle for the healer, and something inside him relished espousing his thoughts to living, listening persons instead of a silent Presence. "It would be bad enough if the FDA limited themselves to stifling the unorthodox and ignoring the dangerous potentials currently allowed on the shelf. But they actively promote some of the most unhealthy and illogical conceptions, ones that somebody has had to have his head way up his ass to come up with: FDA approves the waxing of fruits and vegetables with a wax mixture containing animal fat and sugar; you can't be a vegetarian even if you choose to. One hundred and fifty million people in America have mercury amalgam in their teeth, and a few years ago a news program exposed the fact that the FDA approved its usage without testing the stuff for toxicity. The FDA, despite utterly overwhelming scientific evidence against it, endorses and approves food irradiation. When the public screams in protest about that, the FDA lifts all labeling requirements so said screaming public won't even know they're getting rad-zapped food. It really is the way you put it, Brian. I quote . . ." Gurner spoke in a condescending tenor: "*'Whooo* are yoooo, oh pitiful public, to think yoooo have a choice in this matter?'"

Gurner looked hopefully at the spaghetti pot and then at Dr. Peters. She again tasted a noodle and proudly nodded her head yes. Gurner concluded his talk.

"Heh. I wish I could give my little speech like Stephanie or Brian. You guys say your say and are then at peace. I get so identified with what I propound that I'm sure I lose a couple of years on my life span."

"Healers and environmentalists, it seems, have a lot in common, Gurner."

Willox and Gurner cast a mutually comprehending look at each other. Reeves suddenly injected his irregular face into the middle of that look.

"And reporters, reporters, I believe, sit somewhere between. Let's not forget that reporters, despite their seemingly stoic manner, are also beset by emotional vortexes. If you lady and gentlemen will permit me the firelight, I've a few comments that will surely further confuse matters."

All eyes and ears shifted attention to Reeves. The reporter vigorously rubbed his nose with the back of his hand before speaking. "You, you, Gurner, blew an open hole in my secret thoughts when you said the reporter could be a bridge between common sense and the disguised perpetuation of power. You touched on the private, two-fronted war I've been fighting for the last twenty-five years."

Reeves' face convulsed into doubt. "Any of you, you really want to hear about this?" Reeves rarely voiced a speech and mostly asked questions. Four eagerly nodding heads immediately answered his query. Reeves licked his lips and continued.

"I said a two-, I said a two-fronted war. A. For the last twenty years most of the news-reporting profession has shirked its duty and does *not* report news. That is to say, the major news facilitators—which is what most of the listening-reading-watching public are attuned to—are not giving the facts behind the facts. Hundreds of examples. Let me offer one that relates to the AMA/FDA grievance session you have going tonight.

"A wonderful film, wonderful film and excellent documentary was produced in the mid-'80s. *Hoxsey, Quacks Who Cure Cancer* is its title. It's a captivating narrative and documentary of a Texas man who in the mid-1900s, via a self-discovered herb formula, cured thousands of people of cancer. He boasted an 80-percent cancer cure rate. All kinds of cancer. Documented cures. Proven cures. Hoxsey dedicated his life and his oil fortune to establishing clinics so this concoction could be available to all who needed it. The film also relates how the AMA and FDA dedicated themselves and all their power to relentlessly persecuting Hoxsey's every action. It was war between the two sides for years, even after Hoxsey publicly proved that cure to the world by healing the near-dead, cancer-eaten ghost of a man the AMA challenged him to treat. Many other discrepancies and government nihilisms dictate this story, but finally Hoxsey and his hope-for-thousands cure was forced out of the country. He was 'officially' discredited."

All eyes were glued on Reeves. The reporter noted that fact and continued. "That's just a, just a brief summary. If the world survives ALLIS, see it sometime. You'll really be able to relate.

"So some journalist, some journalist did his job and put together a factual production giving both sides of the controversy. Someone else did his job and made this documentary available to the public. I think certain PBS stations aired it once, but not during prime time. And now, that film floats around, unknown and occasionally being shown at naturopathic conventions. As you said earlier, Gurner, to like-minded persons and not to those who ought to view it."

Reeves stood up, looking something like a spring uncoiling,

and began pacing back and forth. "Front one, front one of Reeves' personal war. Here exists a very probable 80-percent cancer cure. Here also exists evidence of harassment and callous stupidity from two very major guideposts of our country. Why in the hell haven't NBC and CBS and ABC been fighting each other for the rights to show that documentary? Why, I ask you?"

Reeves suddenly stood stock-still, gazing into the fire.

"Why, Harold, for God's sake? Don't leave us hanging."

Reeves sat back down, looking like a tinkertoy house caving in on itself. "You know, big-time, big-time news companies and big-time reporters, these days they got big investments in being who they are. They make huge profits and massive salaries. Besides having to maintain their prestige, inner network competition is stiffer than an old buck's p—" Reeves shot a glance at Dr. Peters. "Er, horn. Competition in this reporting business is stiffer than an old buck's horn. You . . . you don't go blowing fame and fortune, you don't go blowing it all by unveiling too many nasty, revealing, and embarrassing breaks about the demigods in the power seats of today's governments and businesses."

Reeves's voice was suddenly subdued. "Remember in, in the mid-'80s when, for a day or two, newspapers and news broadcasts around the country were wildly headlining this government news release about a Libyan hit team that had reportedly snuck into the United States? Page one across the country was hot with it. And then, that was the last anybody ever heard of it. Nobody even mentioned that the release was a mistake, that there wasn't a Libyan hit team in this country. One feeble reporter a week later broke a story about how the same day of the purported Libyan crisis, the President silently signed into being a law that allowed the CIA to conduct domestic spying. A role that was formerly reserved for countries with Nazi SS and Communist KGB politics. He dared to wonder, this reporter did, if this recent 'loss of another freedom' wasn't a matter of planning, one ignored by the driveling press because of the diversionary, emotionally stimulating and possibly false front of the Libyan news release."

Reeves closed his eyes and allowed a long, loud sigh to escape. No one broke the silence, so he continued.

"That's when I got, I got axed from . . . the big time. That's when the President's press secretary no longer allowed me to attend the White House news sessions. That's when government higher-ups started answering my questions with 'No comment.' I became a Washington reporter who couldn't get any news. That's like being a gardener without seeds. *Newstime* hired me because I could teach their budding reporters a few tricks, but until you and your ongoing ALLIS story came along, Gurner, I was last-legging it there."

Reeves stopped talking and began chewing on his cheeks as he stared at the campfire. Gurner spoke very gently. "What's the second front of your war, Harold?"

Reeves sprung up from his seat again, instantly growing animated. "The most damn-na-ble, damn-na-ble collection of headless honyacks that ever cursed a time period! The most unbelievable fools one could ever imagine!"

Reeves again stared into the fire and entered a voiceless state of suspended animation. Four voices chimed in unison: *"Who, Harold?"*

Reeves pointed his bony finger at the Gang members and practically yelled at the top of his voice, *"You!"*

The Gang exchanged confused glances.

"Not you you. You everybody you. You the public who reads the news and watches the reports on TV. What the hell does anybody do about what they hear anyway? Listen. Again along tonight's subject line. There's no lack of reports on AMA and judicial authorities whisking children away from parents who try alternative methods to combat a disease their kids caught. Chad Green and Caleb Loverro for example, years ago. Two of many children forced by court order to undergo chemotherapy when their parents tried—with success I might add—alternative healing therapies on their kids' cancers. Inhuman and inhumane as such a story is, nobody stops the 'powers' that enforce their standards on the populace. Nobody stops the confusing, costly, nerve-consuming trials those parents then have to go through, trying to prove their parental competency. Everybody reads, and nobody goddamn stops."

The Gang members suddenly realized that when Reeves got wound up, he really cooked. His wild animations also looked a bit like a skinny pocket watch blowing to pieces. "Take the environment, take the environment. Rivers, air, land, and seas. We're tainting them all. And everyone knows it. And everyone with an IQ of six or more knows the consequences. But so damned few get out there and fight. In fact, so damned many still fight *against* the few fighting *for.*

"If the Hoxsey, the Hoxsey film were aired today on every media station in the country, would it legalize the treatment? No. Would it put the people—enough people—up in arms demanding unbiased tests and applications of it? No. Well, that is, four months ago I'd have said no. You may have started something here, Gurner. People may have gotten an unforgettable taste of demanding action as a unit and not merely leaving action up to the whims of higher powers."

All Reeves' energy appeared to drain through his feet into the ground as he slouched into a sitting position. "You add to, add to that the fact that readers don't want to hear most of the facts. . . . They don't want to know about political malfeasance, especially from the '80s and early '90s. They don't want the facts of what our CIA really does or the mistakes the medical profession makes. And if you don't, don't want to lose your 'big time,' you can't go losing your readers."

The skinny and misdressed man offered his familiar misaligned smile and shoulder shrug. "So much for, for this edition of 'Reeves Reports.'"

Dr. Peters recaptured the firelight. "Well, crumb, Harold was so captivating, I forgot about the spaghetti, and it's cooked down to a mush. And the sauce is awfully black. But don't worry. I'll figure out something. Meanwhile, does anyone else want to add to this edition of 'backcountry toastmasters'? The doctor will gladly 'put another log on the fire.'"

All male eyes looked despondently at the pots on the campfire, and then turned toward Willox. The environmentalist slowly stood up. "Well, ahem, I'm . . . just gonna come up with two spur-of-the-moment observations. These are the kinds of observations environmentalists are good at coming up with. They're ones that drive regulatory commissions nuts because they're questions that the commissioners should have acknowledged but didn't.

"The first observation is in fact a question.

"I am Joe Public. Tonight I have listened to the official doctor view and the endorsed government view and all kinds of other views concerning me and the courses of action everyone is prescribing for me. And I wanna ask: why doesn't anybody want my view? Why aren't I involved in the choice-making process for all these decisions concerning me? I'm told I can't have herbs, I can't have Hoxsey, I can't dictate my son's treatments. Hell, it was a secret operation to have my son born with the aid of a midwife, and I *can't* refuse to give him the DPT shot, even though my neighbor's kid became a vegetable because of a reaction to it. And I'm pissed, because I'm an intelligent being and I want the right to make my own choices. I want the *freedom to make my own choices.*"

Willox paused a moment to let his first point sink in.

"Secondly—like I said, this is the kind of observation only an environmentalist could come up with, and that is—it's a darned good thing Christ appeared 2,000 years ago instead of today. We got laws against people like that nowadays. Christ putting spit in some dirt to make mud to put on a man's eyes to heal blindness? Some health inspector would can him. Some FDA board would charge that the procedure has not gone through proper tests, first on bacteria, then on rats, then on monkeys, finally on human volunteers. I mean, Messiah or not, where's his goddamn license?"

A grin began spreading across his face. "I mean, Christ would have been in deep shit his whole life in this day and age. Walking on water? The boatbuilders' union wouldn't like that. Puts them out of work. Dividing and sharing the loaves and fishes? It wouldn't take much before bakers, restaurant owners, and grocery store personnel acquire their fill of the competition. Raising the dead? There's some pretty specific laws in this country concerning grave robbing. And you're for darned sure not going to be able to talk about moving mountains without the military confiscating you and whatever it is that makes that kind of 'weapon' work."

Willox hungrily watched Dr. Peters bury the spaghetti mush and the charred sauce beneath some bushes. "Now we all laugh at the absurdity of what I'm suggesting. But in actuality, it contains more truth than anybody cares to admit.

"Look at it this way. Gurner, you've told me about the powerful hands-on healer you always wished to be. If suddenly you were so gifted by a . . . a divine grace or something; if suddenly you could . . . say hold a prayer service on a hospital lawn and by evening every ailing person inside the building was completely healed . . . how far beyond the patients—or ex-patients—do you think the joy would be felt? The doctors, the nurses, the various technicians, the administrators, and all the staff of a massive medical ant hive: where would they be? No sick folks, no income. And you, oh healer, you perform this feat a couple of times and guards would soon be posted to keep you off the hospital lawn.

"The medical system, like most every other massive and

complex system, is set up for self-perpetuation. I dare say it's geared so nobody can discover and offer easy, effective cures for sicknesses, especially for major degenerative diseases."

Dr. Peters looked up from her rummaging through the meal supplies. "Whoa a minute, Jerry. Every doctor I've ever worked with, every researcher I've ever met is out there giving her or his all to help cure the people in their care. Their methods and medicines may at times seem barbarian to you more enlightened Transcendentalists, but it's still dedicated practitioners using what they've got and what they're trained in to try and help. Often, entire hospital staffs are so overworked they grow numb. And still they're out there doing."

"Oh absolutely, Stef. Individually, in offices and on ward rounds, a bunch of saints are running around in white smocks and blue scrubs. But I said 'it'—meaning the whole darned medical machine. And 'it' cannot afford simple cures.

"Name your disease. Especially the major ones. Massive foundations take up the cause of finding the answer to it. Vast and complicated—and extremely expensive—research happens on all kinds of fronts. Huge investments, huge money-raising campaigns continually transact. And yet, in spite of decades where billions of dollars have been spent and endless strategies and campaigns have been plied, most degenerative disease cures remain elusive. Partial cures and treatments that alleviate the problem's grosser symptoms form the usual mode of action.

"This lack of total success would be understandable, would even justify the time and money spent, had medicine—had 'it'—done *everything*, researched *every* possibility in the quest to end a disease. But have you noticed? The treatments that do find approval, that are available for the public, that have passed the extensive testing required, they're always the costly medicines that only doctors can prescribe; they're always the high-tech machines and therapies that only hospitals can administer. And that stuff is always so complicated and potentially dangerous that a trained doctor is needed for prescription of them. But 'that stuff' isn't all there is.

"Long ago Linus Pauling claimed to have prevented and regressed cancer with vitamin C megatherapy. Dr. Harold Mannor and the E.T. Krebses, mocked as quacks, maintained the same of laetrile. There was William Kelley and his almonds and coffee enemas. There was Max Gerson and his all-inclusive juice therapies. Uh . . . I think the name was Rene Caisse, the woman from Canada who battled medical authorities for fifty years and cured hundreds of cancer patients during that time with her Essiac herbal formula. You know, I'm not involved in the holistic health movement, and these are just a sprinkling of an endless number of purported cancer cures. I've heard some of the discrediting ridicule from organized medicine and I've heard the amazing cure claims they supposedly offer. I don't know. All I do know is that the guys in control of saying what does and doesn't become legal therapy in this country haven't put a pittance of energy into trying to discover what these dedicated and caring alternative scientists witnessed in order to be making their confident claims. All I know is that I'm not allowed the freedom to make my own choices in the matter."

Willox paused as Dr. Peters' face lit up with an idea for dinner, round two. He inwardly groaned as she began slapping peanut butter onto bread slices.

"I read somewhere that it takes tens of millions of dollars minimum for a drug to be researched, tested, approved, and marketed for public use. That's a high investment, and you gotta get return on that kind of expenditure. Nobody's going to test garlic for approval, or comfrey, or echinacea, or beestings if, when approved, the consumers aren't dependent on purchasing it from the testers. Imagine a serious disease cure that every flower bed could cultivate like petunias. No honcho-approved cure consists of something everyone can grow or put together themselves, but the gist is this . . . Science repeatedly refuses to acknowledge clinical data, but the bottom line for a sick individual is clinical; that is, what works. And these homespun remedies work for some. That in itself ought to be enough incentive for research to take the tiniest portion of their budgets and test thoroughly all the homemade and natural 'potential cures' that any 'unapproved' book on the market suggests. Then 'it' could say 'it' has tried everything.

"Personally, I doubt you could get an accurate, unbiased, 'official' testing procedure on natural and preventative cures. Heck, we can rarely get an impartial environmental impact statement. Too many private concerns have too much say-so in the matter. Why would it be different in the big business of medicine?"

Willox reseated himself. Dr. Peters jumped up, dispensing five sandwiches laden with peanut butter and molasses. She exuded vim and vigor.

"Well, gentlemen. Here we have it. We have tonight exposed several of the major problems facing womankind and mankind. Now the question surfaces. What are we going to do about it? We alone can prove Harold wrong. Change starts with us, nowhere else. With the combined brainpower of this group, we really ought to produce some viable solutions."

Johnson held his sandwich away from his body as black blobs of molasses dribbled onto his hand. "Well, er, I guess you'll have to count me out, Stephanie. It's getting late, and I need to write a letter to my wife."

Willox talked with his mouth stuck together from too big a bite of the sticky meal. "Iff's the thame wiff me. Yennie's birffday ith in a few thays, and I fant to thend her a note. Gfflnite, you all."

Dr. Peters focused on the remaining gentlemen. "Well, crumb. Looks like you and Harold and me, Gurner."

Gurner dropped his sandwich into a cellophane bag. "Ah, I'm going to meditate. If any solutions come, I'll let you know in the morning. See you all then."

Dr. Peters glared at Reeves, who was caught trying to hide his sandwich under a rock. "Well, Harold?"

"I, er, I've got a report, a report to get off for tomorrow's news. But if I may say, there you have it, doctor. No one can really accomplish world change by himself . . . and yet here it is, up to you. Sleep tight."

"Well, crumb."

♦ 28 ♦
Communication

August 15, 2008, 1:00 P.M. FDA main offices,
Washington, D.C.

Jim Bowerns' full-throated and agitated voice could be heard
from the hallway outside his office door, had anyone chosen to
listen.

"Vinerson! What do you want from me? At this point in time
he's as untouchable as a shrine . . . by the FDA and your AMA
both."

. . .

"I know, man, how well I know. He's usurped every standard
our organizations have established as law over the past fifty years.
But nothing can be done about it right now. He's not some 'holistic'
doctor you can hang from a license-suspension tree. He's definitely
a quack medicine-pusher, but my hands are tied. I was forced into
signing acquittal papers, and the FDA holds no dominion over
him. I can't fry him. At least not right now."

. . .

"Jack, I'm not stupid. I know that Gurner's every action leaves
organized medicine looking like a flock of headless chickens. I
know he's started a renaissance in this back-to-the-earth, holistic
crap that threatens to undermine decades of modern medical and
chemical advances. But you and I, we have to swallow the
immediate fact that—"

. . .

"For goddamn sure. If he does find an ALLIS cure and wins
the Nobel Prize because of it, he'll be all the more influential and
untouchable. I haven't been sitting on my haunches twiddling my
thumbs. But right now— . . . Jack, listen. Right now: A: We can't
prosecute him; we can't convict him of anything; we can't touch

him. It's fact. And B— . . . Jack, listen. B: It's also a sad fact that he may be the only one who can save our asses from ALLIS."

. . .

"Yeah, it curdles my insides too. But logically—not emotionally, but logically—give me an argument against that statement."

. . .

"No, Jack. UC Davis has slaughtered their last monkey trying that approach. They've bottomed out. I can also tell you that the CDC has run out of theories to try. We're the first to hear if anything breaks, believe me. Not quite one year in the life of this disease, nearly a hundred million deaths, and reputable science faces checkmate. The sad truth, Jack, is that every investigating eye now directs its gaze toward B.C., and Sweden, and Brazil, and . . . and Gurner."

. . .

"No, dammit, and it gets on my nerves. It looks like the Brazilian herb is also *not* the ALLIS cure that the Oregon herb was. Preliminary tests show that it halts part of the disease but doesn't cure it."

. . .

"No, as usual he's absconded. He and his puppets are back on the bomber. Last report has him sightseeing above the Asian continent."

. . .

"Hell, yes. He's a flagrant, power-grabbing son of a bitch, and at present he holds the potential to crumble the corporate and governmental systems that direct mankind's thoughts and actions. No, Jack, I assure you. He's *not* going to be the death angel of the AMA. Or of the FDA."

. . .

"Well . . . I can't tell you details, Jack. Confidential and all that. But believe this. Nobody with any authority likes Gurner. He's made enemies everywhere he's gone and by every action he's maintained. He doesn't play by any of the rules. He embarrasses people . . . the wrong people. He's too good at making things happen. That threatens people . . . the wrong people. When—and I say when, not if—when he finds or reveals an ALLIS cure; when the sure cure is in the public domain . . . well, Mr. Gurner's heyday will quite suddenly come to an end."

. . .

"No, no, Jack. I can't tell you. I'm sworn to secrecy. I just want to assure you that the AMA and its spinoff organizations will not lose their control over the people's health-care choices. The FDA will retain the power to tell people what is and isn't safe. The military will go back to protecting us instead of this nonsensical—what did he call it?—'working-for-us'—role. And the government will not be piloted by direct mandates from the people. Gurner will *not* become a household name."

. . .

"Yes, I swear it. You have my word."

. . .

"The wheels are turning, Jack. The groundwork is all laid. Don't worry. We don't leave things to the last minute."

. . .

"OK, Vinerson. I'll let you know just as soon as I know when he finds the key."

. . .

"Yeah, I will tell my wife that. And you say hello to Mandy from us. And condolences from us on your mother dying from ALLIS . . . oh, and Jack! . . . pray like hell. Pray that Gurner finds something soon."

. . .

"Yeah. It's that bad. As always, what we release to the news media forms such a small portion of the story. But ummm . . . pray that Gurner finds something soon."

✦ 29 ✦
Loggers, III

August 17, 2008, 4:13 P.M. In an apartment complex near Oregon State University, Corvallis, Oregon.

A soft, almost shy knock tapped at the door of apartment 316. A human bulk almost larger than the door frame walked over to answer the summons.

"Ernie! What the holy hell are you doing in Corvallis! You look like a saltwater fish just found himself immersed in a freshwater pond. Man, what brings you to the big city?"

Ernie Slate offered Joe Simpson a nervous smile and an unanimated handshake. "Hey, Joe. Me and the ol' lady are . . . are just passing through, and I told her I hadda drop in on ol' Joe, and uh . . . see how much becoming an educated man is changing him. Still strange, not seeing you cutting with us, Joe."

Simpson motioned for Slate to enter. "Yeah, well, don't think I don't miss wearing that gear and tromping through the woods with you and the other ol' farts. Don't think that a large part of me isn't wishing I was walking through a tall and green forest full of fresh air and good guys working by my side. A man might as well blindfold his eyes and chuck himself into an ant hive as come live in an apartment in a city like this. But things are changing fast, Ernie, and so am I. And this is where I belong for a while."

Slate nervously looked around the small apartment. "Joe, I . . . I . . . I hope that don't mean you quit drinking beer?"

"Oh shit. Monsieur Earn-nay. Please pardon my manners. We got some in the 'fridge. You look like you could use one. Coors or Pabst?"

"Coors! What happened to 'Michelob or nothing'?"

"It's called budget. A forty-nine-year-old logger doesn't get paid to quit work and jog off to the university to solve life's problems. Jean, bless her heart, is working. And with the payments we get from selling our place, we'll survive the cost of schooling. But with five kids, and us not tapping their college funds, luxury is out of the picture for a while."

"Gimme a Pabst, I guess. Thanks."

The old friends sat at the small kitchen table, facing each other, each lost in the bubbles of their own glasses and their thoughts. Slate finally broke the silence.

"Joe, I . . . So you're still gonna follow this schooling notion of yours?"

Simpson nodded painfully. "Ernie, I used to think that the years of hard work and honest logging gave me a wisdom and a practicality that made the rest of the world look foolish. School at the U hasn't even started yet; I'm just running around meeting these professors, getting their advice on how to get prepared: stuff to read and all that. And I'll tell you, these last two weeks I've come to learn that the country loggerman's horse sense is just a drop in the bucket of all the knowing there is to be had. Believe it or not, I can see that in many cases our isolated little ideas are really blinders."

Slate glanced at his watch. "Oh?"

"You might say I've been introduced to facts. Facts of a different nature, Ernie. Facts a few steps beyond how many board feet allowed cut in a day will yield us how many jobs which translates into how many dollars we bring home. We know the facts of tree cutting and log hauling and machinery maintenance inside and out. But we stop there. We put our blinders on and don't attempt any vision beyond today's job and tomorrow's bills."

Slate glanced at the clock on the apartment wall. "Joe, I . . . I . . . well, what the hell's wrong with that?"

"Nothing at all, Ernie. Except that these other facts, these truths that live out there just beyond our vision's end, they keep piling up and piling up. Suddenly, they pile too high and overwhelm something else. Then, when they landslide, they bury us. And we go under, screaming that we didn't know, why didn't someone tell us this was gonna happen. But the sad truth is that we just weren't looking."

Slate glanced at nothing in particular. "Joe, I . . . you . . . lookin' at what?"

Simpson sipped his beer and smiled slightly. "Ernie, keep it in mind, I'm *not* an environmentalist. I'm a plain ol' logger who's turned into a fact seeker. But, since you asked . . .

"Ernie, we're pretty near out of virgin forest. You know how many acres of forest in this country have been logged? You know how few years, at the present rate, before there ain't *any* virgin forests left? You know plain and boldfaced that if the government—the Forest Service—wasn't subsidizing it, in most places logging would go belly up. Not to mention the simple fact that second-growth forests don't have near the ecological diversity of old-growth forests. I still have to face the fact that I helped wipe out the AC herb."

"Yeah, Joe, I . . . that's what I—"

"And logging is so big and important to us, but it's such a tiny part of such a huge picture of blistering *facts*, Ernie. The *hard* facts of chemicals poisoning the land and air and water. And you got global warming and people still wasting vast amounts of fossil fuels. And there's the *glaring* fact that we've got too many people; we're outstripping the land just by sheer numbers. Christ almighty, Ernie, when you start looking, there ain't any end to it. You got ozone depletion, and one out of every five species of life being axed from existence, and radiation everywhere, and what those goddamned A-bombs will do if anybody ever uses them, and there's almost no safe water left in most places and . . . God-All-Peachfuzz, Ernie, I didn't save Myra from ALLIS just to watch her die a slow death from pollution."

"Joe, please . . . I—"

"The amazing thing is, there are *solutions* to all these problems, Ernie. I don't know how to do it, but there's people here know about solar energy and wind power, and recycling, and conservation, and even reforestation and the word we hate most, Ernie, 'preservation.' Christ, 'preservation' doesn't have to mean 'put everybody out of work.' Its real meaning is 'save a little bit of what we got left before we don't have it anymore.' Why, it's a fact that if someone with just half an assfull of brains . . ."

Simpson suddenly noticed that Slate hadn't touched his beer, and was sitting with head bowed halfway toward his beer glass. The big man's face lost its enthusiasm.

"Sorry, Ernie. I get carried away. You look like a twenty-year-old prime stud been told he'll never screw again. You haven't touched your beer, which means you haven't heard a word I've said. What's eating at your insides?"

Slate looked pleadingly at Simpson. "You got any more of that plant left, Joe?"

"That plant? . . . You mean AC?"

"Yeah. You got any more of that at . . . " Slate choked, "at all?"

Simpson shook his head from side to side and watched his friend's eyes cloud over.

"Hundreds of people have asked me that question, Ernie. In letters, by the phone, stopping me in the street and begging. Hundreds have asked me that. Gurner had just enough for one person. It was just enough to save Myra."

Slate nodded and closed his eyes. "I figured as much. I just had to try. You tried and got lucky. I had to just try."

"Who?"

"My . . . my brother."

"Eddie?"

"Um um. B . . . Bernie."

"Bernie! Oh Christ. Your twin?"

Slate nodded.

"Oh, Christ. Ernie, look, I'm sorry. I really am. I know what you're feeling. I felt it when Myra was threatened with ALLIS. I . . . I wake up every morning knowing it could strike Jean or any of the kids, or even me. I'm hoping if it has to hit here again it hits me—but then I know they'd suffer the same way I would if it hit them."

Simpson skirted the table and placed his massive hands on the drooping shoulders of his friend. "I'm sorry, Ernie."

Slate's large bulk shook in quiet sobs for a few minutes while Simpson's mountainous body stood close. His mammoth hands held the crying man's shoulders and poured out as much comfort as they could. Finally Slate shook his head from side to side, sat up straighter in the chair, and wiped the tear tracks from his cheeks with his shirt sleeve.

"Sorry, Joe, I—"

"It's OK, Ernie, Christ a-mighty knows, it's OK."

Slate's face hardened. "What's so damned hard, Joe, it's bad enough, Bernie being doomed like a rat in an ice box and slipping away before my eyes. But I feel like I'm the one who killed him."

"Ernie, that's not—"

"Isn't that funny, Joe? If we'd of let the Friends of the Trees have their way, Bernie and a hundred million other people would be alive today. Even if I wouldn't have cut down that last half acre . . . I really killed my own brother."

"Ernie, no one could have—"

Slate's voice edged toward hysteria. "And you know what I feel like is happening, Joe? I feel like God hit Bernie with ALLIS as a punishment for me, for being the one who creamed a plant species He put on Earth."

"Ernie, listen—"

"Ernie-the-butcher gets his just dues; Ernie-the-knife, who—"

Simpson's great hands had been awkward at offering solace. They were better at a more accustomed role. They grabbed Slate by the shirt front, lifted him from the chair, and began shaking him. Simpson's bellowing voice shook the apartment walls.

"*Goddammit,* Ernie! You're always interrupting me! All the goddamned time! You get your goddamned noggin set in one motion and God Himself can't make you change direction! Now you goddamned well listen to me, and you listen good!"

Simpson continued holding the rag-doll in his grasp, every so often giving it another shake. "Once I had an inner voice tell me not to give some friends some bad whiskey we stoled. I told you that. I had that same feeling about the Squanni Hill cut. You know that too. Well that voice is talking again, and it's talking loud. And it's saying that God's wrath ain't involved in this ALLIS thing one bit. Somehow, somewhere, *mankind* blew it. I can't say just how or where, but I know in my gut that something we did produced ALLIS somehow. Nobody's at fault except maybe mankind in general for ignoring the facts and for electing officials that also ignore the facts."

The Titan hands squeezed Slate's shirt tighter and added vigor to the shaking.

"But you get this through your goddamned knucklebrain. God hasn't singled out Ernie Slate to be his goddamned dart board."

The gorilla hands roughly replaced Slate in his chair.

"Bernie dying is going to be hard enough on you. You gotta quit this additional pounding on yourself."

Slate's eyes had begun to clear. He looked up at the mighty form facing him. "You . . . you really think so, Joe?"

"I said so, didn't I? Do I hafta shake some more common sense into you?"

"No, I don't think so. I think what you said sounded pretty right." Slate gazed at the kitchen table for a few moments, then picked up his untouched beer and killed it in two long gulps. In a few moments his face grew noticeably calmer, as the logic of his friend's words penetrated deeper layers of his mind. "By golly, Joe. I feel better. I always told everybody that they didn't need shrinks. If anybody understood how to handle a problem, it was ol' Joe."

"Well, I'm glad, Ernie. I wish it would help Bernie, but I don't know how to shake a person back into life."

"Well, dammit, Joe, you've helped me. I mean it. It's a damn scary world inside when you think that God has gone from something you use in swear words to Something swearing at you. You've helped me to go on, Joe. I thank you."

"Thank you too, Ernie. You've helped me to go on, too. You've reminded me again what the stakes are. You and Bernie and all those who ache for a hundred million lost loved ones."

◆ 30 ◆
Causes

August 21, 2008, 8:30 P.M. In the jungle forest, on the island of Borneo, Malaysia.

Payanáti, one of three native Penan Indian guides recruited to lead four of the Gurner Gang members through the Sarawak rain forests of the Malaysian section of the island of Borneo, squatted on his haunches, remaining aloof and near the forest edge. While intently watching the four Americans, he purposely shied from their campfire and company. Unable to understand their language, Payanáti was thinking to himself, thinking that more than three decades of foreign invasion had plagued his people, and that he had had his fill of outsiders.

First the monster machines smash through the forest, ripping roads through Penan and Dayak lands. No one asks the Penan for permission. No one of the ruling government tells the tribespeople their plans. Then come the mainland workers with their noisy saws, cutting down the forest as if trees were but bamboo before a machete. They load the trees; the trucks haul them away. The barren ground is left to the rain. The Penan are left with nothing.

The Penan petition the government. The Penan are ignored. The tribespeople—men, women, and children—finally band together and blockade the logging roads, trying to halt the land slaughter that means Penan slaughter. The government has soldiers and power. Our leaders are now in prison. Blocking the logging roads is illegal. We blockade more. More go to prison. We face fines our wealthiest cannot pay. The logging of our lands proceeds, like a river at flood.

Payanáti stared at the white-skinned strangers as they laughed over some obscure joke. He wondered whose side they represented—the government or the tribespeople.

Many outlanders come and try and help the Penan. They end up in prison too.

Then comes the shaking death. My people get sick and die. Now comes more government people, telling us these A-mer-ri-kans search for a plant that will stop the shaking death. They tell us we must guide them safely through what remains of our forests. They tell us we must do as they ask, but so far the A-mer-ri-kans have been unable to ask us anything.

The Indian set his attention to the familiar night sounds of the misty jungle, avoiding as long as possible having to face his next thought and question.

It will be nice, to stop the dying from the shaking death. But the government man said that its sickness is all over the world, in all the countries across all the waters . . .

If these strangers find the plant that cures the shaking death . . . what will happen to what is left of our forest and what is left of our people when the government comes in to take it?

• • • • •

Reporter Harold Reeves, Doctor Stephanie Peters, environmental activist Jerry Willox and the healer Gurner lounged in total laziness by a small campfire. Dinner had been eaten, and Dr. Peters' grilled tofu burgers had not only held together but tasted surprisingly good. Willox, full of food for what seemed like the first time in weeks, inhaled a noisy breath of the humid air. "By golly, Gurner. I'm kinda glad you couldn't zero in on that plant from the air. It's been a while since we've done anything but fly into an area to check it out. It's really great to be trekking and camping in the wilds again."

Gurner, reclined on a tree stump and gazing into the darkening sky, spoke to the universe. "So true, Jerry. And to be eating Stephanie's special menu campfire cooking again. One more Air Force dehydrated meal and I'd have barfed. Listen to those incredible sounds. It's good to be out here."

Dr. Peters, having just proven that campfire smoke does not repel insects, liberally doused herself with a chemical preparation. "Auuuuk. You guys call this steaming, dripping, tangled, matted, hot, mucky parcel of overgrown trees and vines a great place to be? Crumb, everything that flies by us bites or stings or somehow draws blood. Everything that doesn't fly crawls, and weird things are crawling everywhere. Quaaaah, I get the shivers just talking about it."

Willox and Gurner, eyes reflecting the glow from the campfire, gave her a mischievous look. She pantomimed macing them with her repellent. "You jungle baboons can stare at me, grinning like that. But when you wake up to find that paradise has left your bodies looking like a miniature Himalayan landscape because of all the bites . . . don't come crying to the doctor. You tell them, Harold. With Brian gone, you at least be on my side."

Reeves, reposed flat on the ground with his legs and feet elevated onto a log, moved only his mouth muscles as he declared his prophesy. "Malaria. We'll all, we'll all die of malaria before we get out of here. Either that or snakebite."

Dr. Peters glared out a "there you have it" glint at Gurner and Willox, but Reeves' never-ending facetious pessimism set the two nature-loving men to laughter. Willox voiced their mirth. "Jeez, Harold. What would you do if you ever caught one of these deadly diseases you're always predicting?"

"I'd, I'd write my obituary and send it to *The Wall Street Journal.*"

"Ha. You think they'd print it?"

"If, if they didn't, I'd have them forward it to *Macrobiotic Update*. They could list me in the 'Dead Sushi' section."

Payanáti and the other Penan looked quizzically at each other. Their lives had been so serious for so long that the free and bubbling laughter of these outsiders sounded terribly foreign, almost sinful and discordant.

Dr. Peters claimed a log seat by the fire. "Oh, my aching side. I wish we could send some of this cheer to Brian. I wasn't clear why he stayed behind, Gurner, but it sounded ominous. What was happening?"

Gurner moved closer to the firelight. "Ah, Stephanie. Brian is our mission man. For some reason the Supreme Head of the Federation—the ruler of Malaysia—is completely resistant to the idea that I think there's an ALLIS-cure plant in the Sarawak portion of his country. When he welcomed us at Kuala Lumpar, he put the country at our disposal. But the minute I said get us to Borneo . . . it was like somebody clamped a demasculator on his ductus deferens. You know what a continuous hassle it's been to get over here, like pulling teeth every step of the way. Only the ruler having to keep face after publicly promising us support got us here to the island.

"Of course, now that we see first hand what they've done to

the land with their logging operations; now that we see what they've done to the Penan and the other native tribes, how they've terrorized them and destroyed their homeland . . . I can understand why they do not want the worldwide public eye that follows us to focus on their stupidity."

Gurner stepped to the fire, squatted onto his haunches and begin stirring the coals with a stick. "Remember when we finally got to Kuching and nobody would lift a finger to get our show moving toward the upper Rajang country? No planes available, all of the helicopters had 'mechanical problems,' no one spoke the Penan language? We've got three guides we can't even communicate with! On and on like that. As it became clear what was happening, and why, it also became clear that if we did find a solid ALLIS-curing herb here, the Malaysian government might not let it be revealed. Brian had that feeling. So did I. They've been pretty ruthless to this land and to these Indians, and I think they want to keep that fact a secret.

"So Brian is on his way to Bangkok, supposedly arranging for us to explore Thailand next. At Bangkok he's going to alert the media to what the game is in Malaysia. When Brian informs the world that Malaysia may have an effective ALLIS plant whose discovery they are not facilitating . . . well, the rulers may suddenly find themselves under international martial law. That should transform them into angels of cooperation. On the other hand, it may so piss them off that we will all be shot."

Reeves' elongated head lifted itself off the ground as he tried to peer over the log supporting his feet. "Where the heck, where the heck do the trees from these clear-cuts go? I don't see many signs of a timber industry that would require so much logging."

Willox joined Gurner and Dr. Peters by the campfire. "I can answer that, Harold. Part of my environmental correspondence back home was with the Rain Forest Action Network. The facts might give you something to write about.

"Eighty percent of the 400 plus acres of virginal rain forest denuded per day in Malaysia is exported to Japan. Also, most of the members of the Malaysian parliament own logging concessions. You've heard about the natives trying to save their homes by blockading the logging? And ending up behind prison bars? Now the government has laws authorizing timber companies to dismantle roadblocks and charge the costs to the native tribes."

"I see, I see. The Japanese have their chopsticks involved in quite a few Third World environmental degradation episodes, am I right?"

Willox flung some squaw wood pieces into the fire. "Oh Jeez-us, Harold. The Japanese. The Japanese . . . and sometimes the French. Two peoples you just don't want to be stuck with if you're sharing a limited planet."

"Go, go on, Jerry. Maybe your information can be written up into something someone will read, sometime, somewhere."

"Simple facts, Harold. Japan's indefatigable industry carries a colossal demand for raw material. From the Middle East to Southeast Asia to the East Indies to Australia to Alaska, the Japanese are taking, taking, taking, and not giving much back except denuded land, dime store trinkets and high tech merchandise. They take advantage of the developing nations' desperate cash needs to pay minimal prices to plunder their natural resources, and they use the profits to buy out the developed countries' farmland and banks and businesses. What they couldn't do by force in World War II, they are accomplishing by economics.

"And dammit, like most planetary waste, so much goes to absurd extravagance. You mentioned chopsticks. The Japanese alone throw away over 12 billion pairs of wooden chopsticks a year. That's thousands of tons of wood chucked after each meal. They are largely responsible for destroying half the hardwood forests in the Philippines and about one-third of those in Indonesia. I get so—"

"Hold it!" Dr. Peters could tell that Willox's temperature was rapidly rising. "Hold it, you guys, you men! Here you go getting all-fired gloomy and doomy again. In fact, I've got some information that will let you know we are fighting back against the Japanese."

Reeves' notepad turned toward Dr. Peters. "What's, what's that?"

"We Americans—who certainly top the list when it comes to tossing away nonrenewable resources—have an ultimate weapon that'll soon subjugate the Japanese into wheezing mucus balls."

Three voices echoed, "What's that, Stephanie?"

"Cigarettes."

Reeves sat up and joined the other two men in looking blankly at her.

"Cigarettes, I said. Look. With increasing bad press and anti-smoking sentiments flailing the tobacco industry in the U.S., they had to look to foreign markets to beef up their sales. Japan, it seems, has gone bonkers over those little coffin-makers from the West. Of course the manufacturers—humanitarians that they are—are putting their all into advertising and creating Eastern hotshot smoking images. So give 'em time. When Japan becomes the international lung cancer and emphysema capital of the world, slaughtering the last of the world's whales may be the farthest thing from their minds."

Willox looked surprised. "Stephanie! Jeez. I can't believe you're talking like this. You're always so caring, you're always so compassionate, so . . ." Willox looked contemplative. "You think it will work?"

"Ummmm, probably not, Jerry. Humans are so doggone adaptable to their poisons. Their lungs will probably last longer than the planet."

Reeves joined the others at the campfire, filling his notepad with pages of shorthand only he could read. "And what about, what about France, Jerry? They don't stand out in my mind as a world-ruining nation."

"Look at their record, Harold. Their damned nuclear bombs, which they used to blow Melanesia to pieces. No one could tell the French they couldn't detonate their bombs. No armada of facts proving that such an action was ruining a unique part of the world held any sway with them. When the people of New Caledonia—the bomb victims—tried to claim a little nuclear-free Pacific freedom, and a little of their own freedom besides, the mighty French used their military to subdue them. If an environmental group peacefully demonstrated against them, the mighty French planted a bomb and sank the ship—incidentally killing a crewmember who happened to be on board. They ignored the commonsense pleas to sign a South Pacific Nuclear-Free Zone Treaty while continuing to spew deadly radioactivity into the one-time paradise of five million indigenous islanders . . . and into the rest of the world . . . Gurner! Did I say something to make you look like that?"

Gurner shrugged off Willox's question. "Um, nothing, Jerry. It's . . . atomic radiation has been occupying my mind for quite a while. But it's too complicated to dive into tonight. I'll give you my nuclear rantings some cloud-encompassed night when we're all in the mood for ghost stories."

The bony face with the crooked smile injected itself between Gurner and Willox. "Ah, Gurner. Before you, before you turn in. For my 'Reeves Reports' daily worldwide broadcast. Besides summarizing what we have most recently accomplished, my editors gave me directions to secure from you a firm statement as to how close you are to finding a complete cure for the Loggerman's Disease."

"Harold. You know as well as I do, that's like predicting when a certain dream will happen. I won't know what this new plant can do until I feel it and until we test it. If we even find it."

"What do you, what do you mean, 'if'?"

"As you well know by now, up in the air I can't tell the difference between an ALLIS-curing plant that presently exists and an ALLIS-curing plant that has recently become extinct. I tune into what I can only describe as plant energies, and sometimes past energies are just as potent as present energies."

Reeves stopped scribbling notes and looked at Gurner with a semi-disgusted countenance. "Never been able, never been able to get that put into print, Gurner. Editors call it hocus pocus. Editors want verifiable facts."

Gurner sighed and pointed into the darkness. "Well then, my dear reporter, verifiable fact: you see the clear-cuts across this land, the slash and slash-some-more crap that's denuding Sarawak and so much of the world we've looked at. Harold, the answer to any form of your editor's question is dependent on the stray chance that a certain micro-corner of the Earth has been spared. Tell your editors that."

"I have, I have. Many times. They, ah, strongly indicated that they're not interested in news that stays the same all the time. Especially when readers—people facing death—want concrete answers. Tell a person something once and they tend to want to move on to new things . . . readers do, that is."

"But the problem remains the same; so must the answer. The answer has got to be said, over and over, until somebody hears it."

Gurner closed his eyes and withdrew from the conversation. When he returned, his gaze and his voice were knife-edged. "Tell them this, Harold, direct from Gurner. Any time I burp these days it gets news-released worldwide, and gets more attention than the Bible. So let's give them a printable quote.

"Tell them that Gurner deeply regrets that his emotional outburst that day in Oregon left ALLIS dubbed the Loggerman's Disease. That comment was unfair to those of the logging profession. Since then I've come to see that ALLIS could just have accurately been nicknamed a hundred other names. The ORV Disease, for one. You remember the western U.S. and the endless miles of landscape torn up by tire tracks? What unique, unknown life was extinguished under those wheels? Humans with machines can conquer anything, except what they destroy with those machines.

"Tell them that ALLIS could rightly be called the Fast Food or the Pet Food Disease. If Rondonia had gone the sorry way of so much other rain forest acreage—cleared for grazing cattle destined for U.S. markets—the most powerful herb on the shelf next to the original AC herb would probably be gone. Who knows how many other similar plants have paid the price in creating a cheaper hamburger?

"Tell them it could easily be called the Vietnam or the Agent Orange Defoliant Disease. Or be named after any war anywhere that not only killed and maimed people but surely destroyed rare habitat and one-of-a-kind life species. Heh, if you want some environmental justice, say that perhaps the perfect controlling agent for atrial fibrillation used to thrive in the cryptogamic sands along the Saudi-Kuwaiti border. As ALLIS is proving, all the armies in the world are worthless trinkets if because of them something is eradicated.

"Why not call it the World Bank Loan Disease? They and other resource development programs are responsible for flooding and roading and clearing more land and unique habitat than is imaginable. They don't assess the land they loan money to change. I tell you, Harold, if there really is such a thing as a mysterious cartel that secretly controls the economy of this planet, they must have roasted peanuts for brains. Any bird knows that if you foul the nest, you can't raise young in it. What good will it ultimately do them to rule a dying planet?"

Gurner's temperature was soaring. No one dared interrupt his tirade. "You could call ALLIS the Cattleman's or the Sheep Rancher's Disease. How many times have we checked out a piece of land only to kick through the dust of complete overgrazing? Sheep Rancher's Disease might really be a most accurate name. Some years ago, the chairman of some committee, opposing the reintroduction of the Yellowstone wolf, said 'The Endangered Species Act is the villain behind all this. We saw nothing wrong with saving the whooping crane. But the list now is ridiculous. Who cares about a piping plover or a snail darter?'"

Willox added some heat to the healer's thermometer. "Jeez, I remember that, Gurner. That was the National Wool Growers Environmental Committee. I remember thinking that that kind of mind sees only sheep and nothing else."

Gurner incorporated Willox's thought into his speech. "Yeah, sheep, and probably making a living and feeding a family through sheep, Jerry. There will always be that side of it.

"But beyond the economics of it, to me such a statement translates to an insensitive attitude of: Who cares about a form of unique and individual life that God for some sure reason put on this Earth? Who cares or believes that the Master Creator has a Master Plan and maybe a Master Need for everything He so artfully placed here? Wolves and snail darters and giant sea tortoises, aye-ayes and snow leopards, spotted owls, on and on, including insects and plants we don't contact; when a person doesn't give other God-created life room to live, to coexist . . . I'd say he's lost his sense of wonder for life. My favorite quote is: 'He's become a pair of spectacles without eyeballs behind them.'

"And the point might just be coming home. ALLIS is now playing that role. I mean, not that I want any rancher to learn ecology by contracting ALLIS. But the cure for ALLIS, the cure for any old or new or mystifying disease could very well lie in a rare plant, a plant whose seed and survival somehow depends on an unknown action of the piping plover or the snail darter.

"So who needs the piping plover or the snail darter? Or the wolf? That doggone rancher very well might. He might very dearly need everything he's shot, poisoned, and cussed at."

Gurner stirred in the smoky corners of the campfire. "Best answer I can give you, Harold."

"I'll work on, I'll work on it, Gurner. It'll have to be more concise, but it'll get out to the world. Then the choice is theirs."

The fire crumbled, and most of the flames turned into blue and red coals. Gurner tossed his stirring stick into the embers and stood and stretched. "Well, this herbalist is ready for the sandman. Tomorrow will probably be some kind of a day . . . oh, and . . . uh, Stef-un-eeee . . . "

Dr. Peters' insides jumped. A chill ran up her spine, and goose bumps covered her flesh. *What's he thinking?* "I don't like the tone in your voice, Gurner."

"Dear, dear, kind and compassionate Stephanie . . ."

Could he possibly want . . .? Noooo, not in front of everyone.

Not anytime. Not Gurner. "Gurner, what the hell do you want?"

"You're the only one who thought to bring mosquito netting, Stephanie."

Ohhh crumb. How could I have even thought? I should have known. "No!"

"These bugs are really bad out here tonight, dear Stephanie."

"Hell, no!"

"All four of us could fit under your netting, dear Stephanie."

Willox captured Gurner's drift and joined the conversation. "Yeah, Stephanie, Jeez, give us a break. We're your friends, your comrades. Share and share alike, thick and thin and all that."

This blew the top off the meter. "Goddammit, you're the mountain boys who think life is great only when it's inclement and bathless and prickery and seventy-degree slopes and—"

Reeves suddenly realized that his blood was also at stake in this matter. "Malaria. We'll all, we'll all die of malaria. Sure as heck, tomorrow's newsbreak will tell how malaria got three out of the four of us tonight because you didn't share."

"You guys can go fly a kite."

"Really, *Doctor* Stephanie. Could you sleep? Could your conscience really allow you any sleep, knowing Jerry and Harold and I were being hideously tortured and drained by these flying hypodermic needles while you basked, yards away, in the only shelter for hundreds of miles?"

"You're damned right I could. If you crumbums can't even think to—"

"Whimper, whimper."

"Whimper, whimper whimper."

"Whimper, oh I say, whimper whimper."

"Oh c'mon, you creeps! Don't start that."

The three gentlemen as one unit got down on their knees and offered an excellent performance of agony-filled groveling.

"Whimper, whimper" . . . "Oh, please" . . . "Mercy, madam, please . . ."

Dr. Peters raised her arms in a circle of desperation. "Oh crumb almighty anyway. But I get the outside!"

The three gentlemen as one unit fell prostrate, arms extended and fingers touching the doctor's feet.

"Does that mean yes? I think she said yes. Oh thank you, memsahib. Thank you thank you."

"Blessings on you, oh great and merciful one."

"May my words, my words feebly attempt to sing justice to the vastness of your heart."

Dr. Peters, muttering, stormed to the jungle edge for some bathroom privacy. *"Idiots.* The human population of the world is dependent on *idiots* to save it from ALLIS."

• • • • •

As the three Penan natives watched the three male A-mer-ri-kans first grovel beside and then bow before the feet of the A-mer-ri-kan woman, Payanáti found himself hoping that they were on the side of the Malaysian Government.

• 31 •
Reflections

August 22, 2008, 12:01 A.M. Sarawak, Malaysia.

The night couldn't have been deeper, the jungle darker, nor the endless array of insect and animal voices more generous in singing their unique songs to a receptive sky. Two of three Penan Indian guides lay asleep at the forest's edge. The four Americans were clustered as one group under a modicum of mosquito netting. Three of them drifted in and out of various dreams. The fourth lay wide awake, trying to stare beyond the stars.

Well, God. Life is not boring. Exhausting, yes, but certainly not boring. Crazy; painful; hope-filled and hope-failed; but definitely not boring.

We've come a long way in less than a year, You and I. These days I get so wrapped up in herb hunting that I sometimes don't have time to converse with You. But I always think You're guiding me through the moments and into the next step. Guiding me, yes, but guiding me where?

How could I tell Harold that I'm certain an ALLIS cure lies just around the bend? I couldn't, not yet. I don't know which bend. Something helpful is here on Borneo, but again it's not the whole answer. And yet, somewhere, nearby I think, I just tingle with the feeling that We've got an answer.

Gurner whispered to the stars, taking care not to disturb his friends. "And I won't let myself even think it's one more dead plant energy."

The healer paused and listened, both to the jungle noises and to the various breathing rhythms of his sleeping companions.

Oh my friend, God. We've come a long ways. And We've still got a long road to travel.

We've got an unaccountable worldwide disease that has, as of last night's newscast, claimed over 150 million humans. Three out of every 130 people on Earth. It's like a big clock got wound too tight, and now it can do nothing but tick-tock out its death toll.

But the amazing thing. ALLIS is not so unaccountable. You've given me an insight into the whys and whats behind ALLIS. But . . . me? Why give me such a view? Who's going to believe me espousing such an obscure concept? . . . if We even make it to the part where I try to explain the origins of ALLIS. Right now, I've got to put everything into finding that cure.

Gurner rolled on to his side, facing away from the other Gang members. He continued, ground level, staring into the darkness.

Where are We, God? Just for perspective, where are We sitting?

We've got a great "Would have been," a recently extinct AC herb that more than proved itself the complete cure for ALLIS and all of its manifestations.

We've got an abundant AH herb from Canada that allows ALLIS victims to progress to a coma and at that point keeps them alive a week or so longer. Vegetables, but alive. I guess the various nations have accumulated thousands of people in that near-death coma, all being kept alive by an infusion of AH tea.

But with the army now needing to protect that plant from poachers, with the violence now happening in that corner of Canada . . . did We do good, God, or did We do bad, bringing that herb to light?

Gurner turned onto his other side and continued his staring, right into Reeves' back.

We've got AK in Sweden, again in abundance, the herb that raises the temperature of the ALLIS victim back to near normal. Doesn't keep him from dying, but does warm him up a bit. Not such a grab-and-stash war going on over that one, but still lots of people sneak in and steal the herb, people hungry for any ray of hope.

And then We've got the AR beautiful plant in Brazil. That Urueu-Wau-Wau chief didn't have to reveal it to me or anyone else. He knew what the consequences of publicizing that powerful herb might be to his land and his people. But he did. He chose to give civilization the most potent ALLIS fighter to date.

That little fern almost stops ALLIS from progressing. It's amazing. Doesn't heal it but almost stops it. Those near dead stay near dead for a week longer. Those almost in the coma don't enter the coma for a time. Those a few days into the weakness and the temperature decline, when given the herb, they do progress into the disease, but they progress very slowly. No one comes out from the disease. The herb merely postpones the inevitable. Science is centering most of its attention on analyzing that one. And humankind is centering most of its creative resources on sneaking into the Urueu-Wau-Wau reservation and stealing it. Trouble is, this plant isn't very abundant. It's small, it's sparse, and it isn't widely distributed. The cooperating world governments decided that this species must be reserved for research, and are protecting it at all costs. All costs means an incredible international force surrounding the portion of jungle where it grows. All costs means blowing away anyone attempting to steal some. No tiny amount of human folks are trying some amazing ways of stealing . . . and no tiny amount of human folks are getting blown away.

As the snores from his sleeping companions grew louder, Gurner felt freer to voice his thoughts aloud. He repositioned himself onto his back and again fastened his eyes to the stars. "Seems like everywhere We go, God, We create a mess. What will happen to the land and to the people of the land when the real cure is found?"

Reeves, beginning his sentences with double talk even in his sleep, muttered something about burning with a malarial fever while floating on an iceberg in the Great Salt Lake. The other snoozing Gang members joined his restlessness, churning and groaning in a few moments of broken sleep before again sinking into deeper slumber. Gurner listened to the activity, returning to his thoughts after it passed.

Speaking of messes, God. We now have in this world a scapegoat catchword. And that word is "Gurner." Have You forgotten that all I really want is to be alone and unknown in some untrammeled place? This exalted situation of having the whole world instantly fulfill one's every bidding . . . all it really does is generate resentment and hatred toward the fellow stuck in that position. From national monarchs to elected presidents to everybody, nobody wants a stranger barging into their country, telling them that such and such must happen, NOW.

Back at home We got an AMA and an FDA smoldering like an underground coal-seam fire, waiting to burst into flame and consume me the first chance they get. We got a President and most of his cabinet mighty miffed because We've made them look like the bandage-on-an-artery-cut fools they are.

One thing is good. There're no more hordes of people coming to cheer me on like they did at Oregon and Europe. People want flash and show. I'm about as radiant as a smoky candle on its last sputter. Now the general attitude is, "Yes, we need him, but let's not take it any further than that."

But again, what will happen to the "needed one," yours truly, when the miracle herb is found? In fact, what will happen to the entire scene? Right now the world is acting as a harmonious unit. Could cooperation continue, or will there be all-out grab for the cure? Once it's over, will the FDA fan their flames and whisk me into obscurity? Will pissed-off government leaders execute their longed-for revenge? What will happen to this healer when it's all anticlimax? . . .

". . . Well, You don't answer questions in the Kalimantan jungle any more than You do anywhere else, do You?"

End of Book IV

BOOK V

COOPERATION

· 32 ·
Newstime

August 24, 2008. Excerpts from *Newstime* magazine.

THE ALLIS-CURE WARS

An ancient and oft-repeated folk tale tells the story. Parapus, one of the higher gods watching over the activities of Earth, felt a surge of compassion for the humans below. Unlike the immortal gods, mankind inexorably lost its youth and vitality to the process of old age. Moved with pity, Parapus stole from the upper kingdom the magic elixir of youth. With this pirated treasure, the god visited Earth. There, in the mortal world, he offered humankind the drink, showing them the perpetual youth that would be theirs if they but sipped the liquid. Word of the wonder quickly spread, and within a short time thousands of persons gathered before Parapus to drink the potion that would spare them the disease of old age. Latecomers, afraid none of the drink would be left for them, began shoving their way toward the god. This action panicked thousands of other people into fears that they would be unable to obtain the potion. Within seconds, generous Parapus found himself in the middle of a raging mob, all fighting and grabbing for the cup that held the drink. Parapus was knocked down and trampled. The cup was wrested from his hands, but in the melee it fell to the ground. Its precious contents spilled into the dirt. No one received the gift of eternal youth. Parapus, they say, is still angry and will have nothing more to do with humans.

The 2008 version of this story requires but a few word changes to be accurate. Substitute the ALLIS disease for the disease of old age. Replace the youth elixir with the names of the four herbs presently known to combat ALLIS. One could consider the healer Gurner to be an incarnation of a wiser Parapus. Though not a god, Gurner is the bearer of the herbs. And he has learned to avoid crowds.

"A disaster the likes of ALLIS is always a hydra with more heads than that of death statistics," says Dr. Adrian Loca, Psychology Department head for the University of Michigan and noted author on crowd and mass population behaviors. "Fear is one of them."

Fear. Fear of dying from an unknowable, incurable disease. Gurner has revealed the ALLIS-healing properties of four different plants in various locations around the world. Science has so far been unable to unlock the healing secrets of these plants.

Two hundred and twenty-five million people have died of the ALLIS disease. Anyone alive may be next. No one wants to be part of the next set of statistics. People are scared, and because of that fear, Parapus' drama is being reenacted on a grand scale.

West of Prince George, British Columbia, Canada, the Canadian and United States Armies have sealed off a 400-square-kilometer section of some of the wildest land on the North American continent. This mountainous terrain forms the primary habitat of the first effective ALLIS fighter, the AH (ALLIS Hopeful) herb. When ALLIS victims are given regular infusions steeped from the leaves and flowers of the plant, this Saxifrage family member has proven effective in postponing death.

Central British Columbia, following the discovery of this herb, suddenly became a focal point for a mass migration of people. Thousands of persons, many from other nations, came possessed with the singular idea of obtaining AH. Mountainsides of the plant were ripped up and transported to destinations other than research laboratories and hospitals. Researchers feared that a repeat episode of the extinct Amazonian Orchid would soon occur. World governments demanded protection of the plant.

The mountains of the Nechako Range are peaceful now. But the highways and waterways leading to them paint a different picture. Riot squads composed of trained soldiers ward off throngs continually attempting to penetrate into the rugged country. Anything so priceless creates its own market. The underground market for the AH herb brings 100 times the street price of cocaine.

Northern Sweden's AK herb doesn't offer the same life-extending qualities as its Canadian adjunct. An herb that simply relieves the hypothermia symptoms of ALLIS is not as much in demand. Nevertheless, Sweden and its neighboring countries have posted a heavy concentration of armed personnel around the Kebnekaise mountain area in case a research breakthrough reveals the secrets of this alpine moss plant and its market demand increases.

Brazil is "where the action is." Rondonia, Brazil, and the Urueu-Wau-Wau Indian Reserve in Rondonia, to be precise. Less than one month ago a Chief Ianiá of the Urueu-Wau-Wau Indians revealed to Gurner a plant that his tribe had found effective in countering ALLIS. Gurner, in turn, exposed the plant's identity—a small fern of the Hymenophyllaceae family, now more widely known as AR—to the research world. Life in Rondonia has not been the same since.

AR proved to be the most powerful and most promising potential of the tiny ALLIS-cure arsenal. An infusion of AR given to an ALLIS victim noticeably slows the disease process. Persons diagnosed near the coma stage of ALLIS have, when given an infusion of the herb, gained up to seven days' extended consciousness. Persons in earlier degrees of ALLIS postpone the coma by three weeks. In the final analysis, people still die. But the life-prolonging qualities of this plant are the most anything has offered in countering the Loggerman's Disease. Researchers make their greatest efforts to attempt to unravel the secrets of the AR herb. The same is true of those trying to confiscate the herb for their own use.

Gurner must have sensed the potential for destruction of this rare rain forest herb. He refused to reveal its identity and location until a strong international protection force had securely sealed off a sizable section of the forest along the Northern Urueu-Wau-Wau Indian Reserve. Well it is for general humanity he made such a move. AR is a sparse plant growing only in isolated corners of upper Amazon River tributaries in the Pacaas Novos region. Since the plant and its potential were revealed, incalculable numbers of people have tried to invade the forest sanctuary and steal the herb. Seventy-five thousand international troops equipped with air support and advanced personnel tracking devices now protect the area, as dictated by international agreement. Every day fifty to seventy-five persons are killed trying to sneak through the military boundary. Some were attempting to make their fortune . . . others, to prolong their lives.

Finally, science—and the military might needed to keep science's raw materials intact—turn toward the Asian country of

Malaysia, specifically its island portion called Borneo. A brief but dramatic incident occurred there after Brian Johnson, the Gurner Gang "diplomat," broadcast charges that the Malaysian Government was willfully interfering with Gurner and his exploration of the island. He feared that the Malaysian hierarchy of leaders would hamper a valuable plant discovery and oppose disclosure of such a finding.

So anxious—yea, so downright terrified of the ALLIS potential—has the world grown, so utterly dependent has the vulnerable world become upon the possible discoveries of this one man, that the impossible was once again achieved. International boundaries were ignored, language communication problems overcome, and less than thirty minutes after Johnson aired his plea, every warship available in Asian waters—including Indian, Thai, Chinese, Australian, Russian, and American naval vessels—moved full-throttle toward Malaysia. No one felt they were merely playing war games. Malaysia was informed it would cooperate or be flattened. Its rulers instantly raised the white flag, claiming it had never attempted interference with Gurner.

Ten hours later Gurner called for an international protective force to be stationed along the upper reaches of the wild Rajang River in the Iran Mountains near the Borneo-Indonesia border. Gurner, Dr. Stephanie Peters, and *Newstime* correspondent Harold Reeves embarked for the city of Jakarta, Java, to meet with Johnson and begin initial testing on ALLIS victims with their latest plant discovery. Environmentalist Jerry Willox remains in Borneo, Malaysia, to direct arriving field scientists to the jungle plant.

As of press time for this edition, initial reports from Jakarta indicate that Gurner has discovered another ALLIS-effective plant. Initial reports also indicate that this plant is not *the* ALLIS cure every person in the world wishes would be discovered. This herb appears to mitigate the loss of muscular strength associated with the disease, but its healing properties seem to be limited to that aspect.

Botanists have labeled the new plant "AB," and have yet to find a scientific family under which to classify it. AB presents itself as another undiscovered, unclassified, and unknown plant species. AB also appears to have narrowly escaped the fate of Oregon's AC herb. Malaysia promotes massive clear-cutting and timber export of the Borneo rain forest jungles. Loggers were scheduled to enter the pristine upper Rajang jungle area—the only area where AB thrives—within two weeks.

Once again Gurner stirs the world's deepest feelings. Heartfelt gratitude tops the list. Again we have a hope that from this latest discovery a cure will spring forth.

But Gurner also creates our deepest frustration. How many times can you give a person dying of thirst a mere dropperful of water before you drive him crazy? How many times can this man offer an antidote for the deadliest disease and then let us realize that the remedy ultimately doesn't cure a thing? Jim Bowerns of the U.S. Food and Drug Administration asserts that Gurner is playing a game that uses the world as his chessboard while millions die in the process. Many agree with this grave accusation, including Jack Vinerson, president of the American Medical Association.

As always, Gurner arouses questions. Who is this unknown, uncommunicative representative of the herbal and intuitive world? Who indeed is this Joe-out-of-the-woodwork who can, in a few sentences, persuade national forces around the globe to focus their combined power on subduing any nation that interferes with his purpose? No one can consider opposing or obstructing the healer's present quest. As strange as his methods are, his is the only ray of hope in the ALLIS crisis. But many wonder if he doesn't carry a purpose beyond philanthropy.

Gurner doesn't bother to publicly answer these questions. According to Reeves, the single reporter allowed close to Gurner and Gurner Gang activities, the healer doesn't have the mind-set or the time to plot such weighty schemes. Reeves: "The man spends twenty hours a day racing against an alarm clock that will, if it rings, sound mankind's end. He's so busy trying to fit the puzzle of an ALLIS cure together—a puzzle that is terribly complicated because of all the missing pieces due to ecological disasters—that he's never considered the future effects of his work."

· · · · ·

ALLIS AND THE WEARY SCIENTIST BLUES

Scientists began their frustrating attempts to unravel ALLIS as soon as the disease manifested. As the plague grew, so grew the investigation efforts. Gurner came along and discovered an effective herb in a faraway locality, and researchers immediately jogged off to that area. Now, wherever in the wide world Gurner discovers an ALLIS healing potential, there journeys a diverse collection of scientists. Anyone reading updates on the ALLIS progression must believe that the land mass of Earth crawls with the ubiquitous man of science.

"Scientists of every varying background now seem to work as a tuned and cooperating unit," says Dr. H.G. Wilmore of the Hittleman Biological Laboratory and Institute of the Sciences in San Diego. "But don't think it's easy. Tens of thousands of men and women in every aspect of physical research have been pushing themselves day and night trying to unravel this thing. Disappointment, frustration, failure, and fatigue have been their only rewards."

Scientific study has never been more convenient. Money is now no barrier to research. Bills similar to the United States De-ALLIS bill diverting military funds to ALLIS research have been passed worldwide. The military no longer resists the reappropriation of its allowance. Presently, armed confrontations are a thing of the past. Also, many military officers and personnel, including General Jerome Clapboard of the Joint Chiefs of Staff, form the one in every thirty persons who have succumbed to ALLIS.

Dr. Wilmore: "I'd like to say 'when,' but being a realist I'll say 'if' . . . if Gurner finds *the* herb, it's still going to require solid scientific research to unfold the workings of the cure and to reproduce that cure into a safe and effective form that can be mass manufactured and distributed to vast populations. Scientists will be there to answer the call of hard work that follows any viable discovery."

Governments in accord; wars a phenomenon of the past; scientists joining hands in support and allegiance: the world has united as never before. We fervently pray that a breakthrough, scientific or Gurnerific, happens soon, so this piece of Utopia can be enjoyed for longer than the estimated fourteen to sixteen weeks it will take for ALLIS to end human life on Earth.

· 33 ·
Energy

August 28, 2008, 7:50 P.M. The state of Queensland, near the Great Barrier Reef of the Pacific Ocean coast, close to the town of Cairns, near the foot of Mount Bartle Frere, Australia.

Gurner eased his pack from his shoulders and paused to mentally scan the flattish and more open area in front of him. After a few minutes, he turned and called to the four people following his footsteps. "Ho. It's getting too dark. Let's camp here. Something about here feels just right to me. Something feels like this place holds the key we've all been waiting for."

Jerry Willox joined Gurner in viewing the potential campsite. "Jeez, it's nice to be in an English speaking county again. I guess it's a foolish prejudice, but the wilderness in a country where I can communicate seems a bit more friendly and welcoming."

Dr. Peters, covered with branch and vine scratches, dropped her pack to the ground as she joined the two men. "Arrgh. The crummy bugs are the same. Icky, crawly, itchy, all the time and everywhere. The evening forest sounds are the same. Creepy, weird, and unidentifiable. And because Gurner was in such a hurry to get here and wouldn't take time to stock up supplies at Brisbane, the food tonight and tomorrow morning is going to be the same. Plain, tasteless, insufficient in quantity, and not cooked with much enthusiasm."

Johnson, looking as fresh as if he just washed in a city lavatory, joined the crew. "Gurner hasn't been with us in mind or spirit all day. Hello, Gurner. Are you there? . . . Where are you, Gurner?"

Gurner jumped slightly. "Huh? Oh, sorry. Brian, when we flew over the northeast corner of Australia this morning, every atom of my sixth sense began tingling. And the closer we get, the more I tingle. I'm just reaching out, trying to interpret the feelings;

trying not to get too excited in case it isn't what we all hope it is. With over 300 million persons ALLIS-dead, it's hard not to hope."

Reeves, who never could get in shape no matter how long and hard he hiked, practically wheezing, limped up from his lagging position. "You, you think, Gurner, the key may be here?"

"Don't quote me too early, Harold. But all this concentration these past months has turned me into what you could call a fine-tuned plant-detecting radar. Something in this area signals the energy we've been looking for."

"Your face and, your face and your tone of voice are saying something else."

Gurner shot the reporter a questioning glance. *Intuition must be catching.* "You're right, Harold. There's also something black being picked up on the screen. I don't know what it is. To decipher it, I need silence and meditation time."

"Well then, well then, Gurner . . ." Reeves let his pack crash to the ground, and pulling a notepad out of his pocket, the lanky reporter crashed into a sitting pose on top of it. "I must ask, ask you a favor. If our ALLIS-cure plant is here, life will become even busier. Would you, while these three fine associates set up camp and see what miracles they can work on our proposed dinner, would you tell us what you have avoided telling everyone for months? Would you present what you understand to be the cause of ALLIS?"

Gurner shook his head no. "Oh, Harold. Now hardly seems like the time to—"

"On the, on the contrary, Gurner. The eve of the major discovery to its cure could only be the best possible time."

Gurner again retreated. "Ah, it's just a crazy theory that prob—"

Willox paused from his squaw wood gathering and joined Reeves' team. "C'mon Gurner. Theorize at us. We'll only laugh at you and tell you you're crazy. Send you to bed completely mortified. But I really want to hear your ideas. Nobody else has a good theory, but then, nobody else has had any luck on a cure, either. We want to hear any and all thoughts. Don't we, guys?"

"Indeed." Johnson was the only person in the world who could construct a no-impact campfire and not get his hands or clothes dirty. "Gurner, with your intuition, what do you think the cause of ALLIS is? A supergerm released by the army? A discard from biological gene splicing experimentation run amuck? World pollution lowering every human's resistance to a dormant and hidden virus? What's happening?"

"Well, I . . ." Gurner emitted a sigh. "Well, OK. I'll try and make it half believable. Uh, to start things, Stephanie, give us a medical dissertation on the pineal gland, will you?"

Dr. Peters was muttering into the nearly empty food sack. She looked up. "What? The pineal gland? What's that got to do with the price of corn in Iowa on a Thursday afternoon?"

"Please, Stef?"

"Well, OK . . . pineal gland. Pineal gland . . . let's see if I can get a little rote going here . . . named for its conical shape, it's a small reddish-gray endocrine gland located in the roof of the third ventricle of the brain. Um, it's innervated by the peripheral autonomic nervous system, and it does secrete some hormones, the main one being melatonin, which may modulate the hypothalamus gland."

Dr. Peters paused, trying to remember more. "You know, this is all textbook physiology. The truth is, we barely touched the pineal gland in our studies. The structure is of more interest to metaphysicians than to physicians. I seem to remember that it's controlled by environmental lighting, and that a rare tumor called a pinealoma can happen. Overall, it's not a body part doctors philosophize about during their coffee breaks."

Dr. Peters shrugged her shoulders and returned part of her attention to the food sack. "That doesn't tell you much. Sorry."

"But you did, Stephanie, thanks." Gurner sat down to talk while Johnson, Dr. Peters, and Willox, listening intently, arranged camp and campfire accommodations. Reeves folded himself over his notepad.

"Two statements give me a place to start. First, metaphysicians and philosophers and occultists and yogis consider the pineal gland to be man's seat of spiritual awakening and illumination. Just keep in the back of your minds that a steady line of teachers has connected the pineal gland with spiritual dimensions and awakenings.

"Second, you said something about the pineal gland being affected by light. Light is an energy. Again, a connection between energy and the pineal gland."

Gurner cupped his hands together and mimed placing their imagined contents to the side. "OK. Just put those thoughts on hold, but keep them close.

"Now, you've all witnessed me working. I place hands on

people and listen to their bodies, then I'm able to recommend an herbal and/or nutritional course for them to follow. That's what I did with Mary, Brian, you'll remember. That's what I did with little Johnny. Well, the angels don't talk to me and tell me what's wrong. I don't go into a trance and produce what they call a 'reading.' What happens is that I tune into the *energy* of the body, system by system, organ by organ. There is an energy in everything. And to understand what happens in my healing, you have to accept the fact that I can feel it. I can feel the energy of, say a kidney, and tell if it is in balance with the rest of the person's body energies. A team of professional medical persons may examine that same kidney to the Nth degree and find nothing wrong with it. I'm not necessarily talking about physical manifestations when I say an organ's energy is off.

"The second way-out, unprovable thing you have to accept here is that herbs mainly heal with energy. Not only do they contain vitamins and minerals and cell salts and alkaloids and amino acids and allantoins and aloins and on and on with a listing of chemical components that nurture and feed the body, but they also have an 'energy' about them, a vibrancy to their being. You have to accept that a plant's energy directs itself to or is compatible with certain parts of the body. Oregon grape detoxifies and rebuilds the liver, not only because of the berbamine and other chemical ingredients in it, but also because its energy augments the energy of the weakened liver. Uva Ursi is used often in urinary complaints, partially because of its large amounts of tannins and their anti-bacterial properties and partially because its energies give such a boost to that part of the body."

Gurner studied his audience. "You all still with me?"

No one shook their head no, so the healer continued. "Enter the gift I have. I can sense the weakened or overactive energies of the parts of the human body. I can also sense the energies of the herbs and know which ones will specifically balance the out-of-balance properties of the person I'm working on. Poor doctors, they have to prescribe a medicine hit or miss from a grab bag of medicines that might work on a problem. I can specifically tell what plant will work for a certain person and what won't."

Gurner paused, hoping his words would sink into the listeners' minds. Reeves feverishly scribbled notes onto his pad. The healer resumed.

"So. Energy, that little word with no single definition, has a lot to do with what I'm leading to.

"OK. The first persons afflicted with this new and strange disease the world was naming ALLIS, when they came to me, all of them—Mary and Johnny and everyone with the affliction since—when I tuned into their inner workings, the pineal gland, energy-wise, was in a highly weakened state. The meds, in their extensive studies, have scrutinized every bodily component including the pineal. But if science can't see, hear, feel, touch, or taste a thing, usually by a machine, it tends to discount it. Nothing physical has proven itself wrong with the pineal. But a deeper, 'energyless' pineal gland is one of two common threads I find in every ALLIS victim.

"The second thread . . . call it coincidence or call it Divine Planning, but the summer before the ALLIS outbreak began, I happened upon that untouched forested hillside in Oregon called Squanni Hill. Even though my plant energy-sensing abilities were still pretty new, I was blown away by the feeling of power emanating from that AC plant. It just . . . hummed with potency and spirit. With no idea what it was about, I gathered a bunch of it and brought it home to dry. There it remained in my root closet until the first ALLIS-struck person came to me. Some last minute, almost subconscious intuition induced me to throw a few AC leaves into an herbal concoction I'd given him to try. Given him without much hope, I might add. By that fluke he became ALLIS healing number one.

"So, according to me, with ALLIS, we have a pineal gland that on some scientifically unprovable level is not up to par. We also have an exotic herb that hums with energy for the spacey perceptions of a backwoods recluse. You folks are intelligent beings. Are you sure you want me to continue?"

The three male Gang members joined Gurner around the growing fire.

"You bet."

"Yup."

"Continue, yes, yes."

Dr. Peters still nosed through the food packs. "And from a combination of the two we have a proven ALLIS cure. Please do continue. But first. Gurner. All we got for supper are beans. Plain crummy beans. Any herbs around here that might liven up the meal a bit?"

Gurner looked around the immediate area and plucked up a handful of odd looking, broad-leafed plants. "Um, these guys have a pungency to them. Why don't you try them, Stephanie?"

Dr. Peters wrinkled her nose as she took the leaves from the healer. "Great. Thanks. Now do continue."

Gurner took a deep breath and again dove into his discourse. "Hokay. But it does get weirder. My first conclusions from initial evidence said that a weakened pineal gland causes ALLIS. Next logical step: AC strengthens the pineal gland and heals ALLIS. Sounds so simple. But to me that felt like a smile missing about three teeth. Why in the heck was there this sudden affliction of the pineal gland? On a worldwide scale? Something, in some way, had to be a reason behind the reason. And this something had to follow quite a listing of characteristics.

"It had to be all around the world at the same time. It had to be deadly. It had to be something that may have been present for a long time. Diseases caused by unknowns rarely happen overnight, out of the blue. The cause had to be something present for a long time, all around the world, and that could manifest its deadliness all of a sudden, sort of like happens with an accumulated poison. And, if it was affecting the pineal gland in a nonphysical way, it had to have something to do with energy . . . weakening energy . . . deadly, weakening energy. . . . Can anybody guess? . . . Ubiquitous, accumulative, deadly, weakening energy?"

The four listeners looked vacantly at each other. Willox's faced suddenly flashed with a grimace of terror.

"Jeez!"

Gurner nodded. "Jerry's got it. The environmentalist would. Heh, this turns out to be quite the apt analogy. The environmentalist gets it. The government, the medicals, and the news media probably never will.

"You tell them, Jerry. I gotta get rid of some water."

Gurner visited the bushes while listening to the sounds of startled voices from the direction of the campfire. He noticed another plant species beside his feet and reached down to pluck a few of its leaves. Then the healer walked back to the fire circle.

"Here, Stephanie. Put some of these leaves in your bean pot. We might yet rescue tonight's dinner."

"Gurner. This is kind of hard to swallow."

"I know, Brian. But I challenge you. Prove me wrong. I don't think you can. Tell me, in simple terms, what radioactivity is, what its purpose on this planet is, and how it kills life. This conclusion is not simply blaming all of life's problems on nukes. I don't completely disregard scientific approaches and explanations."

Johnson thought for a few moments. "Well, er, radiation is the release of energy from an atom, and ionizing radiation is the dangerous stuff with its gamma and x-rays and its alpha and beta particles. It kills by its high . . . *energy* . . . and its great penetrating power that damages living tissue. But . . . its purpose on this planet? . . . I see I don't really know."

The healer again nodded. "Well, I don't know much either. But I can tell you a few facts that support the vague Gurner theory that we've plutoniumed and strontium-90ed ourselves into this hell of a mess called ALLIS.

"Everything from humans to animals to plants to the Earth has a life cycle. Radiation is part of the normal life-death principle of the Earth. It and its byproducts are rarely a poison when left in the original environment. God did know what He was doing. In truth, over the long, long period of time, the powerful atomic energies help decay the inorganic elements of the Earth into those viable ten inches to two feet of topsoil we all depend upon for sustenance. It's when these radioactive elements are mined and removed, concentrated into condensed amounts, that their power becomes lethal. Mere grams of some of the stuff can wipe out biospheres."

Gurner realized that his communication was too vague. "Look, you remember that chemistry class periodic chart of the elements with all the hundred and some known atoms arranged in columns by numbers and weights? Most life on Earth evolves around just a few of the elements on that chart. Most everything that lives centers on carbon, oxygen, silicon, hydrogen, nitrogen, and a few others. Carbon is the base of our chemistry, right? We need other minerals in minute amounts, but most of them hang within the one through thirty Atomic Number classification of hydrogen through zinc.

"OK. File that, and look at this. Science has noted that the well and healthy cells of a living organism tend to have a firm and rounder shape to them. The same cells, when sick and dying, tend to acquire a flatter shape. Similarly, carbon, oxygen, the elements with the lower periodical numbers that we so depend on for life itself, they have a roundish, fuller shape to their atom structure. The further up the scale and away from carbon the atomic number travels—and the radioactive elements are really high on the scale—the higher the number, the more flat becomes the element's structural shape. Do you see? Move into the atomic shape of the radioactive elements, and the more flat-shaped, like death, the stuff becomes. Of course, talking about the shapes of atoms is just a way to visualize it. But I am convinced that our energy scientists went the wrong way on the chart. They should have moved toward number one, hydrogen, instead of into the dying extremities of radioactivity. Simple analysis states that every time a goddamned atom bomb goes off, every time a nuclear reactor fails or in some way pollutes, every time the incredible volume of radioactive waste modern man creates either spills or leaks or is improperly stored and escapes, every time and all the time we are adding death energy to the world."

Gurner pinched off a few leaves from another nearby plant and tossed them into the boiling pot of beans.

"Mount Saint Helens and Chernobyl and snow samples from Antarctica prove what a few scientists in the mid-'50s, including Albert Schweitzer, were warning us about. That there's no containing radioactivity to a single area. Did you know—in 1956 an eminent authority on radioactivity, a Dr. Ralph Lapp, said that the future is going to be in serious trouble because the upper stratosphere of our atmosphere was accumulating the sorry results of A-bomb testings. And that in forty or so years it would start giving back to us—to our kids, rather—all that we gave it in the form of radioactive isotopes and byproducts. And that life on Earth would then go beyond its maximum safe level for radioactive exposure. In 1956 a prominent scientist was saying this."

Gurner's expressions gained in intensity with each sentence. "The French government still tests bombs in the open air of the South Pacific. In the late '50s and early '60s our own Defense Department and Atomic Energy Commission detonated many big-time bombs thirty to 100 miles up in the atmosphere. Project Argus and Project Starfish were the respective names of these explosions. They did this just to see what would happen to the Van Allen radiation belts that girdle the Earth. Just to see what would happen! God All-the-mighty. I wish there were a way I could tell them what *has* happened."

Gurner's physical gestures added harmonics to his facial expression. "Add all the nuclear reactors for electricity, add all the low-grade medical radiations and food irradiation follies, and especially add uranium/plutonium enhancement for beyond-super-weapons that dear Dr. Lapp couldn't have foreseen . . . and I'd say we have OD'd this little planet with too big a fix of death-dealing, flat-shaped particles."

Gurner paused. Even the local rain-forest creatures seemed to have ceased singing.

"So what do I think the true cause of ALLIS is? I think it's a physical thing—radiation/radioactive energy—attacking our spiritual master gland, bringing its energy down, and in doing that destroying us physically. It's plutonium. It's not God punishing sinners. The only way God's hand is in this is that He gave us free will—the free will to punish ourselves for our own sins, which really translates to us advancing technology without similarly advancing love and understanding."

Gurner's face assumed a fixed and distant stare as he gazed into the fire. "I can't prove it, you know. I can't get in front of a bunch of nuclear physicists and say that I think radiation lowers the spiritual energy in a person, and that by saturating the Earth with it we've also lowered our planet's overall energy. I know with all my intuitive being that radioactivity unleashed is the cause of ALLIS. But in practicality I can only do what you and I have been doing: try and find that cure before it's too late.

"Science, until it learns to look through different eyes, will never find a cure for ALLIS. It's a disease of the subtler-than-physical energies. The AC herb supplied that kind of needed energy to the pineal. AH and AK and AR and AB are only partial answers because they contain lesser amounts of that energy."

Gurner looked up and at his friends. The firelight reflecting from his eyes added an intensity to his gaze. "But I'm pretty excited tonight. I think the plant we'll find here will be the key, probably not by itself, but when added to the others. AC was unique in another way, you know. Competent herbalists rarely recommend just one herb to solve a client's problem. Herbs work best as team members. AC was an exception. Our four current ALLIS herbs alone and together don't have the energy ommph of AC. But if what I'm feeling now is correct, the herb from this area will be the tie-together, the proper catalyst, so maybe—I say *maybe*, Harold—maybe we'll have the energy we need, via combination of the five herbs, to reverse ALLIS."

Gurner paused a final time before concluding his class. "At least, I pray that it be so."

Amens resounded around the campfire.

"Jeez, I hope so, Gurner. In four to five weeks ALLIS could reach a billion people, and I live in daily fear Jenny is going to be one of them."

"You know, Gurner, finding the herbal cure doesn't really take care of the radiation problem."

"No, Brian. It doesn't. But at this point all we can do is try for the temporary solution. Convincing the world of the real cause would take longer than ALLIS gives us. First order is to find any cure, and then try to convince."

Gurner sat back to indicate he was finished speaking.

"Well, let me convince you radioactive gentlemen to come and partake of tonight's supper: beans a la Gurner herbs. The meal certainly smells . . . interesting. Might even move some of the accumulated cesium-137 through your intestines."

Willox slapped his forehead with one hand. "Oh jeez . . . more radionuclear vapors forced into our poor atmosphere."

"You environmentalists. Always worrying about the Earth first. What about our poor cobalt-60 weakened noses? Especially now that the pineal gland isn't there to back it up."

"You government people. Always worrying about your own physical comforts first."

Gurner smiled.

Dr. Peters doled out the beans into individual bowls. "Well, here's to tomorrow. May we find what we're looking for."

The five clinked their bowls together and began munching on the bean meal.

The munching mode didn't last long.

"Gurner. This is really bad. And this time it's not my fault."

"Jeez. Reminds me of moose turd pie. Only I can't say, 'it's good, though.'"

"Sorry, folks. Obviously, I'm better at medicinal herbs than culinary herbs."

"We had a meal something like this once at the employees' cafeteria at the FDA offices. The entire staff, including Jim Bowerns, went on strike."

"I won't, won't report you, Gurner—but I would comment, comment, that this meal is completely . . . energyless."

· 34 ·
Blackness

August 28, 2008, 11:43 P.M. Australia.

If Heaven really isn't "up," as everyone assumes, then God made an awful mistake in choosing His supposed home. The clear, starry and "up" sky of northwestern Australia is simply meant to be looked into while it spontaneously directs a gazer's attention toward the Divine.

Gurner lay awake, gazing and focusing his inner attention up, toward what he hoped was the right direction.

God Almighty. What, what, what is going on here? I know as I've never known before that somewhere near this area grows the plant answer to the world's prayers. And it is not extinct; it is alive. These senses of mine have fine-tuned a little more, and now I can pretty much tell the difference between present and extinct plant species energies. So we do have a long-yearned-for answer.

But You're never One to allow Your seekers to feel like they got it all figured out. I feel like I'm floating inside a black hole. WHY?! . . .

. . . Something about this situation smacks of pete-and-repeat. I feel like I did the day I led those scientists up Squanni Hill to the AC herb logging disaster. Something ominous looms ahead, even though it's supposed to be nothing but rainbows. What is this blackness?

. . . Maybe it's simply a part of me that is facing uncertainty. Maybe ol' Gurner has grown to enjoy this role of having the world depend on him. And of being in the uncanny power position where his words create more conflict AND harmony than anybody has ever been able to create before. Maybe ol' Gurner isn't as ready to return to being a backwoods hermit as he leads himself to believe.

Stars and the "up" direction were also made for voicing one's problems to. "I don't know. I just don't know. All this intuitive power and I can't even decipher my deepest thoughts and motives."

Anyway, soon we'll have the cure for ALLIS, and after a few days of testing herbs on disease victims, the show will rest on the shoulders of those more capable than I. They'll have to somehow make a combination of the herbs viable and distributable for the many humans of the Earth.

And I'll . . . I'll be free. I can vanish. I really do want to vanish. I don't think I'm hooked on being a figurehead. God, maybe You and I will do as We wanted to do back in Oregon. Just take off. Maybe We'll disappear into Australia. Get lost with an Aboriginal tribe and not show Our faces for a few years.

The stars disappeared from the healer's vision as he closed his eyes. His thoughts continued at full pace.

I'll sure miss Brian and Jerry. And kooky ol' Harold . . .

. . . And Stephanie. Dear Stephanie, a beautiful lady like you surely ought to soon find yourself a man whose impulses aren't all bound up in intuitive isolationism. You've worked your way into my spiritual searching . . . and heart. I won't tell you this now, not at this late date, but if we were staying together much longer . . .

Anyway. So. Tomorrow. Find a cure. Be free. Life finally reverts back to normal. All is well.

Gurner's eyes again opened, and he looked pleadingly at the nighttime sky. "Why am I so spooked about tomorrow?"

• 35 •
Standoff

August 29, 2008, 10:29 A.M. Near Mount Bartle Frere, Queensland, Australia.

Sure-footed steps, long strides walking rapidly and with purpose, moved through the rain-forest undergrowth toward the makeshift wilderness camp the Gurner Gang members had established the previous night. Jerry Willox's voice sounded peremptory as he called out to the two individuals seated beside the ash pile of last night's campfire.

"Brian! . . . Stephanie!"

The doctor looked up from her dishwashing. "Hey, Jerry. You're back early. Not even lunchtime yet. Did our herbal bloodhound uncover something already?" Dr. Peters suddenly noticed the solemn undercurrents in Willox's manner. "Well, crumb. You don't look too happy. Something wrong?"

"Gurner wants you two to come and join us. ASAP, I'd say."

Johnson placed his teacup on a log. "What's happening, Jerry?"

"Quite truthfully, Brian, I'm not sure. All Gurner said to me was to get you guys. That, quote: 'This is too big to handle by myself.' Those are the only words he spoke all morning. C'mon. I'll clue you in as we walk. Gurner and Harold are only about ten minutes away."

With facial expressions mirroring the seriousness of the occasion, the three Gang members retraced Willox's path. Dr. Peters submitted an observation and a question.

"I don't like the feel of this. What the heck happened, Jerry?"

"Well, when Gurner and Harold and I left at first light this morning, Gurner was his quiet, introverted self, as he always is when he's, ah, 'listening' to plants. We wandered in no set pattern, as we always do when on a search. He knelt by the plants and meditated on them awhile, and then moved on. When we topped that rise—that one just ahead of us—Gurner grew highly animated . . . really excited. Harold and I assumed he'd found the plant he was looking for."

Willox held some bush branches to keep them from slapping back on his companions. "And I guess he did. He knelt by these bushy little things with a real succulent leaf. He 'tuned into' them, like he does. After a few moments, the biggest, grandest smile formed on his face. I thought his lips were going to rip at the corners. He investigated a few more of the same brand of plants, the grin growing all the time. Finally, he jumped up and let out a totally wonderful and barbarous war whoop. Harold and I were grinning and snapping pictures of the 'historic moment,' the moment mankind was given the ALLIS cure. Gurner started running from bush to bush, I think just to express his joy. Harold grabbed me and we started dancing. The long and winding road was over."

The environmentalist shook his head and disappeared into his own thoughts for a few moments. That was too long for Johnson. "C'mon, c'mon, Jerry. Don't leave us hanging. Keep talking, man."

Willox pointed to a rise in front of them. "They're just over the top of this hill. Anyway, it wasn't but a few minutes after the celebration started that Gurner just froze and stood where he was . . . stood like a statue . . . not a movement. Harold and I were still hugging each other and didn't think much of it. But then five or so minutes passed, and Gurner still stood there, breathing heavy, like a boxer who just gave his all for fifteen rounds and still met defeat. His smile had vanished, replaced with the most burdened look I've ever witnessed. We called to him, but he was in another sphere, and neither Harold nor I felt we ought to interrupt him.

"More minutes passed, and suddenly Gurner took off running. He ran like a possessed man to the top of the land rise beyond this one. He stood there awhile, then ran a circle around us, along a ridge top, back down to a road that cut into the original area, and finally back to the plants . . . the plants he had initially found and was so excited about. He looked at those plants, then he looked up to the sky. He raised his hands, said something aloud that we couldn't understand, and then his knees buckled under him and he fell to the ground, weeping."

"Weeping?"

"Violently. Copiously. He wept for maybe ten minutes. I left him alone. What could I do? Finally, he sort of straightened up and went into another meditation. Still as a rock. After a while he asked me to fetch you two, saying it was too big for him to handle by himself."

Dr. Peters and Johnson looked at each other, and then both looked at Willox. The environmentalist shrugged his shoulders. "And now you two know all I know. Something's amiss, and whatever it is, it's bad."

Willox and Dr. Peters and Johnson topped the rise and looked down upon a lush and scattered forest setting. A natural bowl, a couple-acre rocky depression in the landscape, created an open respite inside the Australian flora. On the ground, in the middle of this bowl, head between his knees, sat an obviously disconsolate Gurner. A few feet away, Reeves squatted on his heels and stared directly at the healer, saying nothing, simply watching the man the way a concerned father would guard a dispirited son. The three gently made their way to the healer and the reporter, as if trying to not disturb them or the painful scene they created.

Johnson stared for a few moments at the herbalist. "Uh, hi, Gurner. What's up?"

Gurner lifted his hand at Johnson's question, shook his head once and let his hand fall. He never looked up.

Willox spoke next. "C'mon, Gurner. I got these guys 'cause you wanted to share it with us all. You gotta tell us sometime, you know."

Gurner nodded but didn't speak.

Several minutes of an uncomfortable silence followed. The voice that finally shattered it held nary a trace of compassion.

"Gurner! Goddammit! Get your head out of your ass and start blowing some air through your larynx. You think you're the only one can carry the weight of the world? You think we got nothing better to do than stand here and watch you mope? We're all part of this show. Now suppose you start acting like it!"

Gurner raised his head and stared into Dr. Peters' challenging eyes. Gradually, a slight smile crept back onto his face. He spoke very softly. "Thanks, Stef."

The healer motioned to his companions to sit down beside him. "Well, my friends. Have you ever heard the saying: 'I got some good news and I got some bad news'?"

Four people stared intently at him. He placed his hand on a

succulent bush-type plant. "This little fellow here, this bush that I can't even begin to classify, is the dream come true. His energy, combined with the other four plant energies, will prevent and reverse ALLIS almost as potently as the original AC herb did. Tests will have to prove this out, but I'm telling you now, this is the one.

"I always thought I'd nickname the tie-together plant AZ, Z being the end of the search. So friends, meet the AZ herb bush, and the bona fide end to ALLIS."

Willox reached out and gently grasped a leaf on the plant, mimicking a handshake. "Great. Glad to meetcha. So why aren't we all dancing and breaking open champagne and dispatching Harold to the nearest phone with the good news?"

Gurner shifted his position. "Jerry. Follow my pointing finger. From the center of this natural bowl we're sitting in, to the top of that ridge, along it to the road, from the road to here, from here to that old mining scar, how big an area do you estimate the land within those boundaries to be?"

"Ah, not too much. Three acres. Certainly no more than four."

"And is it true, Jerry, that for years the world ecology groups have been begging the government of the state of Queensland to not be so efficient in clear-cutting the little remaining rain forest that blesses this area of Australia? That the Great Barrier Reef is being silted in because of it, and the cuts are brutally damaging the fragile land and erasing valuable habitat?"

"This is true, Gurner. Very true. I still don't understand."

The healer continued. "And isn't it also fact that the officials of the state of Queensland have pretty much told the world to go to hell? And that they've increased the cutting?"

"True again."

Gurner pointed to the west. "Well, over that ridge top there isn't a living thing standing. It's hundreds of acres of recent clear-cut."

Stunned silence greeted those words.

Gurner pointed to the south. "And across that road the hillside steepens, and the habitat changes species completely."

Stunned silence continued, hoping that what was beginning to formulate wouldn't.

Gurner pointed to the east. "And beyond those mine tailings, the face of the slope turns southward, grows drier, and the habitat again completely changes."

Silence, still stunned, was still hoping.

Gurner spread his arms and pointed to the whole world. "And for the six-plus billion people needing, in a hell of a hurry, the kind of energy this plant offers to combat our world's radioactive overkill, three acres of a not too densely growing bush herb are all that are left. Once there were hundreds of acres. I can feel that there were. Now there are three."

Silence, if it could have, would have sighed, with all hope fading away.

"The logging operation probably spared this tiny area because the trees were thinner due to the rocky bowl formation."

Silence.

"Scouting parties will have to check it out, of course, but I know there isn't any more of this plant to be had anywhere else."

Silence.

"The government of Queensland has quite literally succeeded in telling the world to go to hell."

Suddenly silence gained a voice. "Goddammit, Gurner! Enough! Will you just shut up for a while!"

Silence. For a long time everyone sat in complete silence, listening to the lack of life around them.

Dr. Peters finally rallied. "For crumb almighty's sake, look. This is bad beyond bad. But we can't just sit here and wallow. I may have an idea. It just popped into my head."

Four people stared intently at the doctor.

"Ah . . . oh crumb, I hate to start this speech by adding to the second half of your good news/bad news, Gurner. But this morning, a couple hours after you guys left, Brian and I received a pretty rough newsbreak. The Aussie helicopter pilot brought it when he came with supplies. I, ah, guess the President of the United States has raised the ALLIS victim quota by one more number. He's about eight days into it. The news hadn't been released because of fear it could cause a greater panic than people are already feeling. But now there's no hiding it."

Silence. It wasn't stunned or shocked silence. Just silence.

Dr. Peters wondered if she had made herself clear. "Like I said, I really hate to pile bad news upon bad news, but these are facts, and we might as well face them."

Silence. It wasn't an emotional silence. Just silence.

Dr. Peters realized she had been perfectly understood. "Well keee-rumm! You characters are a sensitive and distressed lot."

Willox shrugged his shoulders. "I don't feel anything. Jeez, I suppose I should. But all I feel is that he and his predecessors form most of the reasons we're where we are in this ecological disease mess. It might seem heartless, but I can't help but think, 'Gee, maybe there is such a thing as justice in this world.'"

Gurner couldn't disagree. "I don't feel anything. Not even as a healer. I think I'm too overwhelmed by the implications of Queensland's rapaciousness to be jarred by anything else."

"I feel something."

Four people stared intently at Johnson.

"But certainly not too much."

Reeves pointed his pencil at Dr. Peters. "Go on with, go on with your idea, Stephanie. Go on."

"Well crumb, You guys are like a contagious disease. I thought I was all shook up about it. But maybe I don't feel anything either. Anyway. Here's the idea. The U.S. President, a very powerful, *news-making* world figure has ALLIS. We, it appears, have the cure for ALLIS. So immediately Mr. President becomes our first test case for the five herb combination. I don't doubt that the combo will cure him. And with the cure, we also send the message that has haunted us since this journey began. With the cure of the person most watched by the world goes the message of what we as humans have done to this Earth, why annihilating it annihilates us, and how close humanity has come to doing both. It would be an unignorable means of getting that message home."

Silence evolved into a thinking silence. Willox was the first to voice his thoughts. "It has potential, Stephanie. Jeez, it might even change his outlook. Wouldn't it be incredible to have a leader sold on the idea of environment first instead of environment last if at all. What do you think, Brian?"

Johnson nodded. "There're some positive points here. The public's eye, and perhaps even the President's gratitude. It might be a vehicle in which Gurner could espouse his 'Nuclear ALLIS' theory. What do you think, Harold?"

"News is, news is news, Brian. This would be big. Big and important."

Four pairs of eyes focused on Gurner. "Gurner, how about it?"

"No."

The four Gang members stared intently at Gurner. "No?"

"We are absolutely *not* going to tell a soul about this discovery."

"What! Are you mad?"

"Listen. All of you, listen hard. The environmental shape of the world is a mess already said and done. But now we own the potential to create an even bigger mess. We have enough plant material in this three acres to cure maybe 3,000 people. Even if that could be stretched to say, 10,000, so what? You're talking a few thousand cures in a world of six billion in need. Whether you send this herb to President Wolfe or to farmer Maxwell Smith in nearby Cairns, word will be out that there is a cure. And word will just as immediately be out that there's a very limited amount of cure."

Gurner gazed into the three-acre parcel of land containing the newly discovered AZ herb. "I got another old adage for you. It goes: 'First come, first served.'"

Silence was having quite a day with the Gang members. The herbalist continued. "Don't you see? The chaos of ALLIS is nothing compared to the potential bedlam of a limited number of cures up for grabs.

"For one, who would get them, these few doses? The powerful? The rich? The elite? Just the world leaders? A few select from one country or ethnic group or skin color?

"Do you really think that the armies sent here to protect the plants will loyally do that? Let me ask you, Jerry. If no one with a ranking less than a cabinet member could enter the lottery for the AZ combination cure, wouldn't you here and now pilfer a few of the bush leaves for Jenny? How about you for your wife and son, Harold? No high-falootin' lawmaker is more important to you than them? Get an army here, and it's going to be the army that ends up with the AZ herb. It's also guaranteed that these soldiers will have to kill everyone in the world who attempts to get the herb, which everyone else in the world will do because they have nothing more to lose."

Gurner's voice regained its original power and tone. "No! Reveal this herb now and billions will know that they have no chance for a cure. No! Nothing gets said till we assess this situation and see what kind of solutions, if any, are possible."

Dr. Peters vehemently rallied against Gurner's proposal. "That goes against my grain, Gurner. People are dying, and we have a cure. It's a doctor's duty to bring the two together."

Reeves, who rarely voiced opinions, joined the doctor. "And mine, too, mine, too. This represents the biggest newsbreak since newsbreaks began. I have to report it. It's my duty to report it."

Johnson, speaking more gently, chose his side. "I'm afraid I'm with them, Gurner. Call it government idealism, but it seems wrong to not share this."

Gurner stared at the four Gang members, his intuition reading the four-to-one odds. "I can tell you guys are pretty set about sharing this. And there's too much happening to have to take the time to convince you differently."

Gurner closed his eyes, but he still seemed to be intently staring at the four persons in front of him. His voice grew harsh.

"So hear me. Before I'll allow the kind of disaster I foresee happening, I will destroy this plant. Harold, do you hear? You follow your reporting instinct with so much as one peep about this plant, and you might as well write an immediate follow-up report about me ripping every remaining bush out by the roots. This is the gospel. Not one of you or all of you together could stop me if that's what you force me to do."

The four Gang members stared in shock at the healer. They also felt truth in his words. He suddenly appeared as immovable as a mountain, and for some reason no one could muster an argument against his dictate.

Gurner spoke again, in a softer voice. "Somewhere there's an answer. Somehow there's got to be a way where no one gets left out of the healing. Please. Put your minds to it. We've got to come up with something."

· · · · ·

11:40 A.M. Near the world's few surviving AZ bush-herbs.

Crumb. He's gone. He's pushed himself too hard for too long, and he's over the line. I can't believe it. People are dying every second, and he's sitting there with his goddamned EYES shut, talking to his make-believe Whatever. We gotta get the best of him. Oh, if only I had a syringe of morphine in my bag. Or some old fashion chloroform. Or a 357 magnum. Crumb, if science had all five herbs and a knowing of the why behind the disease, they'd have to come up with something. Well, he can't stay awake forever. And if the four of us can jump him . . .

· · · · ·

Crap anyway. What a spot to be in. If I tell the world about this cure, if I give it news it has been yearning for for over a year, I condemn it to death. I'm afraid Gurner has eroded his rational marbles. Never thought he'd censor a news report. Never thought he'd come across with such a heartless threat. We need to think all right, but we need to think about what to do about Gurner.

$$\cdots$$

Jeez, what the heck happened? From the nicest guy in the world to a willful dictator in one fell swoop. He's probably right about the consequences. But I sure don't like the approach he laid on us. Power has gotten to Gurner's head. I hope his God shows him how dangerous a road that can be.

$$\cdots$$

Where did he get such strength? Where did he get such command? None of us could move against him or counter his demand. Where did he dig up such power in his voice and his presence? . . . And how long is he going to keep us from acting on this discovery?

$$\cdots$$

God. They think I'm mad. My friends, the only ones I've really got—or had. They now think I'm a despot demanding my own ways. They're disappointed in me. They think I did what I did for me. No one will ever understand the inner burning that possessed me. I'd say that You took over, but . . . that's not going to apologize to hurt friends. But You did. You filled me with what I had to do at the moment. That must mean there is a way to stretch a few thousand into billions. But how? As far as I know, that kind of dividing only happened with fish and bread. And that was by a Master. I'm just a common man with a gift of listening. How can a common man extend the AZ herb-bush? Help, God. How? . . .

The answer has to be with energy. Bad energy causes ALLIS. Energy from the plants cures it. Science will never find a cure in time because they don't deal with beyond-physical energy. But my thoughts scream that word. Energy. The answer has to be there. But how?

• 36 •
Homeopathics

August 31, 2008, 8:15 A.M. FDA Headquarters, Washington, D.C.

Jim Bowerns glared with disgust at Dan Crimsom. His voice snarled.

"Homeo . . . goddamn . . . pathics?"

Crimsom barely repressed his internal elation. The agent's face twitched slightly between alternating smile attempts and frowning smile suppressions. "No. The report simply says homeopathics. The 'goddamn' must be your interjection. Sir."

Bowerns incorporated large amounts of bile into his glare. "You love to do stuff like this to me, don't you, Crimsom?"

You bet I do, asshole. "Stuff, sir?"

"You love to bring me news that would give Christ a nervous breakdown, and then you love to watch me agonize over being helpless to counter the utter stupidity of that news. Don't you, Crimsom?"

If I can speed your ulcer on its way, Bowerns, then the day hasn't been lost. "Boss. You issued an order stating that *any* news from the Gurner Gang front be brought to you immediately. I'm simply the lesser employee fulfilling the top hat's mandate."

Bowerns almost spat as he plopped into the chair by his desk. "Um hum . . . read it again, lesser employee. Slowly."

Dan Crimsom organized the official papers. "Compiled from the AP, UPI, CNN, CSN news networks. Also ABC, CBS, N—"

"Crimsom! Just read the goddamn report and quit monkeying around! You're giving me a headache."

You ARE a headache. Why am I still here, at this Godawful place, under this exhausting man? "Quote: 'August 31. Brisbane, Queensland, Australia. The healer Gurner, in his search for an effective ALLIS cure, has requested that the top chemists from fifteen of the world's leading homeopathic laboratories be immediately dispatched to the township of Cairns, Australia. Gurner also requests the proper equipment to set up an effective field laboratory. When asked the whys of such a strange request, Gurner Gang spokesman Harold Reeves succinctly stated that Gurner had discovered another potential ALLIS cure plant, but that this species did not appear to offer anything new to the already existing partial plant cures. Gurner is said to hope that the plant's potential could be increased by homeopathic science methods.'"

The chief FDA investigator jumped from his chair and launched into a fuming tirade. "Increased! By the Science of Nothing? By the art of taking a minuscule amount of an unproven substance and mixing it and diluting it and further mixing it and further diluting it until there's nothing left of nothing?"

Crimsom knew the consequences of asking questions when Bowerns was in this frame of mind. With no debate, he asked a question. "Isn't the principle of homeopathics one of increasing the energy of that substance with each mixing until a very powerful medicine is formed?"

Bowerns blew. "Oh for God's sake, Crimsom. Do you work for the FDA or for Mother Goose? That's what homeopathics amounts to, a goddamn fairy tale!"

You will bury your head in the sand, won't you, Jimmy? "Quote: 'Gurner also requested several pounds each of the AH, AK, AR, and AB herbs. These, said Reeves, are to determine if this new herb might possibly combine with the other four plants and produce any unforeseen results. So far, states Reeves, such tests have been negative.'

"Finally, Gurner requested that a large international armed force secure the Mount Bartle Frere area. Troop transport vessels are steaming toward northwestern Australia, and the requested laboratory equipment is at this moment being flown to Australia.

"This report then goes on to say that Reeves was in a very sullen mood, dispersing insulting remarks to any further inquiries. End of news release."

Bowerns sat down in his chair. "Well, I'm glad it ends on a good note. Reeves deserves all the sullenness life can throw at him. But even that P-I-A reporter sees the worthlessness of this venture. Society blindly follows that farce of a healer like baby ducks bonded to a cat follow the cat. But cats eat baby ducks, don't they?"

"Hey, Mr. Bowerns. You're not a blind man. Gurner's the only one offering the world anything on this disease."

Bowerns sprang up from his chair. "And he gave you your life, didn't he?"

"That he did. I'll never forget it."

Bowerns could no longer contain the weeks of frustration. As his pent-up anger roared out at his employee, the protruding vein on his forehead appeared to burst from its fleshly bonds. "At the cost of your soul?! At the goddamn cost of allowing him to become a god in the eyes of the world, a sacrosanct being who can now play impotent games like homeopathic chess . . . using the world as his pawns?!"

Crimsom stared disbelievingly at Jim Bowerns. *You're not a rational thinking man, Bowerns. You're not worth talking to or arguing with. You're not worth getting shook up about.*

When Crimsom offered no protest or defense, Bowerns felt that his point had been made and found unarguable. He began pacing the room, ignoring his subordinate and espousing aloud his thoughts on recent events.

"The President . . . the President of the United States is dying . . . dying, of ALLIS! We're all next!" He wheeled to face Crimsom, glaring accusingly at the man. "Except perhaps you." Bowerns then returned to his pacing and lecturing. "Even skeptics like me know all hope for cure has narrowed down to the Gurner goon. And what does our knight errant, the lifeguard of the world spend his—and our—little remaining time doing? Playing with an ineffective branch of an ancient leechcraft that sensible allopaths overrode long ago."

Bowerns actually stomped his foot on the floor. "And the leaders of the world now meekly do whatever he asks, automatically, without protest or question. Homeopathic field laboratories. It makes me so mad I could spit!"

Spit then.

"The President is dying, and if he doesn't take AR soon, he's dead. Gurner meanwhile wastes precious time masturbating with homeopathics."

Bowerns walked over to the office mirror and began talking to his reflection. "I mean, we've got all the ammunition we could ever want. And we can't use it. Until that bastard finds that cure, he's simply untouchable."

Bowerns stared at the reflection in the mirror, and the reflection in the mirror stared at Bowerns. Both pairs of eyes narrowed at the same time. "But . . . but . . . if the President dies. And if Gurner finds that cure after the Prez goes. Well, I'll bet we can really sock him . . . for playing and delaying with these ridiculous, time-consuming pursuits while great leaders of our country die. . . . In fact . . .! Oh my God! In fact, died, they did, our President and other leaders died, because of Gurner. Died because of his horseplay. Oh my God! I've got something here. I'll put it before the next meeting and we can . . ."

Bowerns wheeled around, catching himself in mid-sentence. "Crimsom! You're still here." He stepped beside Crimsom and escorted him to the office door. "Go back to your investigations. Thanks for bringing me the report. And you just mark my words. Homeopathics, *nothing* will come of it."

Dan Crimsom heard the office door efficiently close behind him, and he tried to twitch a different, incredulous expression off his face. *My God, Bowerns, maybe you are worth getting shook up about.*

• 37 •
Newstime

September 8, 2008. Excerpts from *Newstime* magazine.

A SELFLESS END

The celebrations would have been jubilant beyond description. The victory festivities would have made the largest World War II V-day ceremonies look like small-town ice cream socials. But fourteen hours before the long-desired announcement of a cure for ALLIS, an American President slipped into the same death that has claimed, in one year's time, more than 600,000,000 lives worldwide. On September 5, 2008, at 8:11 P.M., Robert Wolfe, 52, forty-sixth President of the United States, died of the ALLIS disease. Amidst the sweet feeling of dawning success, there hangs a leaden pall of sorrow and confusion.

Robert Wolfe will not be remembered for an innovative or transforming presidency. His directives firmly reflected his Republican predecessors' conservative approaches. With trickle-down economics and massive military expenditures as policy mainstays, the pressing problems of declining social services, national health care, tax reform, and environmental degradation received more rhetoric than action.

Major blows to President Wolfe's popularity occurred this past year. In early June, Gurner incited mass demand that forced the President and the government to acquit him of criminal malpractice charges. Later, again urged by Gurner, the American people compelled Congress to override the President's veto of the De-ALLIS Bill, the initiative that directed the military budget toward promising ALLIS research.

President Wolfe, upon completion of his term, might have rapidly faded from the public's view. But during his last thirteen days on Earth, from the time he contracted ALLIS until he slipped into his final coma, the President displayed a courage that will be remembered for generations to come.

Gurner, one month ago, discovered a fern-like plant in the Brazilian jungles that slows the progression of the ALLIS disease. This herb, labeled AR, is a rare species of rain-forest plant. With its sudden fame as an ALLIS healing herb, the plant has become even rarer. President Wolfe had access to the AR herb, and was in fact encouraged to consume it, but refused. Before he slipped into the final coma, Wolfe left an order that he was *not* to be given any of the herb. The President's final words: "Mankind needs the AR herb more than it needs one dying man to live a little longer. Reserve my portion of that precious plant for research, for finding a cure for the many. I understand now that position is no entitlement for one—be it man or nation—to have what belongs to all."

Such selfless giving evoked worldwide admiration. Perhaps the most notable praise arose from five unlikely persons in northeast Australia. The Gurner Gang—Gurner himself, Brian Johnson, Dr. Stephanie Peters, Jerry Willox, and Harold Reeves—when informed of the President's final request, wept. Willox was heard to say, "He really had it in him. He really gave his life so others could live."

Funeral services for President Wolfe will be conducted at noon on September 9.

$$\cdots$$

THE END OF ALLIS, THE HOPE OF LIFE, AND THE WORK AHEAD

An ALLIS cure! The words ring sweet and gloriously fulfilling. Even a staid news journal such as *Newstime* must be allowed the luxury of expressing its emotions. *PRAISE GOD AND HALLELUJAH!* After one year of hell and 600 million lost lives, an ALLIS cure has been discovered!

But the newly discovered cure is not a simple and readily available medicine. This medicine is comprised of a precise mixture of five of some of the rarest herbs on this planet. A long series of agonizing steps brings these five diverse plants together into a formula that counters the dreaded ALLIS disease.

The AH herb, which calls the mountain slopes of central British

Columbia, Canada, its home, allows a person with ALLIS to progress to the final coma stage of the disease and there remain, in a total coma, for a period of time lasting as long as ten days.

The AK herb, which grows only in the alpine areas of the extreme northern mountains of Sweden and Norway, allows the body core temperature to remain near normal. These two plants still exist in abundance.

Gurner then introduced the Brazilian rain forest AR fern, the single most potent ALLIS controller, which, when administered to ALLIS victims, slows the progression of the malady, adding from three to six weeks to an ALLIS victim's life span. But it is extremely rare. By worldwide declaration, none of the plant can be spared for "mere" life extension. Research personnel alone have access to the plant.

The AB herb, originally discovered in the Malaysian half of Borneo, now also known to exist in the now-preserved highland forests of Indonesian Borneo, prevents the loss of muscular strength in the ALLIS victim.

Finally, very rare, almost extinguished by a forest clear-cutting operation in northwestern Australia, the succulent AZ bush-herb survives in tiny numbers. This hitherto unknown species of flora, when administered by itself, supplies no healing of ALLIS. But given in combination with the other four herbs, this plant—somehow, some way—stops, reverses and cures the ALLIS disease.

The man who uprooted the world, who explored its expanses to bring mankind these healing herbs, is the controversial and highly gifted healer named Gurner. On September 6 at 10:00 A.M., he announced the ALLIS cure discovery.

In his succinct style, Gurner tended to be anticlimactic while announcing the happiest news of the century. He simply stated that a complete ALLIS cure had been found. He introduced a Cairns, Australia, stone mason, Samuel Clems, and a Townsville, Australia, beauty salon operator, Sarah Hevins. Two days earlier Samuel Clems, ten days into ALLIS and almost in the coma, and Sarah Hevins, eight days into the disease and exhibiting very little bodily strength, were transported to the Australian security-sealed field-research site. Gurner then introduced Mary Seamens and Rudi Schroll. Both Brisbane women were deep into the ALLIS coma when helicoptered to the field site. Both women, although somewhat weaker than Samuel and Sarah, managed a promenade before the astonished reporters. A fifth person, Gurner said, Harry

Holms of Rockhampton, Australia, died of ALLIS. He was brought to the field research center but hours away from death by ALLIS. Gurner noted that this combination of herbs doesn't have quite the power of the original and now extinct AC herb that saved Jerry Willox's baby minutes before ALLIS death would have claimed him.

Gurner then presented a series of factual briefs. To quote Gurner directly:

• "It takes all five herbs, AH, AK, AR, AB, and AZ, combined, to generate an effective ALLIS cure. No combination of four, three, or two seems to work. The AZ herb ties the other four together into an effective, ALLIS-curing/preventative medicine.

• "Due to another senseless clear-cutting operation, the AZ herb is almost extinct. There are 3.7 acres of the plant left on this Earth. In those few acres we have located approximately 250 plants. From the usage rates we've determined on these volunteers, that translates out to about 4,000 doses of ALLIS cure available for the world."

This statement sent reporters and observers into an uproar. Gurner, to no avail, tried to shout the growing melee into quiet. He finally regained the floor by having a serviceman fire an automatic weapon into the air. Gurner:

• "Folks, just listen, will you? The homeopathic researchers here, knowing the problem such a fact could create, worked continuously for six days and nights. They have manufactured a homeopathic tincture that uses minuscule portions of the AZ and the other herbs. This homeopathic tincture is as effective as using the plants themselves."

A cry of relief swept through the listening crowd. Gurner continued:

• "What I say is true. Samuel Clems and Mary Seamens were cured by a tea brewed from the five plants. Sarah Hevins and Rudi Schroll were cured by the homeopathic tincture."

Gurner's emotions intensified as he continued speaking: "Listen. If it weren't for this homeopathic key, people would have to repopulate the Earth from four or five thousand survivors. Though I'm not sure anyone would be alive after the war of people trying to secure those dosages for themselves.

• "The homeopathic scientists developing this medicine tell me that the tincture's power can be increased. There is enough ALLIS cure for the world."

A wild, unbridled cheer now hailed from the crowd. Gurner again had to summon weapons fire before he could continue:

• "So do me a favor, will you? Report this news, and editorialize your hearts out about it. We now desperately need a consolidated effort. We need to devote our all to preserving the few remaining plants that are the ALLIS salvation. We need to give all energy to manufacturing, improving, and globally distributing this homeopathic medicine. Tell the people and governments they'll live if they cooperate and die if they bicker and fight.

• "And you might also tell everyone, in as many words as you possibly can, just how doggone close we came to having nothing, including no human life on Earth. Three acres is all that stands between human life and human extinction."

Gurner shuddered as he spoke his next thought aloud. "And it's probably a fluke that the three-acre patch was left alone."

Gurner then unceremoniously returned to the field laboratory, leaving Reeves to answer further questions.

A cure! The world can rejoice. It can also give thanks, both to an aberrant and extremely mysterious healing man, and to an old medical science that American medicine has long suppressed and denied.

ALLIS is still the mightiest of mysteries. Its cause remains as unknown as ever. But we have a cure, and a cure that presents itself none too soon. Estimates for the elimination of the human population are currently set at ten to twelve weeks. The challenge now, through cooperation and indefatigable work, is to distribute this cure to all the populations of the world.

· · · · ·

ALLIS: HEALERS AND OTHER SIDELIGHTS

"Believe me. I almost feel like a fire-breathing dragon for even mentioning this. And because I do mention it, I will certainly become an unpopular man. But it is the living, loving truth. And I can't, in good conscience, ignore it."

Elegant Jim Bowerns, supervisor of the Investigative Departments of the vast Food and Drug Administration (FDA), remains ever relentless in his favorite quest: exposing and prosecuting fraudulent medical and health practitioners. His long targeted yet elusive bull's-eye, the healer Gurner, remains the subject of Bowerns' continued ire. Speaking at a $500-per-plate fund-raising dinner at the Oregon Republican Party's annual convention in Corvallis on September 6, Bowerns lashed out at the motives behind Gurner's actions. His current accusations portend monstrous implications.

Bowerns' speech dominated the evening: "Everyone knows how Gurner fought against and actively discredited the President. Anyone can see that this plant man disagrees with the policies of the President—and therefore of the Republican Party. Gurner fought those policies tooth and nail, and finally overrode them by the unprincipled usage of power he acquired in accidentally discovering an ALLIS Cure plant.

"Don't get me wrong. I acknowledge that we all continue life because of Gurner and his motley . . . er ah, and his crew. But I ask you . . . doesn't something smack of conspiracy? Fourteen hours after the President dies, whammo, he reveals a cure. Given the light of Gurner's unyielding antagonism against the President, I have to meekly propose that the cure was available maybe fourteen hours or even a few days *before* President Wolfe died."

(*Newstime* contacted Harold Reeves in Australia and informed him of the FDA investigator's imputations. Reeves called Bowerns "a raving lunatic," and described the "ceaseless and sleepless workings" of the Gurner Gang in trying to develop the ALLIS cure with the homeopathic scientists as fast as possible.)

Bowerns dedicated the majority of his speech to accusing Gurner and his Gang members of withholding the cure until after the President had died. Reasons why the healer would commit such an action remained vague, but Bowerns' theme that Gurner was anti-Republican and dedicated to usurping party platform met response from many of the delegates attending the convention.

But Bowerns himself suddenly faced a barrage of accusations from one audience member. At the close of the investigator's speech, a booming "Bullshit!" resounded throughout the room, and a giant of a man strode up to the podium, yelling and pointing banana-sized fingers at the astonished speaker.

Ex-logger Joe Simpson, a man involved in the clear-cut that annihilated the original herbal ALLIS cure, clearly did not agree with Bowerns' allegations. Simpson towered over the speaker, yelling, "Prove it, Bowerns. Goddammit, prove it. I've spent my life listening to loggers accuse environmentalists and environmentalists accuse loggers, and everybody talks from emotion and nobody talks from facts. State the facts that prove your insinuations against that man."

As Bowerns, clearly rattled, tried to formulate a reply, Simpson returned to his seat, loudly proclaiming, "That's what I thought."

Bowerns, interviewed after the convention, stated that he knew his observations would grate some persons the wrong way, but continued to call into question the timing of the ALLIS cure. Simpson, interviewed later, called Bowerns a dangerous man, a fool in a position of power.

Presently, Gurner can only be a hero. He saved human life on Planet Earth. But did the healer have additional motives? Jim Bowerns is busy planting seeds that say such is indeed the case.

End of Book V

BOOK VI

VICTORY?

◆ 38 ◆
Newstime

October 6, 2008. Excerpts from *Newstime* magazine.

EDITOR RODNEY MALSON'S
LETTER TO THE PUBLIC.

Never before, in all the history of mankind, has so much been accomplished in so little time. Never before have so many miracles occurred, miracles due to the essential contributions of nearly every living person on this globe. Never before have worldwide events been so directed by the motives of compassion and giving. And never have we seen the results the people of this Earth have witnessed over the past four weeks.

The ALLIS disease is now a specter of the past. This statement, of course, is a gross oversimplification. But in the final run, in the run that matters, the statement speaks the truth.

One month ago an international team of homeopathic scientists developed an effective and simple cure for the uncanny disorder named ALLIS. The days following that memorable date will ever be remembered as the paramount example of humanity at its highest, of human beings reaching out to other human beings, of nations helping other nations.

Our feature story in this week's edition of *Newstime* relates in detail the magnificent, mutual effort required for this cure to become available to all humans. It describes bonding of homeopathic laboratories all over the world in their rush against time to produce billions of doses of the new wonder cure. Absolute cooperation was essential. The rare plants that comprise the formula had to be carefully and nondestructively gathered and preserved and shipped in proportional amounts that fitted the production capacities of each lab. There were no privatized dealings. There was no individual commercialization or capitalization.

A feat nothing less phenomenal than fair, worldwide distribution followed production of the formula. Every military transport device in the world scurried from village to village, farmyard to farmyard, island to island, city to city, distributing both the ALLIS cure and volunteer personnel trained to administer the medicine.

Beyond scientists and the military, we, the people of the world—all of us—have reasons for self-congratulations. In the drama of the purging of ALLIS, everyone helped; almost no one reacted selfishly. It was as if a new and contagious disease, the symptoms of which were giving and caring, manifested and spread throughout the entire world's population. Everywhere people patiently awaited their turn to receive the eight separate administrations of the homeopathic medicine that reverse, cure, and prevent ALLIS. People not only awaited their turn, they made certain that the sickest persons, the persons farthest and deepest into the ALLIS disease, received the dosages first. The healthy, and those just beginning to experience the effects of ALLIS, instinctively waited until sicker victims received treatment.

I personally commend such behavior and cooperation. Because of this harmony, this spontaneous service to others, the final death toll of ALLIS was halted at just over one billion people. One billion amounts to a staggering number of deaths in slightly more than one year's time span. But if we the people of the world had bickered, had delayed the dispensation of the cure by our more normal "me first" attitudes, the body count could have reached a two or even three billion mark.

Close to one sixth of the world's population is gone. Not a person, not a family has escaped the cruel hand of ALLIS. The aftereffects will be felt for decades to come. Governments face a tax base that is approximately one fifth less than last year's. Many businesses are closed due to the death of those behind their operation. Auto sales, home sales, land sales, all economic activity has been reduced. The list of after-ALLIS shock waves is endless.

But we've come through the worst. Not only that, we've come through the worst with flying colors. People have changed their very approach to life. When our actions as a whole prove that we've turned from greed and self-aggrandizing to care and concern, what problem can ever again be insurmountable? Perhaps the hidden blessing, the essential silver lining of the very, very black cloud of ALLIS, is that it spawned a new era of cooperation in the world.

In less than three weeks this year's Nobel Prizes will be awarded. Nominees for this year's awards were submitted over a year and a half ago, but since ALLIS eliminated several prospective candidates, additional last-minute nominations were accepted. The judges, choosing among those who have given so much in both improving life on Earth and in keeping human life going, must have had quite a time selecting the winners.

For *Newstime*
Rod Malson

· 39 ·
Disbelief

October 26, 2008, 9:35 A.M. By a mountain cabin, near
Canyon Creek Summit, near John Day, Oregon.

Jerry Willox and Stephanie Peters sat on the porch steps of a
small log cabin situated on a private land parcel inside the Malheur
National Forest. The two friends were biding time, waiting for
the three other members of the now defunct Gurner's Gang to
arrive for a final goodbye gathering. While waiting, Willox, in an
exceptionally riled state, fumed, half thinking to himself, half
sharing his agitated thoughts with his companion.

I just don't believe it. "I don't believe it!" *I don't. Jeez, I just
DO NOT believe it!* "Do you believe it, Stephanie? I don't believe
it."

Dr. Peters did not outwardly display her agitation. But internally,
she was not the Goddess of Calmness. "Believe it, Jerry. We were
there. It really happened . . . believe it or not." *What am I saying?
I don't believe it either.*

"Yeah, jeez, but how? I mean, why? I mean, his name wasn't
even mentioned. It's as if he never existed, as if he were a wart,
rapidly removed and soon forgotten."

"I don't know, Jer. I guess to a lot of people he *is* a wart, and
a threatening one at that."

Willox had to yell. It made him feel more effective. "Yeah but
Jeez-zus Christ! You don't just up and ignore the wart that saved
the world! . . . I mean . . . wait. That didn't sound right. What I
mean is, he . . . he did it all, Stef. Nothing would have happened
without him, and nothing would be left if he hadn't done so much.
And they didn't even mention his name."

Dr. Peters shrugged, unable to comprehend recent events, unable
to make excuses for what had transpired. She gestured to the

driveway as a dented old barge of an Oldsmobile sputtered into the yard. "Here comes Harold. He looks more bug-eyed than usual. He must have heard the news, too."

Harold Reeves, never able to move his lanky body with any amount of grace, shambled toward the porch steps. The reporter was muttering to himself.

Willox yelled as he waved hello. "Hey, Harold. Whadda ya say?"

Reeves didn't look at Willox or Dr. Peters. He simply stared into space as he walked to them. "I don't believe, I don't believe it."

"See, Stef, he doesn't believe it either." Willox clasped the reporter's hand in a warm shake. "So you heard the news from Sweden too, huh?"

Reeves shot Willox a sideward glance. "What news, news from Sweden?"

Surprised, Willox looked at Reeves. "What—? The absolutely rotten news that Gurner did not get a Nobel prize for anything."

Reeves almost jackknifed himself, so abruptly did he turn to face Willox. "What!"

"The completely *inexcusable* news that Gurner, and all his efforts and all his talents and all his giving, weren't even mentioned during the ceremony."

Reeves, looking breathless and aghast, turned to Dr. Peters. "Tell, tell me he's kidding."

"If I but could, Harold, I gladly would. But it's true. They invited him to be there, so he showed up, and we went with him. They announced that the physics, chemistry, medicine, and economics awards would this year be combined into one category and given, quote: 'to all the world's dedicated researchers who labored long and offered their lives to the finding and manufacturing of an ALLIS cure.' We then sat through forty-five minutes of names that they called a partial listing of all parties involved. The money from this prize goes not to particular persons or groups but as a general contribution toward further ALLIS research."

Dr. Peters watched Reeves' eyes bug wider. "By that point Gurner was twitching in his seat, and I think we all felt something was wrong. Then, in another unprecedented move, they said that the literature and the peace prizes would also be combined and given to—get this—'humanity as a whole.' They said that for bearing the sufferings caused by the disease, for courage in combatting the pain and uncertainty of it, and for unparalleled allegiance to the human race when the cure was found by helping speed and harmonize the distribution of that cure, all mankind deserves the distinctive recognition of the Nobel Prize. Here they didn't mention the names of any 'outstanding' contributors because everyone, they said, was an outstanding contributor. The combined monies from these two prizes goes to a general fund that helps persons left destitute because of circumstances caused by ALLIS. Noble, indeed, but it just doesn't seem Nobel."

Reeves plopped down beside his two friends on the steps. "I don't believe it."

"Well, crumb, Harold, that's three out of three of us."

"They didn't even, didn't even say, 'Thank you, Gurner'?"

Dr. Peters brushed some dust off one of her pant legs. "Harold, they didn't even look at him. It was like the entire auditorium, especially the speakers, were deliberately looking away from him or beyond him or at anything but him. And I know that avoidance wasn't because he didn't wear a tie."

"I don't, I don't believe it."

Dr. Peters brushed a cobweb off her other pant leg. "It stinks. It stinks of conspiracy. But I can't imagine who or why."

Willox suddenly remembered something. "Harold, ol' buddy, if you weren't talking about Gurner, what *were* you referring to?"

"Oh, I was just, just off on other thoughts."

"Yeah? What were they?"

"Oh, just that, just that . . . I no longer work for *Newstime.*"

"You quit!"

"Oh no, no. They fired me."

Willox and Dr. Peters simultaneously exclaimed, "What!"

Reeves lifted his angular shoulders into a shrug. "I was needing, needing a change. You know, hard-to-meet deadlines, approaches to stories that don't please editors, dangerous assignments, no gratitude for long and hard work. Et cetera, et cetera. I needed out."

"Harold!" Dr. Peters glared. "You're avoiding issues. And we've all been together too long to first, not recognize it, and second, let you get away with it. What the heck happened?"

Reeves stared at her for a moment, then let his shoulders sag back to their normal poor posture. "I'm not, not sure, but I think they were forced to ax me. Technically—that is, for the record—I was fired because I turned in a false report. I reported, reported that AZ had no value, and the truth is what the world now knows. According to the magazine's ruling board, I am no longer, quote: 'a factual or trustworthy reporter,' and my services are no longer needed. But between the lines . . . I know Rod Malson, and he wasn't leveling with me. His eyes were saying 'I'm sorry,' but he couldn't admit it. News editors don't call these kind of shots. I don't know who or why, but someone big is twisting his arm."

Agitation filled Willox's voice. "*That* was why you weren't assigned to cover the Nobel gathering! It seemed strange that the guy who was the Gurner reporter from the beginning didn't report the final episode . . . which sure ended in a hell of a strange twist."

Reeves nodded assent. "That was, that was the beginning, Jerry. Rod wouldn't tell me why. He just stated that I was not covering Oslo and left no room for argument. The next day he called me into his office and gave me my walking papers. I wasn't tracking all that well the next couple days."

Willox stood up and began to pace the length of the porch, growing highly animated in the process. "So we've got Gurner being purposely and blatantly ignored, and we've got Harold fired instead of being made a hero because he told a tiny lie that prevented an ALLIS World War III. Something's rotten here. This feels too much like the kind of situation where a Congressman votes against an environmental initiative even though it would be beneficial for the country and his state, even though his constituents want and support it, even though common sense and decency dictate his backing. Then you find he's received huge contributions from the industries that would have to clean up their act if the law passed. Something's coming down on us. Have you gotten any negative letters from the AMA licensing board, Stephanie?"

Dr. Peters was picking small burrs from her shoe laces. "No. Not yet, anyway. Here comes Brian. Let's see what he's got to say."

Johnson's small Subaru pulled into the meadow driveway. As he waved hello and smartly walked toward the cabin, everyone noted how Johnson forever carried the clerk-like appearance of a government employee. As he drew closer, the three noticed the deep gravity of his usually calm expression.

"Hey Brian. How're ya doing?"

Johnson walked past Willox's salutation. "I don't believe it."

"We could have told you that," Willox said. "Are you talking about Gurner not getting the Nobel or about Harold getting fired from *Newstime*?"

"Both. And more. And everything. It's disgusting."

Dr. Peters jumped up from her step seat. "More? What more? I wouldn't have guessed you'd even know about Harold."

"News, as they say, travels fast."

Willox stopped pacing and stood by Dr. Peters. "So travel some news our way, Brian. Like Stef says, what more?"

"How much do you already know?"

Dr. Peters noticed some fresh manure on her shoe and abandoned her preening. "Well, we were at Oslo. We know that Gurner and the Gurner Gang might as well have not existed for all the mention we received. Now we know that Harold was fired from the magazine. And we've unanimously decided that we can't believe it. Any of it."

Johnson claimed a portion of the porch steps. "That's right, you guys came home after the ceremony. Well, Gurner and I stayed for about a day and a half longer. He said he didn't give a damn about the award—didn't want it and the publicity that would follow it. But he said we had to try to give these scientists his theory behind the whys of ALLIS. He wanted to at least plant some seeds so they would research it, and so the nations could begin cutting back on the radioactive wolf we're feeding the world to.

"Well, for the next thirty hours Gurner and I—mostly Gurner—paraded from name-brand scientist to name-brand scientist. He talked isotope dangers and bomb test results and waste release facts and half life clarifications like he was an encyclopedia on the subject. He talked and talked, like life depended on it."

Johnson sighed and unconsciously patted Dr. Peters' shoe. "But I guess even the best gardener can't sprout his seeds in sterile soil."

"What does that mean?"

"Stephanie. The most aroused response Gurner elicited amounted to a couple people saying, 'My, what an unusual idea.' Most of them curled their lips. The general atmosphere was 'Gurner who?'"

Willox began pacing again. "Oh Jeez-zus. I mean, I just d— sorry. I almost said 'I don't believe it' again."

Johnson caught the environmentalist by a pant leg as he paced by the steps. He unconsciously wiped his hand on the cuff. "Jerry, when you and Stephanie were at the Nobel ceremony. Do you remember hearing any rumors about Gurner? Not the simple gossip that always floats around. Conversations where Gurner was the subject and the talk was bad?"

"Ummmm, now that you ask, a few times, yes. Never paid much attention to it."

Dr. Peters held up a single finger. "I caught something, Brian. Some M.D.s in a group were conversing about how Gurner had the cure all along and was leading the world on with his 'good time, government-paid' expeditions. They changed the subject pretty quick when I joined them."

Johnson released Willox's pants. "Maybe with my pedestrian face I'm not as recognizable as you guys. But whatever the reason, wherever I went I heard people maligning him. All over the damned town people were whispering things. Crazy things, like, Gurner could have led science to AC before it was eradicated by the logging operation, and Gurner caused a lot more deaths than necessary by taking so long to find the herbs, and Gurner lied about AZ. Everywhere it was: Gurner did this—negative; and Gurner didn't do that—negative; and, because of Gurner—negative.

"Finally, our exhausted friend said, 'Let's go home. Ain't no more can be done.' Then he said, 'Plus, I've been told that it would be wisest for all concerned if I disappeared into the woods again for a while.' We went to the airport and boarded the plane. Not one person had acknowledged him, said a word to him, thanked him."

Dr. Peters could no longer contain her disquiet. She too began pacing the porch. "Oh crumb, crumb and crumb. Poor Gurner. He must be heartbroken."

Johnson continued. "Well, if he wasn't racked from that experience, he had to be when we arrived in Portland."

Dr. Peters stopped in mid-stride. "Don't tell me there's more."

"There weren't any reporters here in the homeland to meet us."

Three people voiced the word of the day. "What!"

Johnson stood and joined the other two pacers. "It's true, my friends. That's when I knew something must have plugged up Harold. Not one major news distributer made an appearance: radio, TV, magazine, or paper. There were a couple of small-time alternative guys: *In These Times* and a few others whose stories, as Gurner says, reach only the kind of people who already believe the way we believe. Gurner gave them his radiation spiel. Perhaps one of them will print it for the record."

Reeves, perfectly conforming to the angles of the steps, assumed a philosophical expression. "Methinks, methinks I do, I do, that those handling the subtle subjugation of we-uns are more powerful than I first suspected."

Johnson nodded. "You feel that too, Harold? It dawned on me while driving here."

Willox, wiping the cuffs of his pants on a railing post, stared in puzzlement at the two Washingtonians. "What are you guys talking about?"

Johnson looked squarely into Willox's eyes. "Jerry. These are strange events, and they simply cannot be the whims of a wayward public. Gurner is an unprecedented and disturbing threat to many covert power structures. He's moved the everyday people masses as a whole. Almost effortlessly. He's accomplished more leadership upheaval in a year than all the wars and coups and revolutions in history. Covert power structures cannot let something with that potential roam the world at random. He has to be back-numbered, so to speak, put on hold, until people forget who he is and what he can do."

Pacing, by itself, was no longer expressive enough. Willox began to pound his fist into the palm of his hand as he paced. "So that's what Gurner meant when he said someone told him to take a walk in the woods! Well, goddammit, who are the sons of bitches doing this? I mean, is it the Government, or who?"

"Jerry. Calm down a bit. And listen." Johnson placed himself in Willox's path. "There are always rumors—rumors, mind you— of the existence of economic or military cartels that carry more influence and power than any elected government or congress. They may or may not be true, these rumors. But put together all the punches being thrown at Gurner, and I conclude that somebody big is phasing him out. Now, wait, Jerry, before you start yelling about exposing the bastards or something like that. A: you might as well try to capture the wind with a fishing net. And B: it'd be a good way for you to suddenly find everything going wrong in your life . . ."

Willox opened his mouth.

". . . *and* in the life of your family."

Willox shut his mouth.

Johnson continued. "And C: there is only one 'force' that can ever successfully counter such a power. That 'force' is the people as a whole, uniting and acting unpredictably. Example: say everybody everywhere one day decided to quit overheating the planet, and they actively moved to kick their addiction to fossil fuel. Think of all the structures that would fall apart if something like that happened. Now, whoever 'they' are, it seems 'they' are moving to neutralize the one person who could galvanize such an impossible reaction."

Willox opened his mouth to argue, couldn't think of anything to say, looked at Reeves who simply shrugged his shoulders, looked at Dr. Peters who simply raised her eyebrows, looked back at Johnson who shook his head in a slight 'no' motion, and finally said, "Jeez, so crucifixion still happens."

"Yes. 'They,'—the unaccountable 'they'—just don't need to do it physically anymore."

"Jeez, I just don't believe it."

A new voice entered the conversation. "You don't believe *what*, you overidealized environmentalist?"

Four voices in unison registered their surprise. *"Gurner!* Where did you come from?"

"Well, I was told to take a walk in the woods. So I did. I came the back way through the forest from the top of the pass where I got left off from a ride I hitched."

Dr. Peters practically leapt upon Gurner, embracing him and saying over and over, "I'm sorry, Gurner. Crumb, I'm really sorry."

Willox ran up to the healer and grabbed his hand and arm, shaking it vigorously. Because shaking wasn't expressive enough, Willox placed both his hands on Gurner's shoulders and began shaking them. That didn't quite encompass his feelings, so the environmentalist launched a bear hug embrace which engulfed both Gurner and Dr. Peters. From that point, three pairs of entangled legs and arms danced toward Reeves, who was unconsciously leaning against the wrong railing post and, like falling water claiming a floating feather, they absorbed the spindly reporter into their grasp. Johnson made no effort to escape, and so they engulfed him too.

After a couple of minutes, Gurner disentangled himself. "God, it's good to be with you folks again," he said. "To be with you in the peace of the woods and, just for the moment, not having to push on to find the next plant or the next cure or the next anything." He glanced from face to face. "Except . . . what's all the gloom? This is a reunion. You know, a joyous and enlivening event? And you guys look like you're wailing out a dirge. What's up?"

"Well jeez, Gurner. How can we yuk it up when we know that the person who worked forever and a day to discover the cure for ALLIS—and did it—is insulted and ignored? And that he's been told to disappear, or else? And that his trying to expound the cause of the worst disease life has ever experienced to those in the know is like trying to whisper to the deaf? I mean, no, I don't have a 100-percent positive charge racing through me right now."

Gurner softly smiled and grabbed his friend by the arm, leading him back to the porch steps. "Jerry. Did you really expect change to be so fast and easy?"

"Huh?"

"Look, dear friend. Think about it logically. Our cancer-like, gotta-grow, gotta-expand economy is hurting because of all the deaths, and our new Preident is another clone of the clone of the clone of the original guy in the '80s who first eviscerated ecology. Third- and fourth- and fifth-generation clones don't up and change the direction they've been heading for the past quarter-century. Of course he'll be pushing the same old resource development approach he believed in when he was VP: drill more oil, ocean and Arctic; build more homes, cut more trees; drain more wetlands; build more roads and new dams. He doesn't have the ability to consider alternative and sustainable resource approaches."

Gurner waved a hand, inviting the others to join him in sitting on the porch steps. "Nor does he have the support if he did want to. How about Congress? We've got fifteen senators dead from ALLIS. Three of them were long-time creeps on the League of Conservation Voters' worst-environmental-record list—but four of them were pretty good conservationists. The House, the same. More deaths but the same balancing. What can you expect?"

Willox would have resumed his pacing, but Gurner hung on to his arm. "Well, jeez, I did really think that a 15-percent death rate, and the blatant fact that it was almost 100 percent because of environmental carelessness, might show people that treading lightly is more of a necessity than we once believed."

Gurner nodded. "Yeah, Jerry. And one could easily reason that because every person in the world has recently experienced the pain of a loved one's death, no more would anyone promote further death. But already the Irish are planting bombs, and the Jews and the Arabs are flinging accusations and talking about mobilizing their armies. And some skinhead hatemonger just bludgeoned a black immigrant for being in the wrong place."

Gurner's face seemed incredibly peaceful, considering the news he was sharing. "You would also expect thinking people to see that until we control population numbers worldwide, there isn't going to be a hope for saving varied ecosystems. Now would be a regrettable but excellent opportunity to begin measures that would prevent mankind from again staging the lemming syndrome. Not so. Smaller populations mean fewer tax dollars, and so leaders are freaking out. The American approach is going to be to allow a higher 1040 deduction for dependent children; in other words, promote more births. European countries will probably offer reward incentives for couples who conceive. Even China has dropped all its population control restrictions. People everywhere have lost some part of their family, and the coping mechanism for the crisis seems to be a worldwide battle cry of 'Breed, baby, breed.'"

"Jeez-zus! I don't be— . . . This has been a great day for bad news. And you, Gurner, you're all . . . all happy about everything?"

Gurner released Willox's arm only to stand and begin his own easy pacing. "Hey, Jerry. You got to remember that only from the top of the mountain do you get the whole view. We pushed the planet beyond its limit, and it finally pushed back. If mankind as a whole didn't learn from ALLIS, and they again push things to other limits, there'll darned sure be another lesson down the road.

"Plus, governments and majorities never, ever have been able to dance without first doing a lot of stumbling. You know how they work. Nutrition as a prevention for degenerative disease, for example, is espoused by a few outer limit 'oddballs.' The establishments immediately condemn it, deny it, suppress it. Ten years later, when the screaming facts can no longer be ignored without looking foolish, they began to investigate it. Several more years down the road, excited government reports hit the news that proper nutrition as a prevention for cancer and other diseases has real potential. Finally, many years after the original claimants are forgotten, the newest government discovery, advice, and promotion shows that one should cut down on fat and junk food and up the veggie intake. They might even try to claim credit for discovering the fact they originally denied.

"The seeds of this radiation-is-the-cause-of-ALLIS theory have been sown. ALLIS reminders will never leave us, especially since every human is going to have to take the homeopathic medicine as a booster now and then. After endless dead-ends in trying to figure out the whys, somebody will come upon a radioactive inspiration, put it together, reintroduce the theory, be laughed at, disappear from view . . . only to again have someone else, and then someone else after him, resurrect it."

Gurner stopped walking and squarely faced his environmental friend. A trace of excitement touched his calm voice. "Jerry, a real surprise. One of the few private individuals attending my mini news conference at the Portland airport was that logger, Joe Simpson. And he was listening to what I said. Listening intently, because he wanted to know. He told me he's thinking about running in the next election for U.S. Senator. Who knows what hoses God'll use to water the seeds we've scattered.

"Plus." Gurner put his hands in his pockets and nonchalantly shrugged. "Shoot. About this 'Thou shalt disappear' edict. No big deal, other than it's sad that that kind of unhealthy power even exists. But again, remember the view from the mountain top. Nothing that suppresses truth succeeds forever. Whoever they are, they will eventually consume themselves.

"We did what we had to do. I'm getting off a lot easier than many people in history who have done the same. I'm still alive, for one, unlike a couple of Kennedy brothers. I'm also not in jail with a bunch of phony accusations on my head. The FDA is not rekindling their charges against me. They want me forgotten, not highlighted by persecution. So, I did my best, and I'm still alive and free."

Dr. Peters looked into the healer's eyes, and a tremor touched her voice as she spoke. "Yes, you are, a free man you are, Gurner. You're free to disappear into the woods and spend the rest of eternity enraptured in your meditations. Aren't you?"

For nearly a minute Gurner softly looked at Dr. Peters. Twice he tried to say something, and twice he checked his speech before it began.

Dr. Peters said it for him. "I'm really glad for you. I really am, Gurner."

Gurner finally found his voice. He addressed the group. "Look. Part of this reunion was going to be a sweat together. Why don't you all wander down to the creek and fire up the sauna. We can talk more there. I want to spend a few moments alone here, check out the vibrations of the old cabin, see what the last FDA raid left behind for me to collect. I would appreciate just a little time to be by myself."

Johnson and Dr. Peters and Reeves and Willox gathered their towels and began to mosey toward the creek bottom. After hearing Gurner's more cheerful outlook on things, their conversation acquired some lighter notes. But half way down the slope, Reeves, in a moment of recognition, blurted out loud: "What the, what the hell did he mean, *'for the moment'* we're not pushing on and having to find a new plant cure?"

Gurner watched his friends disappear into the forest. He then seated himself on the porch steps, closed his eyes and quieted his mind.

◆ 40 ◆
Repeat

October 26, 2008, 10:05 A.M. On the front porch of Gurner's small mountain cabin in Oregon.

Hello, God. Remember me? Remember any of us? Almost everyone else on this planet has opted to remove us from their mental files. Which is certainly fine. Life needs to get back to normal. Brian's set to go back to work for the government, this time for an environmental think tank that's been created to assess the extent of various ecosystem degradations around the world. They hope to propose a few solutions. Sounds like more rhetoric and paperwork to me, but with Brian at the helm, ideas might be acted upon and not just proposed. Jerry would go back to his life's calling, with more reason than ever to be more driven by his cause . . . which will lead him to more frustration than ever. But he wouldn't have it any other way. Harold, the ol' screwball. He's out of work, but that should last about three days or until some major press needs a super-seasoned reporter to cover a big and tricky story. And Stephanie . . .

. . . Dear, beautiful Stephanie. She could have gone back to a doctoring practice anywhere she wants. Could have easily moved on and forgotten about me.

Might have taken a fair amount of time for me to forget about her, though. I wonder what it would to do my meditation if my mind couldn't forget what her companionship would have been like . . . had I but chosen it . . .

But now. All these guys' plans may be shot.

Gurner never looked up, nor did he open his eyes. But he did speak aloud. "You know, God, it wasn't You who originally phrased the saying 'There's no rest for the weary.' But You should have. You should have put it right in there with the rest of the

Scriptures, because it's a perpetual truth."

I said almost everyone on this planet has forgotten about us. That Chet Alexander fellow who gave me a ride to the top of the pass certainly hasn't. All right, I sort of lied to my friends. I didn't have to hitch from Portland to here because I had a ride all the way with Chet Alexander. He grabbed me the minute I finished my little speech to those few alternative press reporters. And he practically begged me to gather my troops and head out on another expedition. An expedition sponsored by them! Paid for by them. Them, the CDC itself.

The healer opened his eyes and surveyed the autumn-colored meadow while continuing his line of thought. *So, Chet Alexander is apparently one of the biggest big cheeses at the Atlanta Disease Control Center. And he was serious. Hell, he was outright scared. And from what he told me, I reckon he has every right to be seriously scared.*

Evidently, some bio-tech laboratory in northern Florida accidentally unveiled the Mr. Hyde side of genetic recombination. They were attempting to splice an anomalous gene—one that carried a blood coagulating trait—onto a common virus in the hope of creating a cure for hemophilia. Nobody counted on a hunter's stray thirty-ought-six bullet crashing through a lab window and smashing the containment chamber of this rearranged virus. Nobody reported anything—tried to cover it up as usual—but five days later eight of the laboratory workers had strokes. Not just little strokes. Major, multiple strokes. The blood in their bodies turned from liquid to jelly clots. The feds were alerted, and by the time the CDC got there to investigate, ten more unfortunates had curdled circulatory systems.

The CDC acted fast, Chet said. Thirty-one employees work at that lab, and within a day they and their families and everyone they may have contacted were placed in a controlled quarantine. One hundred and seventy-eight people are now in a living hell. They're individually isolated from everyone and everything. Researchers in these weird looking, germ-barrier space suits run all kinds of tests on them. They know that at any minute their insides may congeal, and they'll drop to the floor in agony, dying.

It's sick, God. Sick, sick, sick. I'd ask You WHY? Why this, why now, after so much recent misery and distress? But I know that the only answer—if You offered an answer—would be a silent "You did it to yourselves; I wasn't involved."

Gurner offered the heavens an expression of honest pleading. "You've got to quit giving mankind scientific breakthroughs that we can't handle."

Gurner then returned to his original, inner focus.

Anyway, the containment procedures were harsh but thorough. They should effectively curtail the disease from spreading. But there was that damned broken window. Two days ago, in the nearby town of Newburn, an old bench-sitting retiree fell over from a massive stroke. The government has quarantined the little town in the same drastic manner, and in a sealed chamber they're now dissecting the old man to see if he carries any of those re-formed viruses.

In theory and in hope, says Chet Alexander, the old man's stroke was coincidence and not related to a potential biodynamic plague. In caution and in the name of prevention, says the same man, could I begin a search for a plant that will counter the virus. Viruses snub their noses at antibiotics, and medicine has nothing that will stop this thing if it has gotten out and is airborne.

Gurner audibly sighed, and his posture slightly sagged.

I said I was tired and needed a break from such dealings.

He said so was he, and asked me again.

I said I couldn't and wouldn't do it without my Gang member friends, and that they were burned out and needed a long vacation and some different directions.

He said so were his workers, and asked me to ask my friends.

I accused him of laying a guilt trip on me.

He said he'd do anything to try and prevent the southern United States, perhaps the nation, and maybe even the world from experiencing the holocaust the spread of this virus portends.

I sighed and said, "Holy shit!"

He said, "So you will do it?"

I said that I'd need to go to Florida, to Live Oak and spend some time tuning into the energy of the disease. And that I couldn't even guess at what direction I'd take from there.

He looked at me askance, but simply said that whatever I wanted, however I wanted it, was mine.

I said OK, but right now I absolutely need a little alone time to recharge and regroup.

He let me off at the top of Canyon Creek Summit, and I spent a leisurely half day hiking to here. I'm to meet him in John Day tomorrow.

Gurner's voice sounded tired. "So hi ho. We're back in the saddle again, God. Trouble is, it doesn't feel like the spots rubbed raw from the last roundup have healed."

But even if that genetically altered virus is contained, what about those poor people already exposed to it? Moment to moment, they never know if they're going to pickle. They don't know if they'll have to be quarantined the rest of their lives. And there're quite a few kids involved in that mess. If my efforts could help any of them, I have to try.

And if this thing isn't contained, and does have the capability of spreading like a cold or a flu?

Holy God Almighty. The world population would crack.

Gurner leaned forward so his head could view the sky. *Of course I have to do it. But You listen. Taking off on this journey presents another problem, God. A big one. Brian and Harold, Jerry and Stephanie, none will refuse to be a part of this new escapade. They'll wish there'd been a longer break, but they're healers and will do what needs doing.*

But I want You to know, God. Your monk ain't going to be so monkish if he spends the next several months working with Stephanie. I've held back on that long enough. I, ah, guess I have to also admit, I'm, ah, feeling kind of excited about the prospect.

Gurner tipped his head back and gave the sky a condensed look. "So. I ask You. Is that OK by You?"

. . .

Gurner yelled a bit louder into the silent sky. "I warn You. Silence on Your part leaves me open to interpret the answer any way I want."

. . .

Gurner looked pleased as he spoke. "Well. Son of a gun. Silence does silent remain."

Gurner's face acquired a small grin. "Maybe somebody better warn Stephanie."

So, for the last day I haven't exactly been recharging so much as I've been dwelling on this new disease crisis. Trying to tune into it. Trying to feel its pulse. Trying to ascertain what, if any, cures are possible.

There are plants that combat viral infections. There are lots of plants that stimulate the immune system so viral infections can't get a footing in the body. Maybe countering this new bug is as simple as prevention—just staying healthy so the virus can't invade the body.

There are effective herbal blood thinners. Many insects inject anticoagulants when they draw blood. Maybe the cure has to again come in the form of a combination of plants. I have a lot of ideas floating around in my mind, but no real answers.

Except one. Except one incredible moment of clarity this morning while I was meditating. My plant radar is still functioning. I'm a pretty tuned-in receptor after this last year. I was trying to feel if anything anywhere had some energy to offer this new predicament. All of the sudden, from where I do not know, this wave of power came into my consciousness. It was an energy from some plant that I know will zap this virus. I know it was. From somewhere in this world, something let me know it's there and it's a cure.

But . . . my God. What was next? That energy, that wave. It screamed. Screamed, did I say? How can a life force energy scream? But yes, that's the only word that fits what I felt. It revealed itself to me, and then it screamed. What on Earth?

. . . And now. Now, oh God, I can't feel that energy.

. . . I can't feel it, God. What does that mean?

. . . Help, God. It called to me. Then it screamed. And I can't seem to feel that plant's energy any more . . .

• • • • •

October 26, 2008, 6:05 A.M. In the rain forest jungle, a few miles east of the settlement village of Tena, Ecuador.

Alfonso Hermanez wiped the streaming sweat from his forehead, carefully placed his old chain saw on the top of a large, freshly cut tree stump, and not-so-carefully plopped his own body down against the rough-barked side of another tree's remains. Alfonso had been working and working hard, for a paying job was a gift from God for a poor campesino, and he wanted to impress his employers with his laboring abilities.

¡Ay carumba! If I work this hard much longer, my arms will fall off.

But no. No, Alfonso. The Madonna, She finally smile upon you. Hard work is what you give back to Her in thanks. For She finally answered your prayers.

I am a working man now. Thank you, Mother, I am a working man earning many sucres a week. For too long we go without. For too long my esposa and my little niños and niñas are hungry and must live off what garbage we gather in the Quito alleyways.

For too long my heart cries to give them more, and yet no job possible, no centavos to be had.

Then the great sickness comes and steals pieces of everyone's family. Including my little Frieda and my little Juan.

Alfonso's lip trembled, as it had done countless times over the past year. He gained control more quickly now, for as the time passed, the searing memories faded.

But the hidden blessings of God. Who can understand them? Because of the great sickness, because it showed no mercy to the rich or the poor, my six other bebes now have a chance to live. Because of the great sickness, I am now a working man. A paid working man. Now my little ones have food, and clothing. Someday we may own a little boat, and from the gifts of the sea we will never have to be hungry again.

Alfonso lit a cigarette and puffed on it, enjoying a contentment he had rarely experienced in his hard life.

The ranch boss, he come to me and said, "Alfonso, the sickness killed men, not cattle. But without men clearing the forest and opening up new grazing lands, the cattle will also die. Can you come to work?"

¡Mi Dios! Can I come to work? I show these hombres that Alfonso Hermanez can cut twice as many trees as the best of them, especially once he has a good meal in his belly and a good reason for to sweat.

Alfonso, who was working near the top of a ridge, scanned the valley he and the other ranch hands had been clearing. Seven hundred hectares of virginal, upper Amazon rain forest stood between a wealthy rancher's expanding herd of cattle and the grasses and shrubs the animals would consume to put on weight for the market. The jungle trees were dropped, cut into smaller pieces and moved into slash piles. Fires were then ignited to burn the heaped timbers and the thick vegetation overgrowth that accompanied them. Smoke plumes curled up from many sectors of the valley he viewed.

Mother. It was a beautiful forest, this place. So many animals and so many flowers. Those norteamericanos who study the flowers tried to stop the boss man from clearing this area. They kept saying that many of these flowers grow only here, nowhere else.

But those gringos and their niños are not starving. I am sorry for the forest, but glad for the work and the pay. I am glad the boss man ignored them.

Break time over, Alfonso stood up and lit the kerosene rag torch he would use to set fire to this section of the landscape. As he was about to thrust the burning torch into a large slash pile, a strange chill ran through his spine, and an unaccountable inner hesitation stayed him from igniting the brush. The uneducated ranch hand, unaccustomed to queer imaginatings, shook his head clear and again tried to insert the fire seed into the pile. Again, a curious quiver engulfed his backbone, and a bizarre inner voice screamed at him, forcing his arm to stop before it acted. Confused, the worker stood helpless before the burn pile. Then, out of the corner of his eye, he noticed the ranch foreman weaving a path up the mountain and coming toward him. Swallowing hard, making the Sign of the Cross in front of him, Alfonso forced the torch into the slash, and stepped back as flames began to lick the kerosene-doused material.

Alfonso shivered once again, involuntarily and deeply. He remembered that one of those flower-studying Americans had once caught a cold, a "virus" he had heard the man say. Alfonso hoped he wasn't catching a cold. He certainly didn't want some virus to interfere with his new job.

THE END?

BOOKS OF RELATED INTEREST

PHOENIX RISING
by Mary Summer Rain

This is one of the most compelling and harrowing books ever written about the coming earth changes, as revealed to the author by her Chippewa teacher, No-Eyes, in a spirit journey into the future. An awe-inspiring vision of ecological turmoil from a Native American perspective.

5½ x 8½ trade paper, 176 pages, ISBN 1-878901-62-1, $11.95

DAYBREAK: THE DAWNING EMBER
by Mary Summer Rain

The author delves into the implications of No-Eyes' teachings, answering questions about prophecy, Native American history, and metaphysics. And, in preparation for coming earth changes, there is a comprehensive list (the Phoenix Files) of major high-risk zones (nuclear facilities, toxic waste dumps, oil refineries, etc.) and a suggested pole shift realignment configuration.

5¼ x 8¼ trade paper, 624 pages, ISBN 1-878901-14-1, $14.95

LIVING IS FOREVER
by J. Edwin Carter

A series of dreams leads Hedi Carlton to a small band of idealists dedicated to saving civilization through spiritual insight. When catastrophic events shake the earth, killing hundreds of millions, they find themselves responsible for creating a New Earth of peace and justice.

"This is must reading, for many, many truths were woven throughout the story of cataclysmic changes and aftermath."
— *Mary Summer Rain*

6 x 9 trade paper, 432 pages, ISBN 1-878901-42-7, $9.95

MATRIX OF THE GODS
by John Nelson

After an ecological collapse, the earth's greatly diminished population has been herded into mega cities under environ canopies, controlled and pacified by subliminal programming. The World Council imprisons Rama, the "green guru," for fear he will elevate humanity beyond their rigid control.

"Where do we go when the sky falls and the ozone is depleted, when the trees are gone and the water is ill? . . . Matrix of the Gods *paints a stunning picture of the future of our species."*
— **Magical Blend**

5½ x 8½ trade paper, dust jacket, 288 pages, ISBN 1-878901-97-4, $10.95

RUNNING BEAR: Grandson of Red Snake
by George McMullen

Running Bear continues the saga, begun in *Red Snake*, of a Native American world in transition. Speaking from spirit through psychic archaeologist George McMullen, Running Bear gives a vivid first-hand account of a tragic dispossession. Orphaned in the French and Indian Wars and stripped of his heritage, the young Huron wanders through a land increasingly poisoned by the white settlers. In Running Bear's story, we see how not only was the Native Americans' way of life destroyed, but their connection to nature—and through them, nature's connection to us—was nearly severed as well.

5¼ x 8¼ trade paper, 168 pages, ISBN 1-57174-037-6, $10.95

About the Author:

Bill Hunger, author of *Hiking Wyoming* and a collection of metaphysical family stories titled *When Two Saints Meet*, spends his life working as a farmer, ranch hand, wilderness ranger, writer, massage therapist, yoga teacher, grassroots environmentalist, carpenter, medicinal herb grower and general solitary wanderer. *Clearcut* blossomed into being with the realization that the survival of everyone, in every trade, everywhere, is dependent on cooperating with each other and in preserving the healing gifts of nature *while* we still have them.

Hampton Roads Publishing Company
publishes books on a variety of subjects,
including metaphysics, health, alternative medicine,
visionary fiction, and other related topics.
For a copy of our latest catalog, call toll-free,
(800) 766-8009, or send your name and address to:

Hampton Roads Publishing Company, Inc.
134 Burgess Lane
Charlottesville, VA 22902